The Wannoshay Cycle

The Wannoshay Cycle

Michael Jasper

FIVE STAR
An imprint of Thomson Gale, a part of The Thomson Corporation

Detroit • New York • San Francisco • New Haven, Conn. • Waterville, Maine • London

Five Star, an imprint of The Gale Group.

Set in 11 pt. Plantin.

LIBRARY OF CONGRESS CATALOGING-IN-PUBLICATION DATA

Jasper, Michael.
The Wannoshay cycle / Michael Jasper. — 1st ed.
p. cm.
ISBN-13: 978-1-59414-661-9 (alk. paper)
ISBN-10: 1-59414-661-6 (alk. paper)
1. Extraterrestrial beings—Fiction. 2. Iowa—Fiction. I. Title.
PS3616.O782W36 2008
813'.6—dc22 2007035767

First Edition. First Printing: January 2008.

Published in 2008 in conjunction with Tekno Books and Ed Gorman.

Printed in the United States of America on permanent paper
10 9 8 7 6 5 4 3 2 1

To Elizabeth and Drew: for the past, present, and future.

ACKNOWLEDGMENTS

This book has been ten years in the making, and I've had considerable help along the way. Thanks go primarily to my wife Elizabeth and son, Drew; my parents, Pat and Carolyn; and the rest of my family. Special thanks to editors Gordon Aalborg, Farley Bookout, Alja K. Collar, and especially John Helfers for giving me another chance. And I also owe huge thanks for the insight and feedback from the following wonderful writers: Mark Siegel, Gregory Frost, James Patrick Kelly, John Kessel, Elizabeth Hand, Maureen McHugh, Judith Tarr, Tim Pratt, Greg van Eekhout, Jenn Reese, Lee Capps, Chris Babson, Jim C. Hines, Jason Erik Lundberg, Scott Reilly, Dean Wesley Smith, Kristine Kathyryn Rusch, Gardner Dozois, Andy Cox at *Interzone,* the editors at *Strange Horizons,* the judges and editors of the *Writers of the Future* anthology, and the countless other people who've encouraged me along the way.

Prologue

A dark, soul-curdling shadow haunts me aboard this resurrected ship of my ancestors.

Even with the gathered weight of my people stacked tightly around me, I cannot disperse this shadow weighing me down. Nor can I find the ability to sleep. Sleep—the slow rest required for all but the Navigators—eludes me now, and I spend many cycles looking through the cask skins at my brothers and sisters and envying them their soul-saving ignorance of this journey.

Ignorance of the shadow of memory, too, that lurks just out of my sight, at the outer edges of my vision. The dark echoes of the past hold substance enough to haunt me and push away all thoughts of rest for this interminable voyage.

I pace these black metal halls, wondering if my fellow Elders in the ships around me also suffer from this maddening insomnia.

I want to wish them peace of mind and soul, though the cold part of me that signaled for the firing of the engines of our ancestral ships—the first in over four times four hundred cycles—*that* part of me hopes they suffer the same soul-curdling sensations that I feel.

They know what we had to leave behind in our selfish, mindless haste. They surely remember how the Navigators had to struggle to guide our four times seven ships up from the ground, straining in the wake of the Mother Ship's singular eruption out of our caves. How our departure turned layers of rock to lava before we burst into the cold air aboveground, air that none of us had ever breathed.

I was awake, then, and I saw the aboveground for just a few heartbeats. I saw a land that was desolate, treeless, and blue with ice. Then I had to blink, and we were lifted away.

No, I shall not sleep.

I shall face the long dark-cycles of empty space to remember all we've left behind, even as the very act of recall stains me from the inside out.

Denied the slow rest by this ailment of my soul, I walk the corridors and caskrooms of the ships instead, careful not to disrupt the Navigators in the upper level. I can sense them overhead, practicing their delicate, archaic art of guiding the ship. How they use the long-memorized star charts to pull together the wordless songs of the ancient ones.

I can see the other Elders in my upper eye, meandering just as I do over and around the blisters of the sleeping casks. The casks touch one another, side by side, above, and below to form the walls, floor, and hallways of the ship.

If I stop long enough and stare at a single cask, I can see the resting male or female, adult or child or old one within the skin of the sleep casks, breathing out once for every four times ten breaths I exhale.

Sometimes I see a twitching tentacle, a clenching gray hand, a spasm of anger or fear touching an oval face, and I remember the shadows chasing us in the darkness.

I remember with perfect clarity the echoes of the screams inside our caves burrowed so deep below the surface. I remember the slap of vines against the burning skin of my face and tentacles. The pungent smell of fear and death surrounding us. The taste of blood in my mouth. I remember every detail.

I remember . . . Twilight.

CHAPTER ONE

For the second time that week, a group of armed soldiers filled the alcove at the back of Father Joshua McDowell's church.

As he went through the familiar, almost unconscious movements of the morning Mass, Joshua did his best to ignore them. The soldiers' shadows drifted in and out of focus between the two tall, wooden confessionals carved with tired crosses and the worn faces of saints. The four soldiers were nearly invisible to his old eyes, thanks to their nano-fiber camouflage fatigues.

Taking a deep breath, he continued with that day's reading: "But when you see Jerusalem surrounded by armies, then know that its desolation has come. Look up and raise your heads, people, because your redemption is drawing near."

As if on cue, the lead soldier stepped forward out of the shimmering air in front of the church's new security arch, her black pulse gun the same color as the hull of the ships that had crashed to Earth barely a month earlier.

She wanted to make sure Joshua saw them there. All of them. He turned his gaze back on his meager congregation, the same dozen elderly men and women he saw daily, all of them lifelong Chicago residents, and hoped the soldiers hadn't come for him.

At the end of Mass he watched the slow departure of his few remaining people. Back in January, this Mass would have been packed with parishioners. That had been after the bombings and the ships, but before the riots and the bands of cultists. Now it was March, and winter threatened to linger on for another season.

As soon as he was back in the rectory, Joshua shed his heavy outer robe and musty-smelling vestments. His hands shaking, he arranged his gray hair in an attempt to hide his bald spot, feeling his fifty-eight years mostly inside his chest. His heart attack had been less than three months ago, and the now-familiar ache worsened on cold days.

"They don't know about the colonel," he told his reflection. "If they did, they would've taken you in right away. Have faith, McDowell."

Picking up his Bible, he returned to the church. His shoes echoed down the main aisle and kicked up dust lit by the three dozen stained-glass windows reinforced with safety glass. A bittersweet mix of ozone and gun oil filled the air at the back of the church.

"So," he said to the young woman standing in the alcove, after a glance at her nametag, "Sergeant Murphy. What brings you back here again? It's not every church that has an armed guard, you know."

The female soldier looked at him from behind a pair of wide, gray-lensed glasses. Above the three stripes affixed to her helmet was a blue badge decorated with an old-fashioned rifle and a silver wreath. By the time he looked back at her face, her glasses had turned transparent. Light blue eyes now looked out at him, slightly magnified.

"We've gotten more reports about some recent sightings of . . . ah, *undesirable* groups in the area, sir. Antimilitary protesters, possible new-religion types, and the like."

He stifled a bitter smile at the soldier's description of the cults. Calling what they practiced a new religion was as close to a slap in the face to his work as a person could get without raising a hand.

"With the criminal activity that's taken place here recently, we were ordered to check in on you, sir. Just trying to prevent a repeat of things like the firebombing from down the street. It's not every street that's had such a run of bad luck as yours," the soldier added.

He winced at the memory of the burning apartment complex, followed by the riots only a few weeks ago that had resulted in the destruction of the church's organ and the installation of the new security system. The police and the soldiers with their pulse guns had arrived just in time that night, stopping the band of wild-eyed cultists on their way to the altar.

"Sorry," Sergeant Murphy said a moment later. "That came out wrong, sir."

Joshua nodded, looking away from her at the white metal of the security arch in front of the outer door. The soldiers had turned it off, silencing its low hum. The female soldier moved closer and put two gloved fingers in front of the tiny mike attached to her cheek.

"World's been different since January, sir," she whispered. "*Everything's* changed. We gotta stick together, y'know?"

He looked at the female soldier, with her black cheek mike and ear buds, her tiny blue forehead sensors, her shifting gray camouflage uniform, her blue-black pulse rifle, and her opaqued glasses.

"Yes," he said after Sergeant Murphy had removed her hand from her mike. "The world *has* changed. Too much."

"We'd best be going, sir. Unless you have anything suspicious to report?"

Shaking his head, he forced a smile her way. He wondered how hard it would have been for Sergeant Murphy to call him "Father."

"Okay, then, Mister McDowell. Be careful."

The four of them turned and walked through the security arch without a sound. He stepped through the arch himself and grabbed the outer door.

"Thanks," he called as a blast of cold air peppered with snow slammed into him. After pulling the door closed, he activated the security arch again, turning the air in front of him to static for a disconcerting moment before it cleared. Even through the thick doors and walls of his hundred-year-old church, he could hear the distant whine of a siren, accompanied by what sounded like the rattle of gunfire.

He closed his eyes and prayed that his meeting this afternoon would somehow begin the process of recovering the peace his church, his street, his city, his country, and the rest of his world had lost.

Contrary to what most cultists and former members of his church thought, it was a peace that had been lost long before the ships ever arrived.

The ships came in the middle of a nighttime blizzard not long after the New Year, falling to Earth like more wreckage dropped onto an already battered landscape.

Most people didn't even notice them at first, having long ago fallen out of the habit of looking up at the sky. Like unwatched trees falling in a forest, the rectangular black vessels of alien metal appeared for a few instants on the geo-satellite systems and aviation radar, creating close to three dozen fingers of flashing trajectories. Then they split apart and crash-landed onto the frozen turf of the American Midwest and southern Canada like scattered pieces of a black puzzle.

But Father Joshua saw and remembered the ships. The day they arrived was still crystal-clear in his memory; it was also the same day he'd been attacked on the street by junkies.

He was walking in the Hyde Park neighborhood after a checkup with his cardiologist, a follow-up after his heart attack the previous autumn. The early-winter snow fell onto his face and quickly coated the sidewalk and street, deadening all sounds. His scuffed black shoes, worn on the bottoms, fought for traction in a losing battle with the snow, and he didn't hear the footsteps until too late.

When he turned to see who was coming up behind him, he was knocked to the ground and kicked in the side with metal-tipped boots. Strong, unsteady hands pulled off his coat with a rough efficiency. When Joshua tried to roll away, cold snow up his shirt sleeves and down his tight collar, he got a glimpse of two quivering, wide-eyed faces. The breaths of his attackers whistled in and out of their mouths like tiny screams.

Blur. The men were raging from Blur.

Remembering the stories on the various Netstreams about the brutal drug-related assaults of the past few weeks, he didn't dare fight back, even as his wallet and rosary disappeared into hands that moved almost too fast for his eyes to follow. They took his belongings and dashed off madly down the pockmarked street, outrunning cars as they disappeared into the night.

Joshua staggered back to the hospital, arms wrapped around his own chest as if trying to hold himself together. While he was waiting in the crowded emergency ward, he saw the first newscast on the Netstream about a downed ship in Canada.

"More are on the way," the newsreader kept repeating, as if the face on the wallscreen was caught in a hacker's endless loop.

The ward was especially crowded that night, thanks to the most recent car bomb, already blamed on the suicide cultists. Everyone sitting, standing, or sprawled on the dirty floor paid silent attention to the Netstream, with the exception of the two unconscious Blur junkies lying near the entrance. They twitched and groaned, sleeping off the effects of the drug.

As he watched the Netstream report that additional ships had been sighted in America as well as Canada, something shifted inside of Joshua. He forgot about his stolen wallet, coat, and rosary. A hot, heart-squeezing feeling stirred inside him, an almost desperate need. He wiped cold sweat from his bald forehead. Three, if not four, decades had passed since he'd felt this way before.

He didn't know who was aboard those ships, but he knew he could help them, in some way. He *had* to help them. They needed him.

"More ships are on the way," the newsreader said again to the silent mass of injured and sick gathered in the emergency ward. Low conversations, spiked now and then with shouts of fear, floated around him in English, Spanish, Russian, Korean, and, from a pair of amber-skinned people behind him, what sounded like Farsi. The couple must have made it out of Iran before America declared war on their country three years ago.

Joshua had remained there all night, surrounded by the injured and sick from down the street and around the world, and they watched the news unfurl from the Netstream like yarn from a ball rolled too tightly.

"World-will-never-be the same," a thin white girl sitting next to him said in a Blur-sped voice. She held herself tightly, bare arms like pale sticks jutting from her torn plastic vest jacket. She rocked back and forth, coming down off the drug, and her gaze kept flickering from the wallscreen back to Joshua.

Joshua wanted to reach out and console the girl, but her quivering hands and spastic movements—along with the dull ache lingering in his sides and chest—stilled his impulse. She looked so much like all the others, including the Indian boy who'd come up to Joshua outside the homeless shelter just two days earlier.

The boy's brown eyes were bloodshot, his hands constantly moving. At first Joshua didn't think he was using anything—he wouldn't have been able to see the boy's hands moving at all if the child had been on Blur. He told Joshua he was starting over, getting off using and selling. The boy walked with him all the way back to the church, claiming in his perfect English that he sold only to the rich, dealing with them through their razor-tipped fences at night or passing their armored cars on the street. He went on and on, talking about how Blur hit the user like a mix of cocaine and speed, with a little morphine thrown in to ease the harsh edges.

By the time they'd reached the doors to the Shrine of Our Lady of Pompeii, Joshua had made up his mind. He couldn't let the boy in. Not after all the boy had said and done, even if he was just a child. Instead, as if to compensate for not doing his chosen duty and offering the boy sanctuary, Joshua spent the next few hours talking on the front steps with the boy, whose shaking grew worse as his speech became slower and more garbled.

Then the boy's so-called friends came looking for him just before dawn. And Joshua let them take him. He simply walked back into his church, made sure the security arch was powered on behind him, and closed the doors for good.

Up on the wallscreen in the emergency room waiting area, another black, misshapen ship came into focus, embedded in the ground like a rotting tooth. He patted the cold arm of the shivering girl next to him, but her response was only to grunt and flinch away from him.

Joshua watched for the rest of the night into morning, unable to close his eyes as he tried to regain the fading sense of need he'd felt just a few short minutes ago. The feeling was there, but like a good memory or a blissful dream, it remained out of reach.

The next few weeks sped past in a rush of images: army blockades, black ships hidden under synthetic, translucent bubbles, riots and protests outside the various landing sites. The American president addressed the nation daily, though his message contained little content.

And with each passing hour, Joshua's need to do something about the people aboard the ships intensified, until he found himself on a train headed north. He shivered from the early March cold and sank deeper into his worn plastic seat as the sensory nodes on his wrists sent a symphony by Mahler sweeping over his body.

He stared at the battered landscape of northern Chicago passing by outside his window. His city, like most cities its size, now looked like a series of construction sites in reverse. If it wasn't a terrorist car bomb shattering a storefront, it was a militia-backed "cleansing" fire of a Muslim prayer house. Every street showed the signs of some form of violence, like a missing tooth in a nervous smile. Only so much of the damage could be blamed on the suicide cultists. The arrival of the ships only made the smoke thicker in his city.

As if attempting to distract him from the dismal view outside the elevated train, his sensory nodes filled his nose with the scent of mint, while his mouth tasted chilled champagne. He pulled his coat sleeves lower to cover the nodes, slightly ashamed of the gadgets he'd bought from a Netstream ad a year ago.

He gazed at the digital map superimposed on the back of the seat in front of him. The sorry state of the world was what had first compelled him to talk to the colonel, a former member of his congregation. And then the ships had arrived, and Joshua had started punching in the colonel's Netstream almost every day. The colonel was waiting for him at the crash site.

Would I get to talk to one of them there? Joshua wondered. What sort of beliefs would they have? And would we even be *able* to talk about such things? Could they have learned to speak English after only two months?

He doubted that humans had learned their language first. Humans were no longer the most advanced creatures on the planet; surely creatures who could navigate through space would learn human language faster than humans would learn theirs. The colonel, during one of his late-night Netstream chats with Joshua, had let it slip that the aliens might be using some sort of telepathy to help them communicate.

Aliens.

Joshua felt suddenly short of breath thinking about them, wondering, What in God's name am I doing getting involved in this? But he already knew the answer to that. He'd been called, and not just by the colonel.

The small blinking dot of their train moved steadily to the northeast, out of the city, and the landscape finally opened up around him. The congested buildings gave way to squat two-story houses, stores, parking lots, and narrow roads, and the train picked up even more speed. Few of the buildings he was passing now bore any of the scars from the urban warfare that had been plaguing his city for years. Joshua closed his eyes and let the sensory buds overwhelm his concerns about the colonel and the ships, if only for a short while.

With his eyes closed, he drifted off to sleep. He fell immediately into a dream in which he was walking down a series of straight, unmarked streets. The concrete roads were lined with identical round dwellings that looked more like metal huts. As he walked, he was dogged by the approach of pounding footsteps behind him, coming up on him far too fast, but the footsteps never caught up to him. He was running down the deserted concrete encampment when the slowing of the train pulled him out his dream.

When the train pulled to a stop at the Waukegan train station, Joshua dragged himself back outside into the cold, still hearing the pounding feet from his dream like fading machine-gun fire.

Outside, a young man in shimmering, shifting army fatigues greeted him. Private Petersheim was a thin white man of barely twenty years, with a spattering of acne peeking out on his cheeks from under his oversized, opaqued glasses. The soldier stood next to a boxy blue sedan with black-tinted windows.

"Sorry I'm late, padre," Petersheim said as he stepped up to him, as if hesitant to leave the safe bulk of the car. He ran a pencil-shaped scanner over Joshua's ID card, and the scanner beeped once. With a wink, the soldier returned the ID and shook his hand.

"Not a problem," Joshua said on his way into the warmth of the sedan. He sank into the torn vinyl seat. "Are we ready?"

"Yep," the private said once he was behind the wheel. He handed Joshua a bundle of slick gray and green fabric from the seat between them. "If you would, sir—Father—put these on over your clothes, at least until we get you inside the site. You sort of stand out a bit right now, with your black duds and all."

Joshua ran his hand down the nano-fiber camouflage suit, smiling in spite of his own nervousness. The newly developed smart-fabric shimmered with his touch, trying to match the color of his hand from the brief contact. He was still grinning when slipped the suit on over his clothes. This material was better than any gadget he'd ever seen advertised on the Netstreams.

"Okay then," Petersheim said. "Hold on, Father. We're running a bit late."

They blasted out of the train station and quickly left town. Joshua held onto the dashboard as they rocketed over washboard-like gravel roads and zipped through intersections without stopping.

Due to the headlong way the private was driving, Joshua didn't want to risk distracting him by asking any of the dozens of questions running through his head: Why did the colonel ask for me? What would I say to an alien? And would an alien care if I was *late?*

Short minutes later, Petersheim skidded the ten-cylinder sedan to a halt outside the fenced-off site of the fallen ship.

Joshua pried his hands from the dashboard and squinted through the black-tinted windshield. The bumper of the big car was less than two feet away from a man stretched across the road wearing a rubber *Creature from the Black Lagoon* mask with glowing red eyes, his thin arms crossed over his chest like a corpse at a wake. He wore a bath robe and ski boots.

Three dozen other similarly dressed people carried banners that read "Free Them Now!" or "Let Them Out or Let Us IN!" or other such messages. The masked crowd pushed up to the sedan, all of them reaching the index fingers of their right hand toward the vehicle without touching it.

"One second," the private said, putting his hand to his cheek mike. He whispered something, and three soldiers wearing black body armor emerged from a gap in the chain-link gate.

The first soldier pulled the Black Lagoon man out of the way, while the others used handheld stunners to push back the silent, pointing crowd.

"ET freaks," Petersheim said, giving him an incredulous smile. "Phone home, and all that, y'know, padre?"

"Unbelievable," Joshua said as they were let inside the razor-wire-tipped fence surrounding the site.

He wondered if the robed and booted protestors spent all their time outside the site waiting for something to happen, masks on and ready. He tried to get a glimpse of the ship, hidden under the biggest of five bubble-tents, but the tent was sealed up tightly.

There were aliens inside that ship, he thought. And they wanted to talk with *me,* of all people. Lord, I am truly not worthy. Not of this responsibility.

Joshua gave a start when he felt someone touch him. He looked down and saw Petersheim's pale hand on his upper arm. The camouflage suit had turned a whitish-pink color around the spot where the private's skin touched it.

"Right this way, Father," the private said, aiming him toward the tallest tent. "It's okay. Everything's safe. We've checked it all a million times."

They walked up to the wax-colored wall of bubbled plastic that rose up almost five stories high, like a circus tent. From inside the tent, voices shouted as if from a great distance.

Petersheim threw back the flap. "The colonel's in there."

Joshua nodded and forced his body into action. He took two steps inside into the antiseptic-smelling tent, and in doing so, Father Joshua McDowell became the first person not affiliated with the military to see a crash-landed Wannoshay ship up close.

Chapter Two

Alissa Trang had made only one attempt to film the aliens at the landing site after their arrival, and that had ended in disaster. For Ally, one of the advantages of working at a satellite outlet for CanTechWorld was that she had access to the best tech a small-town girl could find. Sick of explaining for the thousandth time how to use a Netstream speaker remote to a farmer or a factory worker, she'd decided one night to "borrow" the best eyebrow camera in the store after her late shift. Her plan was to grab as much footage of the landing site as she could the next morning, and get the camera back before her manager knew it was gone.

This was what Ally did, what she lived for: making movies of the world around her while her senses were heightened by a couple doses of Blur, and upload her work to the Netstreams for everyone to see. For a small fee, of course. But her rates were low, for now, and she got plenty of hits, especially when she did anything related to the alien ships. That rate would shoot up after today, she knew.

She hadn't paid much attention to all the furor about the ships back in January, when the first ship had landed less than fifteen kilometers north of Sanford. The town had enjoyed celebrity status for a brief time as flocks of 'Stream reporters filled the streets and jammed up the roads before the news of the other ships overshadowed Sanford's fame. The reporters had disappeared as fast as they'd arrived, of course, chasing more alien stories to the south in bigger American cities or east to the sites in Ontario.

But in the meantime, Ally had gotten hooked on learning more about the aliens. Nothing was getting through the information blockade set up by both governments, and even the most cool-headed Canadian had a fiery theory about the secrecy surround the landing sites. Armed Canadian Forces soldiers patrolled the perimeter of each site, supposedly with orders to warn trespassers once, then to shoot to kill in place of a second warning.

That was a challenge too big for Ally to pass up. She just had to get her car working and borrow that camera from the store, and find those extra capsules of Blur lying around her room. Blur was what made the experience real for her; she didn't want to think about the consequences of her temporary "enhancement" with the drug. Or the long-term effects of prolonged usage.

Always grateful for the chance to get out of tiny Sanford, a town of eight hundred blue-collar and farming families south of Winnipeg, Ally woke that morning before the sun had even started coloring the night sky. Her newly repaired beater of a car had started, to her surprise, and she drove away from the quiet town and into the countryside, hoping the heater would soon start kicking out warm air.

Just as she'd hoped, the sun was rising by the time she'd gotten to the outermost fringe of frozen earth a few kilos from the landing site. Excellent lighting and atmosphere. As she walked, the camera affixed to her left eyebrow and covering her left eye recorded everything she saw like a third eye. Gazing at the broken trees and scarred earth a kilometer from the site, everything bathed in the reddish-orange light of daybreak, Ally marveled at how not a single living creature had died when the ships hit.

No one died, she thought, shaking her head, but it was total chaos to many of her neighbors when Armageddon didn't come like the evangelists had been promising. People had lost their minds for a good month or so, and some people had yet to find them again. Ally figured the alien arrival was inevitable, really. She kept her eyes on the night sky and could see well enough to know the stars were too many to not hold anyone else out there.

She zoomed the camera until she could see the huge tent rising up on the horizon, surrounded by smaller tents. Fighting off the urge to squint, which would have thrown off the camera's focus, she got footage of the massive tent that hid the wrecked alien ship along with the six smaller tents surrounding it.

"Come on," she whispered in irritation, then caught herself. Only amateurs and wasters mucked up their own audio.

After barely five minutes of filming, Ally noticed a dark object moving toward her off in the distance. She blinked into the eyepiece to magnify and saw that the movement was a Canadian Forces Jeep aimed at her, bouncing across the frozen earth of what was once a soybean field. She knew that nobody from the 'Streams had been able to get closer than this, and the airspace around all thirty sites had been restricted since the arrival of the ships after New Year's.

"Shit," she whispered under her breath. "Shit shit shit."

Keeping her face pointed in the direction of the site, trying to see around the Jeep speeding toward her, Ally froze. Magnifying the camera lens even further, she saw figures off to the right, walking in front of one of the gray Canadian Forces tent.

She could see that two of the figures were soldiers, but they were walking on either side of someone quite large. Ally immediately thought of the ancient duped Sasquatch from the vids replayed on the Netstreams and almost laughed out loud, but she kept filming. This was no Bigfoot.

The Jeep was less than one hundred meters away when she

slipped her sunglasses over her eyes, hiding the lens of the camera. She popped out the mini-DVD in her coat pocket and slid the still-warm disc into the back of her jeans.

"Hands where we can see them, girl," a projected voice from the Jeep shouted at her. Ally knew the routine all too well. She hoped she had enough credit in her account to make the payoffs necessary to keep these soldiers from strip-searching her out here. At least she had her explosive caplets of Mace packed away in the little pocket inside her sports bra. Just in case.

"I guess that's my one warning," Ally muttered, still taping onto the flex-memory left in the camera, which was being streamed to her system back home. It was going to cost her a painful chunk of cash, but she wanted to have some evidence in case the soldiers got any ideas.

"Looks like we got us another moviemaker," the soldier climbing down from the passenger side of the truck said. Ally relaxed at the female voice, though this woman was as tall as most men.

The driver didn't even bother getting out. "Just grab her disks and show her the way out."

Cursing and spluttering, Ally handed over four of her mini-DVDs from her coat pockets. She said nothing about the disc hidden in her jeans.

"Jesus H. The least you could do is give me a ride back to my car," she said, but the truck was already pulling away. She gave the truck a one-fingered salute and turned her back on them. Idiots.

Half an hour (and two capsules of Blur washed down with iced lime vodka) later, Ally fired up her wallscreen to watch her footage. As she surfed through the footage and came across the shot of the tent and the three figures, she realized she held digital gold in her hands.

She had managed to pick up a three-second bit of a pair of

soldiers marching single-file, with a tall, swaying *alien* between them. The creature looked too big—and too skinny—to be a human, and the awkward, lumbering way it walked . . .

"Oh my God," Ally whispered, grabbing for the remote so she could watch the footage again. "Ohmigod!" She knocked the remote to the floor in her Blur-induced mania.

After watching the snippet twice, riding one of the best Blur highs she'd ever felt, tears filled her eyes. She kept babbling to herself, nonsense words of utter joy, not just at the potential financial windfall she was about to receive but also at the cosmic shifting sensation she felt looking at that far-off image of the alien. That goofy sense of amazement took her back to her childhood, riding a rollercoaster or watching her first movie made completely on her own. It was almost better than Blur. Almost.

She was at the height of her high when she decided to upload her movie to her Netstream. With her vision blurred by tears and each of her fingers operating as its own entity, she hit the wrong button on her remote.

Just like that, her twitchy fingers burned over that day's footage. And she hadn't taken the time to make a backup. All she had was her expensive stream that showed nothing but the soldiers driving up to harass her, their big-ass truck blocking any view of the landing site behind it.

For the next ten minutes, Ally Trang screamed herself hoarse.

Chapter Three

Joshua's first reaction to seeing the alien ship for the first time was to lean as far backward as he could without falling so he could get a good look at it.

Crumpled and broken in many places, the outer hull of the tall, angular ship was made up of a flat black metal that didn't reflect any light. Lit by a ring of lights embedded in the ground, the ship itself stood at least fifty feet high, but it seemed somehow fragile with its delicate lines.

At first the ship appeared cubical in shape, but as his eyes adjusted, Joshua could see more and more angles making up the exterior of the hull as he walked closer. The ship had at least six vertical faces that bent at the top to form a sort of peak. The unfamiliar angles of the dented ship made his eyes ache.

"Good Lord," he whispered.

As they walked closer, he could see grayish foam clustered around the many rents and tears in the hull, while power leads, cables, and thick wires of human design wrapped around the exterior like spider webs. Scaffolding encircled the perimeter of the octagonal ship, and eight crooked spires sprouted from the top of the ship. Most of the spires stretched out far enough to touch the plastic bubble-tent surrounding the ship. Men and women in dark green uniforms walked across the scaffolding, and their shouts died away when they saw him and the young private.

Petersheim moved toward an open hatch just below the

middle-most projection of the ship. The spires made Joshua think, for some reason, of the points on the crown of the Statue of Liberty. Joshua followed the soldier, his legs suddenly heavy.

As soon as he stepped inside the flat black metal walls of the ship, his breath was taken away by the cold. Instead of the institutional odor outside the ship, he could now smell something tangy and earthy, as if a handful of heavy-duty rock salt had been thrown into a fresh puddle of mud after a rain. The odor made the air of the ship feel too close.

Petersheim pulled out a hand light and popped it on. The light flickered red, and then glowed orange, illuminating an irregularly shaped alcove containing a pair of rounded openings.

"They're down there waiting for you, padre," the private said, pointing at the door on their left. "I'll take your camos, sir. They want you to meet him with your priest suit on, for full effect, I guess."

Joshua slipped off the camouflage coveralls with a pang of regret and a shudder of cold; he'd left his coat in the car, and he was enjoying the sensation of nano-fiber covering him, making him feel almost invisible. The private took the suit and handed him the light.

"I'm not authorized to go any farther," he said, pointing toward the left-hand opening and the cold corridor on the other side of it. "Don't worry—you'll see better once your eyes adjust. The smell doesn't ever really go away, though. Good luck, Father."

Joshua thanked the private as the young man walked out of the ship. Inhaling the strange, loamy odor, he left the alcove and entered the cold hallway. After walking for over a hundred feet, his instincts telling him to turn around before and after each step, he turned into a room bathed in blue-gray light.

Inside the room stood Colonel Cossa, along with four other people. A large woman in a gray jumpsuit had her back to

Joshua, leaning over someone resting on what looked like a black metal chair. Two armed soldiers were positioned with their weapons lowered on either side of the woman. The rest of the room was bare, just flat black walls, black floor, and black ceiling, all absorbing the light instead of reflecting it.

"Lieutenant," the colonel said in a low voice. He reached out a slender hand and tapped the woman in the jumpsuit. The woman flinched in surprise at his touch, and then sucked in a sudden, harsh breath. "You're dismissed for now, Lieutenant."

The large woman stepped back and turned, nodding at Joshua. He began to nod back, surprised at both the paleness of her round face and the sweat covering it, and then he saw who she'd been standing over.

This fifth being was *not* a human.

Wrapped from top to bottom in bandages, it was leaning on a twisted piece of black metal that seemed to have been pulled up from the floor of the ship.

Not a human.

Joshua looked at the being's too-short legs and the short, twitching cords on the being's head that slipped out of their wrappings like snakes or fingers.

Alien.

Colonel Cossa stepped forward with a smile. At some point the pale woman in the jumpsuit must have walked past Joshua to leave the room, but he hadn't even noticed.

"Glad you could make it today, Father," the colonel said as he shook Joshua's numb hand. "One of our language experts," he said, nodding at the hallway where Joshua had just came from, and where the woman in the jumpsuit must have just gone. "She's been working with a team of five others to help get our new friends up to speed with English. It's been a challenge, but we're seeing the results at last. Especially with this fellow," he added, looking over at the creature in the middle of the room.

Joshua let go of the colonel's hand and let his own hand drop to his side, useless. His whole body felt useless in the presence of this mummified being. The alien's salty, inhuman aura filled his nose and mouth, flooding his senses until he felt like he could even see and hear it.

"We would've invited you here sooner," the colonel continued, "but the red tape was significant. Plus we had to keep you shielded from the media and other . . . elements."

"I think I know what you're talking about," Joshua said, finding his voice at last as he thought about the Creature from the Black Lagoon outside the encampment. He tried to smile, but his lips stuck to his teeth, making him feel like he was grimacing. He forced his lips together again.

The colonel nodded at that and turned to the creature leaning on the black metal structure. The long-armed, short-legged being was bouncing slightly, giving off more of the salty smell he'd noticed the instant he entered the ship. Salt, and something almost sweet, underneath it.

"But now," Cossa said, "I want you to meet the Wannoshay we've named Johndo. As in John-space-Doe. Johndo, this is Joshua. He's a priest. A man of faith."

Joshua nodded at the tall being whose face was almost hidden in bandages. "Johndo's" wrappings only covered the exposed skin of his face, hands, and feet. A grayish-white robe covered his torso.

"Their skin is extremely susceptible to heat and sunlight," Cossa said. "The wrappings protect him from the air and sun while he adjusts to our environment. We've been supervising the work on drugs that will help him and the rest of the Wannoshay adapt."

Joshua fought back a sudden urge to run from the black-walled ship, away from the soldiers and the tall alien—the *Wannoshay*—with its musky smell.

"In any case," Cossa said, "Johndo has informed us that he and his people need to talk to someone affiliated with religion."

"Right," Joshua said. He remembered this fact from their Netstream conversations. He felt as if his brain was starting to function again.

"He and some of the other have a pretty decent grasp of English, now that the linguists and other language experts have been working with him and his people. But I guess they just distrust us soldiers, even our chaplains. Don't ask me why."

Joshua tried to swallow. When he realized that all eyes in the room were trained on him, he cleared his throat.

"How can I help?"

"Talk to him," the colonel said. "Get him to tell us all he can about his people. Why they're here. What they want. If more of them are coming."

Joshua nodded. "So. Where do we begin?"

Before the colonel could answer, Johndo straightened up with a series of cracking sounds. The musky tones of his odor had gone away, replaced by a sweeter smell, like vanilla, though the smell of salt remained.

Once he was standing upright, nearly seven feet tall, Johndo made a high-pitched humming sound. And then he opened his lipless mouth.

"*Wannoshay,*" Johndo said.

His voice was lilting and high-pitched, almost whistling from his mouth. He reached a wrapped hand behind him until he found the twisted piece of metal. He leaned on it again, as if standing upright left him unbalanced, and then he raised his bandaged hands toward Joshua. Four stubby gray fingers, tipped with black claws, peeked out of the bandages.

Joshua swallowed, blinking rapidly. He could feel his heart

beating too fast, but he managed to meet the alien's gaze and lift his lips into the semblance of a smile.

"*Wannoshay* ha' weagh shun," Johndo said.

Joshua focused all of his attention on the alien's words, and with a jolt of recognition he realized the alien was speaking English, talking about what must have been the weak sun of his home planet. He nodded and smiled without grimacing this time.

"*Wannoshay* ha' cyguls of longh . . ." Here the alien symbolized "darkness," with a four-fingered hand held over the gap in the bandages where Joshua assumed the alien's eyes were, the hand dropping slowly like a sun sinking against the horizon.

Johndo's arms spread wide as he spoke of the cold nights, his four-fingered hands reaching out to the dark metal walls, almost brushing the soldier next to the colonel.

"*Wannoshay* shun, dhyingh . . ."

Johndo continued his story, and Joshua was able to piece most of the events together, though the effort was tiring. He found it easier to understand the alien when Johndo used a combination of gestures, intonations, and the occasional spoken word to get his point across.

With the cooling of their planet, the People (from the forceful way Johndo said it, Joshua felt the word needed capitalization) moved below ground, into caves, turning their backs on the upper world.

After a few minutes more, once he'd grown familiar with the way Johndo spoke, Joshua could've sworn he heard Johndo's low, warbling voice *inside* his head, even when the Wannoshay's mouth didn't move.

The People dug deeper and deeper into the earth with their tools and clawed hands. They built new homes underground, close to the warm, freshwater springs protected from the cold above.

And there they stayed, until they found . . . someone . . .

Joshua was leaning forward, on the verge of losing his balance, when Johndo's words trailed off. The last thing the alien had said had sounded like some sort of name. Something like "my light." Or "twilight."

Johndo lowered his head, as if he'd run out of words.

"Who?" Joshua whispered. "Who did you find? What about *twilight?*"

A shiver passed over Johndo's long body as soon as Joshua said that word, starting at his bare gray feet and rippling up through his bony torso and stopping at his lipless mouth, which was almost hidden in his face. His sweet smell was turning salty again.

"Johndo?" Joshua said, stepping closer.

"Easy, Father," the colonel said.

The warning in the veteran soldier's voice cooled Joshua's curiosity. He'd forgotten about the colonel, not to mention the two other soldiers in the room who now had their pulse weapons resting in their arms.

"For now," Johndo said in a slow, deliberate voice. "Now we live here."

Inhaling Johndo's shifting scents of vanilla and salt, Joshua realized the Wannoshay was no longer talking aloud in his graceful mix of words, gestures, and intonations. Johndo was talking directly to him, inside his head. The priest felt both violated and awed, even as his face grew hot.

"I am glad, Joshua, grateful you came to us. I needed to talk, but only with one of your people's *Elders.* Not a warrior, not a student of battle. Only an Elder like you, for you are aware of the soul of a people. Only an Elder knows what must be taken on *faith.*"

Joshua's ears began to ring. He placed a hand on his chest, where an old pain had started to grow. That high-pitched voice inside his brain was overwhelming. He felt sweat cover his forehead despite the cold of the ship.

"Know a people's soul," Johndo said with another full-body shiver, "and you know their *true history.*"

His voice was fading inside Joshua's head, while his short-fingered, bandaged hands began to quiver at his sides.

"Tell me more," Joshua whispered without moving his lips. "Please."

But Johndo the Wannoshay was no longer talking. Trembling, his shoulders sagged, and the hint of skin Joshua could see under the layers of bandages was gray mixed with traces of pink, like scar tissue.

Putting all of his weight against the flexible black metal behind him as if exhausted, Johndo let out a hissing breath. He stopped trembling and inclined his head toward Joshua.

Your turn, that look said to him.

Looking over at the colonel and his fellow soldiers—one of whom, he now noticed, had been recording the entire conversation with a small lapel camera—Joshua took a deep breath and wiped the cold sweat from his forehead. He held the cold air in his lungs and let the smells of the alien fill his nose. Then he exhaled and began talking.

"The world was created in six days," he began. "And on the seventh day, God rested." He pointed up, his face still warm. "After that, things became interesting."

Stopping for breath half an hour later, he'd covered most of Genesis mixed in with some Darwin, and he was now following that with a condensed version of the New Testament. Johndo seemed to be listening intently, and Joshua did his best to not lose the thread of his narrative whenever the tall alien's body rippled with more of his convulsive movements. He let out a long breath and felt the ache in his chest diminish.

But before Joshua could continue, the Wannoshay made a

clawed fist and punched the metal structure on which he was resting. The black metal dented, then oozed back into shape until the indentation disappeared.

Colonel Cossa, standing just a few feet away, stepped forward, as if he'd been waiting for such an action.

"That's enough for today, Father," he said. "Good work. We'll leave Johndo here, and I'll get you back to your church. But first I'd like to show you something."

Joshua looked back at Johndo, whose wrapped hands were still clenched into fists, and he saw that the other two soldiers in the room had managed to slip some sort of restraints onto the alien's bandaged wrists. The restraints were made of the same dull, oozing metal as the alien's chair, with a narrow band of steel in the middle that didn't yield to the alien's sudden thrashing. He could smell something burning now instead of the comforting, familiar scents of salt or vanilla.

The ship felt cold again, bone-chilling and damp as a cave.

"It's for his own good," the colonel said, touching his arm to lead him out of the room. "Otherwise he'd injure himself. We think it's some sort of reaction to the warmth of our planet. Plus they have a low stimulation threshold, and I think he probably passed it about ten minutes ago."

The colonel tipped him a wink that Joshua couldn't comprehend. "He's never communicated so much in one day with us before. Even with the team of linguists. Now, come with me, please, Father."

They turned away from the sight of Johndo's exposed gray skin, mottled now with purplish-red splotches. Johndo was giving off a keening sound, somewhere between a moan and a shout. Joshua shuddered as he was led down a sloping passage away from the haunting sounds in the meeting room.

At the bottom of the hall stood three more soldiers, wearing full body armor and armed with pulse rifles. At their feet was a thick, ugly hatch made of a bluish metal so unlike the smooth, unshining black metal of the alien ship that it had to have been made by human hands.

Two of the soldiers turned the wheel at the top of the hatch and lifted it, while the third squatted down in front of the opening. Her gun was aimed straight into the widening gap. A sharper smell of mud mixed with salt drifted out from the other side of the hatch.

Joshua felt his heart drop. In the back of his mind he'd been wondering this about the aliens all afternoon, even as Johndo told him about their dying sun, their migration to the caves, and their mysterious discovery far beneath the surface of their frozen planet.

"What is this?" Joshua said, his voice a croak.

"Just take a look," the colonel murmured from beside him. "So you know what we're dealing with here, Father."

Barely breathing, Joshua leaned closer toward the dark opening in the floor of the ship. A soft humming came from below, but the sound was not caused by any sort of machine. This humming came from something alive. This was where the rest of the Wannoshay had been hidden. The rest of the People.

"A light, Private," Cossa said, and the young man on their right popped a hand light. An orange glow filled the small room and the hole at their feet.

At first all he could focus on was the cave where the aliens were gathered. Feeling slightly light-headed, he saw that tunnels extended away from this main cave, which was easily fifty feet wide, its walls made up of black, hard-packed Illinois dirt. Bitter cold rose up from the cave and its tunnels like a wintry wind.

Did they dig all these tunnels in the past two months? Hundreds of aliens, hundreds of the People. How could this be? Joshua wanted to ask about all of this to Cossa, but once again, his mouth wouldn't cooperate.

He stared downward, unable to blink, and looked at the mass of aliens looking up at him.

They flinched away from the light, and a handful of them swung their long arms, striking those closest to them and causing a ripple of movement that was quickly quieted. Their skin was an uneven, pale gray color, as if they'd never been in the sun, and something looked wrong with the long, oval shape of their heads. Other than the wrappings on their hands, these Wannoshay had no bandages or wrappings covering their bodies.

Too many.

The aliens pushed closer to the opening, and Joshua pulled back. He stared dumbly at the strange vertical growth on their foreheads and their writhing hair, until his eyes lost focus.

There were too many of them to have all fit in this ship.

His next thought, to his lasting shame every time he thought about that day later, was one of fear:

Disease. Don't get too close—you'll pick up whatever sickness that these beings carried with them from their world. Leprosy. Contagion.

As he stared, wrestling with his own fears, the aliens below him stopped pushing closer. They looked up at him with their oval faces and black eyes and closed mouths. Silent.

And then, at the same time, as if choreographed, the vertical growths in the middle of each of their foreheads quivered and opened, exposing a black, sideways eye.

"Close it," he whispered, hands in front of his mouth and nose. "Please turn off that light and close the hatch. *Please.*"

The colonel pulled him gently back from the edge of the hole, and the three soldiers let the hatch drop back to the floor, sealing the hole again. The black, liquid metal of the floor shook from the impact, buckled, and then flattened again.

The slam of the closing hatch reverberated in Joshua's ears all the way back to his church, and that hollow sound would echo in his chest and in his mind for many weeks to come.

Chapter Four

Now that both Blur and news about the aliens had their hooks in her, Ally couldn't keep herself away from the Winnipeg slums. For the second time that week, she called in sick for her evening shift at CanTechWorld and hitched a ride up Highway 3 into the city. She had to keep her mouth clamped shut on the short ride from Sanford to Winnipeg, afraid she'd start screaming at the old man behind the wheel to go faster.

Faster.

Everything in the world moved way too slowly when she wasn't using Blur.

And if the rumors about the aliens she'd been hearing were true, she might be able to find more than Blur in the city, so long as she kept her eyes open and her camera ready.

She leaped out of the car as soon as it stopped at the intersection of Portage and Maryland. She knew the elderly driver hadn't wanted to be caught in this part of the city, but she also knew that he'd take her wherever she wanted if she let her skirt ride up higher on her legs, which were covered in black tights.

Ally adjusted the fingernail-sized rectangle of her lapel camera and made sure the recorder in her pocket, connected to the camera, was still running. She smiled, knowing she'd gotten some great footage of the old fart checking her out while he gripped the wheel.

As she hurried along the streets, her gaze moved without thought over the broken windows and the fire-scarred brick buildings that peppered the urban landscape. With her vinyl coat zipped up tight, she wished she had her butterfly knife with her, but one of her housemates had borrowed it last week and lost it. To reassure herself, she touched her trust exploding Mace caplets in one coat pocket and checked that she had all five mini-DVDs in her other pocket next to her recorder.

Her coat rustling with each step, she hurried down Sargent Avenue and entered the main section of the run-down neighborhood. Boarded-up restaurants and businesses stared at her from below dark apartment windows, empty places that had simply given up in the past few years of recession and urban terrorism.

Jenae, her Blur dealer, lived above an abandoned bakery at the heart of the neighborhood.

According to Jenae, the queen of gossip in Winnipeg, the aliens were leaving their ships and the tunnels under them and coming to the city to live. The government had come to some sort of agreement with the Wantas, and Ally wanted to be here when the first wave of aliens arrived, not sitting at home surfing the 'Streams like a waster.

She forced down her growing impulse to simply sprint like a madwoman down the street to her supplier's home. An electric car hissed past her, and she edged closer to the rubble of an old pharmacy on her right. She calmed herself by thinking about how good it would feel to get a pink capsule of Blur in her, and to take a couple more back home to help get through the next few days.

With some Blur, she could face down a dirt-eating, two-meter-tall alien if she had to. Now *that* would make a great flick.

Everyone was waiting for the American president or the Canadian prime minister to hold another press conference to follow the brief one that occurred at the site in Illinois after the priest went into one of the ships last week.

The best either leader could do was give ten-second sound bites that ran at the start of most downloads, urging people to stay at home so that the soldiers could secure the streets for the aliens. That was advice most people had been following for over a decade anyway, ever since terrorism and other acts of violence had covered Canada and America like a virus.

Bunch of scared sheep, Ally thought. They don't realize that there's good material for the Netstreams *everywhere*. And good material means downloads, and pay-per-downloads mean more money in my Netstream account.

After five more minutes of walking, she was pounding on the dented, multi-locked door of Jenae's apartment. Remembering that her camera was still on, Ally flicked it off and contemplated banging her head on the door until someone answered.

The door popped open just as she was about to try it. Jenae pulled her inside without a word. The white woman's usually pale face was flushed red, and her eyes kept twitching and winking at Ally. The skinny young woman shivered as she strode across the floor to the couch, every movement exaggerated and too fast.

Jenae was already whacked on Blur.

Ally fought off a wave of intense jealousy and need, even as the yeasty smell of bread and pastries filled her nose and mouth.

Taking Blur was like a combination of the best, most addictive aspects of every other drug she'd ever taken. When she was on Blur, the rest of the world turned to so much fuzz while she zipped through the simplest of tasks at warp speed. Even peeling an orange became a race for the most dexterous fingers this side of the Red River.

The only things she didn't like about Blur was coming down from it—"flashing"—and the way the world crept in on her while she was sober, pressing down on her with its mundane weight.

But tonight Jenae had Blur, and as a result, tonight Jenae was Ally's hero. Ally already had her money card out.

"What's new up here?" she asked, pocketing the dozen pink capsules Jenae handed her in exchange for six hundred Canadian. There goes most of this week's paycheck.

"Cops," Jenae said. "We-got-'em-everywhere." Her words ran into each other as she rocked back and forth on the dirty carpet.

Ally dry-swallowed a pink capsule and grimaced, the drug burning all the way down.

"No way. They finally figure out Milt's operation upstairs?" She grinned, already feeling her pulse pick up. Finally. *Finally.*

"Nah," Jenae said. "Getting-us-junkies-off-the-street. Busting-everyone."

"Really," Ally muttered. She'd thought the neighborhood had been extra quiet tonight. Nobody was out, not even the hard-core Blur folks.

"Just putting-up-a-show. Getting-ready-for-the-Wannoshit-invasion, y'know."

Ally gave a mock-serious nod. As she spoke, she felt her own words begin to pick up speed. "Oh, that's all. Thought we had something *serious* to worry about. But an invasion—shit. Nothing-to-worry-'bout."

They laughed, Jenae louder than Ally, cackling for ten seconds straight, and then she passed out. Her heels rattled on the floor as she trembled and quivered on her back.

The first time she'd seen this, Ally had panicked, thinking Jenae was having some kind of seizure. But she knew better now. Doing her best not to look at Jenae, she gazed around the filthy apartment with its broken wallscreen and scarred furniture and waited for the Blur to kick in. As soon as it did, she was heading out into the chilly March air to get some more footage.

Unlike Sanford and the kilometers of dead farmland surrounding it, there was always something interesting going on here in the city.

Ten minutes later, Ally left Jenae's apartment with her vision tripled. She jumped down the steps and jogged to the next block of the dark, quiet streets, unable to move slowly anymore. She felt every muscle in her body twitch as if she'd been hit with tiny bolts of lightning. She wondered if she could make it back to her place in Sanford, thirty kilometers away, if she started running now. As usual, she hadn't made any plans for getting back home that night.

She paused for breath on a cracked sidewalk on Ellice Avenue, in front of a broken-down theater whose marquee still announced an old-fashioned movie from years ago. Next door, a convenience store had been burned to the ground.

Trying to stand still was like trying to stop a war raging inside her, but at least it kept the cold from affecting her. Just as she was wondering what had happened to all the traffic, a high-pitched squealing sound filled the air.

She goose-stepped into the shadows, her arms shaking like loose wires, and held her breath for as long as she dared. The squeal grew closer, turning into a buzzing hum as the vehicle downshifted. With a dull gnawing sensation in her stomach, she realized she hadn't seen any traffic on the street all night.

Cops. Something's up.

She moved her hand to her lapel to activate her camera. Already on, the camera beeped at her twice and kept recording.

I must have hit it while I was at Jenae's, while I was waiting for the Blur to hit *me*. Good thing Jenae was passed out, or she would've killed me.

As the hum got louder, Ally finally ran and hid in the recessed entrance to an abandoned Thai restaurant. Sweat covered her face and dampened her armpits as she crouched in the darkness, peeking around the corner. The first electric bus pulled up a second later.

"Oh-shit," she whispered. "Oh-shit-shit-shit."

She pulled the recorder from her coat pocket with trembling hands and looked at the readout. The current disc was almost full. She should've used the camera's wireless feature to stream the footage directly to her Netstream, but she hadn't been able to sit still long enough to teach herself how to do it.

The hum of the electric buses faded as first one, then another, and finally a third bus pulled to a stop half a block from her. None of the buses had windows. When she finally got a new disc loaded, she touched the sensor on her lapel. As always, she wished she'd borrowed the eyebrow unit from work. The footage from the piece-of-shit lapel camera always came out grainy and dark. And the light here completely sucked.

Her right foot tapped on the cold cement outside the restaurant when the doors to the buses opened. Her vision was tripling again as she fought the drug in her system, trying to will herself into sobriety, which almost always made the Blur high even stronger.

The first people to step off the three buses was a line of shadowy soldiers armed with rifles, their shiny camos and helmets blending into the dark green exterior of the bus. Once she'd gained control of her tapping foot, Ally leaned around the corner wall of the alcove.

She held her lapel camera up and out. For the first time she noticed that the lights were on in the apartments above the closed businesses, and the "Open" sign was glowing in front of the old Howard Johnson's, details she'd been too busy enjoying her Blur high to notice before.

Something salty and moist tickled her nose. At first she thought it was a bug or maybe the whiff of ozone left by the electric buses, but then she realized the smell was different. It was a scent she couldn't recognize, and it made her skin turn into gooseflesh.

She smelled . . . aliens.

Wantas.

"Oh-my-God," she whispered, even before the first one stepped off the bus, a dark green Army bag clutched in its big hands. She couldn't see if the creature had fingers or not.

Just a delusion. Nothing to worry about, really.

Most of the streetlights had been broken out long ago, keeping the creatures coming off the bus hidden in shadows along with the soldiers. To her they looked like regular people, but taller and less graceful than most humans.

They walked with a swaying movement, and their legs looked too short. Some bent over onto all fours, which seemed a more natural position for them.

Ally felt a pang of disappointment at not being able to hallucinate something nastier, or at least something less human in nature. Their skin was pale, but with a bluish tint in the weak glow coming from by the running lights of the bus.

She found herself staring at their feet, her lungs full of icy air as she inhaled over and over again. Each bare foot had only four toes. She exhaled, her hot breath clouding up in the cold air. Four toes that were as long as her fingers.

That image clinched it for her—this was no Blur-addled delusion. These were *aliens.*

"Jesus H," she whispered, hugging herself tightly while recording everything she saw, "Fuckin'-better-not-erase *this.*"

She continued filming as the aliens filed off the bus, gathering together mostly in groups of four or six, though sometimes just in pairs. Some teetered, off-balance, while two of the shorter aliens began pushing each other as soon as they stepped onto the street. The soldiers quickly separated them.

Then, in complete silence, the aliens carried their bags off the bus and were led into the hotel by soldiers. They followed obediently, but occasionally one or two would look over in her direction, heads cocked to the side as if *smelling* her, even from over a hundred meters away.

One of them stopped and looked directly at her. His or her—or its—face was hidden in shadows, but Ally caught a glimpse of the alien's eyes. She had to clamp both hands over her mouth to keep from making a sound. The alien shuddered and crouched forward, clenching its four-fingered hands into fists the size of her head.

She watched it all with a disjointed, detached feeling, as if she were floating ten feet above her own body.

Not sure if the strange ringing sensation inside her head was caused by the flashing of the Blur in her system or her closeness to the aliens, she held her breath and stared. Finally, the alien relaxed and straightened up with a sharp, crackling sound. The alien lumbered after the others, shoulders twitching.

Ally forced herself to breathe again, and when she did, her heightened senses picked up movement off to her left.

She peeked through the broken windows of the restaurant and saw a group of cops coming up the street on foot. They checked each doorway, and some of them disappeared into abandoned buildings.

They were less than a block away. Looking for some of the damn cultists, most likely.

With her back against the locked restaurant door, she tried to clear her head. She'd heard the stories about the people who had tried to fire-bomb the alien ships, even with all the soldiers covering the sites. Most of the stories were about the weird suicide cults that had formed and spread on the 'Streams right around the same time the Wantas arrived.

Stifling a sudden urge to scream in frustration, she bit her bottom lip when she realized she was trapped: aliens on her right and cops on her left. She packed the recorder and mini-DVDs into the depths of her vinyl coat, keeping the camera running.

The door to the restaurant was locked, but the window next to her was broken, backed up with plywood. Pushing against the plywood, she slipped into the restaurant as quietly as she could. She bit down even harder on her lip as she snagged her arms and legs on the shards of glass left in the window frame and dropped, bleeding, to the floor of the restaurant.

Short seconds later, a female cop wearing a black leather jacket and faded jeans stopped outside the door to the restaurant, but she left after trying the door and finding it locked. Ally touched the discs in her pocket and sighed, a thrill of discovery washing over her like a sheet of rain.

The Wantas have come to town, she thought. And I've got it all recorded right here. I'm going to make a killing from the downloads.

With her arms quivering from the shallow cuts crisscrossing them and her coat and tights torn and wet with blood, she nearly started laughing at her current situation. But her burst of adrenaline had killed her Blur high, and her muscles began to ache with fatigue.

She lay back onto the dusty floor, her vision going gray, and the cold late-March air washed over her. With a heavy hand, she reached up to turn off her camera so she didn't waste any more disc space. With her arms and legs twitching in their own random dance, her breath whistling in and out of her mouth, Ally Trang lost consciousness.

Chapter Five

Even after all the turmoil the aliens' arrival had caused, Shontera Johnson still had trouble believing that they were actually *here,* in *her* city. Didn't we have enough to deal with?

The few bits of footage she'd had the time to download and watch from the Netstreams had consisted mostly of shots of the fenced-off landing site a mile outside Milwaukee, along with a glimpse of a broken black ship, which didn't convince her of anything.

Give me good solid facts, she figured, not something hidden under a bubble-tent next to someone's soybean field. She'd been working so much overtime at the brewery, not to mention the daily challenge of raising Toshera on her own, that she was too damn busy to worry about the Wannoshay.

So it was a surprise to her when, one day in mid-April, her line supervisor told her and her co-workers that the aliens were coming to the brewery to work.

"It's all part of the integration process," Angie had said. "The mayor wants to show everyone how open and welcoming the people of Milwaukee can be. He even got the unions to okay it. The army guys say the aliens are safe, no diseases or anything bad like that. So it's going to happen, people. Be ready."

Shontera knew Roberta would throw a fit when she heard that the Wantas would be starting the following Monday. Roberta, like many of the other workers, had been at the brewery ever since she dropped out of high school. Rumor had it her

Bible-thumping husband, messed up on Blur, had stormed a church south of the city and killed someone before killing himself back when the aliens first landed. Someone said he'd gotten mixed up with the suicide cultists. Roberta hadn't been the same since.

Back on the line, Shontera stared at the brown bottles, just one shade darker than her own skin, passing by her without seeing them. Unlike the other women here at the plant, she had *plans.*

She wanted to be down South when she was Roberta's age, relaxing in a house with smart walls, something close to the beach. She wanted to smell salt in the air instead of burnt barley and factory smoke. Every morning she'd snap her fingers and turn the eastern smart walls transparent, just in time for the sunrise.

"Shon," someone said next to her. *"Shontera."*

Shontera jerked her head up and blinked. Bottles were backed up behind her sorter, like bugs outside a screen door.

Angie stood next to her, holding an inspection keypad and a stamp gun.

"I need you to inspect the last shipment for me again," she said. "Some of the bottles haven't been sealed right, and they're getting skunked. You up to it?"

"Sure," she said, glad her dark skin hid the blush she felt creeping across her cheeks. She'd been thinking of spaceships falling from the sky and hitting the sandy beach outside her Myrtle Beach dream home with sounds like gunshots.

Angie nodded and walked off, disappearing behind a pallet of twelve-pack boxes.

"Wantas are coming to get you, dreamer," Roberta called out from two lines over. "They already got your apartment. Better start paying attention or they'll steal your *job,* too."

The racket of bottles sliding along the conveyor, on their way upstairs to shipping, kept Shontera from shouting out what she'd wanted to say back to Roberta.

Instead she walked along the line, clicking a stamp on an occasional bottle with a crooked cap or a broken seal before pulling them off the line. After a few minutes her mind began to wander again, but instead of the beach, she found herself thinking about the Wannoshay.

Ever since they came to Earth—"made planetfall," the Netstream anchor's voice blared inside her head—they had caused nothing but trouble.

First was the violence caused by panic and fear, like Roberta's husband in the church, followed by the protestors at the landing sites. Next came the integration riots, which started as soon as the aliens left their ships and moved into the cities. More troops were patrolling the streets now, including Shontera's two younger brothers in the Guard, along with most of the men who used to work next to her in the brewery.

When her landlord had raised the rent on her in March, she and Toshera had been forced to leave their old apartment. She learned later that her former landlord had cut a deal with a businessman who was planning on renting it out at lower rates to the aliens, hoping for some tax cuts and free publicity.

If William hadn't left us, she thought, we wouldn't have had to move in the first place. Slimy bastard, leaving like that in the middle of the night. He had yet to pay any child support for Toshera in the years since he'd run off.

Shontera wondered if William and the Wantas and the government were all in some secret conspiracy to make her and Toshera's lives miserable.

A bottle, broken off at the neck, rattled down the line toward her, and she almost cut herself on it.

"Pay attention, dreamer," she whispered, and the bottles kept coming, never stopping. Like a robot, she clicked the stamp again and again, tallying up the rejects. For her, each day on the line was one day closer to leaving Milwaukee behind, forever.

"What's the difference between a Wanta and a Wannoshay, Mom?" Toshera asked the next morning at breakfast. Baked potatoes, left over from last night, and toast.

Toshera wore her orange sun earrings, and her brown eyes were obscured behind the lenses of her thick glasses. She flattened a mound of sour cream on her potato and sprinkled sugar on it.

Most of the other kids in Toshera's fifth-grade class had perfect vision, but Shontera couldn't afford the lasix surgery. Not if they wanted to get to Myrtle Beach before both of them were old ladies.

"Mom?" Toshera asked again.

"They mean the same thing, honey," Shontera said, swallowing hot coffee. "One is just uglier. I think they like to be called Wannoshay. Why do you ask?"

"The kids at school're talking about them. You know, um, ugly stuff. How they're the reason the soldiers are all over the place nowadays. And they call them Wanno-you-know-whats. Rhymes with 'spits.' I don't get why their kids can't come to school with us."

Toshera pushed up her glasses and watched her mother.

Shontera felt something give inside her chest. Her little girl was growing up so fast.

"They're different, honey," she said. "I don't think they can speak our language yet. Though someone at work said they can understand us, somehow . . . But don't worry about them. I imagine they need their space, too, just like us. Ready to go?"

"Sure," Toshera said, gulping down the last of the milk.

They were almost out of groceries, but today was only Wednesday, with no paycheck until after Saturday's shift. She handed Toshera her keypad and backpack, and they headed out into the morning sun with the smell of burnt hops and stale barley filling the air.

Angie, Shontera's supervisor, had known for months about Shontera's plans to move away, but she'd never held it against her. Shontera took the beer Angie had pulled from the mini-fridge in her office, watching the steam rise from the ice-cold bottle. At first her stomach wanted to turn over at the sight of another bottle of beer after ten hours of staring at bottles on the line, but she twisted off the top anyway and sucked down a big gulp that she could feel all the way down to her toes.

Nothing like six o'clock on a Saturday after a long week of work, she thought. Hopefully all this overtime will get Toshera and me out of here that much sooner.

"Monday's the big day, you know," Angie said, adjusting her bra strap with an expert flip of the wrist. "Hard to believe the politicians were able to pull it off, getting the aliens to come work for minimum wage. Some of the jokers in shipping are calling it the invasion of the beer snatchers."

Shontera grinned and shook her head. "So how come they get stuck down in refrigeration?"

Angie leaned back in her chair, polishing off half her beer. "You really were daydreaming the past few days, weren't you? Roberta's been talking nonstop about how the Wannoshay have this ultrathick skin so they can handle the cold. And they're strong, too. Said she heard all about them from her brother-in-law. He's a cop downtown, on their side."

Shontera took another long swallow from her beer and thought about their old apartment. It all made her want to gag.

"So how come they're just starting to work now? What've they been doing the past few months?" Besides taking over our apartments and setting up in our old hotels, she wanted to add, but she swallowed it with another gulp of beer.

"Stuff like this takes time," Angie said. "Remember how everyone was convinced back in January that the aliens were invading, that when their ratty old ships crash-landed they were just the first wave of some army of killer space aliens? At least we didn't have riots here like they did in Minneapolis. Lots of people got hurt bad when they tried to blow up that ship."

Shontera nodded, thinking about the downloads of the ships in Minnesota, along with the images of all the packed churches at the start of the year. Lots of folks thought it was the Second Coming, or Armageddon, or both. She thought of Roberta's husband and shuddered.

"Guess you're right," she said. "Though if there was an invasion, maybe then I wouldn't have had to move out of my old place."

Angie opened another beer and gave a quick laugh. She leaned back again and flipped the bottle top onto the table.

"This is like nothing else we've ever experienced, Shontera. Maybe like the civil rights stuff back in the sixties—I saw a couple 'Stream downloads about that. People hate anyone who's different, and I'd say these Wannoshay are pretty damn different. Didn't you say your father was one of those Black Panthers?"

"My grandfather."

Shontera shook her head and sipped her beer. Grandpa and Dad were always talking about racism and filling Toshera's head with crazy ideas about protesting and fighting The Man. Shontera didn't have time for all that. When you were a single black mother living in the city, pretty much everyone else was "The Man."

"Anyway," Angie continued, "just like back in those civil rights days, the company's trying to send a message to the rest of the country by bringing the Wannoshay here to work so quickly after they arrived. I think someone's getting paid off. And you know the army guys want to get their hands on the Wantas' tech. Maybe find some lasers on those wrecked ships, use 'em in the good old war on terror." Angie paused to finish off her beer. "But hey, what do you care? You're going to be long gone soon, right?"

"Yeah," Shontera said, imagining soldiers crawling all over the black ships like ants, pulling it apart piece by piece. "It's all too much to think about. And anyway, I need to get home."

She stood up too quickly and swayed a little—too much cold beer on an empty stomach. Angie walked her to the door and patted her on the back, making her T-shirt stick to her.

Angie must have seen something on Shontera's face, because she said, "Don't worry," and then laughed. "What are they going to do, kill us all and take over the place?"

Shontera wanted to laugh, but her mouth was too dry. She opened the door and walked past the second-shift workers on the line, busy sorting bottles and inspecting labels. Even if the economy was crap, people still wanted to drink beer, probably even more so in times like these.

It wasn't until she left the brewery, smelling and tasting stale beer with each step, that she realized she'd taken the long way out, avoiding the refrigeration cellars in some kind of unthinking fear. On Monday, they'd be here.

She woke Monday morning with her daughter standing next to her bed. Toshera's skin was an ashy color, lighter than her usual dark mocha color, and she groaned: the headaches again.

"Morning, honey," she said. "Let's get you some extra-strength painkillers and get you off to school, okay? Two more weeks before summer break."

"Yeah," Toshera said. She put on her glasses with a grimace.

Shontera knew she wouldn't be able to get Toshera to the

clinic tonight after work, not if she got off at six and had to ride the bus back. She wanted to think of the beach and Toshera in her bright red swimsuit in the sand. But all she could think of was what Roberta had said about the aliens in one of the endless gossip sessions the bitter woman led: "They have snakes for hair, and they eat dirt."

In the kitchen, trying to wake up, she put two slices of bread into the toaster.

Snakes for hair. How could that be?

"Mom," Toshera said, breaking her out of her daydreams. "Can we go to the Wanta section of town this weekend? Our teachers say they need volunteers to teach the Wantas English."

"Wannoshay, honey. Wanta's an ugly name."

They'll be at the brewery at eight this morning. In two hours.

"Okay, okay. So can we go over there sometime?"

Shontera smelled something burning. She turned and snatched the smoking bread out of the toaster.

"Go where, honey?"

"Mom! Quit being such a dreamer."

Shontera turned on her daughter, dropping slices of burnt toast.

"No. No, we're not going over to see the aliens. Not this weekend, not ever. Can't you see that we have enough problems right here? Leave the Wantas *alone.*"

Toshera shrugged her shoulder out of her mother's grip.

"Call them Wannoshay, Mom. Wanta's an ugly word. You said so yourself."

That morning, Roberta was early for a change. Her voice echoed through the quiet of the brewery at ten minutes before eight, and Shontera couldn't help but listen to her.

"They all live together and sleep in the same bed. They don't have families like we do. Just a whole bunch of aliens with snakes for hair, all huddled together like rats. They're probably tunneling their way under the city right now, as we sit around with our thumbs up our butts. They've got mental powers, I heard. Telepathy and all that sort of voodoo crap. I even heard they can have sex with any other Wanta they pick, and they think we're childish for having husbands and wives."

"Well, my husband's pretty childish," Maria said, and everyone laughed but Roberta.

Shontera turned away when she saw the flash of pain on Roberta's wrinkled face. Then the first-shift buzzer went off and the line started.

Toshera's painkillers should have kicked in by now.

"Heads up, Shontera," Maria whispered on her way to her station. She pointed at the stairway and the steel double doors leading down to their section of the factory.

Mark Stevens, one of the few men still working at the brewery, stood there. He was sweating through his dress shirt and holding the door open.

A tall, bony person with what looked like thick dreadlocks walked through the door, swaying his back in a strange, jerky motion with each step. His ragged-looking pants were cuffed four or five times.

Another stepped through, then another, all of them with the same build. Before she knew it, a dozen of the lanky, gray-skinned aliens stood on the landing next to Mark. Up and down the line, everyone else had stopped to look.

"Dios mio," Maria whispered, her brown eyes wide.

When Shontera glanced back at the doorway, Mark had gotten the parade of Wannoshay moving again. She looked closer at the aliens as they made their awkward way down the steps. None of them wore shoes, and their hands and feet seemed to have been switched—hands had toes, and feet had fingers.

She thought at first that they were all men, with their

oversized rib cages and long backs, but then she noticed three aliens in the middle of the group with what must have been breasts under the fabric of their T-shirts. The aliens clustered together at the foot of the steps, waiting for Mark to tell them where to go.

They won't even look at us, she thought.

As she watched, mouth dry, the aliens began following Mark again. Without warning, the second alien in the slow parade began to sway. At nearly seven feet tall, he looked like a tower blowing in the wind. The muscles in her stomach clenched when the creature's wide shoulders swung violently from side to side.

He moaned and dropped to all fours, still shaking, and Shontera saw scars crisscrossing the backs of both of his big hands.

Before the shuddering alien could get away—he looked as if he were about to sprint off like a racer—the other aliens put their hands on him, on his back and in his quivering hair. He beat the palms of his hands on the hard metal floor, four fast blows with each toe-filled hand, and then a low hum coming from the other Wannoshay drowned out his moaning.

As quickly as it had begun, before Mark had even noticed the disturbance, the stricken Wannoshay was back on his feet and walking toward the cellars as if nothing had happened.

"Dios mio," Maria whispered again. The wonder in her voice had been replaced with fear and a hint of disgust.

The other aliens hurried past, but one of the females walked slower than the others, her dark eyes taking in everything around her. She wore faded, cuffed-up jeans and a too-short Packers T-shirt that looked twenty years old.

The alien woman was less than ten yards away, and Shontera could smell a musty scent coming from her, a salty smell stronger than the bitter hops-and-barley odor of the factory.

Is she going to try and talk to me?

Shontera's head filled with a strange buzzing sensation, and she wished she would've paid more attention to the article about the Wannoshay that Toshera had downloaded from the Net-streams.

The rattle of glass on glass brought her back to reality. Bottles had backed up for ten yards on the line.

She reached out for a bottle, but before she could check the label and the seal, the bottle slid out of her sweaty hands. It bounced off the rubber bumpers on the belt and would have smashed to the floor if a gray foot hadn't stopped its fall.

The female Wannoshay balanced easily on her left foot and stretched her right leg up to Shontera, at chest level, holding the stray bottle. Her four long toes were wrapped around the neck of the brown bottle like fingers. Her hands hung down almost uselessly at her side, fingers tipped with claws that glistened like metal.

Shontera gazed into the Wannoshay female's eyes. They were totally black, all three of them. The line in the middle of the Wannoshay woman's forehead had parted, becoming a sideways eye that stared at Shontera. A musky smell filled her nose.

"Thanks," she whispered.

" 'Angks," the other woman said. Her wide, lipless mouth moved in a strange, rippling manner when she spoke.

Shontera felt the voice in her head more than in her ears. She shivered and grabbed at the bottle clumsily, her face hot. The buzzing in her head was making her dizzy, and she couldn't seem to get her breath back.

Something ugly inside of her made sure she touched only the bottle when she took it from the alien woman, avoiding any possible contact with the alien's foot or one of her finger-toes.

With the bottle tight in her grasp, Shontera looked back at the line and saw Roberta watching. The older woman's wrinkled face was puckered with concentration. When Shontera turned back to the Wannoshay woman, the alien was gone, leaving behind only a strangely comforting tang of salt that made her yearn for an ocean she'd never seen.

The city bus was late that night, and the sun hung just below the tall buildings on West State Street when she finally returned to her apartment complex. She passed through the flimsy security arch and skipped the rickety elevator.

Panting in the hot air of her hallway six flights up, she unlocked the three deadbolts to her door and stood there for a moment, key still in her hand. Inside, the apartment was stale and hot, like the attic in her parents' house in Lake Geneva.

"Toshera?" she called, hurrying inside and entering her daughter's bedroom.

The air in this room felt like cotton in her lungs. A lump stuck out of the mattress, covered in the thick woolen blankets they had stored in the closet at the end of winter.

"Mama," Toshera said. "My head hurts, bad. The nurse sent me home." Her voice was thick from crying.

Shontera's hands curled up into fists against her legs, thinking about Toshera here by herself all day in the stuffy apartment.

"Toshera, honey, let's get you out from under there."

Under the two blankets, the sheet covering Toshera was soaked with sweat. She wore her heavy University of Wisconsin sweatshirt and two pairs of sweatpants, and her thick black hair was wild and tangled. She was shivering.

"Mama, I'm sorry I'm sick," she whispered. Closing her eyes, she rested her hot forehead on Shontera's shoulder.

"Enough about that," Shontera whispered, stroking her daughter's hair. "We need you to get better, honey."

She pulled out her money card and called up a cab with her

old Netstream unit. They were going to have to go to the clinic and pay the after-hours fee. Another week or two of savings gone, just like that.

They struggled down the stairs, Toshera leaning on her for support. Toshera was crying by the time they reached the lobby. Without really thinking about what she was saying, just wanting to drown out the soft sobbing of her daughter, Shontera started talking.

"They came to work today, Toshera. The *Wannoshay.* I got to meet one. They're really, really tall, and they don't have hair like you and me."

She described the aliens as best she could, and the words fell out of her faster and faster, like the way the bottles on the line flew past when everything was operating right.

She told Toshera about the aliens' gray skin, their smells, their three black eyes, and the way they walked half-hunched over as if they'd rather go on all fours like a horse.

She even told her about the way the female alien had saved the bottle of beer for her, catching it easily with her foot, and then passing it back to her without ever losing her balance.

The cab came at last, and Toshera and Shontera crawled in. It had air conditioning and thick safety windows. The cold interior was as refreshing as jumping into the ocean must feel like on a hot day.

"What was her name?" Toshera asked, sitting up straight.

"Her name?"

Shontera looked at Toshera and thought about those three black eyes staring at her. The Wannoshay woman had no name, for all she knew. No name.

"Nonami," she said at last.

"What kind of name is *that?*" Toshera said with the hint of a grin.

"An *alien* name," Shontera said. She rubbed her daughter's

forehead and smiled for the first time in a long, long time.

"Nonami the Wannoshay," Toshera said. "I like how that sounds."

The cab pulled up in front of the clinic, and the driver swiped her card through his reader with a beep. More money gone.

"Come on," she said, helping Toshera out of the cold cab and back into the stifling heat of the city. "Let's get you taken care of, young lady."

But we'll make it out of here yet, Shontera told herself as they made their way into the clinic. Wannoshay or no Wannoshay.

Chapter Six

Spring came to the Midwest late that year, but with a vengeance, bringing with it a wave of unexpected heat that sucked the air out of Father Joshua's small tent. Wiping sweat from his forehead, he glanced from one of the three flat screens on his desk to another. In spite of the heat and the lack of proper ventilation in his tent, he loved his new job.

The leftmost screen affixed to his hard plastic desk ran a re-creation of the landing trajectories of the alien ships, twenty-nine streaks running east to west. The middle screen was dotted with windows of various Bible passages that he was supposed to be reviewing for Sunday's sermon. The third played a split CNNBC Netstream, the left half streaming a story about an anti-integration protest in northern Iowa, the right half reporting on the first day of work for a dozen Wannoshay at a St. Paul construction site.

"Enter Secure mode," he said into the mike attached to the side of his face like a growth. "Password only, my voice only, active now."

He peeled off the mike, set it down, and stepped away from the desk. After his first visit to this landing site just five weeks ago, the governments of America and Canada had come to an agreement with the aliens: the People (as he now couldn't help but call the Wannoshay) would share the technology from their battered ships if they could be allowed to leave the landing sites and live aboveground. The battered military had been determined to get the aliens *out* of the ships and into cheap housing, away from the landing sites and the precious high-tech secrets of the ships.

Fortunately, through the use of human pharmaceuticals and derm patches, the gray skin of the People had been sufficiently toughened against Earth's sun. Thanks to linguists like his new friend Karin, an expert in Farsi and Arabic and a dozen other languages, the People could communicate with humans in a very basic fashion. The slow process of integration had begun.

Dabbing at his wet forehead with his handkerchief, Joshua checked the time on one of his screens. He was due in Colonel Cossa's tent in ten minutes for a briefing. He grabbed his Bible and his Army-issue glasses and walked outside.

The sky was cloudless, a beautiful afternoon in late April marred only by the occasional shouts of the protestors and other groups massed outside the landing site. The people on the other side of the fence never seemed to leave, much less sleep.

Inhaling the country air, he made his way to the colonel's tent, trying to decide how to start his sermon for tomorrow's Mass. As a challenge to himself, he was determined to talk about something other than the People, but he kept drawing a blank every time he tried to come up with something more relevant.

The colonel wasn't in, but there was a note inside the tent door for Joshua. The note was attached to a long, rectangular package made of black metal that was bent in two, like an old-fashioned notebook computer. The two ends of the outer piece of metal were held together by a black wire.

When he saw the thin sheets of metal inside the thicker, bent piece, he realized it *looked* like an actual notebook, from back when people used paper all the time. He picked up the piece of slick black metal, his fingers wanting to pull away from the icy feel of the thin slices of stacked metal inside. He could almost taste the metal's harsh flavor, just from touching it.

The colonel's careful block letters on the piece of temporary paper read: "Father: What do you make of this? Just found this today along with a dozen others inside flooring of ship. Keep it for a day or two before I pass it on to Karin. We'll talk then."

With sunshine warming his face, Joshua sat down on the front step of the colonel's tent and unwrapped the wire that held the outer piece of metal together and kept the thin sheaves of flat black metal inside. The colonel's note had already dissolved and dripped onto the ground next to him when he unbent the cold metal, the bend disappearing without a seam once the metal was laid flat across his lap.

Before he could marvel at the behavior of the outer metal "cover," the sheaves spilled out, sliding off the now-smooth surface and onto the ground. One of the thin pieces of metal nicked the back of his right hand as it fell.

"Nice work, McDowell," he muttered, looking at all the loose pieces of metal surrounding him like fallen leaves.

Ignoring the tiny cut on his hand, he carefully gathered up the pieces, avoiding the razor-sharp edges. Some of the pieces were square, others circular, some oval, and a dozen were octagonal in shape. Arranging them by shape on the two steps next to him, he soon had four separate piles.

The original piece of thick metal that had held the thinner pieces together now lay limply on his lap like a heavy blanket. Or like Johndo's chair inside the ship. Or the restraints of black metal the colonel had wrapped around Johndo's wrists. The metallic taste in his mouth refused to go away.

Glancing off to his left and then his right, wondering what he must look like, sitting there in front of the colonel's tent surrounded by alien objects, Joshua took the thick piece of metal and rolled it up from one end like a bedroll. The metal cooperated, and he set the thick tube of metal on the step behind him as a back rest.

"Unbelievable," he whispered, the cold of the metal against his lower back seeping through his shirt, cooling him off.

Finally, he picked up an octagonal piece of thin metal from the biggest pile and held it up to his face. Squinting and holding it about two feet from his face with his head turned to one side, he saw that the black metal was covered in spiraling gray and white designs that were made up of raised icons and rounded mandalas. He found an occasional symbol that made him think of Greek characters, while the other symbols reminded him of Aramaic.

I definitely need to show this to Karin, he thought. But not just yet.

With the help of Karin, the language expert in the gray jumpsuit he'd first seen on the day he met Johndo, he'd been understanding more and more of the language of the People. Karin had confided in him that a large part of the comprehension came from what she thought was telepathy, and Joshua had not contradicted her. In any case, the Wannoshay language was much more fun to learn than Latin had ever been. He liked the lilting way it flowed off his tongue, with few hard consonants to get in the way.

But he'd never seen the written language of the People. At first he was overwhelmed by all the meaningless slash marks and jagged scribbles, but when he considered the markings as a whole, he saw that there *was* some sort of organization. He had more luck when he put himself in the mindset of Johndo's manner of speaking, a combination of spoken word, motions, and intonations.

The symbols couldn't be deciphered from left to right, or right to left, he decided. But every time he started to feel something start to make sense, he'd hear the chanting of the protestors outside the fence drifting over to him.

"Let them all free!" one group shouted, only to be answered by "Lock them all up!"

Joshua tried to focus in spite of the battling voices. Usually the people outside were fairly peaceful and quiet, but today was going to be one of those off-kilter days, he could tell.

His head began to ache, but he continued examining the book, turning it slowly and running his hands softly over the raised icons and designs. Everything on the page seemed to have some sort of circular nature; if something wasn't a spiral, then it was a circle or oval, crisscrossed with slashes and wavy lines.

Something about those shapes and designs made him think about Johndo's hands. Stubby fingers that were almost always hooked into a clawing shape, like four fat Cs on the ends of his hands. Joshua glanced at the thin line of drying blood on the back of his own hand, a simple, mundane design when compared to Johndo's.

A pair of Humvees suddenly roared to life three tents down from where he was sitting, making him forget about his and Johndo's hands. Feeling foolish for leaving the remaining pages of this book of the People out in the sun and dust, he gathered up all the pages and unrolled the thick metal covering from the step. While the Hummers hurried past, no doubt on their way to the protestors at the front gate, he made sure not to touch the razor-sharp sides as he placed the pages into the cover.

He winced at the sounds of gunshots outside the fence, and he prayed for rubber bullets. He looked off in the direction of the gate and listened, but all he could hear was the flap of the tents in the breeze. He turned back to the sheets of metal.

Fifteen minutes slipped past as he paged through the metal pages, and the heat of the day was forgotten. He didn't dare to think that he was lucky enough to hold a piece of the People's true history, but he could always hope.

And he could always ask Johndo. Tomorrow.

Tonight, Joshua had to get back home to see if he still had a congregation left for Sunday's sermon.

Early the next day, wearing his short-sleeved black shirt and white collar, he held his right hand up to Johndo, trying to remember the proper word as his Wannoshay friend waited.

"Iwolo," he said at last. His voice fell flat in the black-metal confines of the ship. He ran his forefinger over the shallow, dark red cut on the back of his hand, hoping he'd pronounced the word correctly.

"A scratch," he added. "That's all. *Iwolo.*"

Leaning forward in his chair of smooth, almost-liquid metal, Johndo the Wannoshay blinked all three of his eyes as he stared at the wound Joshua had gotten from the book yesterday.

"Iwolo?" Johndo said, his lipless mouth barely moving. His middle eye closed for a moment. " 'Gratch?"

Joshua had forgotten all about the scratch until he'd walked into Johndo's small room aboard the ship. Lit by a single orb next to the open doorway, the black walls were bare, and the only furniture was the metal chair Johndo was resting on, a second chair that was wider and shorter, a mat on the floor, and a low black shelf at Joshua's eye level that ran the entire width of the room.

The shelf in Johndo's room had always been empty, and this fact had always for some reason saddened Joshua.

"Yes," he said. "From *this.*"

He held up the book he'd spent most of the night studying back in the rectory of Our Lady. After about five hours of fruitless studying, he'd started wishing for some of that Wannoshay telepathy Karin had told him about. The book and its metal pages remained a mystery.

Johndo flinched, pulling his oval-shaped head back, as if the sight of the book bothered him. A bitter smell similar to burnt coffee filled the room for an instant.

Joshua glanced at the doorway to his right, where he saw the armored shoulder of the young soldier who'd escorted him into the ship. He'd never forgotten Johndo's fists from his first visit, punching his chair until the colonel restrained him.

"Is it a book?" he said. "A . . . *neowo?* To read?"

A few thick strands of Johndo's short, tentacle-like hair plucked at the last three bandages covering the slowly healing scars on his mottled gray face. Joshua knew the pink derm patch on the back of Johndo's neck was finally doing its work, but as one of the first of the People to risk Earth's atmosphere unprotected, Johndo's burns had been deep.

"No," Johndo said at last. "Not *neowo,* Yotchooa."

Joshua sighed. He went over to the second chair and rested his back against it. The chair molded itself to his body, taking most of his weight.

"If it's not a book," he said, "what in the world *is* it?"

Johndo took the book from Joshua's hands and carried it to his mat, holding it away from his long torso with his short, curved fingers. Joshua couldn't tell if Johndo was being extra careful with it, or if he simply didn't want to touch it. He had so much to learn about the People, and he felt incredibly tired at the prospect.

Letting Johndo busy himself with the book, he closed his eyes and bounced slightly on the cold metal of the chair. He thought about the three new complaints he'd found on his Netstream when he'd returned home to the rectory last night. One of them had contacted the archbishop about how he'd been gone so much. He hadn't taken a confession in over a month. He never felt like he had enough time, and his congregation was paying for it.

Just before opening his eyes again, he thought of Johndo's

words from their first discussion, the words that Johndo had spoken directly into his mind: “Know a people’s true history, know their soul.”

When he opened his eyes, Joshua inhaled with a mix of fear and awe, an emotion he’d gotten used to feeling on a regular basis around his new friend.

“Johndo.”

Joshua pulled himself free of the metal grip of the chair and gazed at the shelf circling the room. On the shelf, Johndo had placed the sheaves of metal that Joshua had come to think of as pages of a book. They weren’t leaning on the wall so much as stuck to it, in some sort of pattern according to shape: octagon, rectangle, circle, oval. But none of the shapes were arranged in a way that Joshua could see as meaningful.

Bent over and running with his hands slapping the floor, Johndo ran over to his mat and grabbed another sheet of metal, an octagon-shaped piece, and took it to the last empty space on the shelf on the other side of the room. While the shelf and its new contents were at eye-level for Joshua, when Johndo reared up on his feet, the shelf only reached up to his wide chest.

The soldier peeked into the room for a second at the sound of Johndo’s footsteps, and Joshua waved him away.

“Not *neowo*, Yotchooa,” Johndo said again, holding the sheet a foot away from the wall. He hadn’t put it in place yet. His mouth opened in what could have been a Wannoshay grin, the four rows of his sharpened teeth glistening in the light of the room’s orb.

Joshua took one final glance at the ring of pages encircling him—only the gray and white symbols were visible now, the metal blending into that of the wall—and then returned his attention to Johndo. Not knowing what else to do, he nodded.

“True history,” Johndo said in a clear voice inside Joshua’s head. He placed another metal page onto the shelf with a tiny

clicking sound.

White light shot straight out from each of the sheets, cutting the room in half, top to bottom. Joshua choked on his own breath, thinking he'd been blinded at first. When he blinked and inhaled, smelling Johndo's comforting odor of salt and mud instead of the bitter burnt-coffee smell, he saw that he was in a darkened cave filled with the People.

The darkness was staved off by a greenish glow coming from strands of lichen and vines attached to the rough angle formed where the cave wall met the cave ceiling. The walls were ridged and irregular, as if carved out by hand. *Clawed* hands.

Over two dozen gray-skinned, shuddering People stood on all fours, huddled around a trio of lighter-skinned People, males with long bluish-black hair tentacles and scars crisscrossing the length of their bare chests.

Joshua's eyes adjusted immediately to the gloom, and then he saw the same scene sideways, from a slightly higher vantage point. Too shocked to move or speak, he could only watch as the People pushed forward, reaching out to the three males, who inched backward until they were up against the cave wall.

High-pitched voices sang a Wannoshay word that Joshua couldn't translate at first, a word of too many vowels and not enough hard consonants. The voices made something at the top of his head squirm, as if his hair was growing back and reaching for the cave ceiling.

The singing became loud as a scream, yet somehow it never lost its strange beauty. Twitching arms and squirming tentacle-hairs filled Joshua's split perceptions, and the light from the lichen began to fade.

Before a scream of his own could escape his lips, the vision ended.

Gasping for air, Joshua lay on his side on the floor of Johndo's room with his numbed hands plastered over his ears. He couldn't smell anything now except his own sweat.

All he could hear was the People's word that they'd been screaming over and over again like a curse.

He recognized it: *Twilight.*

A tentative hand touched the front of his shirt, and the scream that he had swallowed nearly rose to the surface again.

"Yotchooa?"

Joshua pulled free of the hand before he realized who it was in front of him.

"Johndo," he gasped. "What happened?"

Johndo had left his side. Joshua looked over at his new friend's mat and saw a small pile of unused metal pages. The topmost page of this pile of metal wafers appeared to be blank.

Oblivious to Joshua now, Johndo rushed around the room on all fours, collecting the metal sheets from the shelf, pulling the sheets roughly off the wall, oblivious to the sharp edges even as they cut into his fingers. His breath whistled in and out of his lipless mouth, and his wide shoulders twitched.

"Johndo?" Joshua said, looking at the fresh scratches on Johndo's fingers, dripping reddish-purple blood. Many, many *iwolo.*

Joshua touched the scratch on the back of his own hand as Johndo gathered the sheets in what appeared to be a haphazard manner and closed the cover. He saw the strange designs carved like tattoo or scars on the back of each of Johndo's gray hands, two intersecting ovals inside an octagon.

The room now smelled like salt, and something deeper, more pungent, like rotting fruit.

He slid across the cold floor, closer to where Johndo paused above the book and the mat, panting. Some of the pages sat behind Johndo, pages Joshua hadn't seen on the wall before the vision overtook all his senses. He looked back at Johndo, whose wide shoulders were quivering as his fingers dripped blood onto the black floor. The blood dissipated as soon as it hit, as if being absorbed.

Looking at the expanse of Johndo's elongated spine through his thin T-shirt, he heard a warning begin to sound in the back of his mind that he did his best to ignore.

"Johndo? Were those People . . ." He knew he shouldn't say the word, but he couldn't stop himself. "Were they . . . twilight?"

The soldier standing guard outside the room, having seen something different in the way Johndo was acting, had taken two steps into the room. In the days that followed, Joshua would convince himself that those steps by the soldier saved his life that morning.

As soon as Joshua uttered the word, Johndo turned on him, and the soldier couldn't prevent Johndo from lashing out with a thick arm. His square hand hit Joshua on the right side of the face.

The last thing Joshua thought before the impact of the bloody fingers of Johndo's clawed hand was another word of the People: *Iwolo.*

As his world spun from the blow and bright white light once again flashed into his vision, he saw the soldier grab something on his belt and press a button. Joshua fell to his knees, and Johndo followed suit almost immediately, dropping like dead weight to the metal floor. Johndo's derm patch gave off a trickle of smoke, like a tiny, extinguished campfire.

Not a book, Joshua's reeling mind repeated.

He thought the words first in English, then in bastardized Wannoshay. With one hand held over the bloody, stinging scratches Johndo had left on his face, the other hand pressed to his chest, he wondered if he would ever get the chance to ask Johndo to explain that statement and answer his original question.

He wondered if Johndo would ever be able to answer *any* of the questions that would come later.

With his vision dimming and stinging pain covering half of his face, Joshua stared at the motionless Wannoshay just a few feet away from him and felt something hopeful and good inside of him begin to die.

Chapter Seven

In early May, a few weeks after her painful night spent on the floor of the restaurant, once she'd recovered from the bout of pneumonia she'd picked up as a result of that night, Ally Trang was back in Winnipeg.

She parked her newly fixed clunker of a car on Toronto Street and swallowed a second capsule of Blur. The drug helped her remember the bits of the Wannoshay language she'd found on the 'Streams. She'd been preparing for this day ever since that cold night.

The time had come for her to meet her first Wanta, up close, and film the entire encounter for her Netstream.

She entered the Winnipeg neighborhood flying high, but not so high that she wasn't on the lookout for soldiers or plain-clothes police officers—she knew right away who they were, try as they might to act like they were regular people. But the soldiers on Ellice Avenue seemed more interested in protecting the Wannoshay from anti-integrationists and suicide cultists than they were with her presence there.

They ran a wand over her, okayed her camera, and checked her ID card. She was allowed to walk unescorted through the neighborhood. The government had decided to keep the new Wannoshay dwellings accessible—thinking that would ease the fears of integration—but not *too* accessible.

She passed by the uneven rows of disposable Netstream cams dotting the buildings of the neighborhood, glued to the walls by reporters hoping to catch the first hints of any worthwhile Wannoshay news. She held up both middle fingers to the cams on her way past them. If she were taller she'd reach up, rip them down, and stamp on them.

Bunch of amateurs, letting the cams do the work for you.

As her own camera recorded the renovations taking place in buildings that had been either empty for years or badly damaged in bombings, she was surprised to not see more aliens outside. The sun had been bright all morning, yet another uncommonly hot day, but clouds had gathered as she wandered up and down Ellice.

With the sun gone, the air turned cooler, and less than a minute later she saw three aliens walk out of the old Thai restaurant she'd hidden in on the night the Wannoshay came to town. The window had been replaced recently, and silvery holo-stickers were still stuck to the glass.

Up and down the street, more aliens came outside, sweeping off the sidewalks or picking up garbage that had blown onto the street. The three Wannoshay outside the restaurant were cleaning the new windows under the casually watchful eyes of the pair of Canadian Forces soldiers, who kept their rifles slung across their backs.

Ally's throat locked up when she was five meters from the aliens and the CF soldiers. She stopped. This was as near as she wanted to get to a Wanta. Her legs refused to move her closer. She could smell their salty-sweet odor, and she swore she could hear their muscles creak as they scraped the stickers off the glass and washed the windows.

The aliens made her nose itch and her ears ring. Their long hair was thick and ropy, hanging partway down their broad backs. All of them wore ill-fitting jeans, but instead of faded second-hand T-shirts, all three of these aliens wore shirts that appeared to be woven out of dead grass. They had to have been handmade.

Ally knew she was staring, but she couldn't stop herself. Why hadn't anybody tried to make clothes for the aliens that actually fit them? Surely there was money to be made there.

At the ends of the Wantas' too-short legs, the gray feet she remembered so clearly from a week earlier were still bare, their long finger-toes clutching the concrete sidewalk like claws. The aliens looked like they were afraid of being top-heavy and toppling over if they leaned too far one way or the other.

They were all well over two meters tall.

Thinking about the Wannoshay getting out of the buses on that dark, Blurry night, she almost kept walking past this trio of aliens hunched over their work, silent in their concentration. Then she saw a pair of 'Stream reporters across the street, attaching more cams to a wall and searching for an alien to talk to.

She gritted her teeth when she felt a burst of energy hit her from the Blur. Her confidence doubled as she thought about how great some real footage by a real person, not some clueless hack reporter, would look on her Netstream. Lots of download potential there, and she needed the income—she'd already blown almost all the money she'd made from charging for her footage of the aliens' first night in Winnipeg. She'd been rich with Blur for less than a month.

She forced her legs to step up to the three aliens in front of the restaurant, making sure the tiny camera on her shirt was aimed at them.

"Hello," she said to them.

As soon as she spoke, she felt a slight ringing in her ears, and she wondered if the aliens or the Blur was causing it. In any case, it was a pleasant sensation, and she was all about that.

The Wannoshay towered above her, their long backs turned

away from her. They continued working.

Ally's Blurred brain was going faster now, jumping from topic to topic. She wondered for an instant how the aliens were getting paid, then she tried to imagine what sort of food they'd buy with their money (if they even got paid in cash cards), and finally a Wanta word popped into her head, and she started talking.

"Excuse me," she said. "Hello? Um, *huwatcha?*"

As soon as she spoke her last word, all three aliens stopped their work and looked back at her. Their heads swiveled around impossibly far on their long necks, and the ropy tentacles on heads of the two taller aliens quivered toward Ally as if smelling her. The taller ones appeared to be female, while the shorter, fatter one seemed to be male.

Their hair *moves.* Ally rubbed her nose, trying to get the strange, salty smell of alien out of it.

Holy-shit-their-*hair*-moves!

"I'm-a . . . reporter," she lied, forcing herself to talk slowly and clearly despite the Blur in her system pushing her to go faster, faster. The lie came easily to her Blur-numbed lips, as did another Wanta word. "I am working on a story. About integration. For your people. Could I talk with you? Um . . . *Allola?*"

She pointed at the sparkling clean glass of the window, then at the buckets, sponges, and squeegees around them. She'd heard that the aliens already knew a good bit of English—she'd been secretly hoping they'd learn French first, but the pushy Americans got their way as usual, teaching them English, even those in Canada.

She'd also heard that they often preferred communicating with gestures and tones. Now that she was close to the aliens, she could see why speech wasn't preferable for them—their wide, lipless mouths weren't shaped the same way that humans' mouths were. She made a waving motion with her hand in front of her mouth, trying to pantomime words coming from her.

The shorter alien looked at her intently with his dark eyes, and then the sideways eye in the middle of its forehead opened. Ally swallowed a gasp; for an awful split-second it had looked like the gray-and-black-haired alien's forehead was splitting open. His hair quivered and moved like tiny snakes, but his tentacles were lighter in color and much shorter than the other two aliens next to him.

"Yesh, *allola,*" the short alien said, pronouncing the word with a stress on the first syllable. "We talgh."

Ally exhaled and almost started giggling. The salt smell had been replaced by not unpleasant spicy scent. It was working.

The shorter alien was more hunched than the others, making him seem like the oldest of the three. Further setting him apart from the females, the third eye of the male had flecks of white around the black iris, instead of complete blackness. When he set down his scraper, Ally saw a series of connected triangles and one tiny circle carved into the back on his long hand.

He raised his right hand palm up, dipping his head forward as if to say, "After you."

Inhaling a hint of vanilla along with the salty, spicy smells around her, Ally could have sworn she heard a voice say those words inside her head.

"This-okay?" she said to the two soldiers, who had taken a few steps closer to her and the Wannoshay. The soldier on the left nodded.

"Great-thanks," she called to them, feeling her voice speeding up again. "Thanks-great."

The other two aliens were females, if she was safe in assuming the bumps under their T-shirts were breasts. Their skin was darker, more of a deep gray-black, and she caught the glint of metal in their jet-black hair. The two females also set down their cleaning tools. All three aliens squatted, resting their backs against the brick wall next to the window. They were now exactly Ally's height.

Relax, she told herself. The hard part's over.

"Let's-start-with . . ." Ally took a deep breath and willed her hands to stop shaking and screwing up the camera's shot. "Let's . . . start . . . with names. *Gahawa?* I'm Alissa Trang. Alissa. My-*gahawa*-Alissa."

"A-issha," the aliens repeated. The older male's voice was lower than those of the two female aliens, though all three voices were deeper than a human's.

Ally wanted to examine the scars on the back of their hands more closely, but they were looking at her now with intent black eyes, waiting. She'd have to watch the footage later for details.

"Close-enough," she said, swallowing. She pointed at the male and raised her eyebrows. "Your-name-is? Your *gahawa?*"

The male only stared at her, his oval face blank. The look on his face made her think of Marlon Brando, in his last movie before his death back when she was just a kid.

Feeling foolish under the gaze of those black eyes, Ally touched her chest and repeated her name. She did her best to ignore the two soldiers, who had stopped talking and were watching her intently, probably wondering if they'd slipped up by letting her inside, especially if she was some suicide cultist who had come to wreak havoc with the Wantas.

She reached a hand up toward Brando's chest. He didn't flinch, but his middle eye narrowed and his spikes of tentacle-hair pulled straight back, away from her.

As the sun came out again, Ally raised her eyebrows and gave Brando her best questioning look.

"Gahawa?" she asked, nodding at him. She was starting to sweat.

One of the females snorted and twitched next to him, as if

she were laughing.

"A-issha?" the male said in response to Ally's question.

The smaller female gave another snort and knocked her head against the glass of the window, her tentacle-hairs rattling against the window like hail. Her right foot kicked like Thumper from the old Disney downloads.

Out of the corner of her eye, Ally saw the shadows of the soldiers inching closer, and the two reporters across the street had stopped to watch.

She sighed and wiped sweat from her forehead.

"*I'm* A-issha," she said, her hands starting to quiver again. "*My gahawa* A-issha."

The aliens repeated her name and touched their chests, and Ally tried to come up with a way to get her point across, while the short female—Thumper—continued twitching and tap-kicking her foot as if in response to Ally's edginess.

Ally fought the urge to tap her own feet in response, the Blur making her pulse race.

Before she could come up with a solution, however, Thumper's head dropped, her black hair now clinging protectively to her head. Her thick body shuddered in a wave-like motion, and when Brando moved closer to try to help her, Thumper pushed him back with a high-pitched squeal.

Brando took a half-step back before regaining his balance, and in the process, his hand brushed Ally's shoulder.

A fleeting image filled her head, a vision of a mountainous, black and white landscape littered with caves under a stormy purple sky. The trees of the forest next to the caves were all dead, black fingers poking into the air, rimed with white frost. Inside the trees were the bleached white bones of deformed creatures that she couldn't recognize.

A word echoed inside her head as the world dropped away from her in a vertigo-inducing rush: "Late."

The vision ended as Thumper gave another screech, spun away on her bare feet, and ran off down the street, away from the soldiers.

Ally almost fell over from Brando's touch and the vision that had come along with it. Her forehead was on fire, and she sucked in air as she smelled the alien's odor of burnt toast, with something rotten underneath.

"Go!" one of the soldiers shouted. The other soldier sprinted after the female Wannoshay, while the first soldier glanced at the two Netstream reporters across the street.

"Don't hurt her," he shouted after his partner, "just keep her from leaving the neighborhood. Use the—"

The soldier stopped when he saw Ally and the remaining two aliens staring at him. His fingers had been resting on a small green box clipped to his belt, but he dropped his hand from it as soon as he looked over at them.

What the *hell?* Ally glanced again at the green box on the soldier's belt. Do they have some sort of devices attached to the aliens? Like GPS units, or stunners?

Helpless, she watched the other soldier and the female alien until they disappeared around a corner. She barely had time to check to make sure her camera had gotten a clear shot of all the action.

She closed her mouth, which had been hanging open. She was shivering now as the Blur began to flash in her system.

"Listen," the soldier said. The two reporters across the street were walking off, shaking their heads. The soldier stepped up close to her, his face pinched and tight as he lowered his voice. "You may want to come by some other time, ma'am. Sometimes the Wantas get that way, get a little out of control. Let's just keep that little outburst under our hats, okay? Don't include that in your upload, all right?"

Ally nodded and flipped her hair out of the collar of her shirt so it covered the small camera attached to her lapel, hoping he wouldn't ask for her mini-DVD. But the soldier had already left her, calling out to the two reporters.

Her heart was still beating too fast for comfort, and without the soldiers watching over her, she felt exposed. Keeping her distance from the two remaining aliens, who were now squatting in motionless silence, she hurried back to her car.

She drove back to Sanford shaking and giggling with the remnants of adrenaline and Blur, the image of the frozen forest of bones almost completely forgotten.

She had the footage uploaded to her Netstream in under an hour, and her new Netstream avatar, "Wantaviewer," was born.

Chapter Eight

The day everything went to hell, Roberta claimed she'd lost her money card and kept on saying that one of the aliens had taken it. The brewery had finally cut back to eight-hour days, but the temperatures outside stayed in the nineties. The heat was getting to everyone, but the Wannoshay were taking it hardest. Many of them refused to leave the cool depths of the refrigeration cellars until the end of their shifts.

Nonami didn't seem to be as affected by the heat as her fellow Wannoshay, Shontera noticed. She saw Nonami every workday, on her way to breaks and at the end of shifts, but they never spoke. Nonami was always with other aliens, and ten more had been hired at the start of the past week. Angie claimed they could work all day and all night if the bosses wanted them to.

"When are you going to do something?" Roberta shouted at Angie after the morning break on that day, the last day of May. "I need my money, and I know that damn Wannoshit has my card."

Roberta turned on Shontera, and Shontera felt her face burn.

"I bet *she* knows all about this. She's been talking to them."

"Shut up, Roberta," Angie said. "Shontera's not a thief."

At that moment, a group of aliens were on their way back down to the cellars. They shuffled past Roberta and Angie on their short legs, swaying as they walked. They always looked to Shontera like they were about to fall over.

"Don't you dare look at me, you thief!" Roberta screamed at one of them, her voice cracking. Shontera had never heard her sound so angry, or scared.

The group of Wannoshay hurried past the lines, but the male Roberta had yelled at stopped in front of her, standing up straight. He was over seven feet tall.

The alien raised his right hand toward her, palm up. Shontera leaned forward, squinting to see what was happening. At first he seemed to be simply reaching out to Roberta to explain. Or maybe he wanted to silence her, to permanently stop her lips from moving.

Shontera didn't know for sure, and she probably never would know.

What she did know was this: the alien touched Roberta, and something changed in her. As if she were a balloon full of anger, and the alien had sucked the bad air out of her with his touch.

When he let go of her, Roberta looked at him for a long moment with her face deflated, and then she started moaning. It was loud and high-pitched, full of fear, and it lasted close to ten seconds. Roberta didn't even sound *human*. The memory of it still kept Shontera awake at night.

Roberta's moaning brought the other women on the line running, along with some of the people up in shipping. She'd been that loud.

As his fellow aliens lumbered back toward him, the Wannoshay male stepped away from Roberta, even more unsteady than usual, and then he suddenly bent down. He touched his hands to the floor like a runner waiting for a starting gun. The backs of both hands had a set of what looked like scars, like a strange tic-tac-toe pattern. The other aliens reached out their overlong arms for him.

Staring at the group of Wannoshay, along with the rest of the humans who stood back from him at a safe distance, a pair of thoughts struck Shontera like slaps to either cheek: these creatures weren't like us at all, and I'll never understand them the way I would other people.

After hunching there, quivering, for five seconds, the alien bolted away from the other Wannoshay, galloping down to the cellar on all fours like a huge dog.

Roberta fell forward onto the line, knocking bottles of beer to the floor, shattering them in tiny explosions, one after the other.

Before anyone could make a move to stop them, two of the bigger Wannoshay males bent over the spreading lake of spilled beer and put their gray faces close to the water. The two aliens made a loud slurping sound. Somehow they were able to suck up all the liquid on the floor even as more bottles fell from the line.

With all the attention being paid to Roberta, nobody but Shontera seemed to be paying them any attention. The pointed teeth of the drinking aliens served as filters, keeping broken glass out of their lipless mouths. By the time someone had turned at the slurping sounds of the two hunched aliens, all that was left around them was a pile of broken brown glass.

The two aliens, stomachs bulging, crab-walked down into the cellar after the first one, and Shontera felt herself grinning like a child even as her stomach turned cartwheels at the impossible sight she'd just witnessed. She couldn't wait to tell Toshera about this.

But when she looked back at Roberta and the other humans, her smile faded. Roberta was on her back on the cold factory floor, legs kicking as the others gathered around her, reaching out to her just like the aliens had tried to reach out and help their brother just moments earlier.

Ten minutes later, the noises began in the refrigeration cellars. Shontera recognized the hissing sounds from when the coolers went off-line a few months ago, but this time there was a banging down there that kept getting louder and louder. Like someone was punching at the walls, trying to get out.

Angie hadn't come back yet from taking care of Roberta, and Mariposa and the rest of the women on the line were getting scared.

After another ten minutes, the rattling became a booming.

Then the cellar doors crashed open and one lone alien male, Roberta's Wannoshay, ran out on all fours, his skin glowing white with frost. His mouth was a perfect circle of agony.

Every place his hands and feet touched the floor, he left a crystallized footprint that immediately condensed into a puddle.

Seconds later the remaining Wannoshay came running up out of the cellars, their hands and feet pounding on the concrete floor. Shontera saw Nonami for a second in the middle of the pack. They thundered past on all fours and disappeared up the stairs.

After a sudden explosion, everyone else on the line followed them in a blind panic.

Except for Shontera. She heard the blasting sounds in one part of her mind, but in the other part she kept hearing Roberta's moaning. She walked away from the lines, where bottles of beer had started slamming into each other.

She needed to see what had happened in the cellars.

She walked down the cold, wet steps as if she was in some kind of dream. A smell filled the air, mixing with the smells of barley and smoke. It was the salty smell of the aliens, along with the bitter smell of what she soon realized was blood.

She tiptoed down into the first refrigeration cellar, a square room filled with hissing and churning valves. Half of the valves were broken, spewing out coolant, and fist-sized holes covered the metal walls.

On the floor, three battered Wannoshay men lay motionless.

She recognized two of them as the beer-drinkers, and they lay in a mixture of beer and their own blood, their bodies looking strangely deflated.

A whimpering sound slipped out of Shontera's mouth before she could stop it. She'd never seen a dead person before. Or a dead alien, for that matter.

She felt more than heard the first explosion only two rooms away, her eardrums aching and her sinuses clogging. Maybe this was what the ocean was like when the waves got too rough for swimming.

She was staring at a handful of wires dangling like snakes from one of the holes in the wall, spitting sparks, when something touched her back.

"Leave," a voice whispered, loud and clear despite the noise of the malfunctioning equipment.

Shontera turned and saw Nonami.

"Leave now," the female Wannoshay said.

Shontera's entire body jerked into motion, and she almost fell as she and Nonami jogged past the three dead aliens sprawled on the floor. The other rooms had caught fire. Black smoke filled the air, reaching toward the two women as they ran up the steps, one on two feet, the other on all fours. Behind them, the copper aging tanks in the cellars blew, one after another.

A pair of strong hands reached for Shontera then, keeping her on her feet. A vision of Roberta's alien entered her mind, as if Nonami's soothing touch had placed it there, trying to show her where the alien had gone wrong in trying to help Roberta. How some—like Roberta—refused to give up their anger and fear.

And how his contact with *her* had driven him mad.

Nonami half-carried, half-dragged Shontera through the steel double doors as the explosions behind them continued.

Shontera remembered seeing a set of strange scars on the backs of Nonami's hands as well. Hers were two straight lines around a curly, spiral design.

As she held on to Nonami, another vision filled her head: a cave filled with aliens. The aliens pushed forward, massing in front of one of the two openings of the cave. Four-fingered hands pressed against sheets of black metal, blocking off the opening.

Something was pounding on the other side of the wall of metal, trying to get inside. High-pitched voices screamed a Wannoshay word of too many vowels and not enough hard consonants.

And then they were running through a series of caves on all fours, screaming in high-pitched, panicked voice. The pounding sound grew louder, filling her with panic as well, making the four fingers of her hands curl into rigid claws. Vines slapped her face until she learned to fend them off with her hair-tentacles.

The caves were dark, but she could still see and smell the aliens all around her, and they were running so fast she couldn't breathe. All of them stank with a strange, oily mix of salt and sulfur. She blinked and saw the world go sideways with a third eye higher up on her forehead. Behind her, she saw only blackness and heard only high-pitched screams of despair.

We had to get away from them, Nonami's voice whispered inside her head.

Then they were outside in the hot air of early summer, and Shontera could draw air into her lungs again.

She wanted to ask Nonami what it all meant, why that pounding sound in the caves had scared her and the aliens so much, and what Roberta's anger had done to the alien. But the crowds had already begun chasing the aliens away, waving fists, stun sticks, and broken beer bottles. Nonami simply disappeared.

The brewery erupted half a minute later.

Chapter Nine

As time passed and the four scratches on his right cheek had almost completely faded, Joshua knew he was going to have to return the book of the People back to Colonel Cossa. He'd kept it over two weeks longer than he'd originally planned. He'd missed his chance to share it with Karin and the other linguists, who'd been moved to other projects now that the People comprehended English. He was going to have to figure this out on his own.

He sat in his tent, sweating, with the metal pages spread out in front of him. After another fruitless hour spent rearranging and displaying the different shapes of the pages, he realized he was getting nowhere. He'd never be able to remember the random pattern that Johndo had set up on the ship.

And if I'm able to recreate the pattern, he thought, did I really want to experience another vision like the one in Johndo's room?

He realized the answer to that question was a resounding *Yes.*

That glimpse inside someone else's head, inside one of the People, had been intoxicating. He'd been seeing, for just a few moments, with *three* eyes. How miraculous was that?

He looked away. He wanted to visit Johndo again, but the colonel had declared him off-limits to all visitors after Joshua's attack. While Joshua thought the incident had been mostly a big misunderstanding, he couldn't argue too much with the colonel—Johndo's glancing blow had nearly knocked him out, and the scratches from his claws had been deep.

But let's just forget about all that for now, he told himself. Surely there was a method to how Johndo had arranged the pages.

After sitting, eyes closed, for almost five minutes, he thought he had it. He picked up the book, carefully pulled the pages free, and held the first page, an oval shape, up to his tent wall. With a little pressure, the page adhered itself to the wooden frame of the tent.

Almost afraid to breathe, he arranged the four dozen metal pages against the walls of his small tent. With every page he stuck into place, the air seemed to grow a tiny bit warmer. As he worked, words and phrases flowed through his head like the long-remembered phrases in a prayer.

Three eyes. True history. Hair-tentacles. Twilight.

He stopped when he came to the last eight pages left on his desk. These sheets were all blank, and he couldn't remember where or how they fit into Johndo's pattern.

"Give me strength, Father," he said, looking from the pages in his hands to those resting side-by-side on his tent wall, arrayed like tightly packed works of Wannoshay art. After a moment he began placing the last eight sheets into the remaining gaps.

"And please don't let me blow this place up," he added. Holding his breath, he pressed the final blank page against the wall. Before he could pull his hand away from the page, every single sheet of metal erupted with a beam of pure white light. The beams met in the middle of the room, and a dull roar filled his ears.

Joshua had time to take one quick breath before he was immersed in not just one vision, but a series of them.

The first of the new visions began where the last one ended, in the cave filled with alien singing that bordered on shrieking.

Joshua tried without any success to find the three light-skinned People that had been surrounded by the darker-skinned People that he'd decided were Johndo's People.

He felt himself being pulled along with the convulsing flow of gray bodies surging toward the cave wall, almost melting into one another. The dark-skinned People had found the three light-skinned People.

The wild singing stopped, replaced by anguished screaming and the sounds of flesh meeting flesh. Pieces of long, bluish-black hair flew into the air, landing in the glowing lichen above them like small, dead snakes.

As if in response to the violence against the three aliens, a brilliant white light flashed in the darkness, originating in the passageway behind them. The flash was followed by a quaking sensation that knocked most of the People off balance. The flashing light began to fade, replaced by the green hues of the lichen.

"The ships," someone hissed in a chirping language. Joshua understood the words perfectly. "The ships are waking!"

A heartbeat later, they were all running through the greenish light of the rough-hewn caves, toward the source of the ongoing tremor.

With another flash of white light they arrived in a massive cave where a black ship was roaring to life. The tall, angular ship shook off what looked to be years of accumulated dust and mold and glowing lichen as it began to work its way up through the cave. The swiveling spires at its top cut and drilled through the rock with small bursts of controlled explosions.

In a flash Joshua saw more ships on either side of him in the massive caves, working their way upward. All of them, he knew, without even seeing inside, were filled with gray-skinned People.

In another flash of white he was aboard one of the ships, looking back at the caves that had been the People's home for many generations ("many cycles," Johndo would have called them).

He looked through the walls and saw that more of the darker, gray-skinned People were rushing up the lower ramps and into the ship. Through the dual perspective of his two eyes mixed with the sideways Wannoshay eye, Joshua realized that they were being pursued by a mass of lighter-skinned People, screaming and flailing out with their long arms.

The ramps snapped closed, sealing off the ship with an ear-popping sensation. The People outside threw themselves against the flat black walls of the ships and continued pounding even as the ships lifted up and away from the cave floor.

With another flash, Joshua saw the emerging ships break through the surface of a desolate black and white planet rimmed in blue ice and edged in jagged black mountains, and in another flash they were a mile above it.

The flashes came faster now, almost too fast for Joshua to comprehend: aliens packed into black casks for the long journey, a gray claw glowing orange as it burned symbols into an octagonal metal sheet, and a lone figure threading its way among the stacked casks, its long back bent as if with a great weight.

And with a final blinding flash, the vision ended.

A cold wind whipped into Joshua's tent, knocking the sheets of metal from his tent walls. He tried to pull himself up onto his hands and knees from where he'd fallen, and he miraculously avoided getting cut by the sharp edges of the loose pages as they dropped to the cold ground next to him.

When the last metal page rattled to the ground, he lay on the ground, stunned. He must have arranged the pages in the wrong manner, and now he was paying for it. Too late he remembered the small pile of unused blank pages sitting on a dirty mat from that day in the ship.

"Johndo," he murmured. "I tried . . ."

He slid the pages back into their metal holder, his chest aching almost as badly as it had the day of his heart attack. He set the book on his desk and slid its sharp sides away from the edge before he shuffled out of his tent.

He was resting on the front step outside, trying to cool himself off and piece together the wild events of his multiple visions before they slipped from his mind like smoke, when the glasses in his shirt pocket began beeping.

With shaking hands he slipped on his military-grade spectacles and blinked at a flashing Netstream icon.

Along with the four messages he'd missed while he was working with the book, he saw that there was a flood of news stories scrolling across the inside of his glasses. And the news was not good.

Looks like, Joshua thought, I won't be chatting about this book with the colonel any time soon.

The news reports all focused on an explosion. At first he felt a stab of annoyance at the thought of yet another overreported story about a bombing by a suicide cult or a terrorist cell. He'd suffered through too many of them for the news to have any sort of emotional impact on him anymore.

But this story felt different right away. For starters, the location was all wrong. Instead of a church or an apartment complex where certain types of people lived, this one took place at a brewery in Milwaukee. That city was just a few hours' drive from where he now sat, watching the news feed loop past his glasses for the fifth time.

Milwaukee had been one of the first cities to embrace the integration of the People. That is, its *mayor* had at least embraced the integration process. Others may not have shared his enthusiasm.

Joshua reached a trembling hand up to his mouth, and then his fingers slid over to the healing scars on his cheek. This may not have been an accident, he realized. Just like Johndo lashing out at me.

He spent the next hour behind his glasses, constantly wiping sweat from his forehead to keep his spectacles clean. Terrorism had been everyone's initial knee-jerk reaction, either from the various enemies of the unending war overseas or suicide cultists.

And then the word got out on the 'Streams that some of the People had been inside the brewery at the time of the explosion.

The entire tone of the reports changed from a somewhat familiar dread to a sharper, more hysterical pitch. Reports abounded of People being rounded up like cattle by the American and Canadian military and hauled away from the landing sites and their new apartment complexes.

An hour later, rumors had begun to circulate about *another* suspicious explosion.

So much for the integration process, Joshua thought, unable to stop surfing the 'Streams for more info, even if it was all rumors and guesswork right now.

"Time to go, padre," someone said in a tight voice from above him. Joshua looked up, then pulled off his glasses with a grudging movement. At some point, midday had darkened into early evening.

Private Petersheim, who had been named Joshua's chaplain's assistant back in March, stood over him, hand on his assault rifle. Joshua was shocked to see the anger and fear on the young man's face. He didn't recognize the private at first.

On their way out of the landing site, he bit his tongue when he noticed that the few remaining People still living in and under the ship had been placed under armed guard. Outside the fence, they passed protestors hidden behind their cheap Netstream glasses or watching the latest heartrending news unfold on portable screens in their cars, eerily silent again.

Any second now, he feared, the massed people were going to explode.

On the drive back to the Shrine of Our Lady, he realized he'd left his Bible in his tent. All he had was the book of the People in his hands. He felt like he was somehow responsible for the explosions today. And then he remembered his friend's words.

"Only Elders are in touch with the soul of a people," Johndo had said on that cold day three months ago, when they'd first met. "Only an Elder knows what must be taken on *faith.*"

Forty-five minutes later, the private turned onto West Lexington in the city. He had to slam on the brakes to avoid crushing a clot of pedestrians in the street. The crowds reminded Joshua of the running, raging People of his vision, as well as the huddled mass of People living together in and underneath the ship.

The words entered his head, unbidden: "When you see Jerusalem surrounded by armies, then know that its desolation has come."

Joshua grabbed the book in his lap and touched the arm of the private, who was about to force his way through the people in front of them.

"No," he said. "It's okay. These are . . . my people."

"Oh." The private looked at the people and turned back to him. "You've got a big congregation, huh?"

Joshua saw many familiar faces, though a few seconds passed before he was able to recognize most of them. His eyes had fooled him for a moment, making him think he saw a third eye on the foreheads of the men and women looking over at him, their skin gray in the bright wash of the big sedan's headlights.

He didn't want to speak with the hypocrites, the humans who had no faith except in times of trouble. He didn't feel like reassuring this band of skeptics that no, the sky was not falling, and no, the aliens weren't coming to kill them in their sleep, and yes, God was still in heaven and all the world would still be here when they wake up.

"Do you want me to stay, Father?" Petersheim asked.

Once again, Joshua heard the slam of the hatch closing inside the ship. For the last time.

"Your redemption is drawing near," he imagined saying to his returned congregation. "Deal with it however you may."

From the safe, cool confines of the sedan, Joshua could see old man Ribisi with his oxygen facemask near the entrance, and Mrs. Consiglione rolling her walker across the street, slow as an old car going up a steep hill.

Take me out of here, he almost said.

Then he felt the metal pages of the book the colonel had given him in his hand. He looked down and realized that instead of his Bible, he held an *alien* book in his hands. The metal edges threatened to cut into his hands from his tight grip, and then, the metal pages softened, yielding to his touch.

He ran a finger across a page of the book and the symbols disappeared, melting into the flat black metal, leaving an empty page in front of him.

It wasn't really a book so much as a kind of *journal.* An incomplete record. There were still many pages left to be filled, more work left to be done. Much more work.

"Private," he said. "Thanks for the ride. You can let me out right here. Take care of yourself, son."

Heat blasted him in the face the instant he stepped out of the car. He looked out at the members of his congregation as they came up to him, calling out his name. He recognized them all, every single one of them.

Carrying the book of the Wannoshay in his hands, he took one step, and then another, back toward his church and his returned people.

With his congregation crowded around him, he could only make out snippets of conversation, flashes of sentences from the many voices around him:

"Father, the aliens were running out of the brewery right before it blew up . . ."

"It was the cultists, Father . . ."

"Father, I don't understand . . ."

"Got to put all of the aliens away so they can't hurt us like this again . . ."

"Father . . . Father . . ."

Joshua gently removed the hands reaching out for him.

"Follow me," he said in a voice that silenced those around him. His chest gave one final twinge of pain as he walked up the steps, and then he forgot about everything but his people behind him and the book in his hands.

He had the pages free by the time he walked through the humming security arch. His congregation dropped into the pews, watching him in a shocked silence.

He turned to the lefthand side of his church and began arranging the first of metal pages against the walls. He placed them below the stained glass windows and next to the Stations of the Cross. And this time he remembered to hold back the blank pages of the metal book. He had to get the People's true history right this time, for the benefit of Johndo's people as well as his own.

The heat and energy in the church grew with each page he stuck to the cool plaster wall. He could smell wisps of pine needles mixed with the smell of salt and mud. The heat from the pages of the book made his hands slick with sweat long before he pushed the final eight-sided page with its swirl of almost-decipherable gray symbols against the wall.

Finally, he was done.

As white light filled his church and reflected a rainbow of colors off the stained glass windows, Father Joshua prayed that he and Johndo's People would have time to complete the blank pages of this book, and many books after that.

Chapter Ten

On the last day of May, Ally Trang opened the door to her bedroom closet and was nearly swamped by dozens of mini-DVDs that had been piled at the bottom of her closet floor. They came spilling out at her like oversized coins in plastic casings, coming to rest on top of her bare feet.

"Jesus H," she said, staring at the mess on her floor. She turned to her bedroom door and locked it, afraid her housemates would get curious. "Where the hell did *they* all come from?"

Each disc contained footage of her talks with the aliens she knew as Brando, Thumper, and Jane—she hadn't had the patience to successfully explain the concept of names to them, so she'd made up her own for them. With her hours of footage long since uploaded to her Netstream, she knew she should reuse some of the discs, but she couldn't bring herself to risk overwriting her backups.

She hadn't told anyone in Sanford about her Netstream, and she kept her real name hidden on the 'Streams by using only "Wantaviewer." The 'Streams were safe places for if you wanted to be anonymous, as long as you covered your tracks. Thanks to the regular trickle of download fees, her 'Stream was earning her almost as much as her day job did.

The Wantas had become a popular viewing alternative, much more preferable to the dismal news on other sites, even after the explosion in Milwaukee.

She'd been keeping up with the 'Streams talking about the brewery ever since it had happened a little over an hour ago. It had been the constant flood of images of fire and devastation that led her back to her closet. Sorting through her piles of discs, she'd listened with a rising sense of disbelief to the stories about the three dead aliens they had just found inside the brewery, and the almost two dozen missing humans. Another alien had been found a block away from the brewery, dead of some sort of shock.

A sick feeling grew in her stomach as she thought about her alien friends. She jumped when her wallscreen screen beeped five quick tones, notifying her of a new download from one of her bookmarked 'Streams.

She turned to her half-size wallscreen in time to see an image of a burning grain elevator, flames shooting up a hundred feet into the air despite the five fire trucks blasting water onto it.

"*What?* Another one?"

The images flashed by faster, along with a voiceover. Very little was left of the elevator in South Dakota. Eleven men and women had been inside it when it blew, and eight of them had been killed instantly. Four Wannoshay workers had been scheduled to be working at the site at the time of the explosion. All of the alien workers survived.

She looked over at the discs spilling out of her closet, and a chill crept over her despite the hot closeness of her apartment. She thought of Thumper's lack of stability and the big muscles in Brando's thick arms.

"Evidence," she muttered, her throat aching for the burning sensation that came with swallowing Blur. "This place is full of fucking evidence."

Skin prickling now, she pushed all of the discs back inside the closet, and forced the door shut on them. She collected her car keys and found her money card.

She needed to make another trip to Winnipeg to see Jenae. This was all too much to handle without some pharmaceutical assistance.

Sitting on the floor of Jenae's hot and dirty apartment half an hour later, Ally swallowed her second Blur with her fourth shot of lime vodka and came up gasping for air.

"Why would they blow up our buildings?" she said when she was able. "Especially with people and aliens in both of 'em?"

Jenae rocked on the floor next to her, her bony white arms wrapped around her knees. She'd been using all afternoon, and her shakes were bordering on convulsions. Her eyes were dark brown bruises in her pale face.

"Part-of-their-master-plan," Jenae said. "Takin'-over, y'know?"

"Oh come on." Ally stared at the whitish residue on her shot glass, in the shape of her lips. "Why wait 'til now, after letting the army treat them like such shit for the past half year, ever since they came here?"

Jenae answered only by rocking faster. The Blur was making the other woman sweat, and Ally could smell Jenae's stale unwashedness from five meters away.

She grimaced and breathed from her mouth, waiting for the Blur to hit. She didn't like being sober like this—it made her imagine too many possibilities, none of them positive.

The two young women sat without speaking for a minute, until something rattled against Jenae's door. It sounded like skeletal fingers tapping on the dented metal, and it made a shudder run up and then down Ally's spine. Jenae was at the door and ripping it open before Ally could blink twice.

"Who-the-fuck—" Jenae shouted, but nobody was there. Jenae looked up and down the stairs outside her apartment twice, her skinny body shivering as the Blur flashed inside her.

Ally knew the feeling well—an almost orgasmic shuddering as the heart beat as fast as it could to push the toxic chemicals out of the body. Jenae was going to have a bitch of a headache soon.

Watching Jenae dance like a puppet on invisible strings on the landing outside her apartment, she wasn't sure if she *wanted* to feel the drug tonight. Part of her was waiting for an explosion to come from outside the door. The night felt loaded as a gun, and the person holding the gun was flashing on Blur.

"Cold turkey," she muttered, and poured herself another shot of lime vodka. "I need to. One of these days, for sure."

Jenae spun and marched over to Ally as if she'd heard her. "Drink-up. We're-going-now."

Ally froze with the shot glass halfway to her lips. "Where?"

"To see those alien friends of yours." Jenae's voice was slow and deliberate. "My friends've-seen-you-with-'em, you know. Don'-know-what-you're tryin'-to-do, Ally."

Ally shivered as she swallowed the sickly-sweet alcohol. With numb hands she tried to set down the glass as Jenae filled her pockets with capsules of Blur. The shot glass bounced once on the bare wood of Jenae's floor and shattered on the rebound.

"What," she started to say, feeling like she had a mouthful of glue as she spoke, "What're you going-to-do?"

"Expand-the-customer-base," Jenae said, her narrow face all angles and bulging eyes. She cackled as she spoke. "Wanta-Blur, Alissa? Or should-I-say, '*Wantaviewer*'?"

There was a moment at the start of that hot, nightmarish night when Ally realized she could stop it all. She could have thrown her Mace caplets on the asphalt and taken the Blur from Jenae. Or she could have just walked away, taking her portion of the Blur with her, and nobody would have gotten hurt.

She saw the moment with the perfect, unfettered clarity of an addict at the peak of her high. Jenae stood next to her, laughing and hugging herself as she shook her way through the Blur rush. The sound of Jenae's laughter was mean and sharp, like short, quick punches to the side of Ally's head. The soldiers that had once patrolled these streets had all disappeared.

She stared as Jenae held pink capsules out to the half-dozen aliens around them. Their skin was gray, but on many of their bare arms and faces were mottled patches of pink, almost the same color as the capsules of Blur. The aliens crept up to them like hesitant forest animals approaching a watering hole.

No. That's wrong.

She'd talked too long with Brando to believe that.

They're not animals. They're just freaked out because of the way Jenae was acting. They know what she's offering them.

And they *still* fucking want it.

The warm night air was thick with the muddy, musky smell of the aliens. One of the females, her squirming hair held back in a black metal clip, reached a short-fingered hand out to Jenae. Her long gray body rocked forward, and then back, as if she was trying to get her balance.

The male next to her, wearing cuffed, secondhand jeans with holes and patches just like most of the other Wannoshay, also lifted a hand, palm up. His face wore a spreading stain of pink that ate away his gray coloring. Every vertical eye in the middle of each wide forehead remained closed.

The moment was there.

Ally felt her own hand move, poised to grab the capsules of Blur from Jenae's quivering hand and run.

She could do it.

She *had* to do it.

Then she thought about the images on her Netstream, and Jenae calling her "Wantaviewer." All those discs in her closet to incriminate her, guilt by alien association. Jenae wouldn't hesitate to turn her in as an alien-lover if there was any hint of profit in it. She nearly bit through her lower lip as it curled up with fear and disgust.

The moment was there, but she allowed it to pass by.

Instead, the two Wannoshay took the offered capsules and, following Jenae's pantomimed movements, placed them in their lipless mouths. Their black eyes widened as they swallowed. Soon, more pinkish-gray hands reached for Jenae, the capsules quickly disappearing only to be replenished by the big pack on Jenae's skinny back.

"First time's free," Jenae cackled, her voice going hoarse from shouting and laughing. "First time's totally free, no strings attached, Wantas. After that, though, we got to charge a small handling fee."

Ally watched the transactions, numb and paralyzed.

"Now you fucking did it," she muttered.

At least three alien voices repeated her words back to her: "Nah you fugg-hin' didh idh," one said, like a deep-voiced man with a head cold.

"Fugg-hin' didh idh," echoed another, higher voice.

The screaming began less than a minute later.

Spinning and leaping up and down in a mad dance of agony, the first group of Wannoshay that had taken Blur broke free from the crowd and bounded out into the streets. Their skin was almost all pink now, whether from the heat or the Blur or both, it was impossible to tell.

Most drivers from the city knew to avoid Ellice Avenue, but a new hydro car with American plates flew up the road as if on cue and barreled into two Blur-addled, madly dancing aliens.

The twin thuds hit Ally like hammer blows to her chest, and she tried her best to look away from the wreck. But as always, she had no control, no willpower. She looked at the broken bodies and screamed along with the others.

As the night wore on, hesitant Netstream reporters began to arrive in the neighborhood, collecting their cams now that a story here in Winnipeg was finally evolving. From what they thought was a safe distance, half a dozen began reporting on the madness in the wake of the explosion that day, talking into the cams they held out at arm's length from their faces.

Many of the intrepid reporters never made it back out of the city once the aliens got their first taste of Blur.

The drug seemed to activate the tendency for violent outbursts that the Wannoshay already possessed. Ally was the only person with a camera to survive filming Jenae, laughing and convulsing as she passed out Blur like Halloween candy.

Ally's only consolation, in the midst of the chaos, was that her three Wannoshay friends were nowhere to be seen. She'd spent enough time with them—shot enough footage of them—that she felt able to pick them out immediately in a crowd of aliens.

Also, she couldn't sense that unique ringing in her ears that she felt whenever Brando or Thumper or Jane was near, more of a tickle than a sound. Maybe the Blur was fogging her mind, but she didn't sense her alien friends there that night, and that thought was a tiny victory in this night of madness.

Without relenting, the Blurred aliens danced and fought around her, big gray hands smacking into flesh every few seconds.

Ally made it back to Sanford at half past midnight, amazed that she'd been able to get away from Ellice Avenue in one piece. She'd been sick twice on her way home, and the trucker she'd hitched a ride with had been nice enough to pull over to let her spill her guts both times.

She trudged toward her apartment from the gas station where the trucker had dropped her off. She cried silently as she felt the bag of Blur in her pocket. Seeing the bodies of the Wantas flying into the air after the car hit them, she wanted to pull them from her pocket and throw the capsules into the sewer grate below her. Instead she pushed them deeper into her pocket. This was no time for drastic actions.

Casting her gaze skyward, she looked at the stars littering the sky.

Somewhere out there was their home. She pushed the images of the burning elevator and the black smoke of the brewery from her mind. Now they're stuck here with us. With no way to get back, if they even wanted to.

The thought made her bend over and heave, but she had nothing left inside her. Sobbing in spite of her tightly closed mouth, her body wracked with dry heaves and flashed Blur, she finally made it to her apartment around one o'clock. Her housemate was snoring on the couch in front of a dead wallscreen.

Inside her bedroom, she opened her closet door and gazed at the five or six dozen mini-DVDs she'd made in the past few weeks.

"Evidence," she muttered, her voice hoarse. She set a mint tab on her tongue and felt cool ice fill her mouth, but a burning sensation still ate away at her stomach.

Just like the capsules of Blur in my coat. It's all evidence, linking me to the Wantas.

She'd left her wallscreen on, and she picked up her remote and surfed over to her 'Stream out of habit. The home page for "Wantaviewer" appeared, and her face grew warm at what seemed now like a childish logo and naive stills of Brando, Thumper, and Jane and the rest of their people in Winnipeg.

She started up her most recent upload, and Brando's oval face filled the screen, forcing her to choke down a sob.

Looking away from the screen, she fumbled for an insta-flame on her cluttered desk. She pushed open her window and slid her metal wastebasket in front of it. After breaking the insta-flame in half, she used it to ignite the garbage inside the wastebasket.

She was crying again, as much as she hated the tears. She'd flashed on the Blur long ago, and all she felt now was emptiness and the familiar pain in her muscles and joints.

"Damn it," she whispered over and over again as the fire grew.

She began moving discs out of her closet, making a pile next to the wastebasket.

"Damn it all to fucking hell."

She dropped the first disc into the fire.

Grabbing an old paperback dictionary she'd been using to keep her desk legs balanced, she ripped pages out to feed the fire. More discs followed, melting and giving off an acrid blue-black smoke. She fanned the smoke out into the early summer air as best she could.

With the last disc in the burning mess of plastic and paper, she looked back at her wallscreen. Brando was sitting with his back propped against the wall of his furniture-less living room.

He'd been trying to explain something to her a month ago, she remembered. Her camera, as always, had captured the entire encounter.

"Left them, *Wannoshay,*" he was saying. His sparse basement apartment had been cold enough that day to make his and Ally's breath steam, but he seemed to enjoy the chill. He pointed a stubby finger at his third eye, which had been closed all afternoon.

"Who-did-you-leave?"

Ally couldn't recognize her own voice at first, Blurred into high speed at the time of the recording. She listened to herself repeat her question, more slowly, but the impatient, squeaky sound remained in her voice.

I've got to get off this fucking drug.

She squinted at wallscreen, focusing on the unique design on the back of Brando's big, stubby-fingered hands.

Brando bowed his head in his version of a nod of agreement. His short tentacle-hairs wiggled randomly, like a field of thick, gray-white grass teased by a small cyclone.

"They were . . ."

He stopped, his face going blank as it did when he was concentrating, trying to find the words in English.

He put his right hand palm up, his signal that the game of charades was on. On the wallscreen speakers, Ally heard herself give a hissing exhalation that was half laugh, half nervous squeak.

Brando put both hands sideways in front of him, and then moved his hands over to his right, hands sideways again. The scar design on the back of his hands were clear: two triangles with one tiny circle in the middle of them.

"Um. *Next* to you?" her voice said, filled with a patience that surprised her now, a day later. "Like-neighbors?"

Brando bowed his head again. "Next. And . . . *late*."

His last word came out sounding like "lake," or maybe "light," but Ally had heard him say the word often in their recent conversations to know more or less what he meant. It meant something bad, she thought, something worse than just being tardy.

She'd never know what he meant, now. Not after what happened tonight. Brando was as good as dead to her.

As the stink of burnt plastic began to fade in her apartment and most of the smoke had cleared, she held her speaker remote to her mouth again. Her vision doubled from the tears filling her aching eyes.

"Admin page," she said into the remote. "Password 'atrangviewer001.' "

On top of the image of Brando, lines of code appeared on the left side of the wallscreen. Tiny, moving thumbnails of all the screens of her Netstream displayed on the right, scrolling downward.

What does it mean if an alien is *late?* she wondered.

The thought kept running through her mind as she gazed at all the movies she'd uploaded in the past month. There was the movie from the night the Wantas first came to Winnipeg, along with the dozens of interviews she'd done with Brando and Jane and Thumper since then. The footage of the warm day when Thumper took off running, leading the soldiers on a wild goose chase. So much footage.

"Late," she whispered, fanning an empty mini-DVD case in front of her face, trying without luck to create a breeze in her overheated bedroom.

The people they left were neighbors, maybe. And sometimes neighbors were late, for one thing or another. Late as in tardy.

Or late as in dead.

She looked at the image of Brando underneath the code and thumbnails of her Netstream. She wondered if he was hooked on Blur now, just like she was. Maybe someday they could talk about that, like old friends sharing their battle scars. If he survived this night.

They were screaming for it tonight, screaming for the Blur, even as it drove them insane.

Still smiling through the tears sliding down her cheeks, Ally began deleting every single one of her movies from her Netstream.

Chapter Eleven

Shontera was already sweating as she walked west down Milwaukee's Clybourn Avenue, the big trucks on the interstate to her left making her flinch with every shuddering of their air brakes. On either side of the street sat dead cars, windows broken out, bodies turning grayish-red with rust, bits of window glass sprinkling the ground around them like animal droppings.

The cars had been here back when she and Toshera had lived in the neighborhood, and nobody had seen fit to remove them. Some cars were draped with old blankets in place of windows and windshields, and she kept her distance from them, not wanting to find out what might be inside.

She had two bus tickets in her pocket, bought with the money card the Netstream reporter had given her in exchange for her eyewitness version of the brewery explosion. She'd told the reporter as little as possible about the events of yesterday, keeping her visions to herself.

She had one person left to visit before leaving Milwaukee for good: Nonami.

She wanted to thank the Wannoshay woman for getting her out of the burning brewery, and for helping her get out of Milwaukee and headed south, even if it wasn't the way she'd planned it.

Then, after thanking Nonami, and after Nonami had told Shontera her real name, they would talk, woman to woman, about what had *really* happened that day, and what would happen next.

At noon, with the heat of the day at its peak, the streets of her old neighborhood were empty. The southern side of the street was scarred with fire from one of the anti-integration riots from a month earlier, though some group, either humans or aliens, had been starting the slow process of repairing the broken buildings in the neighborhood.

Okay, she thought, stopping in front of the last apartment complex on Clybourn. This place is as good as any other.

Blotting the sweat from her face with the sleeve of her T-shirt, she walked up to the first apartment on the ground floor. She knocked, wondering if the Wannoshay even knew what knocking on doors meant.

Apparently the elderly female who answered the door a second later did. The aged alien's eyes grew wide when she saw Shontera. Her long, blue-tinged hair stretched toward her like tiny fingers.

"Come!" the female said. Her voice sounded like she had a mouthful of marbles.

Opening the door all the way, the older alien woman bowed her head and reached out a hand. She was a shade taller than Shontera, and her musky smell was sweeter than Nonami's.

Shontera stepped back unconsciously, and then let the woman's cool hand touch her own. She didn't feel either the electric tingle in her chest or the ringing in her ears she'd felt with Nonami, but there was a tiny thrill at the touch of those four fingers. Before she knew what was happening, she'd been pulled into the apartment. She didn't even have time to scream.

Years ago, before Toshera, when Shontera and her former boyfriend William had still been together and life had been much less complex, Shontera had become obsessed with running. Every week she would save up all her leftover cash after the bills so she could buy another related item, one at a time: shoes, spandex, heart monitor, and the new sensory ear buds that would pump motivational music and sensations through her entire body as she ran. William had refused to go running with her.

One night after working late she kept running instead of turning back, leaving the familiar roads of her neighborhood. She turned down a darkened road and came across two men exchanging cash cards and drugs. The two men grabbed her, one calling her a "nosy nigger bitch," and she'd panicked. Jerking her sweaty arms free of the men's grasp, she kicked one in the belly, threw an elbow into the face of the other, and ran off full-tilt. She quit running after that night.

That same wild sense of panic came over her when the alien woman pulled her inside the apartment. The instant the door closed behind her, she snapped out of her shock and tried to wrench her dark brown arm free of the alien's gray, four-fingered grasp. But her arms weren't as sweaty as they'd been that night years ago, and the Wannoshay woman's grip was too strong.

All she could think of was Toshera, sitting with their packed bags in their apartment a few miles away, watching the Net-streams and ignoring the incoming calls from reporters and cops as she waited for her mother to come back.

"Let go," she hissed. "Let go!"

The alien's hand opened, and Shontera fell to the floor, free. She got to her feet and turned, expecting more aliens to come crashing into the nearly empty apartment. But the elderly female was backing up against the far wall of her living room. Her oval face was soft and her tentacled head was bowed.

Shontera let go of the door handle as the adrenaline drained from her. She wondered why she hadn't had a vision pop into her head as it had every time she'd touched Nonami's skin.

"Good god," she said. "You shouldn't *grab* people like that."

"Gra' pee-puh?" the Wannoshay woman said in her marble-filled voice, with both hands held palms up in front of her. The room filled with the scent of lilacs and sugar.

Shontera took a deep breath. Something in the woman's three black eyes made Shontera think of a calm, frozen lake surrounded by black mountains, touched by a wintry breeze. Mixed with the pleasing odors filling the room, Shontera felt herself relax.

Or maybe I'm just crazy, she thought, and moved closer to the Wannoshay woman.

As far as she could tell, the sparse apartment had no Net-stream connection, and not even the wallscreen had been activated. She was forced to lead the other woman outside and draw symbols and stick figures in the dirt, recreating as best she could the brewery explosion and Nonami's rescue.

Outside, Shontera could still feel and smell and see every detail from yesterday: holding onto Nonami as a vision filled her head of the inky black tunnels filled with other aliens, all of them reeking of oil, salt, and rotten eggs.

She was running on all fours, vines slapping her face until she made a path through them with her hair-tentacles. She'd wanted to cry out at the sound and the stench of the aliens' fear, but she couldn't inhale. She could only run headlong into the darkness, hoping to get to their destination—wherever or whatever that was—ahead of their pursuers.

As the sun slipped out from behind a cloud and the air began to grow warm, the alien grabbed her hand. Again the woman's grip was strong. Without too much effort, she tugged Shontera back inside, out of the sun. Shontera started to object, but then she saw the pink flush that had began to cover the woman's arms and face.

Back inside, sitting on the musty, cushion-less couch, she pulled out a bus ticket that she'd forgotten about until now. On her way to the old neighborhood, she'd borrowed an ink pen from an elderly man sitting across from her, and as he watched, she'd sketched the spiral design she'd seen on the back of Nonami's hands.

"It's for an old friend," she'd explained, passing the pen back. His bemused expression had faded when he saw the four fingers on the hand and recognized what the design meant.

She now handed the ticket to the alien woman squatting next to her in the apartment. Pointing at the drawing and touching the unique design of parallel lines intersected by a square that had somehow been etched onto the back of the woman's wrinkled hand, Shontera gave another smile.

"This is my friend," she said, holding up the ticket. "Do you know her?"

She touched the back of her own hands, rubbing the veins and bones and pores that made up the only designs she had on her own hands. The other woman cocked her head and looked from Shontera's drawing to her own hand. With a sudden grunt, she straightened herself up. Her overlong torso crackled with the sudden movement.

"Friend," the alien woman said. "Come here, now?"

"Yes!" Shontera wanted to shout, but instead took a slow, calming breath. "Yes, have her come here now. Please."

As Shontera slid the ticket into the pocket of her jeans, the alien woman pulled something slender and black from the ropy tentacles of her hair.

At first Shontera thought it was some sort of hairpin, but then the woman bent the long, stick-like object in half, and then into quarters, forming a square. She could have sworn that the woman's black, sideways eye winked at her. The smell of sugary lilacs was back.

The alien woman held the square in front of her mouth and blew into it. A greenish-white energy filled the square, like a wallscreen that had been turned on. The hairs on Shontera's arms and the back of her neck were standing up now.

The side of the square facing Shontera had turned black. The woman moved her lipless mouth in a rippling motion, no sound coming from her mouth.

Shontera inched closer to see the other side of the screen. Just as she caught a glimpse of a three-eyed gray face coalescing inside the square, the woman clucked her tongue and the screen winked out. She collapsed the square, and it became a long cylinder that disappeared into the woman's hair again.

They're not sharing *all* their secrets with the media and the military, Shontera thought, grinning at the woman adjusting her blue-black, tentacled hair. They're nobody's fools.

Nonami arrived less than a minute later, bringing with her the strange tingling in Shontera's chest.

Seeing her next to the other alien woman, Shontera was able to note the subtle differences between the women, and an unconscious set of criteria had begun to form in her mind in addition to the designs on the back of each alien's hands: hair color (as in shades of black tinged with a range of unique colors), forehead height (the nameless woman had little room for her third eye, while the woman Shontera called Nonami had a long, graceful forehead that accentuated her eye), skin color (darkness or lightness of grayish-blue), and hair length and width (some tentacles were bigger than others).

In Shontera's newly acquired guidelines for Wannoshay appearances, Nonami was beautiful.

And she had too many questions to ask her.

She waited as the two alien women took up positions on the floor, squatting with their long backs against the wall. They looked quite comfortable like that—hands resting on muscular thighs—more comfortable than Shontera imagined they'd look folded up onto the couch.

Now that Nonami was here, gazing at her intently with all three of her dark eyes, Shontera didn't know where to start.

"Is good, seeing you," Nonami began. After working in relative proximity with humans at the brewery, she had a much better grasp of English than her older female friend did. "How is . . ." Nonami swallowed and pursed her mouth in a strangely human gesture. " 'oshera?"

"Toshera's good," Shontera said, and found herself close to tears at the thought of her daughter. She swallowed hard. "I just wanted to see you again, and . . . to thank you. Thank you for everything."

Nonami smiled. She turned to the alien woman next to her and touched her hair.

"They know you," she said. "I telling them of you. They happy, meeting you."

Shontera relaxed and tried to forget the panic she'd felt when the woman had pulled her into the apartment earlier.

The woman had just been excited to meet me. Hadn't she?

"Tell me," she said, the curiosity she'd felt about the aliens overcoming her doubts and fears. "Tell me what happened yesterday, in the brewery. Tell me where you're from, why you're here. On Earth. Can you please tell me?"

Nonami bowed her head, her third eye closing. She lifted her gray hands, slowly, and held them a yard from Shontera's face. For an instant Shontera was back in the burning brewery, fire on all sides, arms tight around Nonami, helpless. She fought the urge to bolt out of the apartment as Nonami leaned closer, the four fingers of each hand lengthening.

Nonami's middle eye opened wider, demanding all of Shontera's attention.

A familiar, musky smell wafted over her, and Nonami's voice was deep and soft as she murmured, "Show you?"

Home. Home was a land of black rock and deep caves, elaborately dug, deeper than one would guess. My people lived within smelling distance of two of our world's four oceans, though none of us had ever seen them.

Cycle upon cycle, the caverns remained cool, but never as cold-as-death as the aboveground. Passages were dug around icy springs, and in the dark cavern corners were the vines that gave us clothing, lichen that provided our light, and dark fungus that fed us so that Diggers, like myself, could keep tunneling.

My people had always lived in the caves. Many, many cycles previous, however, before our sun began to dwindle, the Ancestors had been able to travel to all corners of the world of Wannoshay.

The Elders of the present shared stories about how the brilliant minds of the Ancestors devised machines that gave the Wannoshay the ability to fly over oceans to see our world.

What they found were three other Wannoshay tribes.

The People of the White Moon dwelt on the far side of the First Ocean, a race with faded skin and bulging eyes who never saw the light of our sun.

Those who did see the sun year-round were the black-skinned People of the Yellow Sun who lived on the other side of the Widening Ocean.

Our closest neighbors were those who lived, like us, in the midsection of our planet. We were separated by an ocean so narrow that it appeared to be a river at certain points. The Ancestors had built clever bridges over the icy water—for our sun was weakening even then—and they shared our knowledge of tunneling, communicating, and flying with these people.

We called them the People of the Twilight.

Eventually, when our fading sun was no longer able to hold back the cold in the aboveground, we entered the caves. Our tunnels went deep under the shallow ocean, and my people joined with the People of the Twilight. That day is shrouded in myth and mystery and story, the most important day in many, many cycles.

We were known as the People of the Dawn until that day, when we cast aside all names for our joined People.

Food was shared. The Drinkers found more springs with every new tunnel the Diggers carved out, and the Gatherers found plentiful plant life and fungi for food.

All was well for many cycles, though neither tribe dared to venture out aboveground, even during our brief middays, which grew shorter every cycle.

Many cycles passed, and the . . . *differences* between the two tribes once called Dawn and Twilight began to be smoothed over. It was a very gradual endeavor. Some of us even tried to join with our new brethren, but that is another tale, for another day.

There in our shared caves, we each had our role, regardless of our tribe. Elder or Navigator, Gatherer or Drinker, Digger or Healer. I was a Digger, and with my hands I helped shape over four dozen new passages deep into the rock of Wannoshay. We Diggers are born with stubborn bones in our hands, and the rock walls submit to us, allowing us to tunnel. Just like the Drinkers have bellies that can expand to hold and carry water for an entire family for a week, Diggers are determined by their inborn skills. I am proud to be known for my stubbornness.

But the bones in our hands failed us the day we dug deeper than we had ever gone before. The rock was black, impossibly hard. When we tried a new tunnel, the black rock stopped us again. We had dug too deeply, and we could dig no more. Our resources had run out.

And so we began the search for the Navigators with their hidden memories of the ships hidden by the Ancestors. Only the Navigators knew how to operate the ships, if their memories could be opened up again. We had no choice but to leave our home.

But now. Now . . .

Now home is Earth, and we have shown our children a hopeful future. They will be the new Wannoshay. Their name is now the People of the Golden Sun. Their name is our victory and hope.

And this, Shontera, this is *my* name.

Shontera opened her eyes with an alien name on her lips, the sound of it echoing in her ears. With so many syllables, but few hard consonants, it was beautiful. It was Nonami's true name.

And I can't pronounce it, Shontera thought.

A sense of longing filled her. She wanted to go back to the world of Diggers and Drinkers and Navigators from Nonami's vision, if only to find out more about how a race that could never see the sun was able to retain any semblance of hope. In the past few years, she'd barely made it through the dreary winters when the sun remained hidden behind the clouds for what felt like weeks on end. She couldn't imagine never seeing the sky again.

"Home," she whispered, abandoning all attempts to speak Nonami's true name, at least for now. She looked up at the two Wannoshay females squatting in front of her. "Welcome home."

Before the alien women could respond, a storm of footsteps filled the hallway outside the apartment. Shontera jumped, her body prickling over with fear, turning the sweat on her forehead and armpits cold. Nonami and the other alien seemed too close to her now, as if they were about to reach out for her again like the two strung-out men in the alley a few years ago.

Loud, high-pitched voices added to the ruckus outside, and then the door burst open. Three alien children ran into the room on all fours, their voices shouting out words in a liquid-sounding, ululating language that reminded her of Nonami's real name. Her inner ear tingled at the sound of it.

She wanted to reach out to touch their flushed pinkish-gray faces and wild hair, but they wouldn't keep still long enough for her to catch up to them.

Feeling a smile stretch across her face, she watched one of the children, a stocky boy—she was assuming he was a male, though it was hard to really tell—tackle another one. They rolled across the sparsely furnished living room, running into the other female alien, who picked them up easily, one in each hand. The third child, a female, giggled and pulled one of the dangling boys back down to the floor. The four of them moved off toward the back half of the apartment.

Nonami gestured at the children and gave what had to be the Wannoshay version of a smile. Shontera saw that her teeth were sharp and pointed.

With a shudder, she looked away, out the window. The sky had darkened, and she could see a group of Wannoshay huddled together in the street. An electric feeling was in the air. She had to leave soon.

She stood up, swaying slightly at first, and reached out to Nonami.

"Thank you," she said again to her, and then she tried to pronounce the woman's real name. Her tongue twisted the words, but it was close enough.

Nonami patted Shontera's hand. "You are weh-come."

Without another word, Shontera left the apartment and hurried out into the street. She forced herself to slow down when she saw more Wannoshay gathering on the other side of the street.

The same sickening feeling she'd felt at the sight of Nonami's sharp teeth filled her as she heard the harsh voice of a Wannoshay standing in the middle of the crowd.

As she walked, she realized that Nonami hadn't even tried to answer her question about what had *really* happened yesterday at the brewery.

She hurried past the crowd of aliens on the far side of the street. Overhead she could hear the low rumble of a helicopter. A pair of aliens walked out of an apartment, and she nodded at them without breaking stride, even as her breathing hitched inside her chest.

The thunder of helicopter blades soon drowned out all other sounds on the street. She looked up and saw half a dozen more helicopters fanned out in the early evening sky. They were the big Army transport choppers that looked like two helicopters fused into one big one, and they were coming closer.

She moved into the doorway of an old house and peeked out at the block behind her, toward Nonami's apartment.

Filling the air with dust and scattering the gathered Wannoshay, one of the six choppers dropped to the street, narrowly missing power lines on either side of it. The choppers hovered five feet above the sidewalks and abandoned cars, and a moment later they disgorged armored soldiers wearing battle gear.

Shontera wanted to cry out as the soldiers began rounding up aliens and pushing them toward the big helicopters. Some of the soldiers held tiny green boxes in their hands that they would lift and point at any alien that gave signs of resisting.

Most of the Wannoshay cooperated, but the occasional young one who lashed out at the soldiers was thrown off his or her feet with a single click of a button on the metal box.

As more troops filled the streets, leading aliens toward the choppers, Shontera slipped out of the doorway. She risked a look back and saw Nonami and her friend followed by her friend's children being led out of the rundown apartment.

Taking a step back, shivering as the breeze kicked up by the choppers touched her clammy skin, she almost returned to confront the soldiers.

She could explain to them how Nonami saved her in the brewery.

She could tell them that she didn't believe the Wannoshay had meant to blow up the brewery, that it had all been some sort of accident.

She could explain all she'd learned from Nonami, and maybe it would help.

But then she remembered Toshera and their plans. They had to leave tonight. They were getting out, starting over.

Watching the aliens being gathered up like cattle, she thought about the strength she'd seen that day in different Wannoshay. She knew the aliens could fight the troops if they so desired.

But for some reason, the aliens chose not to do so.

From across the street, she saw Nonami again. She saw the rest of the world receding as she caught Nonami's gaze. The alien woman's black eyes were calm, though her middle eye was closed so tightly that all traces of it had disappeared.

In that moment Shontera understood why they didn't resist.

Earth was their last chance. Their damaged ships would never fly again, and even if they could, Shontera doubted if many of the Wannoshay would risk another journey through space. Not when there wasn't a home to return to anymore. They'd used up their world.

We are here, Nonami's look had said. We must make the most of it.

A caravan of windowless electric buses rushed by Shontera, filling the air with the stink of ozone. The buses left a hot breeze in their wake as they rushed up Clybourn Avenue. The Wannoshay were being hauled away on the same buses that had brought them here just a few months earlier.

When Nonami disappeared into one of the buses, a fleeting image filled Shontera's head, like a message flung from Nonami's mind to hers. Just like yesterday, as Nonami carried her out of the brewery.

In that vision, Shontera saw a massive black ship—an alien ship—embedded into the ground next to a slow-moving brown river and a grassless field. She had a sudden urge to go find that ship, wherever it was.

But not today. Today, Shontera and Toshera were leaving Milwaukee and heading south.

She started walking again, not looking back. The air was cold now on her sweaty skin, and she could barely catch her breath. After ten more steps, she was running.

Interlude One

I have not seen my new friend in many of his world's short-cycles, and I hope he will soon return, if only to show me that he is not angry like the majority of his people now are.

I wonder if the heat makes them as temperamental as my People. On those days filled with too much sunshine, I myself often choose not to set foot outside, finding shelter instead in cool dirt walls, freshly dug.

But now our shelter has been taken from my People and me.

Watching us now are the protectors with their blue-black weapons and their hate boxes. After what happened only a few hot short-cycles ago with the Late Ones in the work-buildings, I cannot say I blame the protectors for their actions.

In their people's guttural language, one would think, *Wannoshay* translates into *guilt.*

And my people know all too well that soul-curdling emotion.

I ache to see the Father Joshua again, he of the ancient stories and the true history. But there is distance between us now, most likely not of his choosing, or so I hope.

A distance separates us, and a series of barriers. The unthinking anger that infects a growing number of our People here, so much like that of the People of the Twilight back on our home-world, appears to have spread to most of Joshua's people.

And the anger-sickness of the Father Joshua's people makes them productive.

They finally *act,* after so much time spent hibernating and hiding in their homes, pretending and wishing my People had never arrived.

They gather us up in the heat, herd us like mindless animals into their rolling and flying vehicles. Because of the guilt implicit in those two ruined buildings, we can do nothing but cooperate.

One prison, I remind my People, resembles another, whether it is under our ruined ships or in the walled structures the angry ones are constructing for us.

I watch the young constantly. They are already looking for methods to go over or under the newly built walls. I want to stop them, to urge their familial Elders to prevent such troublesome behavior so soon after the loss of trust with the angry ones, but I stop myself. I know the limits of my own power at this unsteady moment in the cycle.

So I retreat into the caverns beneath the round metal homes inside our walled, *cemented* city. I hope this heat will pass soon, and with it, the bitter taste of betrayal coming from both sides of the new walls.

Until that time comes, I will cover myself in darkness and attempt to sleep.

When the first cool breezes at last begin to blow across the flatlands around our walled city, I feel called by my brethren.

The Elders are rested, those distant voices say, and now they are gathering, combining their energy in an attempt to stop the sudden, fatal epidemic ravaging the People. This illness is harvesting our People like the crops that grew this past cycle on this black-earthed land.

The sick succumb to the violence of the wretched excesses of the Blur, or the angry eruption of the soul-sickness carried with us from our old home and what we had to leave behind. Many suffer from a combination of both.

They are all Late.

I am old, my tentacles stunted and weak from lack of use, and my own odors have begun to fade. But I have no choice: I must join those who have already escaped. I am to become a runaway.

For me, unlike the young who climb the walls or tunnel out into an unsteady world, my destination is clear. Getting free of these walls is only the first step of my journey.

For I am needed at the Ship. The Mother Ship.

At this final moment before departure, with my ill-fitting clothes layered on my back and my pack filled with food for four days' hard travel, I try to locate my journal. The book that the Father Joshua mistakenly called a *neowo.*

The journal is missing. I search until the sun begins to fade and my time to leave arrives, the whole time burning with guilt from the memory of the day I last touched it. The day I struck the Father.

But on the actions of that day I cannot dwell. The sun has dropped behind the wall rising up to the west. With the sun's departure, the camp around me comes to life, and the lights of the guards outside are ignited.

The time has come for my new journey to begin.

Chapter Twelve

Tim "Skin" Blair followed his buddies Georgie and Matt out of the pickup, his entire body shivering with cold despite the three layers of clothing he wore. Outside the truck, the early-morning November air was crisp, with just a hint of wind that seeped through his camouflage jacket.

He felt Matt watching him in the gray light, making his shoulder blades itch until Georgie slapped him on the back and handed him one of his hunting rifles. They stood in an empty field a mile from the abandoned Omaha Indian reservation in northeast Nebraska, anxious to begin the hunt.

According to the guy in the bar last night, the alien had been seen in the area the previous afternoon.

"If it gets any colder, my nuts are gonna flash and go south," Georgie said. He rubbed his dark, sleep-bent hair, and one of his fingers stuck out of a hole in his glove.

"Thanks so much for sharing," Matt said as he pulled out his military-grade field glasses and elbowed Skin in the ribs. " 'Least you have nuts, unlike old Skin here, who won't even protect his own woman."

Skin swallowed a response and instead checked his gun for the second time to make sure it was loaded.

The sun crawled over the bluffs of the Missouri River to the east as he glanced at his buddies. Georgie's boyish face had slipped into a grin, while Matt's chubby face frowned at the brown landscape from behind his expensive field glasses, his pride and joy, bought back before they'd all lost their jobs and spent most of the last few months on unemployment.

None of them had ever killed anything larger than a deer before.

Georgie spit on the brown, frozen ground. "Let's go."

Pulling his jacket tighter onto his wiry body, wishing he'd been able to afford a new coat this fall, Skin glanced at the silent forest again.

He'd just started working at the grain elevator in South Dakota when the explosion occurred. A month after that, the Omaha Indians left their reservation. They claimed they'd wanted to get farther south and put more distance between themselves and the alien camps. The Indians on the neighboring Winnebago reservation had followed them a few weeks later.

His face grew warm at the thought of the Indians. His friends claimed they called him "Skin" because of his thinness, but Skin had always suspected that they'd come up with the name years ago when they found out that his mother's step-brother was half Omaha Indian. He wondered if any of his "half-cousins" or friends were still on the rez, or if they'd all wised up and left the ghost town that reservation towns like Macy had become.

"Don't drop that new gun, Skin," Matt said, his jaggedly cut blonde hair flipping into his eyes. " 'Course Georgie gives me the shitty one. I know it's hard for you to carry a conversation, much less heavy weaponry."

"Shut up, Matt," Georgie whispered. "Someone's been through here recently."

They slowed, Matt glaring at the back of Georgie's head. Georgie pointed at some thorn bushes and matted-down grass, but Skin couldn't see any signs in the brown undergrowth.

He knew they weren't going to find anything out here, but he liked hunting with Georgie. After walking around all day, freezing their toes and fingers, they'd all end up at Skin's trailer for home-brewed beer, chili, and football on the all-sports Net-streams that eastern Nebraska had finally gotten installed.

They'd watch the game on the wallscreen he was still paying for, and would continue to pay for, for the next twenty months. Money had always been tight, and he still hadn't found a job after the explosion.

He inhaled icy air and held back a cough. His legs were getting tired already.

"So's Lisa going to be home tonight?" Matt said. "What's she going to be wearing? I always liked the curves on a pregnant lady."

"Don't talk about her like that," Skin said, regretting it immediately.

"O-ho! *Now* he's got an attitude! Where was that attitude last night, when she needed you?"

Skin shut his mouth and walked faster. Matt's soft laughter made his ears burn. He should've taken a swing at the guy hitting on Lisa last night, but he knew he would've gotten his ass kicked. Lisa had pulled him out of the bar and left Matt and Georgie inside, talking to the guy about hunting and aliens.

"Don't pull that macho shit with me, Tim," she'd said in the car on the way home, her hands sitting on her round, tight stomach. "You're not Georgie, and damn it, you're not Matt. I can't *stand* that shit."

The sun stayed hidden behind the clouds all morning. The men moved gradually north, keeping to the shadows and stopping at every clearing so Georgie could look for signs of the alien's passing. At noon they stopped to eat a lunch of salted venison and stale rolls under the overcast sky. Skin felt worn out from Matt's constant talking and the miles they'd covered.

For the first time since learning about the escaped alien last night at the bar, he thought about actually using the gun in his hands to kill it. He knew Georgie needed his portion of the reward money to help take care of his two girls, and he and Lisa themselves weren't exactly living like royalty lately, with the baby coming any day now.

He had no idea what Matt, living by himself in his tiny apartment in Bancroft, would do with the money. Five thousand dollars was a lot of money, even in this day and age.

Caught up in his thoughts, he almost walked past Georgie, who was bent down on one knee examining the grass.

"I think we're close," Georgie said, his dark eyes squinting at the ground.

Matt mimicked Georgie from behind Georgie's back, forcing his soft features into a fierce scowl.

Skin shook his head and checked his gun again. It had one of the new safety sensors that was supposed to make it accident-proof, except Georgie hadn't explained to him how to use it yet. The fact that Georgie had lent him his best gun filled him with pride, too much pride to ask for instructions on its use. The sensor was dark, so he figured the safety was on.

If they caught it, the alien could be strung out on drugs and unpredictable, so he had to be ready to shoot to kill if needed. He touched the sensor, turning it red.

Georgie began talking in a low, impatient voice. Matt nudged Skin and rolled his eyes. Skin knew from years of hunting with Georgie that this meant they were close to their prey.

"Huntin' and killin', ain't nothing better," Georgie muttered, walking slowly into the forest. "Got no room for graymeats, no Wantas, not in this country, not nowhere else."

"Shh," Matt said. His field glasses had turned opaque, and he pointed at a large evergreen seventy-five yards away.

Despite the lack of wind, the tree's branches quivered. Skin never would have noticed if Matt hadn't shown the tree to them.

"Oh yeah, here we go," Georgie said.

They spread out in a loose arc and stepped slowly toward the tree. Skin gripped the cold weight of the gun through his gloves.

When they were twenty yards from the evergreen, he smelled a lingering odor of wet, wormy dirt mixed with a burnt, bitter smell.

They stink, Lisa had said.

He turned to say something to Matt, but before the words could leave his mouth, a figure tumbled out of the tree. Like a gray and black blur, it righted itself and ran into the forest on all fours.

The air exploded with the sound of Georgie's gun.

Matt and Skin, their own guns still resting on their forearms, stared at Georgie with wide eyes.

The fast-moving image of the alien, if that was what it was, kept replaying in Skin's mind like a nightmare.

"Come on, Skin! Move it, Matt, you fat ass!" Georgie yelled, sprinting after the creature into a stand of oaks. "I think I got him!"

Georgie fired his gun a second time, and then Skin heard Georgie's voice shouting in the forest, followed by a strange, piercing shriek that sounded like an animal.

"Holy *shit,*" Matt whispered, and that broke the strange spell paralyzing both of them.

Skin and Matt rushed into the trees and found Georgie on top of a tall humanoid figure, holding it down with the weight of his body. The alien's stubby legs poked out from underneath Georgie.

"Yeah!" Georgie yelled from on top of the alien.

Bright, purplish-red blood dotted the tree trunks and bushes around them. Skin had never seen such a color before.

"Trying to get away from your camp where you belong, huh, Wanta?" Georgie's voice was harsh as he pressed his red face closer to the alien's oval-shaped, gray face. "Don't like your new home? What you going to do now, graymeat? Huh?"

Skin stepped closer for a better look.

"Come on," he said. His voice sounded like a bird's chirp. He coughed. "Take it easy."

The alien reeked of mud and salt. Thick tentacles moved like eyeless snakes across the alien's head, growing out of his scalp like hair. One beat helplessly against Georgie's midsection, giving off a tiny spark with each impact.

Across one side of the alien's head was a purple gash, but the flow of blood had stopped. Along with the wound on its forehead, the alien's face was marred by thin white streaks that radiated out from his mouth, like scars or wrinkles.

The alien's eyes—all three of them—were closed, and his narrow gray face was flat, almost peaceful.

Taking tiny steps, Matt walked up to them with his gun trained on the alien, for once not saying a thing. His expensive glasses were perched precariously on the tip of his nose.

"Georgie," he began. "What are you *doing,* man?"

"Okay, buddy," Georgie said. A change had come over his voice. His hand rested on the alien's back. Purplish-red blood stained Georgie's coat and the finger that poked out of the hole in his glove. "Let's get up."

Georgie held onto the alien's long arms as the alien rose to his feet. The alien's elongated torso and humped back made him look bent over when he stood upright. Judging from the blood on his khaki pants and too-small denim jacket, the alien must have been shot in the side as well.

Skin stepped forward to help him up, but he froze at the sound of Matt's voice.

"Let's take this thing out *now,* Georgie. I've heard all about the diseases they carry. Maybe it's on Blur right now and it's about to flash. It's got those junkie scars on its face. See 'em?"

Georgie brushed off the alien's ill-fitting jacket, gazing at the alien with calm eyes. Skin saw something pink and small fall to the ground.

"Be quiet, Matt," Georgie said, staring at the alien. His face was almost blank, as if the wild adrenaline rush from the hunt had melted away, leaving him devoid of all emotion.

Matt pushed his glasses up onto his forehead with a shaking hand, too shocked at Georgie's reaction to speak.

Skin couldn't take his eyes off the tall, gray-skinned being in front of him. The hunched gray creature was almost as thin as Skin was, and he didn't look dangerous at all.

For the first time in months, he wondered if the explosions at the brewery and the grain elevator had simply been freak accidents, just bad luck and bad timing.

"We got to take you back, man," Georgie said.

"What?" Matt cried. "What are you talking about, Georgie? The reward was dead or alive. I'm not fucking around with some alien that's whacked on Blur."

Georgie continued talking over Matt's shouts. "You have to go back to your camp." Georgie's voice was gravelly, like an old man. "Do, you, un, der, stand, me?"

Swaying, the alien straightened up and opened his eyes.

Deep black, unshining, with no whites at all, the eyes of the alien stared right at Skin.

Despite the cold, a trickle of sweat started from his armpit and ran down his side. His mouth felt so dry it hurt. He backed up, bumping into Matt.

"If you're not going to kill it," Matt said, "we'd better get it tied up so we can haul it back to the truck."

The sky had turned dark blue, and Skin watched his own breath leak out of his mouth in a cloud. Georgie didn't move.

"Come on, man, let's go!" Matt said.

When Georgie didn't respond, Matt poked him in the back

with the butt of his rifle. Georgie jumped, and his eyes fluttered.

"Goddamn graymeat," he whispered, wiping one of his blood-stained gloves on his coat, keeping his other hand on the alien. He looked like he had just woken from a deep, dreaming sleep, and he reached for his gun. "What did you *do* to me?"

The alien answered by dropping to all fours, dotting the frozen ground with blood. His face almost touched the ground for a moment, as if bowing or praying.

And then, almost faster than Skin could follow, the alien reached into his jacket, pulled out a pink capsule, and stuffed into his mouth. His gray arm blurred back into place on the ground.

Skin wasn't sure if his eyes had moved fast enough to see it all happen.

"What the hell?" Georgie said. "Spit that out, Wanta."

He bent over the alien, but his hand stopped an inch from the writhing tentacles on the alien's head, as if he expected the alien's touch to shock him. Three tentacles reached up toward Georgie's shaking hand.

"Get over here and help me!" he yelled at Matt and Skin.

"What do you want me to do," Skin said, "stick my hand in his mouth?"

The alien began to shake, his strange hair-tentacles quivering like a handful of garter snakes. From the middle of his forehead, his third eye winked sideways at Skin.

"Shoot him." Georgie's voice was flat.

Matt moved next to Georgie, rustling the dead weeds. Skin's eyes took in his old high school buddies on his left, and the gaunt, trembling alien on his right.

Everything else—the cold, the bare trees, even the weakness in his arms—faded into the back of his brain.

"He's got Blur in him," Georgie continued, his calm voice

floating into Skin's head like a light wind. "He's gonna flash on us and he'll be moving so fast it'll be like trying to hold on to five aliens. You know how strong these graymeats are."

Skin moved closer to the alien as Georgie spoke, until the alien's smell filled his nose. The muscles of the alien's face were contracting wildly, like a mask of moving gray flesh. His wide shoulders rocked back and forth, and his stick-like arms vibrated with energy. The wound on the alien's head had started to bleed again.

Skin lifted the barrel of his gun a few inches, but he didn't point it at the alien.

Accidents. Explosions. Bad luck, bad timing.

"We did our parts," Georgie said. "Matt spotted him. I took him down. Now it's up to you to finish it."

No. Skin looked down at the rifle in his hands. I can't. Not like this.

Turning the rifle in his hand, he aimed the butt of the gun at the alien.

He glanced at the safety sensor before swinging it. When his eyes left the alien, the alien leaped.

In two seconds' time, Skin was knocked backward, and the rifle flew from his hands.

The rifle flew from his hands and discharged.

With three rabbit-like leaps, the alien disappeared into the trees of the abandoned Omaha reservation.

"Damn it, Skin you let him get—" Matt began, but stopped.

Numbly, Skin looked over at Matt, then Georgie.

Georgie wasn't standing anymore. He was on his back, his head at an awkward angle against a tree trunk. Blood oozed between his fingers from a hole in his stomach.

"Fuck," he said. "You fucking shot me, Skin."

"Oh Jesus," Skin said.

Georgie jerked away from Skin's touch and screamed in pain

from the movement. When he got his breath back, he looked at Matt.

"Get that son of a bitch."

Skin ducked his head instinctively, waiting for the butt of a gun against his temple.

"Not you, idiot," Matt yelled. "He means the alien. Let's get it."

"We'll never catch him," Skin said, looking away from Georgie at the darkening sky. "Plus we can't just leave *him* here."

Matt looked at Georgie without any expression on his face.

"He'll be all right. We'll be back soon, anyway."

"Yeah. Go get the fucking graymeat," Georgie said calmly. He ripped off the bottom of his shirt and dabbed it at his mid-section.

"Go on," he said in a tight voice, and then added in a soft voice, "Don't let me down, Skin."

Skin's arms dropped to his side as he watched Georgie's blood drip onto the ground. Matt picked up a pink capsule from the ground where the alien had stood.

"Here," Matt said, biting the capsule. He held half of it out to Skin. "Now we'll make up for lost time."

"*What?* We don't know what this'll do to us, Matt."

"Take it." Matt grimaced as he swallowed the drug. "Take it, or I'll shove it down your goddamn throat."

Skin set the gelatinous capsule in his mouth, its bitter contents almost burning his tongue. Blur was supposed to do evil things to a human's nervous system, but ever since the camps had been built, Blur dealers had gotten the aliens hooked on the drug. The human population had mostly given up on Blur.

He swallowed the rest of the capsule with a grunt and ran after Matt into the thick trees that hid the alien's escape route.

The drug worked fast. His pulse quickened almost immediately, and the cold air felt warm on his flushed face. He ran after Matt, pumping his tired legs faster than he'd thought possible.

His eyes flicked over every shadowy inch of the forest. He felt liquid and gloriously strong.

They ran deeper into the trees. The alien had bent branches and torn up the hard ground in his mad flight, and his trail was obvious in the dying light, even to Skin. Matt's panting sounded like small screams as the big man pushed his out-of-shape body ahead of him. Skin's hypersensitive ears heard the panicked hooves of at least four deer, running a mile to the west.

"There," Matt shouted, pointing with a shaking hand at a clearing ahead of them.

The remains of an old fire and the bleached bones of a cow were scattered across the circle. Bisecting the grassless clearing were the oval prints of alien feet and hands.

Matt slowed, panting hoarsely, and entered the circle. Skin followed, his arms and legs shaking with the need to keep moving. He felt ready to jump out of his body at the slightest provocation.

"Something's wrong here, man," Matt said between gasps of air.

His field glasses had fallen off somewhere in the forest, and his face looked naked and vulnerable without them.

Matt took another step into the clearing. The woods rustled suddenly, and a gray and black streak hit him. Matt was knocked off his feet without making a sound.

Skin's Blur-enhanced eyes caught the figure of the alien for a split second before the creature disappeared into the forest again. He didn't have time to raise his gun.

Without checking on Matt, he chased the alien deeper into the forest, his body moving before his brain had a chance to make sense of anything.

Images of Matt on his back in the clearing and Georgie holding his bleeding stomach swam through his head. His leg muscles began to cramp and burn. He suddenly wondered what he would do when he caught the alien.

He barely finished the thought before the alien stopped, flattened, and covered his head.

Skin tried to pull up, but he was running too fast. He tripped over the alien's body and crashed into the trunk of a tree.

The world went black.

When he opened his eyes a few seconds later, the alien was bent over him, inches from him.

An earthy, salty sensation filled Skin's mouth and nose. The flat black eyes of the alien watched him in the gray darkness. Swallowing hard, he felt his throat constrict and his chest tighten. His breath caught in his lungs.

This isn't a human in front of me, he realized with a strange shifting in his mind.

The world began to spin faster in his vision. A dull pain began to grow behind Skin's eyes.

The alien stepped back, almost blending into the grayness of the forest, but he didn't try to run.

Lifting his gun, surprised he still had it in his hands after his fall, Skin looked up into the alien's eyes.

"You're not supposed to be here," he whispered.

Pointing the gun up at the alien from the ground, Skin fumbled for the safety sensor. He tried to focus on the reward money, on all the bills he and Lisa had accumulated over the years, and the baby on the way.

"Everything's wrong now, ever since you came here. This is our home." His arms shook as he aimed the gun. "You don't belong here."

The alien took a step back, his elbows jutting out and his

long back straight. He looked like he was getting ready to do a formal bow to Skin. The wind suddenly picked up, rattling the bare tree limbs above Skin's head.

"I have to—" he began, but his mouth wouldn't cooperate with his mind. He couldn't breathe.

Random images hijacked his brain: Matt and Georgie, pregnant Lisa, the internment camps, and the reports of the reward money.

Trying to aim down the barrel of the trembling gun, Skin squinted into the darkness, his lungs burning.

The alien dropped his long arms to his side, made a whistling noise, and the forest fell silent. Skin tried to take a breath, but he could suck no air into his lungs.

The alien lifted his chin in what would have been a gesture of courage and defiance in a human.

"Home," the alien said in a deep, clear voice.

"Have to take you . . ." Skin mumbled. The cold of the ground under him was seeping into his body, numbing him.

His finger touched the trigger of his gun, and a leaden weight filled his chest.

He couldn't let Georgie or Lisa down. Or himself.

"Our home, too," the alien said, gesturing at the trees around him with a four-fingered hand. *"Nee-brash-yah."*

The way the alien said the word was more beautiful than anything Skin had ever heard.

"Home," Skin whispered, his mouth dry even as tears filled his eyes.

More images filled his head. Lisa, on the verge of screaming at him last night. The detainment camps hidden behind high walls and electric fences. Georgie joking with the loud-mouthed guy at the bar. The three white vans that passed him on his way to the elevator the day of the explosion. Matt's face red with laughter. The buses of aliens on their way to the newly built labor farms, then back to the camps. His friends, his people, his home.

He lowered his gun and cracked it, dropping the shells uselessly to the frozen forest floor.

Finally, he was able to take a breath, and he nearly fell over backward from the shock of the icy air in his lungs. The pain behind his eyes tripling in intensity, he got to his feet. He had to get back to the clearing where he'd left Matt. Skin stumbled, and the alien reached out a gray, blood-speckled hand to help him.

Without stopping to think, he touched the alien's thick hand with his own. Numbing electricity coursed through his body, and he fell to the ground, his body rigid.

The last things he saw before losing consciousness were the colorless depths of the alien's black eyes.

The day had turned completely dark when Skin opened his eyes again. His back spasmed for an instant as he sat up on the hard, cold ground and tried to make sense of where he was. He worked his way back to the clearing where Matt had gone down and found him on his side, breathing deeply, as if he had fallen asleep instead of being knocked unconscious by a flashing Wannoshay.

"Matt, it's me," he whispered. He put a hand to Matt's head, surprised that his own fingers weren't cold. "Can you walk?"

Matt's lips moved, but no sound came out. Skin helped him up and guided him through the forest, half-carrying him around the dead bushes and jutting rocks.

Georgie was raving by the time they got back to him. A flare stick sputtered on the ground next to him, covering him in flickering pink light.

"Gray, gray, get the graymeat," Georgie mumbled in a hoarse voice, turning his head back and forth.

"Shh," Skin said. The dull pain in his head was gone, and,

impossibly, he felt no more fatigue in his arms, legs, and back.

"This is going to hurt, Georgie, but we've got to get you back."

Bending down, he eased one hand under Georgie's neck and slid the other under his legs. With a grunt, he lifted the big man like a child and balanced him in his arms. Georgie groaned and pressed his hands on his stomach, but he didn't scream.

"Did you get it?" Georgie whispered. "Did you get the Wanta?"

Matt looked at Skin, the same question on his face. A soft wind rattled the deserted trees of the reservation, carrying with it a hint of mud and salt. He allowed himself a long inhale and exhale before answering.

"He's where he belongs," Skin said.

With Georgie in his arms and Matt leaning on him, he turned away from the forest and walked through the cold November darkness toward the pickup.

Chapter Thirteen

The two priests, one old and male, one young and female, approached the eastern entrance to the camp as government workers strung wire onto the top of the wall. The wire uncoiled through human hands like a metal snake without a head.

A line of six Humvees and two dozen soldiers with pulse guns kept the crowd of protesters away from the fence while the laborers worked. Father Joshua leaned down to tell Juana Mundo that the fence would be electrified again by the time they left that night.

Juana nodded, her slender fingers twitching for rosary beads that weren't there. The morning sun slipped out of the clouds for a moment, and the chanting of the protesters grew louder when they saw the two priests. Some shouted obscenities and threats, many of them aimed at the petite Mexican woman next to him. Joshua was by now a familiar face at the camp walls, and the protestors knew he couldn't be rattled by their taunts.

Squinting into the glare of the early-winter sun, he and Juana showed their identification to the soldiers, passed the Army trucks and the protestors, and entered the detainment camp.

He flashed a quick smile at Juana, a step behind him on his right. The young woman was going to have to learn quickly.

Once they were out of earshot of the constant blare and shouts of the protesters, their shoes clicking on the concrete that covered every square inch of the camp, Joshua realized how tired he was. He was tired of what he saw every day and tired of the work that never seemed to end, here in the camp.

Set up back in June, the camps were supposed to be temporary, a makeshift solution to what was commonly called "the Wannoshay problem." But now, at the start of November, any such talk of a change of venue for the People had apparently been forgotten by the rest of the world.

The sun disappeared behind the clouds again. What he saw in the gray morning light reminded him of the worst sections of Chicago's South Side: the discarded ration boxes piled up outside the huts, the broken bottles on the stained concrete, the clothing limp on the lines.

All that was missing were high-rise tenements, suicide cultists, and Blur gangs on every other corner. Instead, there were government-issued Quonset huts, cheap cement roads, and Blur addicts in every corner of the camp.

Walking at a brisk pace next to Juana, he had to force himself, on this cold morning, not to dwell on the squalor around them on the streets of the camp, just as he tried not to let the past affect his work.

The cold had numbed his ears already, and his breath formed a cloud in front of his face. He caught himself thinking about the words of the other priests from his rectory, most of them claiming that the camps had been built to remove the burden of guilt from the People.

And these were *priests*. Approving of penance through imprisonment. God only knew what the average person without faith, or, heaven forbid, a cultist, must think.

Even the American president and the Canadian prime minister had agreed that the aliens had to be contained, "for their sake and ours."

Juana slowed down next to him, her dark eyes scanning the road and the shadowy entrances to the huts on either side. Her black, close-cropped hair, tousled by the wind, was sticking up in a couple places. She had barely spoken all morning long.

In front of them, young alien voices approached, growing louder. Juana paused in midstep, then set her foot down.

"When a child comes close to you," he whispered to her, "don't pull away or make any sudden movements. Just relax."

A band of five children slid out from behind a hut and galloped toward them on the concrete, using their long, thick arms like front legs. The clumping sound of their long hands and rounded feet was loud in the morning stillness. Fat hair-tentacles bounced on the children's narrow heads.

He saw them anew from the perspective of his trainee. If not for the tentacles, their too-long bodies, and that eye, sitting sideways in the middle of their foreheads, they'd look almost human.

"Favvyer Yotchooa, Favvyer Yotchooa!" they called in bird-like voices as they approached. With a sudden, almost-coordinated movement, they all reared up and stood upright, wobbling next to the two priests.

On Joshua's right, Juana inhaled suddenly. He thought he could hear a clicking sound as the young woman swallowed.

"Good morning, children," he said slowly. The alien smell of rich dirt and salty sweat was strong. He knew their greatest hopes were with the young—they needed to reach the children before they saw the labor farms, the Blur dealers, and the violence and hatred outside.

"This is my new friend, Miss Juana. She'll be working here, too."

The children stepped back to examine Juana. Most of them were already taller than Joshua, and they towered over Juana, who was barely five feet tall.

"Mish Hawana," a boy in the back whispered, and the rest of the children giggled with chittering voices.

Their gray skin, flushed bright pink in spots from running,

was covered in a light sheen of sweat despite the cool air. The pink derm patches developed by the military and civilian researchers had been effective in keeping the People's lightly pigmented gray skin from burning up in the sun's rays and the Earth's atmosphere.

He shuddered as he thought of an old friend whose damaged skin had been wrapped in bandages. He hadn't seen Johndo since late springtime, back in Waukegan. A lifetime ago.

Ezra's fore-eye opened and closed, giving both of the priests a crooked wink. Juana rubbed her hands together and touched the square of white on her collar, but then, to her credit, she met their gazes and smiled.

Bless you, Juana, Joshua thought.

When he looked back at the children, Lucas, one of the bigger boys, had dropped into a crouch. Without warning he started hitting the child next to him. Lucas's open hands pummeled the smaller child until the other boy ran off on all fours, howling.

When Joshua touched him, Lucas screamed and sprinted after the first child. The rest of the children scuttled away as well. Their hands and feet barely made a sound on the concrete, and they left behind an almost-sweet scent of mud and salt.

He heard Juana's sharp intake of breath once again.

"The People," he began, "especially the young, are prone to senseless outbursts like this. Nobody knew about these fits of violence until the People began working in the factories and grain elevators and breweries. But by then it was already too late."

His voice dried up. Annina, the camp doctor—and the only other human in the camp—claimed it was a combination of a chemical imbalance and a hypersensitivity to sun, as well as the movements and possibly emotions of others.

He didn't say anything more about Lucas. Some things Juana

would simply have to learn on her own, without him.

They walked past the Quonsets and the cluttered front yards of stained concrete. This part of the camp was quiet, as most of the healthy men and women had already left for the labor farms that had popped up around all the countryside. Only the old and the young remained during the work days.

Off to the right, dusty-skinned Noah balanced an armload of garbage on his way across a shaded concrete yard, and a newsletter slipped from his grasp when he waved. The paper was covered in unreadable slash marks and jagged scribbles, reminding Joshua of the book he still hadn't returned to Johndo. The book had sat untouched for months back home in the rectory.

When the sun moved behind the clouds again, the camp gradually came to life. Blankets used as doors were folded open and fastened with wire, letting in the cool air that the People loved so much, the cool air that reminded them of their home.

Reminded of his mentoring task, he turned back to Juana.

"See how pale their skin is? Too much sunlight can burn their skin to a horrible pinkish color. And overexposure can kill them."

Juana shivered, as if suddenly aware of the chill in the air. The lack of warmth barely affected Joshua any more.

"The People place great importance in their sense of touch," he said, continuing his lesson. "It took over three months before any of them would get within five feet of me. Hopefully," he added, with a nod at Juana's white collar, black shirt, and black pants that mirrored his own, "they'll trust you sooner."

The tired-looking Quonset huts were arranged in rows of ten on either side of the narrow road, and many had been painted and reworked by their many inhabitants. The long, circular huts often contained a dozen or more of the People, while others contained only one or two.

He had yet to figure out the hierarchy, if there was any. Some of the huts gave hints of the world the People had left behind: synthetic black vines on curving roofs, white-gray patterns on the curved walls giving the rough exteriors depth and the appearance of caves. Others had been left unchanged.

The two priests approached an unpainted, rusting hut and stepped inside.

"Good *morning*, Eli," Joshua said, shouting to get the attention of the old man dozing in the main room of the hut.

Eli had been almost deaf since March, after a brutal fight with another one of his people during an anti-integration protest in St. Paul that had turned into a riot. A meal of wilted lettuce and an unrecognizable chunk of brown meat sat uneaten on the Wannoshay man's foldout table.

Past the table where Eli slept in his chair, the hut stretched off into blackness. Joshua glanced at the cot against the curving western wall, and the thin blanket draped onto it that didn't quite hide a spill of broken concrete under the cot.

Many of the People had secretly punched through the concrete flooring of the camps, but they had been careful not to let any of the human visitors but Joshua see this. He positioned himself between Juana and her view of the cot and called out to Eli again.

Eli jerked awake at the sound of Joshua's voice, and his chair tipped back precariously. By reaching out and gripping the table with his long toes, Eli kept from falling over backward.

"Favvyer Yosh!" he exclaimed. He took Joshua's hand in his short-fingered grasp. His hands were cold and rough.

"Wash bad weekenh' for her," Eli shouted. He let his chair drop forward, and his muddy, bittersweet odor tickled Joshua's nose. "She looksh worsh."

With a crackling sound, Eli stood. His long torso rippled, and he rubbed his stubby fingers together. Before bending to all fours, he touched the four delicate, parallel scars on the back of each hand.

"Let's go," Joshua said, needing to keep in motion. "Eli, this is Juana. Juana, Eli. Come, Eli. Let's go see her."

Eli straightened up again, as if he'd simply been stretching or doing some sort of yoga pose specific to the People.

Joshua gave Juana a nod, following Eli outside. The hospital was always at the top of the list of stops, he wanted to tell her, but he could tell by the determined set of her jaw that she knew where they were going.

As they walked next to Eli down the dirt road, he hoped the younger priest had been studying the camp maps he made for her. Like most of the others of its kind across the plains, this camp covered almost three square miles, row upon row of scraped earth covered with half a foot of concrete, electric fences, and old Quonsets. A young priest fresh from the seminary in Juárez City could quickly get lost here.

"Keep five feet away from the sick, Juana. Some of the elders aren't used to being this close to humans. Or maybe it's my red face and big nose that scares them."

Juana gave a weak smile and picked up the pace.

The camp hospital was a two-story cinderblock fortress that Joshua had lobbied the Minnesota government for six weeks to get built. When he first arrived in Minneapolis after his transfer in early July, the People had been bringing their sick to a huge tent ringed by four Quonsets. Most of them had died in that tent.

At the front desk stood Annina, the camp doctor. Her long black hair hung down in her eyes as she tapped on a chart on her battered handheld. She nodded at them, and Joshua led Juana toward their first patient. Eli was already in Sarah's room.

Sarah was a shriveled-up woman, but her nobility was obvious in her proud chin and clear black eyes. Joshua could barely smell her. She smiled, unveiling a row of pointed teeth that were bright white and spotless. Her long body barely fit on the standard-size hospital bed. There were four long, narrow scars on the back of each of her hands, symbolizing—to the best of Joshua's knowledge—her connection to Eli.

"Favvyer," she whispered. Joshua felt a sharp stinging sensation deep inside his chest. On his right, Juana simply stared at Sarah's wasted body. Outlined under her sheet were the elongated ribcage and the curved spine that distinguished their people.

Sarah should never have left her home planet, Joshua thought, to die here. Even if their planet, according to the stories Johndo had told him, had grown too inhospitable. He couldn't imagine anything more inhospitable than this camp.

"You are looking especially beautiful today, Sarah," Joshua said, trying to focus. Father, watch over her, his mind managed to whisper. The rest was silence.

They left Eli standing hunched over at her side, his thick hands cradling her slender, scarred hands.

"This is what the camps are all about," Joshua began, but the words faded like his prayer for Sarah. He wanted to tell Juana about the anger that coursed through him at night, when his head was filled with images of Sarah and Eli and the rest of the People locked up here in the camps.

He wanted to tell her about the unholy hatred he felt for the blank-faced Blur dealers lurking outside the camp walls, waiting for the trucks to return from the labor farms. He wanted to tell her how the administrative job Father Miller had talked about would end his sleepless nights.

He wanted to tell her to leave this place now with her soul intact.

But again, he said nothing.

They left the hospital an hour and a half later. He usually

stayed longer, but he could tell that Juana was close to sensory overload. The young priest hadn't even been able to remain at his side for the last three rooms.

Outside, the clouds had been burnt away, and the sun beat down on empty brown streets. The wind skipped around the huts and threw dirt on them, streaking Juana's black pants.

They walked down another row of houses, and Joshua saw the Quonset that Ruth used to share with six other Wannoshay. Her family. She had passed away late Saturday night, succumbing finally to her respiratory infection, and he'd hoped to anoint her body and ease her transition to heaven. He and Ruth and her family had discussed it last week, and they all had agreed. But when he came to visit late on Sunday, her body had already been removed from the hospital.

The People did not bury their dead, he knew, and he tried to grant them some amount of privacy and dignity by not prying too deeply into their rituals.

"The People have a very loosely organized culture," he said.

The People take care of their own, he continued silently, wondering what had happened to Ruth's body. Who am I to try to influence them, to change their beliefs?

"But everything here is so . . ." Juana's voice cracked.

"So structured? Yes, but it's not their choosing." Next to them, the schoolhouse loomed over the huts, the tall eight-sided structure built by volunteers from the People during Joshua's first week in the camp.

At the time, he hadn't been able to believe how quickly it had been built. Since that time, he had witnessed countless times the strength of the People, along with their drive to complete a task once it was started.

He also wondered, late at night when sleep wouldn't come, why they didn't use that strength to break through the concrete and pull down the walls that kept them in these camps. But again, he knew it was not his place to ask.

As they entered the drafty schoolhouse, he felt another pang of guilt.

If I leave, I will miss the children the most. They have restored my faith on a daily basis.

He corrected himself: *When* I leave.

Half of the children showed up for their language lessons on time. The rest straggled in without apologizing, and Thomas and Elizabeth came in half an hour tardy.

"Loosely organized," Joshua said under his breath to Juana, who tapped her pen on the Bible in front of her.

They used scripture passages to teach English to the People. The children learned quickly, despite the problems they had with pronunciation. Today's verse was from Saint Matthew, the parable of the prodigal son returning home.

Juana spoke a line from the Bible, and then the children would try to repeat her words. Most of the children had difficulty with their t's and j's and other hard consonants. Joshua was content with being known as "Yosh."

Juana fiddled with her collar as she repeated the lesson at the front of the classroom. Her Mexican accent had thickened as her frustration grew, and the children giggled at her rolled r's and clipped endings. Joshua watched for any sudden movements by the children in their seats, any bursts of energy or violence. Juana was starting to sweat.

"Shovinosh," Joshua said, with an edge to his voice. Elizabeth clapped a hand over her mouth, and David's fore-eye snapped shut. The room was quiet.

He turned to Juana. "It's a good idea to learn their language as well, Juana. Continue."

As they recited, he was reminded once more of the sound of birds who cannot sing. They try so hard to learn our language, yet what have we done for them? Locked them up and surrounded them with miles of electric fence.

Father, give me strength.

Elizabeth peeked over her Bible at him as if reading his thoughts. She blinked all three eyes at him in succession until he smiled. He pointed at her Bible with what he hoped was a stern expression, and then walked over to Ezra, who had started beating both hands slowly against his desktop. Joshua rested a hand on the boy's shoulder and kept it there until Ezra relaxed.

Ten minutes later, Juana dismissed the children with a weak wave and a hesitant "*Wanniya,*" which roughly translated to "goodbye."

David's quick, hiccuping laugh echoed through the room as he and the other children pushed each other on their way out the door. They left behind papers scattered on the floor and across their desks.

"They like you," Joshua said to Juana, who was still gripping the lectern. "But they feel your nervousness. Just relax. They're used to disorganization, and they'll take you for a ride if you let them."

Juana dropped into a chair and crossed her legs in front of her. She gave Joshua the look.

Eyebrows raised, mouth half open. He'd seen it on four previous priests in the past six months.

"How can you maintain your spirit here?" Juana asked.

"Don't you enjoy doing the Lord's work?"

"*Sí,*" Juana answered with a quick smile, then her face tightened. "But there were all those deaths from the attacks. You cannot deny the fact that they had something to do with it. All the Netstreams said that they were seen at the grain elevator before it blew up. That it was *not* an accident."

Joshua lowered his eyes for a moment, looking down at his hands. When he lifted his gaze again, Juana was shaking her head slowly, looking at the papers littering the floor.

"And the way these children act sometimes, all this hitting? Maybe the government tried to integrate too fast. We're supposed to forgive the Wantas, I know, but they *are* aliens . . ."

Joshua stood up and moved the desks back into straight rows. The metal feet of the chairs scraped against the floor.

"You'll see, Juana. The People live and breathe and feel just like you and me. They're misunderstood. We're all trying to learn." He slid the last desk into place.

Safety for us and atonement for the People. The words burned in his ears, echoing like a metal hatch slamming shut.

"Let's go see our next parishioners."

Juana followed him outside. They walked deeper into the camp, until they were standing in front of a heavily vined, rusting hut. The afternoon sky was dark again, promising snow.

"Should we knock?" Juana asked.

He nodded, but Juana's knock on the doorframe was drowned out by the wail of a siren cutting the air. He felt his chest tighten. The sound rose and built until he could see the flickering red lights of a police car.

"It must be in the square," he said to Juana, who had been staring at him, eyes widening at the sound.

The tightness in his chest forgotten, Joshua led Juana away from the hut. They ran five blocks to the west and north, following the siren. In front of him, the huts flashed red in the spinning lights of a black-windowed Minnesota State Police cruiser. Juana was thirty yards behind him, staring at the cruiser as if frozen.

Two officers in black helmets and thick body armor eased their way out of the car. One swung a shotgun back and forth in an arc while his partner pulled two bodies from the back seat. With an air of carelessness they dropped the bodies in the middle of the concrete road and drove off, engine fading as they rushed back to the western camp gate.

Joshua forgot about Juana and the police and ran up to the bodies in the road. They were barely more than boys, just old enough to work in the fields, and they were both covered in their own purplish-red blood. Deep bruises and jagged cuts crisscrossed their gray skin. Just boys. They were alive.

"Get Annina from the hospital," he yelled at Juana, who had been inching closer. "And come right back here."

The smell of coppery blood—so much like our own, Joshua thought, but lighter in color, almost purple—made him want to gag, but instead he pulled out his handkerchief and wiped the thickening blood from the closest boy's face.

Under the swelling and cuts, he recognized Matthew, who should have left that morning on one of the trucks for the labor farms. At Joshua's touch the boy moaned deep within his wide chest.

"Shh," Joshua said, looking down at Matthew's injuries, too many for him to even try to stop all the bleeding. He loosened the boy's ill-fitting clothing and straightened his long body in the dirt.

His hand touched the blood from a wound on the boy's neck, the contact filling his mouth with the same metallic taste he'd first felt when he opened the metal book Colonel Cossa had found on the ship all those months ago. Swallowing hard, he moved to the second boy, a young man he didn't recognize.

"Hold your hand there," he told the boy, but instead of obeying the boy opened his hand and swung at him. His strength was gone, though, and his arm fell back to the ground before ever reaching the priest bent over him.

Joshua sat between the two boys and took their dry, four-fingered hands in his. He tried to clear his mind to pray, but no words would form.

Help me, Father. Work through me, Father.

But nothing came to him other than the rush of wind in his ears.

Giving up on prayer, Joshua looked down at Matthew.

"Where were you? Who did this to you?"

"Fence off this morn'," Matthew murmured through broken teeth.

He was one of Joshua's first students, and his English was strong. He'd loved his new name when Joshua gave it to him. Joshua hadn't been able to pronounce their real names, and he realized now how arrogant it was for him to rename them from his Bible.

"Went city," Matthew continued. "Wanted fighting. Men chase, catch us. We found some fighting, we did."

Footsteps echoed through the square. Joshua hoped it was Juana and Annina, not any of the People running up on all fours to see what the sirens had heralded. Matthew's lipless mouth moved again, but no sound came out. His fore-eye opened wide, stretching taut, and then closed. His hand slipped from Joshua's grip.

Annina ran up and began working on the two boys. She spat obscenities under her breath as she touched bruises and welts. His throat too tight to breathe, Joshua stepped back to give her room. He was covered in purplish-red blood.

Alien blood.

He almost fell over his own feet as he backed away.

There's nothing else I can do here.

The wind blew on him again in a blinding burst of anger. There were no tears in his eyes, and the only thing he could feel was a deep ache on the left side of his chest.

Juana brushed past him, a small, dark figure that floated across his vision. He glanced up and saw aliens on every side of him.

This will be my last day here in the camp.

"Joshua," Juana whispered from the ground. "We can't just leave them."

Without realizing it, he'd taken two steps away from the bodies.

Juana knelt, taking Annina's place next to the boys. Annina turned and walked away. He looked down at Juana. There was a tiny drop of blood on her collar. Purplish-red soaked into pristine white.

Almost half a year here. It's taken that long to open my eyes and see the truth.

"We couldn't save them," he said.

Looking up at him, Juana's eyes tightened at the corners. It was a tiny movement that nobody else could have seen, but he saw it.

"If we can't save these boys," Juana said in a soft, calm voice, "we can at least help them in our own way."

The crowd of aliens, the too-old and the too-young, moved back when Juana pulled a vial from her shirt pocket. Matthew's elderly mother was there, and she nodded stiffly at Juana. Her three black eyes were dry.

Her brown finger anointed Matthew's forehead with oil, above the third eye, then the boy's lips and chest. Whispering the prayers, Juana's voice hummed with an ancient rhythm.

She repeated the sacrament over the other boy.

The humming in her voice was picked up by the People gathered around them. Soon the air vibrated with alien mourning mixed with one human's words of prayer.

Within minutes, the wordless throbbing was deafening.

Juana crossed herself, her hand trembling the slightest bit. She left the two bodies at rest and knuckled away the dampness at the corner of her eyes.

The alien voices continued rising to an impossible pitch, an inhuman sound of sorrow and pain. With his eyes squeezed shut tight, Joshua's eardrums felt like they were about to burst. The song was both hauntingly beautiful and horribly inhuman.

He wanted to scream, but before he could, the song ended. He opened his eyes again. He and Juana were surrounded by the People, a quivering wall of gray, alien flesh. Annina had already slipped away from the crowd, abandoning them.

For the first time ever in the camps, he felt a flickering of danger, of fear. With his ears ringing, he pulled Juana out of the circle.

Energy built as they pushed past old and young, male and female. The hairs on his arms and the back of his neck were standing up.

When they were outside the circle, an ageless female voice began to sing. The words were lilting, almost indistinguishable from one another in the People's exotic language.

The breath taken from his lungs, he stepped closer to the circle of energy to listen. Juana listened as well, a look of peace on her face.

The only words of the song that he could make out were life, death, sorrow, and a word that he'd heard them say before but had never quite comprehended. Now, in context—in *song*—he understood it.

Forgive.

They *had* been listening to what I'd been teaching them.

The People—the Wannoshay, the aliens, the others—had heard me. They understood.

The lone voice was joined by soft female voices and low male voices. Joshua smelled hints of incense and ozone. He tried to turn away, but he could not. His fear was gone; he needed to listen.

The two bodies in the middle of the circle glowed with a wavering light. The light grew stronger as the song sped up. The words blended together. The bodies appeared to be lifting up into the air, as if the gathered hands around them were raising them up.

He saw young Lucas, the bully from this morning. The boy was unmoving, free from his fits of aggression and mindless violence.

Joshua took Juana's hand and pulled her to the ground, onto her knees next to him.

"Pray," he told her, his final lesson, but Juana's head was already bowed.

Pure white light filled the camp, pouring from the two bodies in the middle of the circle. The energy of the People swirled around and lifted the bodies higher.

Before he closed his eyes, he saw the bodies start to dissolve into the air, as if melting into the tentacle-haired, three-eyed beings standing below them.

"Father," he murmured, a prayer that he could hear only in his mind, "let me have the spirit to continue my work here."

The wind blew hot onto his skin.

"Father, let the walls crumble so one day the camps will be no more. Father," he whispered, "give me the strength and the grace to endure, here in the camp."

Joshua finished his prayer with dust in his throat as the wild energy of the Wannoshay spilled onto him, and, using every ounce of strength left in him, he opened his eyes.

Chapter Fourteen

Ally needed to make Jenae stop laughing.

Even as the aliens pranced and convulsed around them in the throes of Blur, their high-pitched screams threatening to pierce her eardrums, all she could see was Jenae's crooked teeth as the skinny white girl laughed at the madness she and Ally had created around them.

"Wantaviewer," Jenae croaked, repeating the alias over and over, until her voice was lost in the screaming of the aliens around them—Ally had to read her lips as they formed the syllables at high speed.

And then she heard the horrible thudding of alien bodies as they were crushed by the oncoming car, sounds she knew were coming but couldn't prevent from happening. The screams of the aliens sounded human.

From farther away came the actual sound of human voices screaming: the Netstream reporters, under attack as they returned to report on the breaking news.

And Jenae continued laughing.

The Wantas crowded into the street, some of them crawling down out of apartment windows like giant spiders, dropping to the ground and raising their hands palms up.

More Blur, those four-fingered hands seemed to say.

Ally turned away from those aliens and took slow, unfeeling steps closer to the two Wantas wounded by the runaway car.

Turn back, a voice told her. Wake up, you goddamn fool.

"No," she said, and with that the streets cleared of everyone but her, Jenae, the two dying aliens, and a small, hunched alien lying face down in the street. The hunched alien's body formed a T with the two injured aliens. The only thing moving on the hunched alien's body was the writhing tentacles of the alien's hair.

His hair, the voice in her head said. You know him, don't you? If you won't turn back, at least admit the truth.

She heard a whimpering sound like an injured animal, coming from her left. It was Jenae, her skinny body shaking as she flashed from the Blur. She moaned and writhed, spittle flying from her mouth as she struggled for air. Her ratty hair flew around her face, and for an instant, as her head fell forward and her face contorted, Jenae the Blur dealer could have been mistaken for a small, undernourished Wannoshay.

Ally grabbed Jenae by the shirt, but she was too heavy, and they both toppled forward. Jenae had finally stopped laughing.

Ally stepped over her and tried to run toward the three aliens, but they were farther away now. Slipping away from her, as if the street was expanding. The two injured aliens were females.

"Jane," Ally whispered. "Thumper?"

The face-down alien turned his head toward her, all three eyes so wide that she could see that they were rimmed in strange slivers of white. Brando.

His usually comforting smell of salt and mud had changed. She could barely smell him. In the blink of a Blur-addled eye, the alien was on his feet, squat legs quivering with power.

Brando growled at her, a low rumbling that turned her blood to ice. He closed his middle eye and pulled three chewed-up capsules from his mouth. Turning his hand over, palm out, he offered them to her. Brando smelled now of madness: sickly-sweet syrup mixed with bitter onions.

When she shook her head to tell him no, no-no-no, Brando

the Wanta threw the capsules in the air. Leaving the two dying aliens behind him, he sprang at her with a shriek that nearly turned her bladder to icy water. His clawed hands reached her, touching her an instant before the discarded capsules of Blur hit the ground.

Ally woke with a scream lodged in her throat. She clamped her mouth shut, her breath clouding up in front of her before it dissipated onto the opaqued windshield. Her fingers and toes were numb. She stared at the shadows of the stranger's garage where she'd parked her car that morning, trying to dispel the nightmare.

"Jesus H," she muttered, sitting up slowly. The cheap vinyl of the passenger seat crackled under her. "I've about had enough of *that* shit."

She raised the seat and scrabbled for the door handle next to her, fighting against the weight of the two sleeping bags on top of her. She could smell her own unwashed body like a musky sock under her nose, but she was too cold to care.

"Shit!" she shouted through clenched teeth. No matter how much she prepared for it, the cold always came as a harsh shock. She hurried around the driver's seat and started the car. She cranked the heat and blew on her hands as the engine groaned and threatened to stall on her.

The violent dreams about that night had been haunting her ever since the last day of May. They'd gotten worse since she'd been thrown out of her apartment in August for not paying her share of the rent. Guilt-ridden from her night of handing out Blur to the Wantas, Alissa had quit both Blur and her job. A week later she sold her wallscreen and all her related Netstream equipment, including her lapel camera and recorder. Everything she owned now fit into her car, her new home. And her money was running out.

Without Blur, Ally's life had become so slow that she had to keep checking her watch and her pulse to make sure that time—and her body—hadn't stopped altogether.

To keep herself moving, she spent the last few weeks cruising through Winnipeg, watching different neighborhoods for houses where the family was gone all day. She had plenty to choose from, and all she had to do was vary her neighborhood every week or so. She just made sure not to get too close to the Sargent neighborhood, where she swore she could still hear Jenae's crazy laughing along with the aliens' screams echoing up and down Ellice Avenue. Jenae had disappeared since that night, and Ally hoped she'd met the same fate as most of the 'Stream reporters.

Once her car had finally warmed itself, Ally backed out of the garage. With Christmas music fading in and out of the old radio-only Netstream wedged into the dashboard of her car, she cruised through town, away from her nightmare memories.

"This is what I *wa-a-a-ant* for Christmas," she caught herself singing along with the grunge rhymers on the 'Stream. "A toke and a *smo-o-o-oke* and spaceship full of *way* too much." The words didn't make much sense, but the fuzzy guitars and the rhymers' voices were addictive. For a few minutes, she didn't feel quite so cold and alone.

By the time the song had ended in burst of feedback mixed with sleigh bells, Ally was accelerating on Route 85, heading west out of the city. If she kept going into the countryside, she'd end up passing one of the labor farms, where Brando was most likely working, along with Thumper and Jane.

What are *they* gonna get for Christmas? she thought, turning down the music. Besides another day on the farms, cleaning barns or cutting down trees or digging ditches?

Checking the gas tank—half-full—Ally kept driving. The flat landscape of dead fields, broken only by random clumps of leafless trees, helped her organize her thoughts into some semblance of order. She sped down the highway and aimed her car in the direction of the first, and largest, labor farm.

In hindsight, the labor farms had been more or less inevitable once the camps were created. Sentiment against the aliens had been strong enough after the explosions that volunteers had crawled out of the woodwork to help construct the camp walls and concrete flooring for the huts and tents that would temporarily house the Wantas. From sunrise to sunset, human volunteers helped to pound metal spikes into the ground, pour concrete, and string wire around the giant squares of the camps. The sooner the Wantas were contained, the better, people thought.

But after a few months, the people living close to the camps began getting nervous. They reported strange moaning sounds that would wake them late at night, along with bursts of whitish-blue light that would shoot from the middle of the Quonset huts of the camp. Some described the lights as beacons to more alien ships, and others were convinced the voices were hypnotic messages to encourage the humans to let them free, or at the least, to slip them some Blur to help pass the time during their imprisonment.

So the aliens were put to work, night and day, on the factory farms that had taken over almost all of the smaller, family-run operations, and the labor farms were born. Some were livestock farms, while others were for processing grains and hemp, and some were both. The Wantas were tasked once again with the labor that humans no longer wanted to do.

All of the labor farms were located far from the nearest town, and, as a result, they were mostly forgotten.

Punching the button for the heater again, trying to warm up her frozen toes, Ally bit off another length of grape-flavored stim-gum from the rope she'd bought earlier. She'd felt childish for buying the gum at the time, but she was thankful now for the sugar and caffeine the gum gave her. She'd gotten hooked on the stuff back at the rehab center during her two-week, state-paid stint back in August.

The other residents at the center had plenty of theories about the aliens, most of them wrongheaded and ignorant. The only tidbits of useful information had come from a guy her age named Gregor, who claimed he'd actually been inside both a camp and a labor farm.

"They don't guard the farms as tight as the camps," he told her, his shaky hands constantly running over the blonde stubble on his head. He was there to get off Blur, just like Ally. "Just a couple soldiers with guns and those remote control clip-ons they wear on their belts just in case one of the Wantas tries to make a getaway. Back when they still lived in the city, I saw one of them get hit by a blast from one of those clip-on jobs, and it dropped him like he'd been hit by a sledgehammer."

"Why do they let this shit happen?" Ally whispered. Explosions or not, she was sickened at the thought of one of her friends knocked out like an animal.

"The Wantas? They're just biding their time, y'see," Gregor said, "just waiting for the next big thing. They're not going to fight. Something else is happening with the aliens. I just don't know what the hell it's gonna be."

Ally bit into another stale gumball from the vending machine in the basement and grimaced. "Were they using?"

"Oh yeah," Gregor said, and his eyes went distant on Ally. He'd only been at the health center for three days, and it was going to get worse for him soon. "They had lots of Blur to go 'round. Maybe that helped them pass the time while they were waiting for . . . whatever. One of them put his hands on my shoulders and showed me how it felt for *him* to use Blur." He shuddered. "They definitely get their money's worth out of the shit. I couldn't stop pacing for a week after that."

Their talk had been interrupted by the five o'clock meal, and Ally had never gotten another chance to get more details out of Gregor. He got tired of the center when his withdrawals hit, and he left the treatment house against medical advisement.

Just like so many other people she'd known in the past few years, Gregor had disappeared from Ally's life. Blur used them up and left them old, which was how Ally now felt in her cold car, cruising past the snowy fields of the farm.

"Just like that," Ally whispered, chewing her gum hard enough to make her jaws hurt. She wished she'd asked Gregor if he'd ever heard the aliens talk about being late.

An empty Canadian Forces Humvee, draped in shimmering camouflage that continually shifted colors, was parked next to the entrance to the factory farm. On the other side of the tall chain-link fence topped with razor wire were two dozen long, low buildings connected by gravel drives. The heavy stink of manure filled the air, mixed with the nauseating odor of ammonia.

A beefy, bored-looking soldier stood next to the fence. His rifle rested against the fence, and his eyes were hidden behind a pair of opaqued glasses; he was either surfing the 'Stream or napping. He wore one of the ubiquitous green boxes on his belt.

Ally thought about turning around, but she couldn't think of anywhere else to go. She drove up to the reinforced metal gate and smiled at the soldier, who had picked up his rifle the instant he heard her car.

"Don't shoot," Ally said in what she had hoped was a light voice, but turned out to be little more than a squeak. She breathed out of her mouth to keep from gagging from the smell of pig shit. Her car rumbled as if it was about to stall on her, and she goosed the gas pedal to keep it running.

The soldier looked at her from over the tops of his still-opaqued glasses with the hint of a grin. "Help ya, miss?"

Ally didn't hesitate, surprising herself with the quick lie. Usually she needed Blur to do things like this.

"Got a delivery for the main office. New computer stuff, boring shit."

"What kind of delivery vehicle you driving there, miss? Is that a damn *hybrid?*"

"Hey it runs, okay, big guy. And yeah, it's a hybrid. Got it a couple years before the electrics got so popular."

The soldier had forgotten her as he walked around the car. "Those things were supposed to be recalled the year after they came out. This baby could blow up on you if—"

"Hey, you know, I'd love to chat, but I'm running late and I'd really like to drop off this stuff, 'kay?"

"Hmm? Oh sure, let me beep you in. I got you covered. Just drive that thing carefully, and don't run into anything, eh? It could blow you into tomorrow, y'know."

As the gate swung open, Ally nearly laughed out loud. Her piece of shit car was finally doing some good, as a distraction.

She drove past a row of new tractors nearly twenty feet high, parked next to shiny, dark green combines with their big teeth sticking out inches above the ground like reaching arms. She parked in front of one of the smaller buildings.

Act like you belong here, she told herself. Hold your head up high, look busy, and nobody will notice you.

Hurrying away from her car with a distracted look on her face, Ally walked through the gate leading into a courtyard that connected the farm buildings. She slipped into the first of the buildings and found ten Wannoshay inside the barn, cleaning up manure, scooping out feed, and herding pigs from one stall to another.

She pulled up short at the sight of the aliens. That awful night in May came rushing back to her, like a nightmare.

Nah you fugg-hin' didh idh, a voice whispered inside her head. *Fugg-hin' didh idh.*

The long building was impossibly long, easily the size of a hockey rink. Ally wanted to cover her ears as well as her nose from the noise and stink of the pigs.

Still hiding in the shadows of the entrance to the barn, Ally relaxed and waited for her nose to start itching and her ears to start ringing. Then she'd know she was getting close to Brando.

When she saw a soldier approaching from the far side of the barn, she slipped back outside.

So many pigs, she thought. So much pig shit. I may never eat bacon again.

The next three buildings also held pigs and a handful of alien workers, but no Brando. But when she walked into the tallest building on the complex, the ringing sensation inside her head returned, and she followed it down a side corridor.

She nearly cried out in relief when she saw the short, hunched alien stacking bales of dried hemp. The sweet, musty smell of the hemp filled the thick air and made her smile. She knew that if she wanted to get any kind of buzz off this stuff, she'd have to smoke a joint about as big as one of the bales stacked next to her.

Only five other Wantas were working there, and the others were far enough away to not notice her as she approached. With all the hemp around her, the barn felt twenty degrees warmer.

Setting his round bale on top of the others, the male Wannoshay Ally thought was Brando suddenly stopped. With his back to her, Ally could see the steam slowly coming off his bare skin in spite of the chilly air, and she realized he was naked from the waist up. She'd thought he'd simply been wearing a tight gray shirt. Swirling patterns covered the flushed skin of his long back, and his pink derm patch was like a horizontal pink scar at the back of his thick neck. Ally held her breath and stared.

"A-issha?" the alien said, not even turning around. "You come to see me?"

Ally was able to breathe again. For the first time in months she felt the almost forgotten itching sensation in her nose to go along with the ringing in her ears.

"It's me," she whispered. "Are you okay?"

Brando slowly turned, and there was something wrong with his face. Ally thought he'd been injured somehow, or if he'd changed like the way he'd been in her dream.

Turn back, the nightmare voice whispered. Wake up, you goddamn fool.

Still steaming, he stepped closer, and Ally breathed in his salty smell, smiling like someone who'd finally scratched a hard-to-reach itch. She couldn't see Brando's mouth, and his middle eye was clenched as tightly as his lips, hidden in his gray skin. His two horizontal eyes had a hard glint to them, as if he was afraid to blink.

"Are you okay?" she said again. She remembered now how much she'd missed talking to him, trying to figure out his people's history and telling him about her own past. "And the others?"

"Ah," Brando said, his mouth barely opening. From farther down in the barn, Ally could see some of the other aliens looking at them. "She is . . . taken in, into us. You call her . . . Thumber?"

"Thumper?" The ringing in Ally's ears tripled in volume, and she stepped back, her stomach twisting as she thought about his words. "What do you mean? How she get taken *into*—" Ally felt her knees go weak. "Oh my God. Did you *eat* her, Brando?"

Brando closed his eyes for a moment, and the pain on his face made him look remarkably human. She could see what may have been a smile as he shook his head in a gesture she'd taught him months ago.

"She Blurred. Attacked fellows, attacked soldier. Died at camp, after soldiers . . . We took her in, sharing all her energy."

Brando opened his eyes, and Ally could see the condemnation in them, or at least she could imagine it. She wanted to explain what had happened that night in Winnipeg, wanted to tell Brando why she gave Blur to the others. But it was too late for explanations, and she knew it.

"What can I do to make things better?" she said.

Soft footsteps approached from farther down the in the barn. She ignored the footsteps. She didn't care if she was caught, not anymore.

"Show you?" Brando said, his soft voice in her ear. Somehow he had gotten up and moved behind her without her knowing.

"Okay," Ally whispered. "Show me."

His hands were rough, but his touch was gentle as he rested his palms on her shoulder. Out of her peripheral vision, Ally could have sworn his stubby, toe-like fingers were growing. She knew if she looked back and up at his face, Brando's sideways eye would be open again. But before she could turn around and look him in the face, her vision went black.

She saw only the blackness of space for long moments, until her closed eyes adjusted, and she saw the stars, a spill of them too many to be comprehended. Her breath quickened with awe and fear, slowing only when Brando's voice filled her mind, no longer speaking in his halting English.

She wouldn't realize until later that he was speaking to her in the words of the Wannoshay, and she'd understood every word.

"Our voyage here went wrong quickly. We knew nothing of the location of your planet other than the few facts our Stargazers, those brave souls who dared the aboveground, had shared with our ancestors us many cycles ago. Yet the flight was made easy by the Mother Ship; the Navigators in the ships behind simply followed her trajectory most of the long, sleepless journey. Our plan was to land together on a less-populated area of your planet, a portion of your planet similar to the one we had left."

Ally watched the stars begin to blur, and then planets streaked by—was that Jupiter? Saturn? Mars?—until Earth loomed large in her vision, a now-familiar ball of serene blue and white and green. Looking at it through Brando's point of view, she realized its beauty, mostly forgotten after years of looking inward and strife.

Brando continued talking, his voice high and soft.

"But the instant the Mother Ship entered your planet's atmosphere, we lost contact with her. The Navigators panicked, I'm ashamed to say. We landed on our own, and most managed to do so without casualty. But in the process, all of the ships were damaged beyond hope of recovery. And, for many of your world's short-cycles, the Mother Ship has been out of contact with us. Until now."

A city rushed into view on the planet far below Ally. Rising up out of pastures filled with black and white cows, it sat next to a quiet interstate. The city was bisected by a muddy, slow-moving river. Ally flew over the sleepy city, which looked smaller than Winnipeg, but much bigger than Sanford. She stopped in front of a gray domed structure surrounded by four similarly shaped, boxy buildings. On the other side of the buildings, down a steep hill, was a tall black building cast into shadow.

"This is where the Mother Ship landed. We cannot go there now, not without creating more problems, so we wait in the camps and work on the farms. We do not know what you call this city, but we do know that it is not far from here.

"The People cannot continue without the knowledge and guidance of the Elders. They wait for us in the Mother Ship, silent to our pleas.

"I hope you and your fellows never have to live in the dark times that we have known, dark times we fled our home to be rid of. Yet those dark times are continuing for us today. They continue for me because Yuallawo—the one you call Thumper—is taken into the rest of us, and my *xiowaya,* my . . . student, the one you call Jane, is mad. She is *late.*"

In sudden flashes, Ally saw the female Wannoshay she called Thumper on that day in the neighborhood, before the explosions, suddenly break into a mad sprint, running past the soldiers, scampering on all fours headlong down the trash-strewn street. Then she saw Jane, always quiet and in the background, her face lined with tiny scars around her mouth and eyes, huddled against a brick wall, long arms hugging her thick legs, rocking back and forth, eyes closed. She was flashing from Blur.

"She is sick, too sick to learn any more. She is *late,* like more and more of the People have become, and she is lost to me. Just as the Elders are lost to us all, without your help. All of us will soon be the same way. *Late.*"

Ally opened her eyes and blinked away tears. Half a minute passed before she could get her breath back, and when she did she saw Brando's long, three-eyed face gazing down at her, his mouth partially open. His yellowed teeth were broken and sharp. She struggled to find her voice.

"Late?" was all she could manage.

Brando tottered and didn't answer her. Instead, he walked over to a bale of hemp and dropped onto it, sending up a cloud of fragrant dust.

"Brando?" Ally said. Her voice was just a croak. Something wet covered her cheeks, making the dust in the air stick to her and form tiny rivers of mud. She felt guilty for never learning his real name.

"Tired," Brando whispered, letting his shoulders slump forward until he looked much shorter, almost shrunken. "All of us tired, many of us becoming *late.*"

"What do you mean?"

Ally wanted to sit next to the Wannoshay she knew only as Brando and try to comfort him, but a shaking hand on her shoulder, clutching at her jacket, interrupted her. Three of the other aliens who were supposed to be working in the barn had crept up to her and Brando, hands held out, reaching for her.

"Blur?" the first alien, a female, asked. Her shaking was the worst.

"All of us, Blur," another said, a younger male. He pushed the female to get her out of his way, and she swung at him. Soon all three were fighting, and Ally had to pull Brando to his feet and away from the ruckus. His grip on her arm was weak. She felt him reach for her with his other hand, grabbing at her coat.

"Take this," he whispered, shoving something into the inner pocket of her coat. "It can help you."

Ally almost flinched away from his touch, fearful of another vision of his alien homeworld, but she let him tuck the long, narrow object inside her pocket. They hurried away from the fighting Wannoshay. Ally wondered if Brando would let her take him from the farm.

They were almost at the door when it burst open. The big guard from the front gate ran inside, holding up the small green box he'd been wearing on his belt. Without seeing Ally and Brando, he pointed his clip-on at the first of the three aliens, and all three panicked and tried to flee outside. The first alien reared up and then fell flat onto his back when the soldier clicked the device at him.

Ally pulled Brando outside only to see more aliens filling the courtyard between the buildings. They were fighting with one another in an eerie silence, even as more security guards and soldiers ran up. The only sounds were the thud of alien hands on alien bodies, accompanied by the clicking of the clip-ons and bodies hitting the cold ground.

"What the hell kind of delivery you making, girl?" the soldier from the front gate snarled as he caught up to her. "Come with me."

"Wait!" Ally shouted, trying to pull free from the grip of the beefy guard. She saw Brando slide down to the ground once she'd let go of his hand.

"What's it mean?" she yelled at Brando as the guard pulled her away. "What's it mean if one of you is *late?*"

Brando's face was etched with pain as he pointed first at the fighting aliens, and then he pointed south.

"Find them," Brando said, and Ally heard his voice clearly inside her head. The object he'd stuffed into her coat wriggled like a snake, almost making her cry out with surprise.

Brando lowered his long arm and balled his stubby fingers into a fist he held in front of his chest and said, "Elders."

"Where?" Ally tried to scream the word at Brando, but the air was knocked from her lungs as the soldier grew tired of pulling her and slung her over his shoulders.

Ally kicked and punched at the soldier, but he ignored her. When she looked back at the aliens outside the barn, surrounded by soldiers with their clicking clip-ons, dropping Wannoshay like flies, she couldn't see Brando anymore. Her only consolation was that they weren't screaming like they had been that night in Winnipeg, back on the last day of May.

The guard put her down and pushed her toward her car.

"Fuck you," Ally said to the guard, swallowing her tears of anger and sudden sadness.

Even as more soldiers pulled up in a Humvee, Ally got into her car and fired up the engine. The guard watched her for a few seconds longer to make sure she was leaving before turning to go back to help his comrades with the aliens. Ally drove from the chaos inside the labor farm and never looked back again.

Back on the gravel road, she pulled back her coat pocket in order to see what Brando had placed into it. Careful not to touch the object, she saw that it was a short, thick piece of alien hair.

She pulled over. Unable to stop herself, forever a victim of her own lack of willpower, she reached in and grabbed the still-warm hair-tentacle.

She immediately had a vision, but it was nothing like the painful, nightmarish hallucinations she'd had after quitting Blur. This vision was crystal-clear and breathtaking.

From a great height, she looked down at fields of blue grass and black earth spread out on either side a yellow-green river that slowly flowed around caves of black stone. A soft, blue-tinted sun rested on the horizon in front of her, cut in half like a faded eye by a frozen ocean in the horizon.

Shadowy gray creatures ran on four feet across the fields, headed either toward cities of white and red towers or toward the entrances to vine-covered caves. Their hair-tentacles danced as they loped over the rising ground.

"This is what we think of when we say home," Brando's voice whispered in his chittering voice inside her head. "Even if it exists now only in our minds."

The sky of her vision suddenly went dark as black ships burst from the ground and filled the air. The gray creatures had disappeared, and the river had frozen solid in the shadow of the ships. The sun on the horizon of the once-peaceful landscape was now growing smaller and smaller with each breath she took, and then the landscape fell away beneath her. She was flying aboard one of those ships now, aiming for the cold depths of space beyond the white and black and blue planet below her that would soon die, making all life on and under its surface extinct.

Blinking hard to make the vision stop, Ally flung the piece of hair into the piles of clothing that filled her back seat. She felt like throwing up.

Brando did this to me, she thought. Infected me with something to punish me for the Blur. All the Blur. All my fault.

She squeezed her eyes shut and felt herself rocking in the driver's seat. A low moan slipped from her mouth. When she opened her eyes, it took her half a minute to realize where she was. It took another half minute for her pulse to go back to normal.

Ally drove slowly from the labor camps, too sickened to touch her rope of gum. She kept the Netstream in her car silent as she rolled away on the gravel lane, imagining she saw black ships crisscrossing in the overcast sky out of the corner of her eye.

"A toke and a smoke," Ally sang softly under her breath as she smacked the palms of her hands against the steering wheel, willing herself not to cry. "And a spaceship full of *way* too much."

She turned onto the deserted road and punched the gas pedal. The unfamiliar city that Brando had shown her flashed through her mind, and on a green highway sign she could see a name written in white block letters: Iowa City.

Ally kept her gaze locked on the ruler-straight road in front of her. Afraid of what she'd see, she didn't dare look too closely at the sky above her.

Chapter Fifteen

Late in the afternoon on the fourteenth of December, unaware that his very pregnant wife was at home counting the time between her contractions, Skin was out hunting again with his old buddy Georgie.

A few yards away from him, Georgie was making slow but steady progress over the light dusting of snow on the field, moving with a practiced ease in his upright walker. Even now, guns out as they crept through the flat, easily navigable field outside Bancroft, Skin was never completely sure if they were hunting deer or aliens. Nobody had ever caught the runaway alien they'd encountered last month, and with each passing week he heard of more sightings in the area.

Skin hadn't seen Matt since that day—every time they'd asked him to go hunting, Matt refused. He'd been keeping more to himself in his apartment, as if afraid to speak anymore.

What did I do? Skin wondered, glancing over at Georgie's red face as his buddy worked the walker over a rut in the field. Were they coming here because I let that alien go that day? He'd never told Georgie or Matt about his conversation with the alien.

Georgie, meanwhile, had survived the gunshot wound, but his spinal cord had been severed in one of his lower vertebrae. He'd never use his legs again without the help of his walker. Skin was filled with guilt for the first two weeks after the accident, until Georgie finally blew up at him.

"I don't blame you, Skin," Georgie had said, sitting in his temporary wheelchair. "But if you keep looking at me like you're about to fucking cry, I *will* start blaming you, right after I kick the ever-living crap out of you."

Skin and Georgie had started hunting together again the next day. Georgie's spinal injury had been low enough for him to keep control of his upper body down to his waist, which made him perfect for the latest in upright walker technology.

Lisa had done some research about the walkers at work, and she'd told Skin that a large portion of the tech had come from what they'd managed to learn from one of the Wannoshay ships, after stripping away yards of the bendable metal from the hull and dissecting it. Skin vowed never to tell Georgie that.

They'd been hunting for almost two hours, and Georgie was sweating hard in spite of the mid-thirties temperature, his hands red from working the levers on his walker. The slick black strips of metal running up and down each of his legs were attached to wide, wheeled boots that articulated at the ankle. The strips of metal followed impulses from Georgie's torso as well as his hands, which worked the joystick-like levers at his hips. His rifle was strapped to his back, loaded with the safety on, ready for him. If he saw anything, he could lock himself in place by pushing the levers down. It was a surprisingly effective system.

Something rustled off to the north, where the reservation started, but before Georgie could position himself and get his gun, Skin's handheld 'Stream beeped three times.

"Shit," Georgie gasped in frustration. "I thought you turned that thing off while we're hunting."

"I usually do," Skin whispered back. He popped in an ear bud and slapped a cheek mike onto his face. "But Lisa wasn't feeling too good this morning."

"Oh. Yeah. I sort of forgot about the baby. Sorry, man."

Skin waved him off and punched on the Netstream on his

belt. "Hey, Lisa. Are you—"

His voice caught in his throat as he heard his wife moan on the other end of the 'Stream. He wished he could've afforded a unit with a screen, because he needed to see her face right then.

"Tim," Lisa said. "I think it's time. I'm on my way to the hospital. Jimmy's driving me there. I . . . oh boy . . ."

"Lisa? I'll be right there, okay? Lisa?"

"Sorry. Another contraction. I'll be at the hospital. Meet me there. Ow. Oh boy . . ."

"We'll be right there, just keep talking to me, okay? And don't let Jimmy drive too fast and get in a wreck. That kid is crazy behind the wheel. You okay?"

Still talking to his wife, Skin led Georgie back across the snowy field back. The walk was taking so much time that he thought he was going to scream. He forced himself not to go too fast, but all he could think of was the baby coming two weeks too soon.

"Screw it," he said. "Sorry, Georgie," he added as he wrapped his arms around the walker supports at Georgie's upper thighs and lifted. He carried Georgie, walker and all, to the truck, not even surprised at how light Georgie had felt in his arms. All he could think of was his family in the hospital and needing him. Once they were both in, he gunned the pickup and roared off toward town.

At least I got to *hear* Randolph Timothy Blair being born, Skin would think later, after the mad drive to the hospital. He had his ear bud cranked to the max so he could hear the birth over the roar of his truck's engine, with Georgie next to him screaming to either slow down or speed up.

The Netstream faded out every time they came close to a factory farm, though the closest alien camp was across the river in Iowa. Skin had grown used to the interference; rumor had it the military had put up communications buffers around all the camps and labor farms in the area to make sure the Wantas couldn't talk to each other and plan more trouble.

They made it to the hospital ten minutes after Skin's son Randy was born. Skin was convinced Lisa would never forgive him, but her sweat-stained face was all pride and teary relief. He didn't think he'd ever be able to let go of Lisa, but he finally did when the nurse handed him his red-faced son.

With his tiny boy in his arms, not even an hour old, he wanted to believe that his boy would grow up in a better world. A world that was not all violence and fear, a world where people didn't hole up in their own houses as if they were under attack.

I want more for my boy, he thought. Looking at the sleeping baby in his arms, he knew there had to be something he could to do make the world better. And he had a pretty good idea of where to begin.

A week later, after Lisa and the baby had been home for a few days, he rose at dawn and went out once more into the cold. He didn't bring any of his hunting gear with him, and Georgie was going to have to stay at home this time.

Yellow-white sunlight had already burned all traces of night from the sky by the time Skin drove into the reservation town of Macy.

He rolled down his window and breathed in the cold, clean air swirling around him. He always felt like he was stepping back in time when he went to Macy, or any of the other towns on the rez, as if he was entering a time before the world went to hell and people holed up in their own houses out of fear of the world's violence.

In Macy he was greeted by empty streets and boarded-up houses. Even the pack of wild dogs he usually saw roaming the town was nowhere to be seen. He stopped in front of the blackened husk of the old brick school that had once housed all twelve grades. He remembered going to basketball games there with Georgie and Matt in high school. Now the school was ruined, just like so many buildings in the bigger cities, as if the violence of the world had finally made it here.

Nebraska had always been behind in the times, he thought, touching the gas pedal. But the bad times had caught up to Macy, at last.

He stopped in front of his half-cousin Rich's house, the sight of the crooked shutters over the windows and the overgrown lawn filling Skin with a sudden sadness. The town was so quiet that he could hear the wind whipping a faded American flag a few houses down.

He was staring at the flag and thinking about heading back home, when something struck his passenger window.

"Tim Blair, you skinny little shit!" A thin old man with long, silver-white hair rapped on the window again. "What the hell you doing in my town without my goddamn permission?"

For as long as Skin could remember, Shermie Powell had claimed to be the president and CEO of Macy, Nebraska. He could be seen at school gatherings, games, church outings, and especially at the yearly pow-wow held in the arena outside town, presiding over the crowd in his best suit, a shiny black number that had lapels so wide they looked like wings.

Ever since he'd fallen off the back of his brother's pickup truck while they were flying down Highway 75 on their way to a football game in the early nineties, Shermie had never been the same. At first people thought he was charming, but as the years passed and his hygiene grew worse, the cigarillos he constantly smoked making him smell like spoiled tobacco, he became more of an embarrassment. People from Macy began shooing him away from get-togethers like they did to the ever-present pack of dogs that roamed through town. His indignant response was to get louder and bathe less.

As teenagers, Skin and his buddies had traveled to Macy to smoke ditchweed with Shermie and the other hermits who lived next to the river, until the Indian kids heard about it and beat them up and told them to never come back. Shermie had always claimed that the rez was the rez, and white folks were always going to be visitors there.

And now, a decade and a half later, Shermie Powell was sitting next to Skin in his truck.

"Shermie," Skin said. "You've . . . gotten old, man. And I can tell you still don't believe in bathing very much, huh?"

"Don't talk to the president and CEO that way," Shermie said, his sour breath blasting Skin in a vile cloud. "I've got bigger concerns than taking a bath. I'm a man in search of his people."

"Well," Skin said, about to tell Shermie what he'd heard about the migration of "his people" to Oklahoma, but the crazed look on Shermie's face made him stop. "Maybe they're in the woods, or gathered at someone's house."

"Bah!" Shermie said. "You're not blood, kid. You don't know what's going on here. There's been bad shit going around for too long. People want to get away from it. They think it's the Wantas' fault, but it's deeper than that, I tell you."

"Yeah," Skin started to say, but Shermie was on a roll. There was no stopping him now.

"And people are scared, boy. They're so scared, they've left their tribal lands. Turned their backs on the places that made 'em who they are. All because they're scared, worried their kids'll get sick or the aliens'll start attacking the rez. It's not natural, being this scared. Makes folks do stupid shit."

"Tell me about it," Skin muttered, thinking of the news 'Streams that he and Lisa, in frustration, had stopped watching. There was only so much devastation a mind could take before overloading.

Shermie reached into his suit coat and pulled out a tiny pair of ancient wire-rimmed glasses and an equally old piece of yellowed paper. Skin didn't know what to say as he watched Shermie slip on the glasses—transforming him temporarily into an aristocratic-looking older man with his long silver-white hair and delicate bifocals—and unfold the paper.

"I'm glad I found you today, Tim. Got a copy here of the Macy Constitution, written by yours truly, and nowhere in here does it say anything about what to do if everyone in town moves away. Now," he said, lifting the paper closer to his face, "let me read it to you, from the beginning—"

"No, really," Skin said, thinking the trip here had been a bad idea, after all. "I believe you. Trust me, you don't need to read that whole constitution to me. Let's get you back home."

Shermie looked at him from over the tops of his spectacles. "You haven't been listening to a word I been saying, have you?"

"What?" Skin said, baffled.

"I don't *have* a home anymore. It's been abandoned. They left me here, their president and CEO. And what the hell am I supposed to do with no people to lead?"

Skin looked at the ashy color of the older man's face. "What *have* you been doing out here, all by yourself?"

Shermie scrunched up his face and stuck a pinkie up his left nostril. He pulled the pinkie out and flicked off whatever he'd found up there before answering.

"Meditating. Working on the Constitution. Smoking the peace pipe. Communing with ghosts. The usual stuff." He pulled out one of his hand-rolled cigarillos and began searching his pockets for a light. "But that's not why you're here, is it?"

"Just thought I'd come up and see you, that's all, and make sure you weren't putting too much ditchweed in your pipe. In case you needed someone to talk to here, all by yourself."

"Yeah," Shermie laughed, popping a wooden match into flame with a thumb and lighting his smoke. "Well, I've always got the grayskins to talk to."

Skin tried to smile, but his face had gone all tight at the mention of the aliens. Maybe this hadn't been a waste of time, after all.

"So you've seen some of the Wannoshay from the camps?"

"That's what they're called?" Shermie's voice was all innocence and naivete.

Skin had to laugh. "You've been out of the loop, man. Do you even know about the explosions?"

A strange look flashed across Shermie's dark face. "Don't be giving an old man a hard time, now. It's been a tough winter already, and it ain't even Christmas. Of course I know about the Wannoshay. Let's go for a drive, why don't we?"

Skin wasn't surprised to learn that the place Shermie was leading him was less than a mile from where he and Georgie and Matt had first found the alien. He pointed out the clearing where he'd accidentally shot Georgie.

"So you shot him and just *left* him?"

Shermie walked up to the tree where Georgie had propped himself up and waited for Skin and Matt to return. One of the five flare sticks he'd used was still jammed into the ground like a spent sparkler. The others had blown away or melted with the first snow. Skin could have sworn he could see what looked like two different shades of blood on the tree.

"He told us to," Skin said, but he knew his argument was weak. He stared off in the direction he'd chased the wounded Wannoshay. "We were scared and angry at the alien, so we chased him. I caught him, too."

"But you let him go, didn't you?"

Skin turned back to Shermie, his throat suddenly tight.

"How'd you know that?"

"Lucky guess," Shermie said with a shrug. He watched Skin for his reaction, then added, "And anyway, like I said, I talk to 'em. Come on."

Skin straightened up, feeling the shock on his face. He tried to hide it, but Shermie's eyes were too quick. The old man burst into laughter as they walked into the trees.

"Bullshit," Skin said.

"Don't look so surprised. I kid you not. You know I've got to have *someone* to talk to. They found *me*—I didn't even have to go looking. Told me all about you and your buddies."

Skin wondered how long a person had to live on his own before he completely lost what was left of his mind.

"Okay," he said. "If you know them so well, tell me what that Wannoshay said to me when I caught him."

Shermie stopped walking. He gave Skin a crooked smile and pulled his jacket up over his shoulders, hunching his shoulders up high and standing precariously on his tiptoes. His back was ramrod straight. With his arms held elbows-out and his chin pointing up, Shermie looked disturbingly familiar to Skin.

" 'Our home, too.' " Shermie's voice quavered with the same raspy, sing-song quality as the alien's voice. " *'Nee-brash-yah'*."

Skin's bladder almost betrayed him, Shermie's impersonation—*alienation?* he thought, almost laughing out loud—was that good. He had to look away from the tottering old man pretending to be a Wanta.

"How . . ." Skin swallowed. "How could you understand them? Most folks can't do that without lots of training."

"Time, my boy. We had lots of it, sitting around in my cold little house, ever since the camps went up. They like it that way, you know. Cold. Reminds them of the caves they lived in on their home planet." Shermie waved a bony hand in the air in the general direction of the sky, as if that clarified his explanation. "Way out there. Before their sun petered out on 'em. Something else happened there, too, something they never wanted to talk to me about . . ."

Skin was tired of being played for a fool, and he couldn't stand Shermie's smirk. It reminded him too much of Matt, before Matt stopped coming around. Matt and his deranged cultist friends.

"Where do they hide out then? Or do they camp out in Macy with you? Where the hell *are* they, Shermie?"

The old man smiled and nodded. "Thought you'd never ask. They're right here," he said, pointing at the trees around them with his chin. "Been here for the past ten minutes."

Skin's immediate thought, when the first alien stepped out of the woods, was if he'd ever see Randy again. By that time he could tell from the rustling in the undergrowth that this alien wasn't alone. He had to fight the urge to run and hide behind the blood-stained tree.

When he caught the first whiff of the aliens' salty scent, he steeled his nerves and focused his attention on the first alien to keep from feeling overwhelmed.

This one was different from the one Skin always thought of as *his* Wannoshay; this alien was a bit shorter, with thicker hair-tentacles and a more hunched walk. The gray skin of his bare chest was pebbled with light pink splotches, like the remnant of a bad sunburn. He wore only a pair of cuffed-up, faded jeans, and his chest and torso were smooth, unbroken by nipples or a navel. His long, leg-like arms were held elbows-out in the same manner that Shermie had been standing only a minute earlier.

Then the others came out of the woods. Also shirtless and clad only in cuffed, dirty jeans, no shoes, they stepped away from the trees with barely a sound, snapping the random twig or swishing past a tuft of dead grass with their short legs.

There were only twelve Wannoshay men there, but to Skin, standing next to Shermie in shock, he would have sworn there were twice that number. He didn't think the tall creatures would ever stop coming out of the trees.

How the hell did they all manage to get away from the camps? he thought.

Next to him, Shermie just laughed.

As Skin watched, some of the aliens twitched their arms and hair-tentacles in small convulsions. He thought of how it had felt that day on Blur, and he gave a shudder, wondering if these aliens were addicts. At least four of them had the telltale facial scars of alien Blur junkies that Lisa had told him about, including the last alien to emerge from the trees.

Skin let out a slow breath when he recognized this last alien. *His* Wannoshay.

This alien stepped up to the first, shorter alien, touching him on the chest in a strangely respectful manner. Along with the Blur scars on his face, Skin's Wannoshay had a whitish-gray welt across his forehead, and his three black eyes were as familiar to Skin as his wife's. He'd seen those eyes in his dreams nearly every night for the past month.

"Weh-come," his alien said, turning and nodding his narrow face at them. Three of his hair-tentacles lifted up, as if waving. Skin couldn't answer. He could only stare.

Shermie nodded and said, "Thanks." He elbowed Skin. "You're in *their* territory now, son," he hissed. "Show your respects."

"Um," Skin said. "Thanks. Thank you very much."

The other aliens that had been milling around stopped what they were doing at the sound of Skin's voice. They all turned, opening their middle eyes, and watched him. He swallowed.

"Are your wounds healing?" he said. He touched his own forehead in the same spot where the alien's wound was. "All right here?"

Shermie was smiling at him again, but this time it was less sardonic and more compassionate. "Mind if I step in here?"

Skin looked over at the old Indian man with his wiry gray hair pulled into its tight ponytail and shrugged. At some point Shermie had pulled on his bifocals, giving him the look once again of a hippie college professor with bad taste in old suits.

"I suppose you can talk to . . ." he began, but he never finished his sarcasm-laden sentence. Shermie was already speaking in the chittering language he'd heard the other aliens using.

Communing with ghosts, Shermie had said earlier.

Right, Skin thought, thinking about the nightmares haunting his sleep for the past month, ever since their hunting trip.

Shermie's thick, callused hands were moving rapidly through the cold air, forming patterns and gestures—driving a car, a flat landscape, a wall, perhaps?—as Skin watched in disbelief.

Over half of the aliens had lost interest already, moving off toward the trees to huddle together again. All the aliens had a pink derm patch on the back of their necks, almost hidden by their thick hair. Some of the aliens were missing hair-tentacles, as if going prematurely bald. Skin wondered if there was some sort of black market out there for Wanta derm patches, Blur, and food for these runaways.

The remaining aliens came closer and bent down in front of Skin and Shermie, bringing them eye-to-eye.

These four aliens seemed somehow older than the rest, though he had no criteria for judging their age other than their size: they were shorter, with thicker, finger-sized hair tentacles.

"Wise Shermie," Skin's alien said, though the words came out sounding like "why chernee." The alien's mouth didn't seem to want to cooperate with the English words. "We are glad, seeing you again."

Nee-brash-yah, Skin thought, shocked at being able to

comprehend an alien standing less than five feet from him.

The alien and Shermie began a fast conversation, the alien giving apologetic bows to Skin every few seconds, as if to say "Sorry we can't include you." But Skin could sense urgency in the high-pitched alien language in his ears, and he didn't feel slighted that they didn't include him.

Instead he watched the other aliens on the far side of the clearing. They had spread out into a small, irregularly shaped circle, and were throwing a rock three feet in diameter to one another. He couldn't find a pattern to what they were doing, other than trying to keep the rock in constant motion without getting bashed in the face by it.

Then another big rock was added to the mix. Hissing filled the air, and Skin hoped it was laughter. The alien faces weren't smiling, but he didn't know if that was due to the seriousness of the game, or an inability to smile in the first place. He watched the game, half-afraid to watch in case someone was hit, but unable to completely tune them out as Shermie and his alien talked.

"Tim," Shermie said, and it took Skin a moment to realize the old man was speaking to him. "Tim, we've got a situation here."

Skin glanced one last time at the group of younger aliens, who had added a third and fourth big rock to their game of group catch. One of the aliens did a handstand as a rock was coming toward him, catching the rock easily with his finger-toes. He remained upside-down even after launching the rock at another alien. Their voices grew louder as they game intensified, and Skin could smell them even more now, a sweeter smell than he remembered coming from his Wannoshay last month.

He turned to Shermie, his mouth dry. "A situation?"

Shermie nodded. "They need to get more of the young out of the camps. The young are the most unstable, more prone to violence and the new sicknesses. Awoyana here"—he pointed at Skin's Wannoshay—"is trying to get a bunch of young men together here, before more of the People are hurt inside the camps."

"What, like an army or something?" Skin felt his tentative sense of hope for the aliens turn sour again. "Is that the situation?"

"Damn, kid," Shermie said. "Not so loud. Some of them can understand a good bit of English. Take it easy."

Skin took a shaky breath, and as he let it out he noticed that the game of four-rock catch had stopped. The younger aliens were barely even breathing hard, but there were pinkish splotches on their faces and exposed chests. Feeling sick from the sudden rush of panic, he found himself staring at the bare alien chests around him, wanting to see nipples there or some other hint of human features. Those chests were twice as wide as his narrow chest. The tall aliens inched closer, the rocks held tight in their gray hands, and one held by four finger-toes.

"What," he began, and then cleared his throat. "What do you want me to do?"

With a rippling of his mouth, Skin's alien—Awoyana—gave what could have been a smile.

"We must stay," he said in a familiar voice. "You must see Elders."

Awoyana touched Skin's shoulder, and the touch made something clicked in Skin's mind. He saw a small city next to a river, next to an empty highway. Following the ribbon of a muddy river, he next saw a group of five old buildings that lined a grassy square. Down the hill from the buildings—*Pentacrest,* a voice whispered inside his head—and next to the banks of the river, a huge black structure sat leaning to one side. The blackness of the structure was the same color as the eyes of Awoyana and his fellow aliens.

Skin recognized it, of course. It was his nightmare image, and he'd always woken up before he could get closer to it.

"I'm supposed to take *you* to *my* leader," Skin mumbled. Shermie gave a loud laugh next to him and clapped him on the shoulder.

"So you'll help us?" Shermie said.

"Help how?" Skin couldn't get the image of the black structure from his mind. It had too many angles, and it looked broken, somehow. Broken and impossible. He realized he should have been keeping up with the news 'Streams after all.

Awoyana watched him in silence, his hair-tentacles swaying softly above his open third eye.

"They can't leave here," Shermie said, talking fast now as the other aliens moved closer. "At least not yet, not with attracting too much of the wrong kind of attention. The military's blocking all communication between the Wannoshay, and Awoyana needs to get in touch with their Mother Ship to learn what to do about the sicknesses. That's where we come in."

"Sicknesses? Mother ship?" Skin couldn't help but repeat everything Shermie was saying, feeling like an idiot. "What the hell are you *talking* about, Shermie?"

"Listen, just trust me here, okay. Awoyana can't leave—I mean, how is he gonna make it from here all the way across Iowa without someone seeing him? But something bad is affecting all the aliens inside and outside the camps, and they need to talk to their Elders in the Mother Ship. You owe it to them, 'specially Awoyana here."

Skin looked at the rocks held by the tall aliens next to him. He felt a mixed sense of guilt and responsibility that felt exactly the same as when he looked at Georgie after that day in November.

It wasn't my gun, he wanted to say. It wasn't my fault.

"I don't know how I'm going to explain this to Lisa," he said instead. "But I'll do whatever I can to help. Okay?"

"That's my boy," Shermie said, and rattled off a quick series of chittering words to the aliens.

"What do we have to do?" Skin said, finally able to breathe easily again. He nodded at Awoyana and the other aliens, who had lowered their rocks and stepped back from him.

"How would you feel about a road trip," Shermie said, peering at Skin from above the tops of his bifocals with a devilish glint in his dark brown eyes. "To Iowa City?"

"Oh boy," Skin said. "I don't think so, Shermie. Not now, not—"

"Skin," Awoyana said, pronouncing his nickname as "shin." Skin stopped talking and turned just as his alien was taking the largest of the four rocks from one of the younger aliens.

With a sudden grunt, Awoyana launched the rock directly at Skin's head. Before Skin could even take another breath, he'd caught the rock in midair. He continued holding his breath as he waited for it to slam into his face. But nothing happened. He held the rock easily, as if it were hollow.

"You are strong, more than you think," Awoyana said, pronouncing the English words laboriously. "You can help all of us, not just Wannoshay. You are *strong,* remember you are. And Skin, we thank-you."

Skin dropped the rock to the ground, where it made a divot in the hard earth before rolling away. He turned to Shermie with a dazed look in his eyes, but Shermie only shrugged as he stuffed something from one of the other aliens inside his coat.

When Skin turned back to Awoyana and the other Wannoshay, they had disappeared back into the trees.

"You're weh-come," he said. Under a sky heavy with snow, he and Shermie began the long hike back to his truck.

Chapter Sixteen

New Year's Day in Lake Geneva, Wisconsin, was unlike any New Year's Shontera had spent in Milwaukee. Usually she woke up late on January first with a headache, eyes sore and throat parched from too much partying and too little sleep the night before. And compared to last year, when she woke up to find her wallet emptied and William gone without a note, this New Year's Day was a vast improvement.

She woke at six a.m. sharp, wide awake and ready for her shift at Quick Mart in an hour. She'd get time and a half for going in today to man the cash register and monitor the recharging stations and the old-fashioned ethanol pumps, and the money would come in handy. It always came down to money.

She stumbled to the bathroom, ears full of the almost numbing silence of her parents' big house. Even after half a year away, she still missed the city with its hum of traffic and the shifting sounds of the people in their apartments on all sides of her. Out here, on the two-acre lot where her parents' rambling old house sat, she felt cut off from the world. Toshera and her parents, on the other hand, loved it here.

Leaving the bathroom, Shontera sniffed the warm smells of bacon and coffee and smiled. Toshera must have made everyone breakfast again. Shontera winced, thinking about the headaches that had come back, after a few months' respite, to bother her daughter again. Toshera usually did her cooking when she was having trouble sleeping. Shontera had to do something, but her health insurance didn't kick in for another three weeks.

Putting the negative thoughts out of her head, she walked downstairs and was rewarded with a plate of hash browns, scrambled eggs, sausage, and toast waiting for her at the kitchen table. Mom and Dad were still asleep, but she could hear Toshera in their bedroom, jumping on their bed to wake them up.

Shontera was reaching for a fork and knife when Toshera came bouncing into the kitchen in her robe and crooked chef's hat.

"Is everything okay?" she asked, pushing up her glasses. "I made deer sausage from Grandpa's stash! What do you think?"

Shontera set down her fork and kissed the fingertips of both hands.

"Delicious. Of course I haven't had a chance to eat anything yet, but I'm sure it's all wonderful."

"I hate that you have to work again, today," Toshera said, watching Shontera eat with a big grin on her face.

"I know, honey. I hate it too." Shontera swallowed the food and a good helping of guilt. Toshera hadn't had the easiest time getting used to her new school, where there were only four other black children in her grade. "Let's do something fun tonight when I'm off, okay? Now you'd better get Grandpa and Grandma down here before I eat their breakfasts too."

Toshera padded down the hall to her grandparents' room again. Closing her eyes, Shontera chewed a mouthful of deer sausage and took a deep breath to dispel the guilt swirling around inside her.

As she was inhaling, she saw behind her eyes a long black tunnel, peppered with openings punched through the walls every few feet, lit with a greenish glow that came from strands of lichen growing overhead. The walls were ridged and irregular, as if carved out by hand.

The empty tunnel filled her with an inexplicable fear, its emptiness like an omen that something bad was coming soon to fill the rough walls of this tunnel and all the other passages connected to it.

She held her breath, afraid to let the vision slip away. She'd been dreaming about this place for the past few months, almost every night.

In the vision, she moved down the hall in a flash, and the tunnel opened into a room bigger than all the cellars of the old brewery, combined. Filling the room was a monstrous ship made of a strange black metal that refused to shine in the weak green light.

She'd never seen this ship before in her dreams, and it took her breath away. Spikes jutted from each side of the humming, multi-sided ship, each spike slowly quivering and lifting up above the ship as if sniffing the air while the ship itself began to rise.

Then she felt the air being sucked from her lungs when she sensed something—*many* somethings—filling the tunnels behind her, running headlong toward her and the ship with a wild madness and desperation. The ship began rising, its spikes digging through the solid rock above it.

She ran for the ship, even though she couldn't see any doors or openings. She didn't want to see who or what was stampeding toward her from the tunnels, but the ship was leaving without her. The ship wavered in her vision as it pushed upward, through the rock.

The Mother Ship, a voice whispered inside her head. Nonami's voice. Iowa City, her voice said.

Shontera couldn't breathe.

"Mom!" Toshera said, pounding on her back.

Shontera's eyes flicked open, and she grabbed at her throat. Something was lodged there.

The Mother Ship, she thought to herself, her brain starving for oxygen. She was lying on her side on the kitchen floor, the linoleum cold and hard underneath her. Her lungs began to burn from lack of oxygen.

"Mama!" Toshera screamed, still pounding on her back, and Shontera came back to the reality that she was choking.

Making her left hand into a fist, she drove it into her stomach with all of her strength with her right hand, and the chunk of deer sausage that had been stuck in her throat shot across the kitchen and smacked into the stove.

"Shontera? Toshera?" Shontera's mother called. Pulling her robe closed, she ran into the kitchen, followed by Shontera's father. "What happened?"

"I'm okay," Shontera tried to say. She couldn't get the sensation of breathlessness and wrongness from her head. The kitchen felt suddenly too hot, despite the cold air seeping in from the crack in the window above the sink. "I'm okay."

She sat up and took Toshera in her arms, wiping away her daughter's tears. Her mother touched her back and her father stared at the three of them from the safety of the doorway, his brown face still puffy with sleep.

"I thought you were gonna die," Toshera whispered through her tears. "You weren't even breathing, Mama."

"I'm sorry I scared you, honey." Shontera rubbed her throat. She wanted to close her eyes again, but she was afraid of what she'd see. She didn't want to see those tunnels and that ship—the Mother Ship—anymore.

"We're a mess," she said to Toshera. "You know that? Now I'd better get Grandpa to give me a ride into work so I'm not late."

Because right now, she thought, with Toshera and her school problems and headaches, and me with my visions of the Wannoshay ships, we're not making a very strong start to this New Year.

The following Sunday, on Shontera's first day off in the New Year, her parents came home from church arguing about the aliens.

"Those boys must have done something," her father was saying, shaking the snow from his driving cap and running a hand over his bald brown head. "Why else would those men have got into a fight with them?"

"You're getting snow all over my kitchen," Shontera's mother said. "*And* you're in a state of denial about what happened up there in Minneapolis. Those alien boys were beaten, for no reason other than for what they were."

"Come on, Melonee, you can't be—" Her father stopped when he saw Shontera and Toshera at the sink washing dishes. His voice had been rising, and there was more than a trace of anger in it.

Shontera's mother stood, arms folded, and shook her head at him, her tiny gray dreadlocks quivering with the movement. "I can't be what, Mr. Johnson? Can't be serious? Can't be *right* about the Wannoshay? You of all people should know better. You're always talking about how your dad and uncle were so involved in the civil rights movements back in the Sixties."

"They had a talk today at church about the alien boys up in Minneapolis," Shontera's father explained, his voice returning to its soft, grandfatherly tone as he touched Shontera's shoulder and kissed Toshera on the forehead. "Got Mother all worked up about the crimes of humanity against the Wantas."

"Wannoshay, Grandpa," Toshera said before Shontera could shush her. Toshera peeked up at her grandfather and gave him a winning smile, and his smile grew wider. Shontera's mother threw her arms in the air and walked out of the kitchen.

"Turns out the fella who helped those boys in the camp in Minnesota used to work at the landing site over in Waukegan. Even though he's Catholic, seems like he did some good work over there. Our minister wants to get him to come talk to us Methodists, but he can't get a hold of the fella."

Shontera put the last of the plates away, enjoying the chance to get her hands wet and soapy like she did when she was Toshera's age, when they hadn't been able to afford a dishwasher.

"Dad," she said. "Do you really think those alien boys deserved what they got?"

She looked from her father, dressed in his best dark blue suit, to her daughter, eyes almost hidden behind her glasses, wet sleeves rolled up past her elbows.

"Not you too," her father said, rolling his eyes and sighing dramatically. Shontera hoped he was exaggerating just to get a giggle out of Toshera, which he did.

"Dad," Shontera said. "Answer the question, will you?"

"Oh, I don't know. I've just heard things about them, being like animals sometimes, losing control. It's scary to think about—they're not from this planet, for God's sake. This is our world. Maybe they should go back where they belong."

"They probably can't," Toshera said from behind them. She had left the dishes in the sink and was now rearranging the flowers on the center of the table. "They wrecked their ships pretty bad when they landed, so they're stuck. And maybe they were like the pilgrims at Plymouth Rock. They left England 'cause they *had* to."

Shontera looked at her dad, and they both turned to Toshera.

"What'd I say?" Toshera said.

"That's my girl," Shontera's father said, hugging her on his way past her. "Gonna be president someday. Or even better, an astronaut." His soft chuckle followed him out of the room.

"You may be right, honey," Shontera said. "About the Wannoshay, I mean. I'll bet they have no choice but to stay here."

In silence, she and Toshera arranged the synthetic flowers on the vase on the table, pushing the faded flowers toward the middle. Bright pink carnations and yellow daisies with silky petals moved through their hands.

The reports of the occasional deaths in the camps were told at the end of the reports, like afterthoughts or bits of trivial data. Shontera hated that her daughter had to grow up in times like these.

"Toshera," she said at last, after a glance into the living room where her father was tapping on his handheld Netstream in his easy chair. "How would you feel about a nice drive today?"

Waukegan was a little over an hour away from Lake Geneva. For the first time in months, as she sat with Toshera next to her in her father's battered old gas-guzzling Buick, Shontera felt as if something had clicked into place inside her mind, that she was finally taking control of her life, and Toshera's as well. She hadn't felt this way since early summer, walking through Nonami's new neighborhood. Before she'd betrayed Nonami by running away.

At half past one they arrived at the outskirts of the locked-down landing site. Shontera knew that Toshera had seen images of the landing sites across the Midwest and Canada before and after the camps, but that didn't stop her daughter from gasping and gripping the dashboard when she saw it firsthand.

The temporary buildings and the alien ship that the bubble-tents had once hidden were gone. All that remained were the deep divots of the caved-in tunnels that had been carved underneath the ship. The tunnels reminded Shontera of those in her vision, and she couldn't help but reach up and rub her throat. The broken tunnels were surrounded by surprisingly few random pieces of the alien ship that had been left behind by the military. The rest of the ship had disappeared.

"Oh God," Shontera whispered.

The scars left by the blown tunnels stretched for over five square acres, and all of it was surrounded by a fifteen-foot-high chain-link fence tipped with razor wire. Yellow "No Trespassing" signs were attached to the fence every ten feet.

Shontera had thought they'd be able to see what the Wannoshay had built under their ship, and maybe get some sort of idea about a people that had managed to fly here from millions of miles away in their ships, but dug these tunnels with their with their bare hands and feet.

She'd hoped that Toshera would be able to experience some of the magic that Shontera had felt ever since Nonami had handed her that dropped bottle of beer.

But all she was left with was this destruction, ringed by chain links and razor wire. Just like one of the internment camps.

"Where is everyone?" Toshera said. She stared open-mouthed at the remnants of the tunnels, her bottom lip caught in her teeth. "Where did they take the ship?"

"The military have it, probably. So they could learn all they could about the Wannoshay technology." Shontera put the car in park and got out, leaving it idling. The icy wind whipped her coat open, slipping under her shirt and chilling her skin.

"I just thought," Shontera whispered, more to herself than to Toshera. "I thought there'd be something here. But this is a . . ."

A *graveyard,* she wanted to say.

She looked back at her daughter, still sitting in the car with her seat belt fastened.

"Mom," Toshera called out, pointing. "Look at the *fence.*"

Shontera squinted at a clump of long, dark objects hanging just below one of the "No Trespassing" signs on the fence.

Hundreds of aliens had lived in those tunnels, she thought, walking closer to the fence. She tried to focus her gaze on the tunnels, at the rough walls and the passageways that had been caved in. But she kept coming back to the dangling black objects hanging from a faded wooded sign on the fence like a warning.

Shontera was twenty feet away when she saw the individual ropes that made up the hanging black objects. At eighteen feet she saw that some kind of nail had been jammed through the black ropes—the *hair,* Shontera told herself, *hair*—in effect nailing them to the fence. She was fifteen feet away, smelling the faintest hint of salty dirt, when she saw one of the Wannoshay hair-tentacles lift up and point at her like an eyeless snake.

Shontera froze.

Toshera, she wanted to call out. Lock the doors, girl.

The hair-tentacle pointed at her like a finger now, and she found herself moving closer, thinking of Nonami and what the alien woman's real name had felt like in her mouth when she'd tried to say it.

"Oyawnahallo?" she whispered, ten feet away. Eight feet. "Ohalloyawna? Ohallolo?" Four feet. "Nonami, what do I *call* you?"

When she was a foot away from the fence and the ruined tunnels it was guarding, Shontera pulled both hands from her coat pockets and raised them. Her left reached for the upraised, outermost strand of Wannoshay hair (staring at me, she thought), while her right reached for the black metal spike that pinned the pile of hair against the sign.

She could smell the musky, salty-sweet smell of aliens, and again she thought of Nonami. The cold wind rushed up, almost blowing her off-balance.

And then she touched the thick, corded hair and the cold black spike, and the world spun away from her. Shontera was back in the cave from her vision earlier that day, trapped between the roar of the ship rising up through the rock in front of her and the onrushing creatures coming up behind her.

The tentacle in her hand moved, giving off sparks that stung her bare palm, and the scene behind her eyes changed. She was now looking up as a black sky rushed toward her. Blotting out the unfamiliar stars were other ships, smaller than the ship she'd seen in the cave.

They flew in groups of four, warping the air in their wake. The roaring of the engines of her own ship, mixed with a strange keening sound like the wailing of mourners at a funeral, was so loud she couldn't breathe. The sound grew as the star-littered void of space rushed past her and enveloped her and the other ships.

Shontera didn't know at what point she had spun around, but suddenly she was running back to the car, nearly falling over the ruts in the ground. She couldn't catch her breath, and she felt like she was choking again. The piece of metal in her hand had changed shape, fitting now in the grip of her fist.

"Oyallohawna," she said as soon as her lungs would cooperate with her. She stuffed the hank of hair and the piece of metal into her coat pockets with numb hands. "Nonami's name is Oyallohawna."

She fumbled for the car door and dropped heavily onto her seat. Gasping for breath, she gunned the engine and waited for her daughter to ask her what she'd seen. But Toshera's eyes were closed, with a single tear streaking down either side of her face. Shontera took a deep breath. She wiped Toshera's tear away and rested a hand on the back on her daughter's neck.

"You okay?" she asked.

Toshera nodded, then looked up. "Can I touch it?"

"Touch what?" Shontera stared at her daughter, who was staring at her coat pocket. "No, I don't think so."

"Why not? *You* got to."

Shontera looked back at the fenced-in tunnels and the tiny pile of alien hair she'd left on the cold ground. She sighed.

"Okay, just for a second," she said, and before she could finish her sentence, Toshera was reaching into her left-hand pocket. Before she could stop her, Toshera had the thick black tube of hair in her hand. Her small face tightened for a second, then she smiled up at Shontera, eyes wide.

"Wow."

"What did you see?" Shontera pulled on a glove and eased the hair tentacle out of her daughter's loose grasp. Once it was back in her coat pocket, she zipped it shut.

"See?" Toshera's eyes were still wide behind her thick glasses. "I didn't *see* anything. Why, did you?"

"I—" Shontera stopped. "I don't know."

"I didn't see anything, but my headache"—Toshera reached over and pulled Shontera close for a hug—"it's *gone*, Mama."

Her thin arms squeezed her so hard that Shontera could feel them shaking. Shontera closed her eyes and hugged her daughter, fear and relief coursing through her. She knew she shouldn't have let Toshera touch this thing, but at the same time, she knew she'd had no choice but to let her.

"You feel up to riding some more?" she said at last, her voice husky as she reluctantly let go of her daughter. Toshera nodded, eyes still lit up by her smile.

Shontera turned the Buick around, and they left the wasteland of the landing site behind. She knew that I-94 would take them right to Minneapolis, and if they were lucky, they'd make it there before dark. She hoped her father didn't mind if she kept the car a little bit longer.

As they drove, Toshera pulled out her portable Netstream and located all the Catholic churches in the area, and then searched the news sites for the name of the priest her grandparents had been talking about that morning. By the time they'd driven past Milwaukee, only an hour into their drive, they knew the priest's name (Joshua Christopher McDowell), his church (Our Lady of the Lourdes), when he'd transferred there, and more details about him than he probably knew about himself. Toshera was almost bouncing up and down on her seat.

After the six-hour drive across the entire state of Wisconsin, passing the time by talking about aliens, school, the beach, and anything else that came to mind, Shontera and Toshera found Joshua's rectory nestled behind the tall, three-steepled Catholic church made of brown bricks. They were able to find the church easily from its spotlight positioned at the topmost steeple, like a beacon for the weary travelers.

Shontera left the headlights on and the engine running when she got out of the car. She had Toshera lock the doors behind her while she walked up to the rectory entrance. Through the thick, frosted glass of the door, she could see a light, but otherwise the place looked empty, almost deserted.

The only sound was the mutter of the Buick. After knocking three times, each hollow rap of her knuckles making her wince, Shontera turned back toward the car and her daughter, angry at herself for wasting her day off by running all over the countryside. They still had at least a six-hour drive ahead of them before they got back home.

The clicking of a pair of locks and the rattle of the door stopped her. A round-faced, white-haired man older than her father peeked out at her through the gap in the door.

"May I help you, miss?" he said in a suspicious voice.

"Yes," Shontera said. "We're looking for Father Joshua. The one who works with the aliens."

The priest drew back the tiniest bit, as if he were going to shut the door on her, and then he sighed. "Joshua. Right. That would figure. And you are friends of his?"

"Well," Shontera said, glancing back at the car, where Toshera was giving her an enthusiastic thumbs-up. "Not really. We just . . . we just wanted to *talk* to him."

The priest gave her one last appraising look, and then smiled for an instant.

"You might as well shut your car off and get your little girl. Joshua spent the day at the camp, but he'll be in shortly. You can wait for him inside."

Shontera rushed back to the car to collect Toshera and the keys.

"He's here," she said, "or at least he'll be here soon. He was at the *camp* all day. With the Wannoshay."

The rectory was cool and quiet, lit only by lamps with low-wattage bulbs. Not a single wallscreen could be found in any of the three rooms Shontera and Toshera passed through, and the small sitting room where the white-haired priest left them was decorated mainly with musty books lining the walls. A painting of Mary holding Jesus adorned the only wall with a window. A tiny line of winter air slipped in through the thick, cracked window, as if trying to cool off the bright halos above the heads of Jesus and his mother.

They sat and waited, the hum of the road filling Shontera's ears in the stillness of the rectory. Next to her, amazed by the feel of paper after growing up with Netstreams, Toshera turned the delicate pages of one of the books while they waited.

Shontera had so many questions to ask Father Joshua, and she wanted to start with what she saw today at the landing site. If he used to work there, he would surely know why the military had felt it necessary to wreck the tunnels.

Half an hour passed, and Toshera began to complain about being hungry, but fortunately, she made no mention of her headache returning. Shontera was feeling more and more certain that this Father Joshua never existed. She was about to collect Toshera and slip back outside when a priest burst through the front door and clomped down the hallway to meet them.

"Hello!" the smiling, red-faced priest called in a hoarse voice. Standing a few inches shorter than Shontera, the priest wore all black: coat, shirt, pants, shoes. Even the ear buds in his hand were black.

"Father Joe caught up to me," he continued, "on my Net-stream on the way home. He told me you were here. I'm Father Joshua." He winked at Toshera and smiled at Shontera as he took her hand.

"My name is Shontera Johnson," Shontera said, shaking his hand. She felt a surge of energy with his touch, as if his boisterousness was contagious. "And this is my daughter Toshera."

"Nice to meet both of you." He sat across from them and crossed his legs casually, like an old friend. "So what brings you out to this neighborhood on a night like this? I saw you have Wisconsin plates, but this is probably more than a nice Sunday drive, isn't it?"

"A nice *long* Sunday drive's more like it," Toshera said, and the priest gave a hearty laugh.

"We hate to bother you on a Sunday like this, all uninvited," Shontera began, "and you just having worked all day . . ."

"Think nothing of it. The past few weeks I've had all the energy in the world. The other priests are jealous, think I'm hooked on some kind of drugs or something. Me, on Blur . . ." A pained look passed over his face so fast that Shontera convinced herself she'd imagined it. Joshua gave a short cough and sat up straighter. "But enough about me. Tell me about you, Shontera. Why did you trek all the way over here to our fair city?"

"The Wannoshay," Shontera said.

Joshua was nodding already, and some of his blustery demeanor seemed to melt away like the stored cold dissolving off his jacket. His eyes became somber, almost sad.

"I thought so. You had that look about you."

"We saw the landing site where you used to work," Toshera said. "It was pretty creepy, sir."

Joshua smiled, and Shontera saw what had to be another flicker of pain in his eyes.

"The soldiers were very thorough, cleaning up that site, as you saw. I spent some fascinating days there with the People—the Wannoshay—back before the explosions last May. And please," he added with a grin, "don't call me 'sir.' 'Joshua' is just fine, or 'Father Joshua,' if you like."

"I was at the brewery in Milwaukee," Shontera said. She felt like she was unable to speak in anything but the simplest of sentences. "The one that blew up."

"Her friend Nonami saved her," Toshera said, taking her mother's hand. "And then when Mom went to visit her, the soldiers took Nonami and all the other people away."

Joshua wriggled out of his black coat, and his face turned red again as he leaned forward and cupped his chin in his hands.

"So you actually *spoke* to one of the Wannoshay, by yourself? Amazing. Were you able to understand much?"

"Too much," Shontera said, and she felt an emotional dam burst inside of her. She began talking, sharing with the balding priest everything she knew about the aliens and all she'd learned from Nonami. Joshua listened, barely moving the whole time. Toshera and Father Joshua wore a matching expression of wonder as Shontera told her story, including the most recent additions: the visions and dreams of the caves and the black ships.

Fifteen minutes later, Shontera finally ran out of words. Her throat was dry, and she felt shaky all over.

"Wow," Toshera said. "You never told me all that, Mom."

Shontera could only smile. Father Joshua leaned back in his chair, his hand over his mouth. She thought she could see the hint of tears in his light blue eyes.

"Lord in heaven," Joshua said. "This is something to hear. And to think all this time I thought I was just getting senile or going crazy. Because you know what? You're not the only one who's been having visions."

Joshua wiped at his eyes and his smile grew wider.

Shontera felt giddy at the sight of his smile, and she nearly laughed out loud when the priest asked her another question: "Have you ever heard of a town called Iowa City?"

Chapter Seventeen

Father Joshua knew he shouldn't be feeling this good. He knew his heart wasn't what it used to be, and he weighed thirty pounds more than he should have. He knew in his heart that his faith should have been shaken by the deaths of Matthew and the other boy whose name he finally remembered as David. He should have felt worn out and sick after so many sleepless nights, haunted by the nightmare images of the black ships bursting out of the caves of the alien world, and, inside the ships, the rows of the People crammed head to toe under a blanket of pliable metal, twitching and cooing in their restless sleep.

He should have been overwhelmed by these negative factors in his life, but he felt as if he'd been lifted above them all, first by Juana's actions at the camp that day, then by energy flowing from the beings he used to think of as the People, and now by the woman and young girl sitting in the car with him.

Last night, all three of them yawning and bleary-eyed from their shared stories, Shontera had surprised him by agreeing to go with him to Iowa City. She'd even volunteered to drive so she could take Toshera along as well, instead of going out of her way to leave the girl with her grandparents.

Part of him expected her to change her mind in the morning, but she and her daughter were both dressed and waiting for him in the sitting room when he got up at seven the next morning. He should have known better than to doubt them after seeing the way Shontera had been so absorbed in his stories about the aliens, as if she needed to hear that the Wannoshay were not the violent, hopeless cases the media had made them out to be. He was among kindred spirits.

He'd told them almost everything he knew about the Wannoshay last night. How every night, back in the rectory, he would work on the elastic metal book of the Wannoshay, studying it with the same intensity he'd had while poring over the Bible as a young man. He also talked about the doubts of his fellow priests, the deaths of the two boys in the camp, and the wave of energy from the Wannoshay that had passed over him after their deaths.

"I thought I was going to go blind at first," he'd said, feeling his face grow warm at his words. "But the energy and light that came from the bodies of the two boys didn't burn me. The camp went white for almost a second, which at the time I thought would hurt the People gathered around me, because they can't handle bright light. It took my eyes almost ten seconds to adjust after that; all I could see was black splotches. When I could see clearly again, the bodies of both boys were gone."

Two pairs of deep brown eyes watched him, barely blinking. He could see the similarity in mother and daughter in those eyes and the way they held their heads at the same slight angle as they listened closely to his story.

"The People have a phrase for it. They don't understand the words 'dying' or 'death.' They call it something like 'leaving the body' or 'taken into the rest of them.' I think a lot gets lost in the translation, and I haven't been able to get any of them to talk to me about it anymore. All I know for sure is that I've *never* seen the People bury any of their dead. Even now, they simply . . . disappear, after death."

Toshera had looked at him with a shocked look on her face,

and Joshua realized he'd said too much, given the young girl too much to think about. He patted her hand and lent her his coat so she could wrap herself in it. Joshua continued in a lighter voice.

"Something happened to me when those boys . . . left us. The same thing happened to Father Juana, and she became so full of the Holy Spirit that she volunteered to go to another camp, one worse off than mine, and use her skills there. She's a good priest. One of our best."

They had talked for another ten minutes after that, and then he'd fixed them up with blankets and pillows in the guest room of the rectory. He wasn't able to get to sleep until nearly two a.m.

Early the next morning, when he should have been thick-headed and grumpy from lack of sleep, Joshua instead was wide awake and brimming with excitement about going back to the town where he'd attended college for two semesters before transferring to the seminary.

He hoped that the hints his dreams and visions had given him about the aliens falling sick was just something, like so many other things recently, that had gotten lost in translation.

Shontera let the car idle, goosing the gas pedal every few seconds. Cold air poured from the vents, and Joshua felt nostalgic from the stink of gas and exhaust. He'd gotten spoiled by the electric buses and the train.

"Wake me up when you get there," Toshera said from the back seat, buried under her blankets.

He hadn't even packed a change of clothes. All he had was his portable Netstream, his Bible, and, tucked at the bottom of his bag, the metal book from the landing site. Traveling light, he thought. Just like Shontera and Toshera, wearing yesterday's wrinkled clothes.

We all must be crazy, Joshua told himself, and smiled just the same.

They drove through the light early-morning traffic of Minneapolis, driving south in a course roughly parallel to the icy Mississippi on their left. He fought the urge to look back at the three steeples of Our Lady of the Lourdes, promising himself he would come back to this Lady, and not leave it behind like he did the other Lady and his people back in Chicago.

Toshera was asleep by the time they made it out of the city, barreling south down Interstate 35. Joshua had sent a Netstream message to Father Joe to let him know his whereabouts, and he was relaxing back into the vinyl seat, which had finally softened and warmed with his body heat, when Shontera glanced over at him.

"Do you think this is all some sort of punishment?"

Her voice was soft, almost lost in the humming of the wheels and the rumble of the engine.

Joshua blinked, the steady motion of the car on the smooth interstate almost lulling him to sleep. A light snow fell outside, just enough to turn the fields and the shoulder of the highway white. The asphalt, salted and sanded countless times already that winter, remained free of snow.

"What do you mean by punishment?" He felt his voice turn into what he thought of as his "confessional mode," and he tried to stop himself from sounding so condescending.

"The aliens coming here," Shontera said. She kept her dark brown eyes focused on the road in front of her, and her hands gripped the wheel tightly. "Are they God's way of punishing us for not having faith, for not being good to each other?"

"I don't think punishment is the right word," he said, talking before he'd stopped to really consider his answer. This wasn't the darkened room at the back of Our Lady of the Lourdes, and Shontera was not a member of his congregation. They were just two adults, talking in a car. He had no obligations to her other than the truth, as best as he could understand it.

"I don't think God works that way," he said. "I think of the Wannoshay coming here as more of a test, a challenge. Maybe even a wake-up call. A way for humanity to realize it was headed in the wrong direction, eating itself up with violence. Maybe the Wannoshay are our second chance."

"Really?" Shontera glanced at him, eyebrows raised. For an instant she looked like Father Juana, back in the camp classroom.

"Think about it for a second," he said as Shontera turned on the wipers for two swipes, just enough to clear snow off the windshield. "During the hard times in your life, you've probably felt like things were never going to work out, that you were just going to keep sliding down and down until life became unbearable. But you made it through, and you're here right now, trying to help a people that a year ago you never knew existed."

"Yeah. I guess."

"And you're probably stronger than you were before."

"But I'm not sure I'm better *off* than I was before." Shontera lifted one of her hands from the wheel and chewed on a fingernail. "I never could have predicted I'd be doing anything like this, a year ago."

Joshua smiled at that and glanced at the green road sign passing next to him. The Iowa border was only ten miles away. Snow as gritty as salt was piled up on either side of the road now, drifting into miniature mountain ridges painted white, and more continued to fall.

Staring at the whiteness filling the land outside the car, he felt a tiny twinge in his chest, thinking of that horrible, wonderful day in the camp last November. He suddenly missed Father Juana and the young woman's intense faith and boundless energy since that day. He wondered what sort of unnatural radiation and strange power the energy of the dying Wannoshay had contained as it washed over him. Did Juana feel this healthy and energetic?

He rubbed his face, wishing he hadn't lost touch with his junior priest so quickly. Part of him had been hurt when he realized Juana no longer needed him, and he hadn't tried to contact her through the Netstreams.

A sudden thought struck him, and he turned back to Shontera.

"Did you know that the People—the Wannoshay—have their own version of God?"

A strange look passed over Shontera's face, as if considering what an alien god must look or act like.

"At least, as far as I can tell, they do. Just like all the other religions in the world believe in some Supreme Being. All the Gods—with a capital 'G'—out there just run together, I think, like all the rivers here run into the Mississippi, which runs into the Gulf of Mexico, which runs into the ocean." Joshua had to laugh at his words. "Okay, now I'm getting poetic. I guess I didn't get enough sleep last night."

"That's okay," Shontera said, nodding her head as she stared at the road ahead of them. "It makes sense to me. I'm just surprised my friend Nonami never told me about her God. I'd imagine it takes a lot of faith in a higher power to pile into a spaceship and leave your planet behind."

"Or faith in your Elders," Joshua said. "Or your pilots. I've heard that the Wannoshay called them Navigators. Why do you look so surprised?"

"I'm sorry, Father. I never expected a minister to say that you could have faith in anything but God."

Joshua felt his face grow warm. "Faith comes in all varieties, you know. In the Supreme Being, in people, and in science." He thought about that for a second. "Probably in that order, too, I guess. Just don't tell Father Joe I said that, though, in any case."

Still smiling, Shontera nodded and turned the wipers on again. She left them on low to keep the snow, now falling in big, round flakes, off the windshield. The rear of the car slid a tiny bit to the right when she touched the brakes. On either side of them, the fields were hidden by new snow.

"So tell me more about what your friend Nonami showed you that day, if you can remember it."

"That's funny," Shontera said. "I was just thinking about her. There must be something about driving that makes you remember stuff, don't you think? Anyway, she told me that her people were called the People of the Dawn. Which was funny, I guess, because their sun was really weak, almost burned out. It probably was nighttime all the time there. Though she made it sound like they never went aboveground. Too cold."

"People of the Dawn," Joshua said. He liked the sound of that.

"Yeah, you could tell by the way she said it, it was supposed to be capitalized. Then there were others she called the People of the White Moon, who lived on a different continent from her people. And there were some *other* people, the People of . . . something. She didn't seem to want to talk about them too much. The People of the Twilight, that's it."

Joshua gave a start at that name, recognizing it from his talks with Johndo, but he waited for her to continue. The young woman had acted as if she'd never confided her thoughts about the aliens with anyone else before, so he was careful not to interrupt.

"But what I was really trying to remember," Shontera said, "was Nonami's real name. I had it yesterday, but then it slipped away. I never could pronounce it."

Joshua nodded, thinking about the names he and the other humans in the camps had come up with: Sarah, Eli, Ezra, Elizabeth, Noah, David, Matthew. So many more names. Through his thick coat, he rubbed his arms against the cold wind slipping in through the window next to him.

We have so much to learn, he thought. And time, along with the rest of the world, doesn't want to cooperate with us.

As Shontera continued talking and wondering about the real names of the Wannoshay, Joshua listened and watched the snow come down. The sky was turning overcast and gray, a darker color than the snow-covered ground, when they passed over the Iowa border.

Joshua was driving thirty miles below the speed limit, his eyes aching from glaring through the windshield at a road covered in bright, freshly fallen snow.

He'd been driving for two hours now, and Iowa City was still fifty or sixty miles away. Shontera dozed next to him after fighting off sleep all morning. To keep himself relaxed, he'd been mentally compiling all that he'd learned in the past day from Shontera and Toshera, adding their stories to what he'd learned at the landing site and in the camp.

He kept revisiting the images from his dreams: white light from the two dead boys, lighting up a series of tunnels dug into the dark brown earth of the Midwest, and the black heights of the Mother Ship at the end of those tunnels. In the dream, the white light of the Wannoshay had morphed into a harsh, blue-tinted sun. And then the light had winked out, replaced by the seemingly endless black expanse of space slowly creeping past, while his body was crushed by the weight of so many other of the Wannoshay. He had a sense of being awake for far too long, of being incredibly exhausted, but unable to sleep.

Slowing for a big blue Chevelle fishtailing its way into a turn, Joshua took a long breath and glanced in the rearview to make sure some fool wasn't following him too closely in the middle of the snowstorm. He didn't think Shontera would want to anger her father even further by banging up his Buick after borrowing it for a few days longer than her planned Sunday drive.

After the Chevelle turned off into an empty parking lot—the big car spinning as the joy-riding driver slammed on the brakes—Joshua caught up to a snowplow and followed it through the small industrial city of Waterloo. The blade of the plow threw snow twenty feet into the air on either side of the truck, and Joshua kept a safe distance behind it, glad to be able to see the road again.

His thoughts drifted to the book the colonel had shown him all those months ago. He'd never figured out where in the damaged ship the soldiers had originally found the book. After the explosions, everyone but Joshua had forgotten about the book, and he'd never told anyone that he still had it.

He thought about how, when he ran his hand down a page, the symbols on that page disappeared, gray icons melting into black metal. He'd tried countless times to create some sort of symbol of his own on the empty metal page, but none of the tools he used—finger, ink pen, plastic stylus, laser—made an impression.

Just before leaving the rectory that morning, he'd packed the metal pages in his small overnight bag, hoping he'd be able to find Johndo again and return the book to him. He hadn't had the presence of mind to give the book back to him the last time he saw Johndo; he'd been in too much pain from where his alien friend had struck him.

"Maybe," he whispered. "Maybe I will see him again."

Next to him, Shontera stirred, and then she woke with a start. Her face was panicked for a second until she realized where she was.

"Sorry I fell asleep," she said. She glanced back to check on Toshera, who was also waking up. "Where are we?"

"Almost there. I thought a shortcut would be better than taking I-35 all the way to 80. I heard on the 'Stream that the interstate in Des Moines is closed because of the snow and a wreck. Iowa City's coming up soon, right after Cedar Rapids."

"Great," Shontera said. "Are you doing okay?"

"Yep. Just thinking and driving."

"Told you driving makes you think too much."

"Nah," he said, smiling in an attempt to cheer himself and remove the memory of Johndo's clawed hand slamming into his face. "It's good to think and clear out the cobwebs upstairs."

"Where did you get *that?*" Shontera said, nodding at his face.

Joshua dropped his right hand from his right cheek. He hadn't even realized he'd been fingering the three horizontal scars there.

"Would you believe a bar fight?"

"Nope."

"Didn't think so. I had a run-in with one of my Wannoshay friends. He got overexcited, I guess, and he hit me. Just about knocked me out. They're powerful people."

"I'm sorry. I've seen what they can do, when they get all worked up. That's partly what caused the brewery explosion, I think. It's like they sometimes have some sort of, I don't know, nuclear meltdown or something."

"I think that happens a lot with them," Joshua said carefully, trying to get a grasp of how Shontera truly felt about the aliens. "My friend the colonel has a lot of theories about why these things happen. My best answer is simply that they're aliens, and they can't help themselves. I hate to think what *I'd* be like, trying to get by on a totally new planet."

Shontera glanced back at her sleepy daughter in the back of the drafty car.

"Maybe," she whispered, "maybe they just learned to react with violence by watching *us.*"

Thinking about Sergeant Murphy and her pulse gun, the last line of defense against the suicide cultists, protestors, and terrorists from around the world, Joshua nodded. He was about to say something more about it, but he was cut off by a scream from Toshera behind him.

"Look out look out look out!"

Sitting nearly sideways in their lane was a stalled truck. Even as Joshua tramped on the brake he knew he wasn't going to be able to stop in time. He'd have to go for the ditch on one side of the road or the other.

He held his foot on the brake and turned into the swerving motion of the big car. They slid to the left, into the empty oncoming lane. The Buick narrowly missed the truck, passing it on the left, and the car's front bumper missed the rear fender of the truck by half a foot.

For a wild, triumphant moment Joshua was almost able to pull the Buick out of its skid, but the snow on the far side of the road was too deep, and the Buick slid sideways across the road.

Two shadowy objects flashed past in front of the windshield, the shapes both about the size of a tall man, and then the Buick hit the snow piled on the shoulder of the road with a loud thump. The car fishtailed to the left.

He jammed both feet onto the brake this time, and the car cooperated with an abruptness that made his head snap forward. His forehead hit the steering wheel, and then all he saw for the next few moments were stars dancing around in the bright snow in front of him.

He closed his eyes, and an instant later the screaming started.

Chapter Eighteen

Ally sat in the middle of the electric bus, knees pulled up to her chest, and tried to let the staticky hum of the bus lull her to sleep. But she kept thinking about her desperate situation, and that kept her from sleeping. She had almost no money after buying her bus ticket. Her nerves had been so damaged from her repeated Blur use, followed by months of poor eating and sleeping in her car, that she felt as if she were carrying weights on her wrists and chest. She was even down to her last rope of gum. When that was gone, she didn't know what she'd do to keep sane.

Even the snow outside was little consolation. Usually she loved watching a good blizzard, but that was back when she lived in an apartment, not a car. And now she didn't even have a car anymore, having sold hers for a fraction of what it was worth so she could afford the bus ticket to Iowa City. Her only other possessions were twelve capsules of Blur she'd had for over a month, and their presence in her inner coat pocket was another reason she couldn't fall asleep.

Try one, the voice in the back of her mind whispered. Just one to help you get through this unending damn bus ride. You could be running up and down the aisles, driving people crazy, burning off some energy and having fun. They wouldn't dare kick you off in the middle of winter.

Ally tried to silence her inner Blur-voice, but every time she relaxed and her eyes began to close, she would snap awake with a sudden lurching movement, as if a soldier had used one of his clip-on weapons on her, but in reverse.

With a shiver of longing and need running through her at the thought of using Blur, Ally grimaced at the memory of the clip-ons and the damage they'd caused back at the factory farm. Brando had surely gotten hit by one of them. She wondered if all of the aliens had been tagged with receivers somehow, like animals, so the soldiers simply had to point and click at a misbehaving Wannoshay. Maybe it was in the derm patches they'd given all the aliens to help them deal with the sunlight.

Two seats ahead of her, on the left-hand aisle, sat two big guys with crookedly cut hair, wearing the long blue coats with the flickering, morphing logos on the left-hand sleeve that many of the suicide cultists and cultist wannabes liked to wear up in Canada. They kept turning around and looking at the other passengers, as if gauging what sort of fight the others would put up.

Glancing over at the old woman in the seat across the aisle from her, Ally slipped a hand into her pants pocket and touched the capsules of Blur yet again.

No, she told herself. Not yet. Maybe in Iowa City. As a reward.

The electric bus droned on. Ally had just fallen into a half-doze when the bus came to an abrupt stop. Waking with her arms flailing for the seat in front of her, her heart pounding, Ally thought for a mad instant she was back aboard the alien ship from her vision, floating high above the dead, frozen horizon. And the alien ship had just hit the brakes.

A high-pitched whirring sound filled the air, bringing Ally back to reality. The bus shuddered again, evoking shouts and cries from the other passengers. Ally glanced out the window and saw a white, featureless world outside, drawing closer to her. A loud snapping sound came from the front of the bus, followed by a whiff of ozone.

The driver began swearing. None of that sounded very promising.

Half an hour later, the bus was sitting in front of a truck stop where the two all-terrain vehicles had towed it, and the passengers were being herded inside the stop to wait for a replacement bus. The driver said it would be anywhere from one to four hours before the other bus arrived, thanks to the snow.

Checking her pocket one last time, Ally gathered up her rope of gum and caught herself looking under her bus seat for a bag she hadn't brought with her. All she had was what was on her back. Everything else was in the car she'd sold to the kid in Winnipeg, a city that felt as if it wasn't just hundreds of kilometers away, but in a different lifetime.

Inside the truck stop, the wait staff wouldn't let the bus riders sit in the restaurant unless they bought something, so Ally sat in her booth in front of a cup of coffee she'd paid for with the last bits of change in her pocket. She hadn't eaten since lunchtime the day before, but her money was too tight to buy anything more.

The sky grew darker as late afternoon crept closer, and every now and then she caught herself imagining black ships darting in and out of the snowy skyscape.

Names ran through her head. Yuallawo, who was a *xiowaya*. Some aliens called Elders. Jenae. Brando. Wanta/Wannoshay. Jane. She wondered if she would see any of them again. She wished she'd learned what Brando's real name was, now that she knew the aliens understood the concept of names—she'd just been bad at trying to explain it to them that day. No surprises there.

Time passed, and the snow continued falling. Ally's coffee grew cold, but she kept sipping it every five minutes or so. The other passengers were complaining to the driver, who sat at the counter of the diner with his hand on his forehead, talking into his handheld Netstream as he cast furtive glances outside.

She had her fingers wrapped around a pair of capsules in her pocket when she heard a low rumbling outside. A few seconds later a light blue pickup swerved out of the snowstorm and slid to a stop next to the gas pumps. Fresh snow flew up in a sheet from the tires, and the pickup missed the pump by less than a foot.

"Crazy shits," she said, watching a tall, thin man run out of the driver's side to start pumping gas. A smaller man nearly fell out of the passenger door, hidden in an oversized, bright orange poncho. The man in the poncho leaned into the wind and worked his way gingerly through the drifted snow toward the restaurant of the truck stop.

Well, Ally corrected herself when she saw the chains on the big tires of the pickup, maybe not *too* crazy. But crazy enough, being out on a day like this.

The door to the restaurant whooshed open, raising more shouts and cries from her fellow passengers, as if that was all they knew how to do. Snow flew into the booths closest to the entrance, and she half-stood to see the man in the orange poncho fighting with the door. The wind had caught it, and nobody was helping him.

She caught a glimpse of gray-white hair under the hood of the poncho, and she was at his side as quickly as if she'd taken Blur ten minutes ago. Someone had to help the old fart.

"Get *in* already, pops," she shouted over the wind, pulling the man in by his coat and jerking the door closed.

Sudden silence filled the restaurant as the others turned back to their empty plates and cups. Ally glared at the backs and tops of their heads and headed back to her booth.

The man in the poncho followed her and dropped into the seat across from her. Her booth had one of the few open seats in it. She cringed.

The man in the booth across from her pushed his hood back and pulled off his poncho, revealing what had to be an ancient suit, all wide lapels and pin stripes. With a practiced ease he pulled his long, straight hair back in a ponytail, and Ally could more clearly see his leathery face and squinting brown eyes. She felt the cold coming off his skin and smelled a bitter whiff of his body odor. He stopped squinting when he pulled a delicate pair of eyeglasses from inside his coat so he could look at the menu.

"Thanks, missy," he said at last, peering at her from above the tops of his bifocals. "Been a long damn day of driving, let me tell you. And we still got a ways to go in this mess."

"No prob," she said, but he was already talking again.

"Yeah, we've been on the road all day, in this damn snow, coming from my hometown." He gave her a proud smile, all crooked yellow teeth. "Surely you've heard of Macy, Nebraska?"

Ten minutes later, Ally didn't think the old guy would ever shut up about his hometown. Macy this, Macy that. As if she gave two shits about the place. She was starting to wish she'd left him outside to fight with the wind and the door until the wind and door won.

"The kids in town," the man who'd introduced himself as Shermie was saying, "now they *loved* to play ball on the concrete slab next to the school. Any time of the year, even if they had to shovel the snow off the cement, they'd be there, shooting hoops and running. It was a thing of beauty, you know, seeing a full-blood kid running, hair behind him or her like a black flag waving in the wind. Beautiful. And the kids could *play.* No bones about it."

Ally tried to ask which reservation Macy was on, but the old man cut her off.

"At least they *used* to be able to play," he said, without missing a beat. "Now, with everyone living down in damn Oklahoma, who knows if the kids have the same quality of life? As president and CEO of Macy, I was very involved with the quality of life in town, you know. But all that went away when people got wind of the ships. And then the aliens started coming around the rez."

Ally sat up straighter and felt her pulse quicken for what felt like the first time in months.

"Aliens?" she said in a low voice.

"Yep," Shermie said with a satisfied grin. "You could say I know a few of 'em. Firsthand knowledge and all . . ."

Just when the conversation was starting to get interesting, the tall, thin man from outside clapped a hand on Shermie's shoulder and dropped into the seat next to him.

"What are you doing, old man?" the younger man said in a quiet voice. "You're not talking too much, are you?"

Ally could tell the two men weren't related at all. The old man was obviously Native American, and this younger guy was white all the way, with light brown hair flecked with snow. Tall and skinny, his hands were almost blue from the cold outside. He had the same look of impatience and nervous fear in his eyes that Ally had noticed in her mirror more than once in the past few months.

"What did you tell her?" the younger man said. He still held onto Shermie's shoulder, squeezing it.

"Relax, Tim," Shermie said. He shrugged out of the younger man's grip. "Let me introduce you two, at least, before we start arguing again. As if your bitching and moaning all the way across this boring-ass state wasn't enough. Alissa Trang, Tim Blair. Tim, Ally."

Ally shook Tim's hand, which was cold as ice after pumping gas for his truck without gloves. "Nice to meet you, Tim."

"Call me Skin," he said, rolling his eyes at the old man next to him. "Everyone does, except for Shermie here."

"Um, okay, Skin," Ally said. "So. Where are you guys headed?"

"Iowa City," Shermie said.

"Chicago," Skin said at the same time, his elbow digging into Shermie's side.

"O-o-okay. Whatever you say."

She was definitely interested now. Aliens and two misfits in a pickup beat a mindless ride in a slow-as-hell bus any day.

"Look," Skin said in a resigned voice. "It's a long story. How much of it has he told you?"

Ally grinned. "He hasn't even gotten out of Macy yet."

"Figures," Skin said, relaxing a bit. He waved for the waitress. He ordered protein sticks, fries, and hot chocolate for himself, and Shermie ordered a chickenburger. Stomach grumbling, Ally resolutely stuck with her cold coffee.

"So," she said. "What's in Iowa City and Chicago? I'm going to Iowa City, too, by the way."

"You a student there?" Skin said.

His harsh expression was softening, and Ally guessed it wasn't so much meanness but nervousness and fear making him so short with her. He also was turning the conversation away from him and Shermie back to her. Not bad for a farmboy.

"No, I'm not the university type." Ally swallowed hard as Skin and Shermie's food arrived, the fries and the burger giving off a wondrously greasy smell. "I'm doing a favor for a friend who wanted me to go there for him. Never been to Iowa City before."

"Neither have we," Shermie said around a mouthful of chicken.

"So, Shermie," Ally said with her sweetest grin. "Tell me more about this firsthand knowledge you have of aliens."

"Damn it, Shermie!" Skin hissed. "What *didn't* you tell her while I was outside?"

"Relax, Tim," Shermie said. "No reason to be all secretive, is there?"

"I just think it's a good idea to keep our mouths shut," Skin whispered. "If people know we've been talking to"—he gave Ally a nervous look before turning back to Shermie—"*them,* instead of reporting them to the cops, we could get in big trouble. Don't you worry about that, old man?"

Shermie answered with a shrug.

"You've been talking to them too?" Ally said in a low voice. "What did they tell you about Iowa City?"

"We have to go there," Skin said, shoulders slumping in defeat. "There's something there we have to see. Now what we're going to do when we find it, I really don't know."

A sudden wind rattled snow off the windows of the restaurant, and Ally shivered at the sound. Her bus wasn't coming, she knew that now. She'd been itching to help herself to the food that Skin had barely touched on his plate (Shermie had been doing so for the past few minutes, having downed his own sandwich in record time), but now her hunger was forgotten. The reality of what the guy across from her was saying finally hit her.

"Are you talking about the Mother Ship?"

Skin's mouth dropped open, and he pushed his plate away from him. Shermie's eyes were also wide with shock.

"It's huge, right?" Ally said, fighting the urge to jump up and down. I'm *not* crazy, she wanted to shout.

"This big black eight-sided thing's bigger than most of the buildings in Iowa City. And it's crashed right next to the river, right? That's what I saw, when"—she almost said Brando's name, but her voice wouldn't form it—"when one of the aliens showed it to me in a vision. They can do that when they want to, y'know, instead of talking out loud."

Ally knew she was babbling, so she shut her mouth and

watched the two men across from her.

"Tim . . ." Shermie began.

"Oh Christ—" Skin said at the same time.

"We have to. She's not just making this up. She knows about the Mother Ship, for crying out loud."

Skin sighed. "I know, Shermie," he said, never taking his eyes off her. "Ally, can we give you a ride to Iowa City?"

"That's a boy," Shermie muttered.

Ally swallowed hard and felt the tightness in her shoulders drain away, tension she hadn't even known was there until just then. She put her hands under the table to hide their shaking, and in the process touched the capsules of Blur in her pants pocket.

"Yes," she said. "Thank you."

"Better eat something, girl," Shermie said, pushing Skin's plate toward her. Ally dug into the food, hoping she didn't look like too much like the starving junkie she knew she was.

As she ate, Skin waved at the waitress for the bill. Ally and Shermie grabbed the last few fries from Skin's plate and stood up. She gave the other bus riders a big grin as she walked past them, and they gave her dull, sheep-like stares in response.

"Y'know," Ally said before they walked into the wall of snow outside and all sound was swallowed by the wind, "I wonder how many other people got visions like us?"

Chapter Nineteen

In the brutal white light of a late-morning blizzard, Father Joshua dreamed of his old friend Johndo.

He could see the elderly alien clearly in the dark space behind his eyes, his gray skin ravaged by exposure to Earth's unforgiving atmosphere and sun. Johndo had been telling him about the arduous flight from their world, the way he and his fellow Wannoshay were packed together like cattle in the sleep-ships. For some reason, Johndo kept looking behind them, as if they were being pursued.

Joshua was about to find out how the sleep-ships worked, how it was able to keep so many of the Wannoshay alive as they flew through space, and he was almost there, a heartbeat away from understanding the alien physics, when Toshera's screams woke him.

The sound was a shock to him in the silent coldness of the stalled Buick, awakening the pain in his forehead. Joshua touched his right eyebrow and looked at the red smear of blood left on his shaking hand. Shontera was staring through the windshield, seemingly ignoring her daughter.

"Toshera," he said, turning to the back seat, "are you hurt?"

The girl shut her mouth with a snapping sound and shook her head. Tears stained her dark face. She pointed back up the road, toward the snow-covered truck they had nearly driven into the ditch to avoid.

"We hit one of the people standing next to the truck, Joshua.

There was a thump, I swear I felt it. We ran *over* somebody, Father. I think it was an alien."

Joshua turned toward the windshield, the sudden movement making his forehead throb. Through the layer of snow on the glass, he saw two dim figures standing in front of the outline of the truck, less than twenty feet away.

"Oh Lord," he whispered. "Shontera, are you seeing what I'm seeing? Shontera?"

Shontera didn't answer. Instead she reached for Toshera and pulled her into the front seat with her as Joshua opened the driver side door. The bitterly cold world outside the car blasted over him with a strength that made his head spin even faster. He pushed himself through the drifting snow on the road, trying to find the tracks the Buick had made, but they'd drifted over.

How long have I been out? he wondered. And how long had poor Toshera been screaming?

Panting for breath, he crossed the road, but all he found was the truck. It appeared to be empty, and the two figures he thought he'd seen standing in front of it were gone. He bent over, head pounding now, and looked into the locked truck. Peering through the layer of ice on the outside of the truck, he saw that the seats were empty.

As far as he could make out, he and Toshera and Shontera were the only other living things around, no other humans or aliens. There were no bumps on the road that could've hidden a body, and the ditches were clear and trackless, thanks to the snow. Nothing out here but the Buick and the abandoned truck and the snow.

He must have imagined the two figures, standing unsteadily on their thick legs. Just like Toshera had imagined the Buick hitting someone in the first place.

With Toshera's screams still echoing in his head, he turned

back to the car sitting sideways in the road. They had to get out of the way before some other driver came plowing through just like they had.

Over the howl of the wind he heard Shontera trying to start the car. He walked back to the Buick as fast as his aching head and the drifting snow would allow. Joshua crossed in front of the ragged front bumper of the Buick as the car roared into life, but he stopped when he saw something hanging from the edge of the front bumper.

Without thinking, he grabbed the ropy black object with a gloved hand and pushed it into his coat pocket. His face turning numb, he hurried around to the passenger door. Once he was in, the wind slammed the door shut behind him.

"Thank you, Daddy," Shontera said from behind the wheel as the engine started up on the third try. "Thank you for keeping this big old Buick in good shape. Are you okay, Father?"

Joshua nodded. "Nobody's out there."

"I *saw* someone," Toshera said from next to him in the front seat. She had the lapbelt snug around her waist, with two pillows in front of her for added protection. "I *did.*"

Shontera flicked on the wipers and urged the car forward. "We believe you, honey. Right, Joshua?"

"Of course," Joshua said.

He was distracted by what he'd found on the bumper of the car. He took off his glove and ran his hand up and down the length of it through the thin material of his coat. It was long, and it was flexible like wire or rope. He pulled his hand away when his fingers started tingling. He gave Shontera and Toshera a guilty look, but neither of them had noticed his sudden movement.

They bumped over a snowdrift in the middle of the road, and Shontera coaxed it out of a small slide.

Joshua touched his forehead again. The pain in his forehead

flared up again. He tried to calm himself with the thought of Iowa City as they crept east and south through the storm, and when he touched the strange object in his coat pocket, he felt himself relax a tiny bit. The snow came down harder as they inched closer to the Mother Ship and the answers that waited for them inside.

Chapter Twenty

Driving through the worst blizzard in over a decade, traveling from the north and from the west, they arrived in Iowa City at last, in the middle of the early January day, just as the temperature reached its high of nineteen degrees.

Separated by less than thirty minutes, six people limped into the city in two vehicles: a beat-up blue pickup with tire chains, and a brown Buick with a nasty divot in its front bumper. The pickup contained a young white man in his late twenties in the driver's seat, with a woman of Chinese descent of about the same age in the passenger seat. Between them sat a Native American man easily twice their age. The Buick held a similarly disparate group: a white priest in his fifties, a twenty-eight-year-old black woman, and her eleven-year-old daughter.

Snow covered the roads and sidewalks like a rumpled blanket, broken only by the occasional tire tracks of an intrepid driver, and it continued to fall, forming a wall of white that threatened to overtake both vehicles.

They arrived in silence, all of them too tired to speak after so long in their vehicles, creeping over snowy roads. The northerly wind pressed against the windows, filling both pickup and car with a low howl and icy air. They drove past cars parked and forgotten on the side of the street, transformed into rectangular snowdrifts outside their frosted windows. Street signs were hidden under a layer of white, while trees had been transformed into frozen towers of swaying snow.

Without remarking on it, all the travelers marveled at the silence of the snowbound city, bathed in snow-muted, midday light. They were too tired to say anything, especially the most obvious, painfully ironic comment: Iowa City looked like an alien world.

For the trio riding in the pickup, the silence was broken by a snowplow roaring past, throwing thick, wet snow onto the hood like a bully kicking sand on a smaller kid on the beach. Behind the wheel, Skin flicked on the wipers to no avail, and he had to crank down his window and use his bare hand to loosen up a corner of the sheet of slushy snow. Leaning forward and squinting through the tiny gap in the windshield, he followed the snowplow deeper into the city until he saw the five buildings from the vision that had been given to him by Shermie's aliens.

"The Old Capital, uh-huh," Shermie said in a gravelly voice. He was pointing at the domed building in the center, surrounded by the bare limbs of ancient oaks and elms. "The Pentacrest, uh-huh, uh-huh. We're almost there. Hang a right up here."

Too tired to even question Shermie's knowledge anymore, Skin followed the freshly plowed trail left by the snowplow. A sudden gust of wind loosened up the snow covering the hood of the truck, throwing it onto the windshield like mist as they passed the old buildings on their left.

When the windshield had cleared, Skin slid the pickup to a fishtailing stop. The road dropped away in front of them, creating the impression that it simply stopped, or continued on into a snowy nothingness.

"Almost there," Shermie whispered, with a hint of impatience in his voice.

"I know," Skin said. "But I'd like to see where I'm going before we try to get down this hill. It's a steep one."

When the last bits of snow on the windshield blew off, they saw it. At the bottom of the hill, in the middle of what had once been an open field, sat a towering black structure, over eight stories high.

"The Mother Ship," Shermie murmured. "Uh-huh."

Lodged somewhat crookedly into the ground, almost touching the banks of the frozen river directly behind it, the ship looked as if it would fall over at the slightest provocation. It was twice as tall as the block-long building made of red brick and glass it had landed next to. The top of the ship was nearly level with them, and it was tipped with vicious-looking spires that jutted out in eight different locations.

If the road had continued straight on instead of down the hill, Skin felt like he could have driven his pickup right onto the uneven roof of the Mother Ship.

"Holy shit," he whispered.

His right foot pressed so hard onto the brake that his leg had started shaking. This was the ship from the dreams that had been haunting him for the past two months. The ship that Awoyana had needed him to find. He couldn't stop staring.

A razor-tipped, chain-link fence over fifteen feet high protected the lower section of the ship, while half a dozen olive-drab tents sat on the near side of the fence. On the roads surrounding the field sat a pair of dark green Humvees next to an electric sedan labeled "ICPD," blocking access to the ship. Soldiers with pulse guns, black helmets, and thick body armor were already standing outside of the Humvees at the bottom of the hill, along with a pair of police officers in matching black riot gear.

From a snow-covered lean-to next to the chapel, almost touching the frozen river, a camouflaged tank-like vehicle that he recognized from the endless Netstream footage from the war on terror as an enhanced Bradley Fighting Vehicle had begun rolling toward them.

Incongruously, a tiny chapel sat between the ship and the brick building, an island of calm next to the chaotic wreckage of the mammoth black ship and the armored vehicles.

"Oh shit," Ally said. "What's the plan now, fellas?"

"We'd better get moving," Skin said, thinking of Matt and Matt's strange new friends. "We look suspicious just sitting here. They probably think we're suicide cultists."

"Jesus H, you're right."

Skin felt like someone was pushing against him with finger tipped with a sharp fingernail, almost a claw. He couldn't take his foot from the brake as he looked down at the scarred land around the ship. The torn-up ground had yet to heal from where the ship had apparently skidded to a stop a year ago, less than ten feet from the river. No snow stuck to the divots in the ground or the exterior of the ship, and none of the military tents or vehicles rested on the churned-up ground.

"Tim. Let's *go,* son." Shermie spoke in a soft tone, but his words were clear and sharp.

Something in the old Indian's voice made Skin release the pressure of his foot on the brake. They began to roll down the snow-dusted hill toward the ship and the armed personnel in front of it. The wind intensified as they crept down the snowy hill, the truck sliding every few feet.

As the wind blew more snow into the windshield, Skin squinted off to his left. With a nasty shock of recognition, he saw four vans (white vans, his mind shouted, passing me on my way to the grain elevator the day of the explosion) parked side-by-side next to a big pickup, all of them covered in snow. Their front bumpers were up against the chain link fence surrounding the Mother Ship. A finger of numbing cold traced itself down his back.

When Skin looked back at the road a second later, he didn't

even see the big brown gasoline-powered car parked at the bottom of the hill until his pickup nearly slid into it a second later. And then armored soldiers and police officers surrounded his truck, weapons drawn.

Fifteen minutes earlier, Shontera had found the Mother Ship without making a single wrong turn or needing Joshua or Toshera to consult their Netstream map. After driving all morning long, even with their near-miss with the ditch and the truck outside Cedar Rapids, she felt completely free of any fatigue the moment the spires of the black ship came into focus in front of her.

She felt as if she'd been led there by the familiar tingling in her chest she used to feel whenever she was close to Nonami. The tingling had been growing stronger the closer they got to the Mother Ship, guiding her as they drove through the snowy streets.

After sliding down the steep hill toward the two Hummers and the electric sedan, holding her breath the entire way down, she came to a stop at the first roadblock. Four soldiers and a pair of Iowa City police officers, all helmeted, armed, and anonymous, popped out of their respective vehicles and hurried toward her.

"Can we help you, miss?" the first soldier said as soon as Shontera's window was down, eyes hidden behind opaqued glasses.

Before Shontera could answer, the passenger door of her father's car opened, and six pulse guns lifted in unison to point at Father Joshua. The red-faced priest held one hand in his coat pocket and lifted his other hand into the air.

"It's okay," Joshua said, his voice calm in the swirling wind and snow. "We're here to help."

"Let's just take our hand out of the coat real slow, father," the first soldier said.

Shontera realized that the soldier was female, her curves hidden under her black armor. The soldiers on the other side of the car were inching closer to Joshua, guns still aimed on him, and Shontera could smell ozone and gun oil. A gust of wind threw snow into the car, hitting her like cold pellets of sand. Toshera called for her from the back seat, but Shontera didn't dare make any sudden movements.

"Joshua?" she said, feeling like she'd walked into some sort of trap of the priest's devising. "What are you *doing?*"

"We need to get inside the ship," Joshua said. He lifted his gloved hand and showed the soldiers something wriggling and black, like a furred snake. Shontera recognized it immediately.

"Drop it," the soldier next to Shontera said, but the young woman's voice had lost its authority.

A whitish-light poured off of the object in his hand, spreading up his arm and filling the car. When the light reached his chest, something twinged in Joshua's face, and he almost dropped the piece of Wannoshay hair. Incredibly, the pulse guns lowered when the soldiers saw the light coming from the hair. The air had turned electric and impossibly warm.

Shontera felt her length of Wannoshay hair quiver once from where she'd buried it deep inside her coat. She felt like she was riding once more on Nonami's back, rushing out of the burning brewery, and many creatures were running after her. And then the feeling stopped when Joshua dropped to one knee outside the car and let go of the hair-tentacle. The light vanished.

The soldiers sprang into action with the graceless movements of those awakened from a deep sleep by a siren or an explosion. They grabbed Joshua by either arm and pulled him up. Toshera called out his name, and then she called out for Shontera in a thin, panicked voice. Shontera took her daughter's hand as slowly as she could without drawing attention to either of them.

Two of the soldiers poked the hair as it quivered on the ground, melting snow with a hissing sound and giving off a series of sputtering sparks. The smell of the pulse guns had been replaced by something sharper and more unpleasant, like scorched meat. The hair twitched twice more, and then stopped.

When the Wannoshay hair tentacle went still, so did everyone else. The wind died, and the world went silent.

Shontera watched the young female soldier, who looked from Joshua to Shontera and Toshera without moving her head. In the back seat Toshera bit her lip and squeezed a pair of tears down her cheeks.

Shontera risked a look at Joshua, and saw that his face was pale and his forehead was wet with sweat in spite of the cold. The blood rushing through her head was loud as a waterfall.

"Damn it," the soldier next to Shontera hissed at last. "Should've recognized him sooner."

Still not moving her armored body, she winked at her Net-stream glasses and whispered into her cheek mike. After a long moment, her glasses cleared.

"Father Joshua McDowell? Can you confirm your identity?"

Joshua muttered a low "Yes" that was almost completely lost in another cold gust of wind. With a shaking hand he pointed at his chest and opened his jacket.

The first police officer, as if afraid of finding more alien tentacles in Joshua's jacket, reached a gloved hand inside and retrieved the priest's wallet. She passed Joshua's ID to a soldier next to her, who ran a pen-shaped reader across it and gave a nod.

"Should've recognized you from the 'Streams." The lead soldier stepped back and opened Shontera's door. "I'll need you and your friends to come with us, please. Mr. McDowell, if you could pick up that . . . thing . . . on the ground there, sir, we can take you to see the colonel's tent."

Shontera was relieved to see that color was slowly coming back to Joshua's face, but he still looked weak, the exact opposite of the boisterous man she'd met last night and talked to all morning. He bent with a grimace and picked up the Wannoshay hair and stuffed it back inside his coat.

Shontera stepped outside and felt the tentacle in her own coat wriggle once more. She did her best to keep calm and not react to the movement. With most of her face already turning numb from the cold and wind, it wasn't a hard task to accomplish.

Once she'd helped Toshera out of the car, Shontera turned and got an unimpeded view of the Mother Ship. It seemed bigger now, more ominous than it had felt only a few minutes earlier.

The lines of the towering craft kept wanting to shift every time she looked at it, so she forced herself not to look. She pulled Toshera's hood down low over her daughter's eyes, and they followed three of the soldiers toward the clump of dark green tents next to the fence.

"We're going in there soon," Toshera said, pointing at the Mother Ship. Shontera couldn't tell if her daughter was asking a question or merely stating a fact.

As they approached the tents, something shimmered in the air between the tents and the fence. Shontera blinked and suddenly inhaled freezing air. There were *more* tents behind the dark green tents, extending out and away from them. The hidden tents, she could see now, were draped with what looked like the same camouflaged material she'd seen the soldiers wearing outside the camps and labor farms. This camouflage was much better than any she'd seen before: the tents had been all but invisible until she had pretty much walked right into them.

Shontera wondered why the soldiers and police officers weren't wearing the camouflage material as well, and then she shivered: the soldiers and cops she'd seen so far were there to make their presence *known*. There were probably countless invisible soldiers wandering all around them, and she'd never even know it.

She wanted to say something to Joshua about this before they entered the first hidden tent, but he was walking slowly behind them, head down and hunched forward against the cold wind. He was muttering something to himself about seeing the colonel again.

Shontera gave the ship one last glance, and that look made her grip her daughter's hand even tighter. The ship filled her vision with a liquid blackness broken only with distorted angles and sharp-looking spires.

We *are* going inside that ship, she thought, and soon.

With that sobering thought, she led her daughter into the tent. She wondered if anyone had been watching them, and if so, she wondered if it looked as if she and Toshera had simply disappeared into the snowy air, winking out of existence altogether.

"I don't *care* about Macy, Nebraska, sir," the soldier outside the driver's side door was saying in a low voice. "I understand you've come a long way, but I'm going to have to ask you and your friends to turn around."

Ally recognized the exasperated tone in the woman's voice, having used it countless times on the customers at her old job, during her old life in Canada.

"Come on!" Shermie began, about to launch into another tirade, but he stopped short when Ally gripped his arm through his poncho.

"Listen," Ally said, leaning forward. "My grandpa here is good friends with some important people on board that ship, and he needs to set up a meeting with them. Is that too much to ask?"

"Your *grandfather,*" one of the soldiers next to the lead soldier said. "Wants to set up a *meeting.*"

"Quiet," the first soldier said, her exasperation replaced with a controlled anger. She lowered her pulse gun and looked in at Ally. "Miss, that ship's empty. I don't know who you folks have been talking to, but you've been misinformed."

"But . . ." Ally stopped when she heard the whine in her voice. That pissed her off. She caught herself wanting a capsule of Blur, as if talking faster would help them get past the soldiers.

"Turn it aroun—" the soldier said, but the attention of her squadron and the police officers had been diverted. The armed men and women were looking at a pair of people approaching from the left side of the pickup.

"Oh *shit,*" Skin whispered. It was the first thing he'd said ever since the soldiers had stopped them ten minutes ago. His face held a trapped, guilty look that made Ally's stomach drop.

"Now what?" the lead soldier said, glancing over at the figures approaching them. "Do you know these people?"

"Nope," Skin said, too fast, and then Shermie was leaning forward, almost on top of Skin.

"Good lord," Shermie hissed. "That's Bobby Blackhill and . . . Steven French?"

"No," Skin said. "Don't—"

"Bobby! Steven!" The old man's voice carried through the open window, and the two burly men approaching the pickup lifted their hands and waved. The soldiers stepped closer to the pickup, and the snowy air around the two approaching men shimmered in a way that made Ally's eyes want to cross.

"*Told* you," one of the two approaching men said in a deep voice. "It's Shermie Goddamn Powell! I'd know that orange poncho anywhere, even if he is inside a truck."

A moment after the big man stopped talking, the two men were suddenly surrounded by soldiers that appeared out of nowhere. There were easily two dozen soldiers emerging from both sides of the truck, pulse guns shimmering into visibility as they were lifted free of whatever camouflaging material that had been covering them.

"Those are my people!" Shermie said, grabbing Skin by the arm and giving a joyous look at Ally. He didn't seem to notice, or even care about, all the soldiers and guns focused on him. "They came here!"

"I know," Skin said. "And now we're fucked."

"Out of the truck!" the lead soldier said, grabbing Skin's arm. "Slowly. Come out this door only."

Behind the first group of green-clad soldiers, the two big men that Shermie had claimed were fellow Macy men had already been surrounded by the newly arrived soldiers. The two Macy men had been cut off from the truck.

"What the hell are you boys doing here?" Shermie called out. His wrinkled face was filled with delight to see the two men in their long blue overcoats.

"Had to leave the rez in Oklahoma, man," the first man called out, ignoring the soldiers around him. "It's bad there, man. Overcrowded, not much food. People all desperate—"

"Quiet!" the lead soldier said. Her glasses went opaque as she whispered into her cheek mike.

"Freedom of speech," the other Macy man said. "And we can peacefully organize here, ma'am. It's our constitutional right, y'know."

"Don't fuck around here," the soldier said. "Move these two back," she said to the fresh squadron of soldiers.

Ally followed Skin and Shermie out of the driver's side door. She didn't bother zipping up her coat, but let the icy wind and snow blow onto her. She was shaking now, and not just from the cold.

She'd gotten a good look at Shermie's two friends, and it was dawning on her just who they were. The two men, shouting now at the soldiers, wore the short, crooked haircuts and dark blue overcoats trimmed in black that were the unofficial uniforms of suicide cultists.

"Leave those boys alone!" Shermie shouted, making a move toward his fellow Macy men as he continued to yell. Then his gravelly old voice was cut off as a soldier slapped an adhesive patch over his mouth.

"Oh no, you didn't!" the first Macy man shouted, surging like a fullback through the soldiers around him. Ally saw the flash of a gun turned butt-first, and looked away before the gun made contact with the man's head. She still heard the dull sound of metal against skull.

Skin stood still as a sleepwalker next to her, while Shermie struggled against the half-invisible arms holding him back. The second Macy man kicked and swung at the shimmering soldiers around him until one of the pulse guns went off.

Ally squeezed her eyes shut and held her breath until the nausea from the blast subsided. She wanted to disappear herself, just like one of the cloaked soldiers. But then she thought of Brando and the other Wantas in the labor farm, creeping up to her and asking for Blur, just one more capsule, one more rush.

Nobody noticed her hand slip into her pocket faster than she'd ever moved on Blur. Instead of pulling out a capsule of the drug, however, she pulled out Brando's last gift to her: a shank of his hair, still wriggling in her hand.

The instant she held the hair-tentacle aloft, a white surge of energy covered her. She held tight to the hair as the energy spread out in all directions from her with a hot blast of wind. Falling snow turned to water, dropping to the now-wet ground like rain inside the hot, twenty-foot circle of energy created by Brando's hair.

With a synchronized clatter, every single pulse gun held in the hands of the soldiers and police officers dropped to the wet, snowless pavement.

"What the *hell?*" the lead soldier whispered into the sudden silence. "Another one?"

Everyone turned toward Ally. She stood at the center of the warm circle of alien energy that came from the quivering tentacle gripped in her hand held above her head. Feeling foolish, she lowered her arm, and when she did, she saw a matching light coming from the ship. She had to squint to see it, but there was something there near the lower level of the ship, glowing like a beacon.

"Sorry to interrupt," Ally said, pointing at the ship. "But I think our friends are waiting for us. You want to keep them waiting?"

All eyes turned toward the ship as the white glow coming from Ally's hand began to dissipate. Snow returned to cover all of them again, sticking to every last inch of wet, exposed skin.

Ally could now see a tall gray figure standing inside the circular door at the bottom of the ship, its outstretched hand giving off a matching white glow.

"Supposed to be empty," a soldier muttered. "What's going on here, Sarge?"

"Our friends are waiting . . ." Ally said again, but as soon as the words were out of her mouth, the gray figure outside the ship faded from view.

The lower level of the ship shimmered where the figure had been standing. A black circle formed where the broken ground met the alien ship. The circle widened until it was large enough for a person to walk through.

The Mother Ship, Ally thought, is now open for business.

Father Joshua kept having things happen to him that he thought would never happen ever again. Like the twinges of pain that crisscrossed his chest when he'd held up the Wannoshay hair tentacle that had been jumping around in his coat pocket like a fish pulled out of the water. Or the unnatural buzz that being so close to a ship of the Wannoshay caused in his fillings, a sensation he'd forgotten since the camps had arisen. Or the fact that he was now sitting across from Colonel Cossa once again, talking about the Wannoshay.

"I first came here in early November, after we started getting reports of missing Wannoshay," the colonel was saying. "And the aliens that were going missing weren't just the young ones, out looking for adventure or trouble. The older Wannoshay were also disappearing from the camps, including your old friend, Johndo."

Joshua almost knocked over the untouched cup of coffee sitting on the metal table in front of him at the mention of his Wannoshay friend's name.

"You may get a chance to see him again," Colonel Cossa said. He glanced around the small room lined with dark green canvas that seemed to absorb all sound. He lowered his voice anyway. "We've discovered a small group of the Wannoshay aboard the Mother Ship."

"I *knew* it wasn't empty," Toshera whispered, flashing Joshua a victorious smile.

"This is restricted information, you know," the colonel said. His dark eyes widened and the corners of his usually tight, unsmiling mouth lifted with an almost child-like excitement. "But Father Joshua knows I'm not one for sticking to the rules when my gut tells me otherwise. I've only been burned once when it comes to the aliens, and that was the day of the explosions. And even on that point I'm willing to give our first visitors from space the benefit of the doubt."

Joshua was struggling to find his voice again. The twist of pain he'd felt half an hour earlier while holding up the strand of Wannoshay hair had been growing inside his chest, but the colonel's enthusiasm was contagious.

Johndo, he thought. How in heaven did you get here, and what are you planning to do here?

As if reading his mind, the colonel answered a question from Shontera that Joshua had been too distracted to hear.

"How they got there we don't know yet, what with the nonstop military presence here, both covert and not, but I have my suspicions."

Joshua swallowed. "Tunnels?"

The colonel looked at him and nodded. "Most likely. We should have been watching for such a thing, but most of our attention had been elsewhere, what with all the goings-on elsewhere in the world. Our troops are spread pretty thin these days, fighting terrorism here and overseas. We pretty much forgot about the Mother Ship."

Joshua rubbed his chilled arms through his jacket. He kept thinking that a soldier draped in the same invisible fabric that covered the exterior of the tent was standing a foot away from him, listening in on them.

The colonel paused in the middle of his conversation with Shontera and Toshera to touch the bud in his left ear. His face went blank for a moment, and his hint of a smile disappeared.

"Everything okay?" Joshua said, placing his hands on either side of his cup of coffee, activating the rewarmers in the metal sides of the cup and chasing away some of the chill growing inside him.

The colonel gave a quick nod.

"A small disturbance outside. A group of people in a truck,

getting some of the local protestors worked up. Nothing to worry about. As I'm sure you've seen, we have more soldiers here than at first meets the eye."

"How exactly does that work, anyway?" Joshua said, pointing out into the hallway where the high-tech fabric hid them from the outside. He still wasn't sure he'd seen the soldiers unwrap themselves from the thin air like that.

"We've been researching the Wannoshay metals," the colonel said. "They're as much a liquid as a solid, it seems. And the metal has been quite useful in enhancing our troops' camouflage skills. Suffice to say, we've made huge strides in our relations with the Wannoshay, even with them holed up in those godforsaken camps. And now I think we should—"

The colonel paused again as something buzzed in his ear bud loud enough for Joshua to hear. An instant later, the unmistakable thunder of a pulse gun discharging filled the air.

"Stay here," the colonel said on his way out of the inner tent. He muttered something under his breath that sounded like "cultists."

Joshua hadn't even seen the man get out of his chair. He sat for a stunned moment, looking down at his bare hands, remembering the riot at his old church in Chicago. The looters—cultists, most likely—had torn up the cushions in most of the pews and were advancing on the altar when the pulse guns began to go off, blowing all of the cultists off their feet.

Outside, the roar of the pulse gun was not repeated, but a strange electricity now filled the air. Joshua recognized the sensation immediately, and he was on his feet in a heartbeat, followed closely by Shontera and Toshera.

They slipped out through the Wannoshay-enhanced fabric of the outer tent and into the driving snow and wind.

Remembering the general direction of the pulse gun blast, Joshua looked up at the roadblock ahead of them, where a sky-blue pickup sat almost touching the old Buick. The surge of electricity came from there.

Joshua squinted through the snow and saw white light spreading in a circle from a small figure holding something aloft. The small figure was a young woman, and she was holding up what had to be a piece of Wannoshay hair. She had somehow caused all of the roadblock soldiers, along with the now-visible covert soldiers surrounding them, to drop their pulse guns. She'd also melted all the snow around her in a wide circle.

"That's so cool!" Toshera said next to him. "Just like you did, Father! But even bigger!"

"We'd better stay here, Father," Shontera said, but Joshua was already hurrying toward the crowd of soldiers and civilians. All of them stared at the girl with the hair, too shocked to move.

Joshua pushed against the bitter wind on his way to the truck. He wanted to feel the power of the energy of the People one more time. From the growing pain in his chest, he knew firsthand how fleeting that energy could be.

He was just at the outer rim of the circle of energy when it began to dissipate. The attention of the crowd shifted, turning on Joshua. With a nervous smile, he tried to think of something calming to say, but then he realized they weren't looking at him. They were watching the ship. The Mother Ship.

Joshua had thought that the blackness of the ship couldn't have been more complete, but then he saw an even darker black circle at the base of the ship. That circle, he was positive, hadn't been there when they'd arrived at the site barely an hour earlier.

As the soldiers around him bent to pick up their dropped weapons, the whole time muttering about how the ship was supposed to be empty, Joshua saw the colonel step closer to the three people from the truck.

He turned and gave Joshua a meaningful look, as if to say, How convenient that all of you arrived today, of all days.

"Come with me," the colonel said, pointing at the old Indian man, the thin white man, and the young woman with the Wannoshay hair—now looking dull and useless—in her small hand. "Take these two cultists out of here," he added, gesturing to the two Native American men almost completely hidden by camouflaged soldiers. "I've had enough of their shit in the past few weeks."

"But—" the old man in the orange poncho began. His voice died with a look from the colonel.

The soldiers opened up a gap to let the colonel and the trio from the truck out of their protective circle. Joshua had to jog to keep up with the tall man, the three civilians, and the five soldiers Cossa had pulled from the crowd around the pickup. Shontera and Toshera caught up to Joshua a few steps later.

The colonel was headed for the Mother Ship.

"Holy shit," the young woman with the alien hair said as Joshua caught up to her. She was looking at him with her dark eyes wide. "I'm sorry, Father. But you're—aren't you the priest from the ship in Waukegan? I've seen you all over the 'Streams."

"Joshua McDowell," he said, holding out a hand as they hurried through a gate in the chain-link fence. The girl was much too thin, he thought, and her eyes had the deep-set, desperate look of a junkie. Probably Blur, or something newer.

"Alissa Trang." She moved the piece of Wannoshay hair from her right hand into her coat pocket with a crooked smile before shaking his hand. "I came all the way down here from Canada. Nice to meet you, Father."

"Nice to meet you too, Alissa."

Her eyes widened with amazed glee for a second as the ship loomed higher and higher above them.

"Can you believe this is *happening?* Jesus H!—Um, sorry, Father. Anyway, that's Skin and Shermie up there," she added, pointing. "Skin's the pissed-off looking white guy."

"And that's Shontera and her girl Toshera back there." Joshua reached into his coat pocket so he could show her his piece of Wannoshay hair. "Looks like we all had the same thing in mind today, huh?"

"I'd say," Ally said, and then they were at the entrance to the Mother Ship. "This is all really frickin' weird."

The blacker-than-black circle was wide enough and tall enough for three of the People to easily walk through side-by-side and upright, without hunching over. The strange hum of electricity that Joshua had heard while they were first talking to the colonel had intensified, and now the sound filled his ears. The circular doorway gazed out at Joshua and his companions like the third eye of one of the People.

Joshua touched the hair-tentacle from the near-wreck a few hours ago, feeling the pain in his chest subside for a moment. He'd finally come home.

Nobody at school was going to believe this, Toshera thought as they crunched across the snow and stepped over the broken ground at the base of the alien Mother Ship. They're actually going to let me go inside!

Holding hands with Father Joshua and her mother, Toshera followed the colonel, the soldiers, and the others into the ship. Toshera grabbed her mother's hand as tight as she could, almost afraid to take a breath now that she was inside the ship. The air was even colder here, and as Toshera finally exhaled and breathed in, she could almost taste the smell of the aliens her mother had described to her so often. It was salty, with something sweet underneath.

This part of the ship was empty, and the round door silently closed behind them, cutting off the sunlight. Her eyes slowly adjusted to the dark as she tiptoed across the floor. She half-expected to get shocked or zapped by the touch of the alien ship. The rubbery metal all around her absorbed almost every sound.

"The metal must be some kind of malleable material that hardens over time," Joshua said next to her, as if talking to himself. "I thought the floor would be uneven because of the way the ship was jammed into the ground."

Nobody said anything in response to his comments as they gathered together in the alcove. Toshera counted three doorways leading into the ship.

"Follow me," the colonel said, and he turned to Joshua. "This ship is four times as big as the ship you were in, but for the most part they're all set up the same way. I know the way to the Elders."

The colonel walked toward the middle doorway, but when he was less than five feet from it, the door slid shut, followed by the two doors on either side of it.

"What's going on?" Skin said. He was standing closest to the colonel, and he'd almost gotten caught in the left-hand door as it slid shut.

"This has never happened before," the colonel began.

"Should we force it, sir?" one of the soldiers asked.

"No. I think I know what the problem is. Joshua, try the door."

Joshua stepped up to the middle door as ordered. The door opened, but slid shut the instant the colonel moved toward it.

Toshera wanted to ask her mother what the problem was, but she didn't dare say anything. When she looked up, her mother had her hand in her coat pocket, and her face was distracted.

When she looked back at the colonel and the priest standing inches away from the closed door, Toshera figured it out.

"Step back," she said to the colonel. "I think you're too close to the door. Um, I mean, *sir.*"

"I think you may be right," the colonel said as he moved

back from the door. The middle door slid open before he finished his sentence. "Someone doesn't want you people to have a military escort, it looks like."

"What should we do?" Joshua said. "We could try holding the door open for you while you and the soldiers run through."

"No. I think this is one of those times, just like your first day in the ship at Waukegan, where we have to defer to the aliens' preferences. That's what my gut's telling me, at least. You remember the way, Father?"

Joshua nodded and shook the colonel's hand. The two men Toshera had just met, Skin and Shermie, walked through the middle doorway first, flinching the slightest bit on their way through. The doors had slid shut fast on the colonel, and it wouldn't be good to get caught in the middle of it before it closed.

Shontera and Toshera walked through the middle doorway into a branching hall, followed by Joshua. The door hissed shut faster than Toshera's eyes could follow, cutting them off from the colonel and the other soldiers.

As soon as the door was closed, her mother gave out a cry and pulled up short. She started hitting at her jacket, as if trying to get rid of a bee that had flown inside.

Toshera knew what it was before her mother pulled the hank of alien hair from her coat. Her mother gave a small squeak, as if the hair had given her a shock, and she ended up throwing it against the wall. The hair gave off sparks and squirmed from where it was stuck to the wall. The four others gathered around it.

"What the hell?" Skin said. "Does *everyone* have one of those but me?"

Looking at the piece of alien hair made Toshera think of the ruined tunnels at the Waukegan landing site. There had been a lot of hair-tentacles there, jammed to the fence. Too many.

"It's pointing," Shermie said. "Maybe it's like a divining rod. We should take it with us, don't you think?"

"Don't look at me," Ally said. "I already got to use my Wanta hair."

"Wannoshay," Toshera said automatically.

Joshua made a face, as if something inside him was hurting, but he reached out and picked up the hair-tentacle. It was still moving, and the end that Toshera thought looked like a snake's head (or an eyeball, she thought suddenly, watching the end move) pointed at the doorway to the left, away from the middle doorway.

He held up the tentacle to her mother as if asking her if she wanted it back. Shontera shook her head: no thanks.

"I think it wants us to go this way," he said, walking past Toshera and the others. Without a word, they followed him to the doorway on his left.

The passageway began to go down an incline into shadowy half-light. Toshera concentrated on her feet, squinting in the gloom and biting her lip. In front of her, Joshua ran his hand along the wall to his right.

Occasionally the wall stopped, opening into another passage. Every time that happened, they would pause as Joshua consulted Shontera's hair-tentacle, letting it lead them like a divining rod. Without fail, the hair-tentacle pulled them down what felt like the coldest of the passageways, always leading farther down.

Toshera was starting to lose her enthusiasm as the cold air slipped through her coat and clothes. Their footsteps were muffled by the metal of the passageway, and the ship made soft settling noises as they ventured deeper into the heart of the ship.

They turned left at another fork in the passage. Shivering in the cold, Toshera felt completely lost now, after all their turns and the curving of the passageway itself, but she knew she'd be safe with her mother and Joshua with them. She wasn't sure the skinny guy or the old Indian guy would be much help in a fight, but the girl named Ally looked like she could hold her own, even if she was twitching like a Blur junkie with every step she took.

After five minutes of walking huddled together in almost complete darkness, Toshera saw a soft glow in the passageway ahead of them. She had to squint to make sure she wasn't imagining it, and when she did, she felt the hint of her headaches return.

No, she prayed to herself. Not the headaches again. I'd touch Mom's Wannoshay hair again if that's what it takes to keep them away. I'd braid it into my own hair if that's what it took.

The salty smell was stronger, and an icy breeze blew up from the direction of the lit doorway, making Toshera so cold she wanted to stop walking.

"They're in there," her mother whispered, and her voice was picked up and repeated in the high hallway: *"there there there . . ."*

In front of them, Joshua stepped up to the opening where the light was emanating. Shermie hurried up to Joshua and grabbed the priest by the arm. Shermie's dark eyes glittered in the light from the opening. Toshera wondered if the two old men were getting ready to fight. But instead they stood frozen in place for a long moment outside the room, staring inside. Toshera could now hear soft noises like whispering voices coming from the glowing room.

This was going to be awesome, she thought. She wished the two old guys would hurry up and decide who'd go in first.

Joshua looked at each of the people around him, his gaze holding on Toshera for a long moment that warmed her. When he looked away, she glanced at the others. She wondered if they had met some of the Wannoshay up-close, like her mother had done. She couldn't wait to meet them for herself.

"All right," Shermie said, letting go of his grip on Joshua's arm. "Thanks, Father, for getting us here. I'll go first, if that's okay with everyone. I know their language, and if anything bad's going to happen, I want it to happen to me. I've lived a long, full life."

Before Joshua could argue with him, Shermie took a long stride and entered the well-lit room. The priest followed a moment later.

"Let's go, honey," her mother said, watching Skin and Ally enter the room.

"Finally," Toshera whispered. She hoped the sudden burst of fear that had jumped into her chest wasn't too obvious in her voice. She had to be strong for her mother and her new friends. Hand in hand, she and her mother stepped down into the bright room.

Once inside, she was temporarily blinded by a half-dozen white globes pressed to the walls. She blinked fast to force her eyes to adjust, and once they did, Toshera was face-to-face with the first Wannoshay she'd ever seen up close. She felt tears squirt from her eyes and fall down her cheeks until she could taste them on her lips. There were eight of them, and they were as scary and wonderful as she'd hoped they would be.

In the middle of the room, the Wannoshay wore long black robes and rested on metal chairs that looked as if they had been pried up from the floor. The Wannoshay must all have been old, because they looked much more hunched over than the 'Stream images Toshera had seen before, and their hair was lighter and shorter than any of the hair-tentacles she'd seen anywhere else.

The half-circle of Wannoshay had been waiting for them, that much was obvious. Their eyes glowed, and even from this distance, she could see a tiny bit of white surrounding the black irises of the sideways eyes.

We found the Elders, Toshera thought, squeezing her mother's hand. And they were beautiful.

Chapter Twenty-One

Shermie Powell was in dire need of a smoke. He stood in the brightly glowing room with his hands held palms-up, four humans behind him, eight Wannoshay in front of him. Nodding at the creatures he thought of as snake-hairs, he licked his lips and wished he had a cigarillo or a filtered joint or even some ditchweed to suck on. Smoking always helped him focus while he was talking with them.

Instead of the tall, long-torsoed creatures he'd met in the Nebraska countryside, these eight beings looked partially shrunken, like humans suffering from calcium deficiencies. And the strange tentacles at the top of their heads were shorter and grayish-white, like human hair.

Just being this close to them, feeling the intensity of their dark, three-eyed gazes, smelling their musky scent, Shermie felt the hairs on his arms raise up under his heavy poncho. He put on his glasses and tasted something metallic on his tongue as a horrible thought hit him: I've forgotten how to speak to them.

The other humans crept into the circular room behind him. Shermie saw them only from the corner of his eye, but he relaxed at their presence. He kept his face turned toward the eight aliens, peering over the tops of his glasses as he moved to the middle of the room. Before any words could be spoken, the first alien on the left nodded at him from his chair of misshapen metal. And then Shermie remembered what to do first.

The white light from the globes in the walls seemed to

brighten as he twisted his arms inward, making his elbows stick out at a sharp angle. He arched his back and gave his best formal bow to the alien Elders.

"I bring news from your escaped Wannoshay to the west," Shermie began, in English, and then he repeated it in the snake-hairs' language. "News, and this."

Trying to maintain the awkward angle of his elbows, he dug into his coat pocket and pulled out his piece of Wanta hair. He felt it squirm in his hand, and for a second he thought of the thick black hair of many of the Indian men and women from Macy. This tentacle-hair felt like a braided ponytail cut from one of those absent members from his tribe.

The ropy lank of hair wriggled in his hand until it was pointing like a finger at the Elders.

"I come from Macy, Nebraska," Shermie whispered in the alien tongue.

There were more nods and abbreviated bows from the Elders arrayed before him. The room went dark for a moment, and Shermie felt something inside his mind, as if probing it. A flashing series of images filled his head: the people of Macy leaving, the first time he met Awoyana, the other snake-hair boys playing catch with the rocks. He heard the gasps of the others behind him, and he wondered if the Elders were touching them as well.

When he looked up, the hair-tentacle was hovering in the air, giving off a soft glow. He hadn't even noticed it leaving his hand. The warm white light tickled Shermie's skin at first, and then turned into a caress.

As if on cue, the snake-hairs began talking, all at once. At first their words were sing-song gibberish, coming at him from eight different directions, and Shermie felt an instant of panic. But when he looked back at Skin and Ally and the others, he relaxed.

I'm not alone, he thought. I've got my ad-hoc tribe here.

As he relaxed, the words of the Wannoshay returned to him, and he was able to understand the Elders. They were talking to each other not just about Awoyana, but about groups of aliens from different parts of the Midwest. They mentioned the aliens in Milwaukee as well as aliens from camps in Winnipeg and Minneapolis. After half a minute of rapid-fire chatter, the Elders turned to Shermie.

"You know our language," they said, all of them speaking together, in a sort of eight-part harmony. "You have shared your stories with us. Now we want to share ours with you. We need your help in spreading our true history."

Shermie nodded and cleared his throat.

"Okay, folks," he said, turning to the group of staring humans behind him, "they want to tell us *their* story."

The snake-hairs began with a familiar tale Shermie had heard before, back in his rundown shack outside Macy, Nebraska. He began translating for the humans behind him.

"Their sun lost its heat," he said, warmed by the glow of the floating hair-tentacle in front of him, his fingers no longer itching for the comforting cylinder of a cigarillo. "They knew they would have to leave some day, but they couldn't until their astronomers—the Stargazers—found another world to move to. So they went underground, far from the cold, and many generations passed."

Shermie glanced at the humans behind him as he spoke. He thought that the priest was following along with the snake-hairs' words, but judging from the confused look on his face and the sweat on his forehead, he was having trouble keeping up with them.

Shermie listened to the Elders explain their ancient ships, their deep sleep, and their seemingly endless time spent jammed together on their journey here. He translated as fast as he could, his own face getting hot and sweaty from the effort.

"They hadn't had much choice in leaving their world. They had waited generations, caring for the ships of the Ancestors, biding their time until their Stargazers sent back the location of another, suitable world. They started up their ships that had been waiting, unused, for many generations, and they made the long voyage here. They all slept the deep sleep until the ships came crashing down to Earth.

"And then, after only a short time here—'four times four times ten short cycles,' as they call it—their people began to grow ill. The sicknesses struck many down," he said, and stopped. He squinted up at the eight old snake-hairs in front of them, who were holding the last note of their story in perfect, unwavering clarity.

"Sicknesses?" Shermie repeated. Hadn't Awoyana mentioned something about this? Shermie had forgotten about that, until now. Until it was probably too late.

The Elders continued their story, answering his question in song. He glanced back at his human cohorts and saw that all of them were absorbed in the story he was translating for them.

"The sicknesses fill the camps now," Shermie said, his voice cracking. "And there are many variations and apparently many different causes. Some suffer from Blur addiction, to the point where the drug is the only things the aliens can ingest. They burn themselves out—that's the only way I can translate it.

"Then there are those who were struck down by the heat last summer and still haven't recovered. The heat caused many outbursts of violence, and still others are recovering from the wounds suffered at the hands of their brothers and sisters. They fill the camp hospitals, leaving little room for the newly sick.

"And then there are the Wannoshay who suffer from what they call 'soul-curdling.' They keep beating themselves up—not so much physically, but mentally and emotionally—for something they did in the days before they ever came here."

"That," Joshua said behind him in a low voice, "sounds like what we Catholics call *guilt.* Oh, Johndo."

Shermie listened to the Elders as their song slowed. One by one they stopped singing, until only one continued the song. It was the tallest one, the one at the far right of the line of metal chairs.

He took a shuddering breath as the mixed song of the eight Wannoshay came to an end. The Elders sat back on their bouncing chairs of thin black metal and waited for him to finish translating.

"If nothing is done to stop this sickness," Shermie said, his words echoing around him in the flat black walls of the room, "none of the Wannoshay will survive to see next year."

He swallowed, needing a sharp kick of tobacco more than ever before in his life.

"They will either die from this illness, or kill each other from it. The soul curdling drives them all crazy. And once the strongest of them kill the weakest, the Elders fear they will turn to humans next."

The other humans behind him shuffled and muttered back and forth, and the ship felt suddenly colder.

"So our mission," Shermie said, as if trying to convince himself as well as his human counterparts, "after the explosions and the camps and the labor farms, and now this strange sickness that's affecting them, is to convince the rest of the world to help the Wannoshay."

He didn't dare look at his fellow humans for fear of the looks of disbelief that would be reflected back at him. He felt the same emotion coursing through him. This was the last thing he'd been expecting to hear from the Elders. They wanted them to do the impossible.

With a whisper of air, the glowing hair-tentacle that had been hovering a few inches in front of him dropped to the floor with a dull thud.

Interlude Two

The shuddering guilt-sick and the Blurred are now everywhere I look, every place I turn, every face I see.

All of them, Late.

Coming here, they have been coming here for the past four times four short-cycles. More with each new sun, bringing with them more energy and suffering, all suffering, all carrying their own version of the sickness. So many sicknesses, so many. The smells of all the new arrivals are overwhelming.

They fill the halls of the Mother Ship in a weak replication of our journey here, but instead of casks they lie discarded like trash against the walls, twitching on the comforting metal floors. Twitching with sickness. They press together as if wishing for the spent energy and security of the sleeping casks, but the casks are no more, no more.

None of us will travel again, I fear. I fear.

And the masses of sick, once they have arrived here, continue to suffer. They wake only to attack one another in a fit of Lateness before succumbing again to their own lassitude.

I walk these halls, an insomniac again. Feeling the sickness around me threatening to take hold of me, I try to distinguish the different variations of the ailments. Some wear the scars of the Blur hard upon their faces, and their twitching has been sped up by this human drug infecting their bloodstreams. Others have retreated within themselves, into the memories we as Elders had thought we'd been able to block. It is these who I fear for the most, the People whose souls are curling in upon them.

The sicknesses are threatening to take hold of me, taking hold of me.

So many of them, Late.

I will focus all of my energies on my People. I will try not to think that their unseeing eyes are seeing the abandonment of Twilight on our home world. Yet I can tell by their moans and whispers that they are reliving those final moments with their inner eyes.

Others of the sick rage, while still others freeze with some combination of both symptoms, along with the taint they brought with them on the ships—the mixture of Dawn and Twilight.

My People. They are dying around me, and I know of only one cure, only one.

But that cure is an impossibility, one which I should not even entertain. Not unless all other options have been attempted; attempted, and then attempted again.

For I do not relish the thought of what it would cost us all to attempt to one more journey.

Until that desperate measure comes to pass, hoping against time and the forces of this too-warm plant, I shall entrust myself to the Father Joshua and his friends and hope that they will prove sufficient. Sufficiency is all we ask. I do my best, using what wild energy I can spare without succumbing to any of the sicknesses myself (I cannot let myself succumb), trying to ease the suffering of the afflicted.

I cannot let myself succumb.

All of them, Late.

I must not succumb.

For we have no place left to run.

Chapter Twenty-Two

The Old Capitol Mall in downtown Iowa City had never witnessed this kind of desperate commerce before, and one filmmaker, someone who had been gone for far too long, managed to capture it all.

The footage begins with a hand. The camera holds tight on it, drawing into harsh detail the four thick gray fingers being held palm-up. The square-knuckled hand is reaching out for something, waiting with the slightest quiver to it, alone in the dim light. A Wannoshay hand.

And then a pair of battered black gloves blur across the screen, from out of nowhere. Just like that, the short-fingered hand is now holding what looks like a dozen pink capsules.

The camera pulls back in time to show the other gray hand passing the gloved figure something dark and lumpy. The smaller figure glows with the flickering red of a dying light stick. The camera moves closer again, smooth and confident, yet the object wrapped in brown paper—payment? food?—is not identifiable.

A sigh from the perspective of the filmer, something that would have been edited out in most Netstreams before upload, but a choice has been made at some point not to do so. That choice is like a signature; Wantaviewer's work has always carried that kind of untampered authenticity.

A quick flash of widening perspective and the area surrounding the owners of the hands comes into focus: overturned shelves, torn piles of paper piled into long beds, and a wall of broken screens. A few of the shelves still remain standing, but all the books and miniature discs from the old store are gone, the books most likely burned for heat, and the discs turned into tools or weapons, or possibly used for barter in the open area of the old mall, in the dried-out fountain area. A pair of metallic books sit untouched next to the alien Blur user, glinting in the fluttering light cast by the Blur dealer's muffled light stick.

The figure in the dark jacket is moving away by the time the camera has zoomed out. After dousing the light stick with a flick of his or her wrist, the dealer slips out through the broken door at the far end of the old store, never to be seen again.

Without zooming, the camera holds on the alien standing alone. The lighting effects from the camera illuminate the delicate white scars on the face of the female alien and show the glistening layer of condensation covering her features.

All that moves are her hair-tentacles, dark blue-black cords that flop and quiver across her head. Some stretch down as if trying to get a better look at (or possibly to smell) the capsules. Her hand remains there, palm up and at chest level, holding the pills for a long, silent moment.

And then the capsules disappear into her thin plastic jacket, and she takes three long steps on her short, thick legs in the direction of the camera. One moment she is there, looming like a gray, growing shadow—surely she has seen the person filming by now—and the next moment she has dropped from view.

She has gone into the tunnels under the mall-turned-camp.

With barely a pause, the camera follows her. Without the Blur dealer's light stick, the visibility is next to nothing, so again the lighting effects from the camera are activated. Down a ten-foot drop (the operator grunts and swears, a female voice) and then a choice of paths.

The dim heat-display coming from the alien's body appears

in the passage ahead—the camera operator is fast, switching modes almost instantaneously like that—and the camera follows it down smooth, rounded walls covered in minute scratches. Claw marks.

This tunnel is so well-used it appears to be more than a couple years old, but that's impossible. This camp was the abandoned husk of a mall a year ago.

A year ago, the world was just learning about the aliens called the Wannoshay.

Moving through four turns, left-left-right-left, the tunnel always the same width, symmetrical and scratched. The walls slide past in blue-gray murkiness. There is a slight pause as the image freezes for a second on a widening gap in the tunnel. The tunnel ends in an oblong room, glowing with a sickly blue-green light.

In this room are over a dozen of the Wannoshay, including the sweating female with the Blur bought from the abandoned store. Pulsing and twitching, kicking out where they lay or pacing as they stood, the aliens here remain in motion, a sharp contrast to the calmness of the female alien the filmer has followed here.

When the camera finds this alien again, however, she is shivering as well, but in a controlled way that makes it obvious she didn't want anyone to see her doing so.

Even more unsettling than the sight of the restless aliens are the sounds they make. They hum and sing in low voices that are almost too high-pitched to hear. Birdsong has never sounded so mournful or pained. The melody is threadbare without sounding like moaning, accompanied by occasional scratching at the dirt floor with feet or hands as if trying to reach a persistent itch.

The camera operator makes another sound that is added to the soundtrack, a sudden exhalation of air that sounds like a mix of satisfaction and horror.

The female alien with the freshly bought Blur starts passing out capsules, one to each alien stretched out on the floor. After a closer look, it becomes obvious that the number of aliens in the room as well as the amount of Blur held by the female have been underestimated. There are easily three dozen aliens here, packed tightly into the rounded dirt walls under the old shopping mall. More wander into the room at the whispery sound of Blur capsules rattling together.

The female Wannoshay leaves another capsule with one of the motionless and bedridden aliens, and from all sides needy hands reach out to her. Whether they long for the drug or simply for a touch, it is not clear.

One of the first aliens to ingest a capsule stops humming. He's an elderly male with short, white-tipped hair-tentacles, and he rolls onto all fours and then slaps himself in the forehead—third eye closed tight enough to disappear. The sound of flesh meeting flesh, coupled with the low growling that has begun in his long chest, make the rest of the sick aliens fall silent.

His shoulders hitch four times in succession, as if he is hiccuping or sneezing, and then he begins to shake. The shaking leads to convulsions that make his body appear liquid, rolling with waves of agony.

And then, instead of doing the expected and collapsing onto the bed of shredded paper below him, he leaps to his feet. His hands are up and swinging, but none of his blows land on his neighbors. The female with the Blur has grabbed him from behind and eased him back to the dirt floor with a gentle, insistent strength that is surprising to witness.

The elderly man, as soon as he is on his back again, stops struggling. In what must be a trick of the camera's lighting mechanism, a flash of white light leaps out of all three of his eyes before they close.

In that moment of brightness, all movement in the room stops. Every single Wannoshay in the cave turn almost expectantly to look the elderly man.

The 'Stream footage holds on this tableau for ten seconds.

The silence is complete; even the filmer must have been holding his or her breath. The light begins to dim. The only movement is the occasional drip of sweat from a motionless body or a minute twitch of a muscular shoulder or hand. The aliens watch the dying man. The camera holds steady during the stretched series of seconds.

Somewhere from the darkened back corner of the room, a high voice begins to moan with heartwrenching sadness, and the body of the elderly Wannoshay man begins to lift into the air.

All but four of the gathered Wannoshay reach up for him. These four stand in the right-hand corner of the cave, distracted by something offscreen.

And the dying alien releases more of the intense white light that had slipped from his three eyes earlier. It starts in his eyes and chest, bursting out of him so quickly it's impossible to remember what he looked like in the moments before the light covered him.

In the last second of 'Stream footage remaining—before the camera was apparently overwhelmed with light and energy and ceased to work—the four distracted aliens turn completely toward whatever it was that had distracted them.

When the camera freezes for a final time on a screen of white, peppered only with faded dots that on further examination turn out to be sets of black alien eyes opened wide, the twelve eyes of the four distracted Wannoshay are half-lidded, as if preparing for sleep.

If you look closely enough you can see their bodies in the

process of hunching over. The others stand tall on two legs, arms lifted into the air and awaiting the energy coming from the levitating alien at the moment of his death.

The scene remains locked in that instant, a tortured breath torn forever caught between living and dying, and even the *thought* of looking away refuses to enter your mind.

"You piece of total fucking shit."

Ally leaned back from her wooden editing chair in front of the wallscreen and rubbed her eyes. Her voice was more resigned than angry, as if she'd been swearing at the footage since the instant it was made, and the curses had become almost a mantra over the course of the past few hours. Her heart just wasn't in it to be mad at her equipment any more.

Not after what she'd seen—and filmed—yesterday.

She looked back at the frozen white wallscreen dotted with random circles of black and wondered what good would have come from the lost footage if her camera hadn't locked up from the rush of light and energy in the dirt-walled cave.

Probably not much, she decided.

The events following that burst of light, with the dying or maybe even dead alien floating almost five feet off the ground, were hazy at best in her mind. She had been over forty feet away from the Wannoshay sick room, yet the footage had been crystal clear, thanks to the zoom capabilities of the eyebrow camera the military had entrusted her with (thanks to Colonel Cossa, she thought with a wry grin, amazed at the company she was keeping these days).

Before she realized the camera had stopped working, someone else had entered the cave from a side tunnel she hadn't noticed at the time.

This new arrival had distracted the four aliens at the outer fringe of the gathered Wannoshay.

"You're too late to help him," she'd whispered to whoever (or whatever) had just entered the cave, and the sound of her own voice had surprised her. She thought of her talks with her Wannoshay friend Brando from her days back in Canada, and remembered how he would use that word. "You're . . . *Late.*"

All she'd been able to see was a shadow approximately the same size of the surrounding aliens. She'd thought she was still taping at the time.

The shadow made a whistling sound, and then the white energy spilling out of the floating man from the inside out was channeled across the room in a river of light, toward the shadow. Somehow the shadow creature absorbed all of the energy without any of it piercing the shadows or illuminating the intruder.

She'd felt an aching sense of loss coming from both the aliens around her and from herself. She'd talked with Father Joshua about what she'd seen, and he told her about the transforming power of the energy of the two Wanta boys that had washed over him.

A part of Ally had *wanted* that, probably a bigger part of her than she was willing to admit. Make me better with your energy, she'd thought.

But the dying alien's light had been stolen. The energy thief had slipped away as soon quickly as it had appeared, and the four witnesses were left facedown on the dirt floor.

Ally would never know if they were killed or simply incapacitated, because a cold fear had gripped her heart and filled her with panic. The aliens inside the sick room were starting to realize what had happened, and they were growing angry.

She'd turned and fled back through the tunnels under the camp, trying to remember the way out, wishing with every step for one last capsule of Blur to help her move faster, faster.

Thinking back on it now, she was glad that she hadn't had to make a choice about how much of the footage she needed to cut. She didn't want to introduce the shadowy creature she thought of as the energy thief to the minds of the people who used her Netstream to download the latest footage of the Wantas. She needed to send the right message to people about the aliens, and it couldn't contain even the slightest hint of danger.

"It was for the best," she muttered, as if assuring herself for the umpteenth time. "It was a *good* thing my piece of total fucking shit camera chose that exact moment to lock up on me. Really it was."

With a sigh, she stared at the last image of her footage and shivered. She thought about how the dying alien's energy had been pulled away, like a beam of light sucked down by an irresistible gravity. Did that old alien disappear from existence after that? Did he know his energy hadn't been dispersed to his brothers and sisters, but instead to some greedy bastard who took it all for himself or herself?

Ally hoped not.

She yawned and stretched in the overly warm editing room she and her friends had set up in the Iowa Memorial Union during the weeks since their visit to the Mother Ship. Outside, the sun was coming up, and she hadn't even realized the night had passed. The last time she'd checked the time was four in the afternoon.

She clicked down the heat from the remote built into her chair; she was always hot these days, it seemed, even in late February. She wanted to blame it on the lack of Blur, but she was feverish with a different kind of want these days.

It wasn't the burning need for Blur—she still had all of her capsules left over from her bus trip from Canada, the pills lined up next to the three smaller screens on her editing desk like tiny pink bombs. Most days she forgot they were there. Other days she looked at them and clenched her jaw at all the time she'd lost under the influence of capsules like them.

There was just too much she wanted to do these days to muck around with Blur. After that chaotic night in Winnipeg, many of the aliens were now hooked on Blur and sick from it. She owed it to the Wantas to help them however she could, even if it meant making movies again.

"Wantaviewer's triumphant return," she said with a smile.

Aiming her editing joystick at the wallscreen, she looked back at the image of the energy coming from the fading Wannoshay. Father Joshua had more knowledge of the aliens than anyone else she'd ever talked with, even more than Shermie, who spoke their language fluently like the crazy old bird he was. In the past six weeks since meeting them, she'd learned more than she could have ever imagined about the Wantas.

But nothing beat the firsthand knowledge she could have gotten from one of her oldest friends. Wherever Brando was these days, if he wasn't sick or already dead.

She realized that she'd known Brando almost a year now. She knew she should've done more for him. She couldn't remember anyone in her life, outside of her family, who she'd been able to remain friends with for more than six months.

My oldest, closest friend is a Wanta, she thought with a sad laugh.

She shook her head and told herself to focus on the job at hand. They needed this footage put together and on the 'Streams today. Public sentiment about the aliens was still dangerously low, but she liked to think that her recent set of downloads was improving the average Joe's perspective about the Wantas. Her download numbers had never been higher.

She made a few adjustments to the footage, trying to clarify some of the fuzzier images (even though it went against her instincts—she was from the old-fashioned film-it-and-upload-it school of vid-bloggers), and got ready to save the footage. She knew this footage would open some eyes, though a part of her hated herself for putting it on her 'Stream.

It was sensationalistic journalism, aiming for the heartstrings, going for the gut. But it was going to take shocks like this to get people out of their secluded home fortresses and wake them up before an entire race of beings went extinct right in front of their scared, do-nothing selves.

With a final click of her editing joystick, she uploaded the interrupted footage. An icon shaped like an old-fashioned movie camera in the corner of the wallscreen flashed red, then blue, and beeped. The footage was live and ready for anyone to download and watch.

"Learn from it, you bastards," Ally whispered. "Learn *something.*"

She was dozing in her editing chair in front of the frozen wallscreen filled with alien energy when Shontera and Toshera came at eight a.m. as usual. Ally shook herself awake and croaked a greeting to them. Her mouth was painfully dry.

" 'Morning," Shontera said, rolling her eyes and smiling at Ally in a motherly manner. "Another all-nighter, Wantaviewer?"

"Yeah," Ally said, fishing around in her desk for an unopened bag of water. Her throat was starting to hurt. "How are you two doing?"

"Good," Shontera said with a quick glance at her daughter. When Toshera wasn't looking, she pointed at her right temple and shook her head. The sadness in her face told the rest of the story: Toshera's headaches were back.

Everyone's sick, Ally thought, nodding at Shontera with what she hoped was a supportive expression.

She still had a hard time believing that she and the black woman next to her were almost the same age. She felt like a failure compared to all that Shontera had done in her life, and

Shontera's maturity and warmth made her feel like a shallow teenager.

"Got the footage from yesterday uploaded," Ally said. "It's good stuff."

Shontera paused in the act of passing Toshera a keypad.

"I thought you didn't have to have that done until the end of the day."

"I can't stand not having fresh footage sitting around for no one to see." Ally yawned and began flipping through her list of To-Dos from her handheld 'Stream. "And I didn't see the point of making anyone wait. Especially our friends outside."

"Hey, Ally," Toshera said from her chair next to the window. "It's supposed to be fifty-*eight* today, can you believe that? And it's not even March yet."

The young girl perched on the edge of her chair, looking out at the Mother Ship, which filled half the window like a black shadow in the morning light.

"Wow," Ally said, not sure what else to say to that weather report.

"That's right," Shontera said to both Ally and her daughter. "If what the Elders say is true, the warmer it gets, the more violent the sick will get. I guess they didn't have to worry about the heat down in the tunnels, you know?"

"I'd go crazy living underground," Toshera said, absently massaging her temples. "Not being able to see the sun or breathe fresh air."

Ally felt something cold creep down her spine as she listened to the mother and daughter talk. Staring at the wallscreen again, her handheld 'Stream forgotten, her eyes lost their focus.

The black dots in the frozen screen of white began to swirl and shift, forming an image that was both familiar and alien to her tired mind. She didn't dare look away from it.

The white of the screen morphed into a frozen field a

hundred times bigger than the field next to the student union, and this white field, tinged with blue, was unbroken by any ship.

The perspective began to move over the field at an impossible speed, zooming over black rocks that now littered the field. The rocks became more numerous, growing larger and sharper until they formed jagged mountains passing by scant inches below the onrushing camera. Tufts of thick blue grass stubbornly poked out of the crevices and gaps in the mountains, all of it looking frigid and dead.

And then there were caves, hundreds of them opening up from the mountainside. As she stared, the vine-covered entrances to the caves began to shimmer and disappear, as if sealing themselves off from the world, protecting the inhabitants who were fleeing the blue-tinted sunlight illuminating the aboveground world.

A line of caves still remained open to the outside world, though, and even as the skies around her darkened, she felt as if she needed to go back to these vulnerable entrances. Something could get in, or out. She wanted to go back and help close them if possible, but already the caves were blurring out of the frame. It was too late to go back.

Bad technique, she thought in her critic's voice, teasing the viewer like that. Wantaviewer. Her hands were fists and she wanted to scream. Teasing Wantaviewer. Too late to go back. Late.

Inside her head, Ally felt an image or idea trying to come into focus. Something just out of her field of vision, past the corner of her eye.

"Ally?" Someone was calling her, and it took three more repetitions of her name for her to realize she'd been asleep sitting up. Shontera touched Ally's back and said her name one more time.

"Whoa," Ally said. "Sorry 'bout that. Must've dozed off."

The wallscreen in front of her had gone black, and Shontera was bent close, worry in her dark brown eyes.

"You were moaning," she whispered. "And saying something about being late?"

Ally's face grew even warmer than usual. "Sorry. Been working too hard."

"Let me know if there's anything I can do to help. I'm just working on some 'Stream calls and message board stuff today. Why don't you get some rest?"

"Good plan," Ally said. She gave Shontera a sheepish smile, glad that Toshera hadn't paid any attention to her while she had been in la-la land. "Thanks."

She rolled back to her desk, but before she left for her room in the other wing of the union, she couldn't help but check her 'Stream for downloads and messages. Barely three hours had passed since her upload, but she'd already had almost a hundred downloads of the new footage, and half that many messages.

I should do this later, she told herself, but she was already running her finger down the screen to access her messages.

She was used to crank messages on her 'Stream, but the anger of the first few responses to her footage was enough to make her catch her breath. Many of the notes were written all in capital letters.

"Why?" the first message all but screamed at her from the handheld's rectangular screen. "Why should we help THEM? What have the Wantas done for us?"

Unable to stop now, she scrolled through the rest of the messages, even as a dozen more people downloaded the footage, and more messages continued coming in.

"Good riddance, I say! They were sick before they ever got here."

"At least they're contained in the camps."

"FUCK THE WANTAS! GIVE EM BLUR TILL THEY BLEED!!!"

"We never should have allowed them to live with us in the first place."

"Fucking Wantas got what they deserved."

Only a handful of messages had anything helpful or positive to say. And two of those message-writers had offered to help somehow.

Ally tried to focus on *these* people, the ones they'd been able to touch with the footage they'd taken and uploaded in the weeks since meeting with the Elders. The ratio of bad to good responses was almost overwhelming, and she knew that.

But they had to start somewhere. Spring was on its way, and then the heat of summer. According to forecasters, this summer was going to be the hottest in decades.

Ally dug through the junk on her desk and found a stim tab and her eyebrow camera. She picked up her coat and waved goodbye to Toshera and Shontera. Shontera gave her a questioning look, but all Ally could do was give her a smile on the way out of the office room.

Wiping sweat from her forehead, she put the stim tab on her tongue and headed for the stairs leading down and outside. Sleep was out of the question now. There was too much footage to grab, too much work to be done. She had to get the word out, one upload at a time.

Chapter Twenty-Three

His early-morning walk around the roadblocked area surrounding the Mother Ship and the student union had become a favorite part of Father Joshua's day. Some days, when he knew the People would be moving about in the open air inside the Old Capitol mall encampment, Joshua walked up the steep hill and followed the twelve-foot-high wall surrounding the detainment camp set up in the abandoned shopping mall. The camp's presence in the heart of the city was unlike any other camp he'd ever seen; the others were out in the country, on cemented plots of cropland, living in shacks and used Quonset huts.

But the weather today was unnaturally warm and sunny, just as it had been all week, and Joshua knew the People would remain inside. He settled for two big circles around the Mother Ship for his morning walk. He'd visit the camp later, if he had time.

While a chain-link fence surrounded the Mother Ship, the various types of vehicles parked in front of the fence was what created the true barriers for the towering black ship. Some were official vehicles, like the Hummers or the lone Bradley armored vehicle next to Danforth Chapel that Joshua was now passing, but the majority of them belonged to private citizens.

Every day people drove their cars, trucks, and vans to the site of the Mother Ship, some to protest, others to "keep an eye on things," and yet others to simply become part of the controlled chaos that now filled Hubbard Field and spilled over into the rest of Iowa City.

He walked through the growing crowd and slipped past the first roadblock of Hummers and police cars, surprised that the vehicles had become so familiar to him. He unzipped his jacket and watched the activity inside the fence. The air was filled with the soft, lilting sounds of Wannoshay voices, singing.

This morning he counted close to a dozen new structures that had cropped up around the Mother Ship, seemingly overnight. Made of the same dull black metal as the big ship, the structures came in various sizes, and they were scattered in no logical order across every open space next to the ship. Many of them were rounded like caves or the Quonsets in the Minnesota camp that he remembered all too well, while those closer to the fence were all jagged angles, with the occasional spire sticking from the top.

The overwhelmed military and police officers could do nothing to stop the Wannoshay from taking over the field, entering it from above ground and below ground, so they agreed to simply watch over the entrances to the Mother Ship and do their best not to interfere.

At all times, the People sang in their native tongue, songs that Joshua could almost understand, though the words seemed to have been used wrong, in the wrong order, possibly. Their true meaning eluded him.

The high-pitched hum of their songs had become as much a part of the background noise of the Mother Ship as the trickle of water from the melting snow or the Iowa River flowing behind the black ship. He wondered why the People had never sang in the camps, but then he remembered the song of forgiveness he'd heard during the last few moments of the two boys in the Minneapolis camp. Maybe that was when the singing had started, he thought.

Joshua paused to greet a group of young Wannoshay men and

women before returning to his walk. Two of them, he noticed, had a familiar twitching in their arms, and half had the facial scars that came from Blur abuse. Their chat through the fence was brief, and then the People ambled on four legs back to their black-metal shantytown around the Mother Ship.

More of the People came to the site each day, carrying or wearing bits of flexible black metal, most likely salvaged from their original ship before the rioters and cultists had destroyed them. They used the flexible metal to build the structures in which they were staying.

Late at night, on his way through the new encampment after a long day of working with Johndo and the other Elders, Joshua often could have sworn he heard, along with the burbling songs of the People, the scratching sounds of digging.

As he ambled past the encampment and grew close to the colonel's invisible tent, he greeted the soldiers in their shifting green-and-yellow camouflage uniforms. He wondered how many invisible soldiers patrolled this and the surrounding areas. Security had been tightened in the past few weeks, as rumors flew about the alien sicknesses and the violent outbursts increased.

More humans were visiting the site as well, watching the activity from the other side of the fence with a mix of fascination and morbid curiosity. It seemed that Wantaviewer's Netstream downloads were raising awareness faster than any other means imaginable.

Wiping sweat from his forehead, Joshua saw the Mother Ship on his right, behind a group of soldiers reinforcing a cut in the fence with barbed wire. Coming up in front of him was a fifty-person-strong group of masked protestors. He slowed, trying to remember what Private Petersheim from the Waukegan site had called them that day, when they'd almost run over one of them.

The name clicked when Joshua saw the bathrobes and rubber

monster masks.

"ET freaks," he whispered, moving in a wide arc to his left to avoid them. They were strung out the length of the eastern side of the fence, shoulder to shoulder, masked faces and index fingers pointing at the People within.

From what Joshua could see on his way past, the People were ignoring the humans and going about their business, singing softly to themselves. The People darted about from structure to structure in the warm sun, as if trying to get back to shelter as fast as possible. A few moved more slowly, and they were headed for the lowered ramp of the Mother Ship, where all the sick had gathered.

The sight of one of the young People limping away from him toward the Mother Ship, long arms flailing occasionally in some sort of violent spasm, made Joshua cut short his morning walk. It was time for him to get to work. He'd been keeping long hours, both inside the Mother Ship and in the research station inside the student union. He and the colonel, along with a surprisingly helpful and industrious Shermie, worked on ways to help the People recover from their many-symptomed epidemic.

Joshua passed through the checkpoint outside the second of two gates leading to the Mother Ship. He hurried to catch up with the young Wannoshay limping toward the ship. Gray faces poked out from tents, calling his name, but he could only nod and hurry past.

Before he could catch up to the young Wannoshay, however, the shirtless boy stumbled. He landed face first in the dirty slush of melted snow, hair-tentacles waving and beating at the ground, exposing the pink derm patch on the back of his neck. The patch was the same color as the splotches on the boy's arms and spreading across his wide, ridged back.

Approaching with slow, deliberate steps, making sure the boy could hear him, Joshua squatted down and reached out a bare hand to the boy's quivering shoulder. He waited for the now-familiar shock he felt whenever he touched one of the People, but the boy was so ill that Joshua felt just a tiny spark, like a weak spit of static.

He turned the boy over, surprised at how heavy he was. The boy gave off a too-sweet smell, like overripe apples.

All three of the boy's eyes were closed, and the Blur scars radiating out from his lipless mouth confirmed Joshua's worst fears. Keeping just out of reach of the boy's long arms, he waited for the inevitable lashing out that the sick couldn't help but do when agitated. But, except for his dancing hair-tentacles, this boy was still.

"Let's get you inside," Joshua murmured. He inched closer. "We've got people inside who can help."

The boy groaned and began muttering something in a high, quavering voice. It took Joshua a moment to realize the boy was speaking in English.

"Don' let her . . ." the boy said, slurring the words together. Joshua leaned closer. "Don't let her . . . take me . . . take me . . ."

"You're safe now." Joshua wanted to simply pick the boy up in his arms and hurry him inside, but he knew such a sudden movement would do more damage than good, and could even kill the boy in the muddy snow next to him. "No one will hurt you—"

Joshua felt something give in his chest, as if a hand had reached up and squeezed his heart. The boy's sweet smell had turned sour, like the hot sweat of the fevered. He looked down.

All three of the Wannoshay boy's eyes were open and locked on Joshua's chest. The clenching sensation inside Joshua's rib-cage intensified, making him want to cry out, but the air had left his lungs. He fumbled inside his coat for the transmitter that connected him instantly with the colonel, but his fingers acted as if they belonged to someone else's hands.

Not again, Lord, Joshua thought as images of Matthew and Eli and Johndo and all the other People he'd ever met flashed through his mind. This can't happen now.

"Someone . . . *touched* you . . . wild energy . . ."

The three black eyes widened almost impossibly, showing traces of white at the edges as the boy spoke in a tight whisper, slurring his hard consonants.

"Protect us . . ." the boy wheezed. "Protect us . . . from . . . ourselves . . ."

At the moment when Joshua thought his heart would stop, the tightness in his chest disappeared, as if at the press of a button. The world went gray for a few seconds as he fought to stay conscious, and he was only able to do so by looking down at the boy next to him. The young Wannoshay's face was ashy-white, and his black eyes were nothing but razor-thin slits.

"Bro-deckh ush," the boy had said in his fading, gasping voice. The sound of it was burned into Joshua's head, echoing louder than the hatch of the Waukegan ship slamming closed. "Bro-deckh ush bruhm ourshelvshs . . ."

He pulled out the transmitter in his coat pocket and hit the Call button for the colonel.

"Send help to the front of the ship," he told the soldier on the other end of the connection as he sank back into the wet snow. "Fast," he added, looking at the motionless boy next to him.

A group of People from the surrounding black structures came running up on all fours, and Joshua wondered for an angry instant where they'd been a few seconds ago when his heart was being squeezed by the boy.

Then he was pulled to his feet and, following the four People now carrying the stricken Wannoshay boy over their heads, he was led inside the Mother Ship by a mixed group of soldiers and the People. By the time they were at the top of the ramp the pain in his chest had fled, and he felt as strong physically as he'd felt since that day in the Minnesota camp, sitting above two other Wannoshay boys.

"Wild energy," he whispered, and waved off a questioning look from one of the soldiers helping him.

He felt like he'd been pulled and manipulated by too many puppeteers, both human and alien, and he needed to talk to Johndo about the boy's message to him. Father Joshua hoped the boy's plea for protection would not be the young Wannoshay's final words spoken on this world.

Joshua loved watching the Elders work, even if he couldn't figure out how their tech functioned. As far as he could tell, they accessed data in the Mother Ship by simply grabbing a piece of wall and manipulating it with their hands or fingertoes. Making their work even more opaque to Joshua, the Elders used no tools or equipment as part of their healing rituals.

After fifteen minutes of watching three of the eight Elders work on the boy inside the laboratory of the Mother Ship—the air filling with waves of power that Joshua felt as if he could touch, like branches on a tree—Joshua knew it was time to see his old friend Johndo again. But before he could leave, he had to know about the boy.

"Will he make it?" he asked the female Elder at the boy's feet, who was securing him with a thin metal blanket attached to the bed. The two dozen other beds in the lab were also occupied.

The Elder nodded and touched her right temple with a shaking hand. She'd been sick herself for the past week, and the "soul-curdling" was taking a toll on her in addition to her long hours in the lab. Her blue hair-tentacles were only as long as index fingers, and her wide shoulders were not hunched forward like the other Elders. Her name was Iyalloshay.

"He arrived here just in time," Iyalloshay said in a voice Joshua heard only inside his head. "He had high levels of what your people call adrenaline in his system, caused by some sort of fear that lead him here. Did you see anything that may have caused this?"

"Nothing," Joshua said, wiping sweat from his forehead. "He seemed to be afraid of someone coming after him. One of the People. A female, I believe."

Iyalloshay's eyes narrowed the tiniest bit.

"That is . . . disturbing." She looked down at the boy stretched out on the table next to them, his breathing shallow but regular. "Thank you for your help," she said. "We'll take care of young Yowinnoh here."

"Thank you," Joshua said, pulling himself grudgingly away from the busy wonders of the lab, even though his mental chat with the Elder had left him hot and shaky. Outside, he hurried down a sloping corridor and up a narrow side-passage, careful not to step on the sleeping sick and keeping out of the way of the humans and Wannoshay tending to them.

He'd forgotten all about the day that Johndo had given him the scar on his cheek—the wound refused to completely disappear from his face—until he walked into Johndo's small room aboard the ship.

He'd been busy working with the colonel in the student union for the past week, and he hadn't seen Johndo at all during that time. The change in his friend was shocking, and the fear from the day Johndo had attacked him returned with a rush.

Johndo squatted with his back against the wall, hands on his thighs, eyes closed, ignoring the two metal chairs and the mat in front of them. The low black shelf encircling the room was empty again. Johndo sang softly under his breath, and every few seconds he would shiver and his song would stop in mid-note, then pick up again. Johndo's skin, while not anywhere near as light as the boy Joshua had encountered that morning, was a much lighter gray than usual, with pink splotches on his chin and forehead.

Like so many of the People, Johndo was sick.

"Talk to me," Johndo said without looking at Joshua. "Talk, talking, talk."

His voice melted back into his song, the words rising from his lilting tune and then disappearing again. The room smelled like burnt coffee with a hint of salty sweat. Johndo's breath rattled inside his chest, and his hands turned into fists.

Father, protect us all, Joshua thought and stepped into the room.

"Johndo," he began, "my old friend. I miss our talks. You know, we have known each other for quite a long time now."

"Many cycles." Johndo still hadn't opened his eyes. "From cold to hot to cold to now hot again. Your world has so many cycles, so different from *Wannoshay.* Many, many cycles. But no Wannoshay cycle."

Joshua cleared his throat and tried to start again.

"We have shared histories together, Johndo. We have learned each other's languages. We have become friends."

Johndo opened his two lower eyes and looked steadily at Joshua, as if he knew what was coming next. Taking a deep breath, Joshua ran a hand across his chest and tried to forget about the crushing sensation he'd felt there earlier that morning.

"Johndo, I ask two things of you today, my friend. I know you are tired, but we must talk. First, I ask you to teach me your true name. Second, I ask you to tell me all you know about this sickness that is killing the People. Please. Tell me all of your true history, so that we can help you."

Johndo's black eyes regarded Joshua for a long moment that stretched on for almost a minute. His short hair-tentacles quivered like waving fingers, while the rest of him remained completely still. Joshua met his gaze, feeling the strength of his own faith mix with the wild energy of the People that the boy had spoken of earlier that morning.

I'll take whatever help I can get at this point, he thought. From heaven above, or elsewhere.

At last Johndo spoke one word as his arms reached up to Joshua, his fingers stretching and encircling Joshua's head.

"Twilight," Johndo whispered, and then Joshua was gone.

The three we found guilty were not the first, and we knew they would not be the last to shed blood in the caves. Caves we had created, caves they had overtaken. Their souls had already suffered the curdling, yet they had grown immune to the sensation, as if souls to them had become a luxury, something they did not need to survive.

The People of the Twilight were a cursed race, even if they were our cousins and of our bloodline. We once had an ocean separating the People of the Dawn from those of Twilight, but their Diggers could burrow deep and far.

With the help of their Mystics, they were able to tunnel deep, and they broke through the rocks far under the yellow ocean. They punched through rock we could not break, and they began to encroach upon our landmass.

At much the same time, with tunnels spreading like fingers throughout the black rock of our world, we had reached the end of our resources on *Wannoshay*. We were out of space.

Tunnels need rock to support them, and our claws had never been sharper than they were nearly four times four times four cycles ago, when the tunnels of Dawn first met up with the tunnels of Twilight. Our Diggers thought at first that they had miscalculated and done the unimaginable—breached the surface of our frozen world.

But the cold wasn't caused by the surface of *Wannoshay.* It was the presence of the People of the Twilight.

Meeting them for the first time was like looking at my People as through a distorting pool of water. Their arms were thicker than ours, their skin a few shades lighter (as if dipped in frost and stained permanently from the cold they loved so much). Their hair-tentacles were blue instead of black.

They spoke a fast and low-pitched language that took us many cycles to understand, but the main reason for the delay was due their nature. And their faith.

We thought we had met our match the day our tunnels met theirs, but something amazing happened instead. As we would learn later, the Twilight People had lived their lives singing songs about us, the darker-skinned of their race who had ascended from the world aboveground and watched over them from what your people would call the afterworld.

When their tunnels first met ours, their Diggers immediately prostrated themselves. They thought they had reached the afterworld and come face to face with their gods.

I am ashamed to admit that my People waited to inform the Twilight People of their mistake. In the cycles that would slowly pass, however, the People of the Dawn could not help but do so; we were prone to mistakes and weaknesses just like any other of our race. We were no gods.

The People of the Twilight did not take this new information well. Once awakened by our heresy, their anger was quick to surface again, and in the warmer climes of our tunnels, their outbursts came often. Much blood was spilled in the caverns, and there was talk of sending those who had spilled the blood of innocent into exile.

Even the unions of Twilight and Dawn appeared to be

doomed, as lover turned on lover and children were born with the taste of violence in their mouths.

So when the Stargazers returned, after being away for so long we assumed they were lost forever, our thoughts returned to our ancient ships. To escape this dying, overcrowded world. We'd managed to keep the knowledge of the ships hidden from our new guests, but we knew someday they would be discovered.

When the time came for us to climb aboard our Ancestors' ships and burst free from our dying world, we left without them.

We abandoned the People of the Twilight, and it is the memory of that weakness that is killing us. Our souls are being eaten up with guilt over the abandonment of our coarse cousins and violent bloodmates.

We left *Wannoshay* and Twilight and fled to your Earth. And it is here that we will all die for our sins. We are dying for them right now.

Joshua felt himself falling backward as the cold fingers released him, but he never hit the metal floor. Johndo caught him, and he was whispering something over and over to him, like a mother cooing over her newborn child.

"Iyannoloway," Johndo said. "Iyannoloway."

Joshua couldn't speak. He was remembering his first vision he'd had with Johndo, the crowd of the People surrounding the three lighter-skinned males. Dawn versus Twilight. Twilight versus Dawn.

"I am called Iyannoloway," Johndo said. "You asked for two things of me. I gave you both. But please, call me what you wish . . . my friend. Call me . . . friend . . ."

Joshua fought the urge to break free of Johndo's arms. He tasted something bitter as bile in his throat, and it felt like betrayal. He swallowed the taste and focused on forgiveness, just as the People sang on that day in the camp.

"Iyannoloway," Joshua said. "Johndo. We're all sinners."

"Not sin. Weakness. Fear. Not sin, Joshua."

Joshua took a deep breath and met Johndo's eyes. He was glad to see all three of them were open and focused, two horizontal and one vertical. He couldn't help himself; he had to ask.

"How many? How many were left behind?"

Johndo's eyes began to close as if in admission of his guilt, but Joshua inched closer and held the gaze of the Elder Wannoshay.

"More than we could fit on our ships. More than the number of our People aboard the four times seven ships and the Mother Ship combined. Hardy and strong, the People of the Twilight. They had many children, many families. Easily four times more of Twilight than Dawn. Our ships, not big enough . . ."

"Johndo," Joshua whispered. "If there wasn't room for them, what could you have done?"

"Made room!" Johndo said.

His right arm shot out, but Joshua had been ready. Johndo's clawed hand slapped at the air five inches from Joshua's face. Johndo let his arm drop onto the metal floor with a slapping sound.

"Could have made room for more," he said in a defeated voice. "Made room, made room . . ."

"Would your ships have made it here with more People aboard?"

Johndo just looked at him, and in his white-rimmed eyes Joshua could see the answer to his question: all the justification in the universe was not going to undo the fact that they had left their people behind.

"I have something for you," Joshua said, needing to fill the silence of the small room. "Something your people lent to me, and I've had it for too long. I'll bring it by tomorrow. We can talk more then. Now, rest."

Johndo reached out a short leg and snagged his woolen mat with two finger-toes. He spread it out in front of him and lay back on it. His right arm twitched once more, and then was still. The room was filled with the smell of wet dirt and chocolate.

Father Joshua stood over the Wannoshay Elder, the leader of People. Below him, Iyannoloway, better known as Johndo, lay flat on his back, ankles touching and wrists tight against his thighs. Even his short tentacle-hairs were motionless, looking more like gray dreadlocks than ropy fingers. His face was gray and smooth except for the vertical line bisecting his forehead.

"We'll come up with something to help all of you, old friend," Joshua whispered, rubbing the soreness in his chest and stepping backward as quietly as possible. "Now rest. You've done enough penance for this life."

Chapter Twenty-Four

Skin rubbed his unshaven face, trying to stay awake for just a little longer to close out of his current Netstream search and discussions before he called Lisa for an early-morning chat. Hopefully, he thought, an argument-*free* chat, but there were no guarantees on that.

The headache he'd had since talking to her yesterday, when she'd informed him of her new plan, had slowly grown worse as he finished up his research for the colonel and the others working to help the Wannoshay. He'd spent all night in front of a pair of screens, flipping through various 'Streams for information and gossip about the aliens and trends in the world, the whole time wishing he had some home-brewed beer at his side.

Now, at half past five in the morning, the first screen was showing a split-view: his research on the left, and on the right, a live shot of the river and the Mother Ship that was almost the same angle as the view from his hotel room.

The second screen ran a repeating download of his family and friends celebrating his son Randy's two-month "birthday" from a week ago. Skin had missed the party, and he was torturing himself by watching and rewatching the download of it. The footage of his son rocking away on his bouncy chair on the floor, grinning toothlessly up at Georgie's daughters, was accompanied by Lisa's voice on top of the footage, asking when they'd get to see him next.

You know the answer to that, sweetheart, he thought, popping the top of his fourth can of coffee that late night, which was turning into early morning.

"The hell with it," he said, and punched in his home address on the remote. The first screen cleared and displayed his home 'Stream number and address. He'd been waiting until a decent hour to call her. "I don't care if it *is* really early. I'm in enough trouble as it—Hi baby!"

He put on his best smile as soon as he saw Lisa's face flicker into focus on the right-hand screen. "Sorry to call so early. I just wanted to talk about your idea from yesterday."

Lisa, in spite of being only partially awake, wasn't hearing any of it.

"What's to talk about, Tim? We're coming to Iowa City."

Skin hoped she hadn't seen his wince. He knew that tone of voice too well, was too familiar with that set of her jaw.

"Me and Randy will be there by lunch time today. We're tired of not seeing you. I'm glad you found a job you love, a *purpose* in life. But we need to be with you. And if you give me a hard time about it, I'll bring Georgie along. Or Matt."

"Lisa," he said, "do you realize what's going on here? Aliens are dying, and some of them are attacking each other, and humans. Their sickness may even be contagious. This is *no* place to bring a two-month-old. It's crazy."

"Two months and nine days." Lisa's voice remained deadly calm. "You don't know what's going to happen with the aliens, if their ship is going to just explode or blast off into space or something. That's the thing—you *can't* know, Tim. They're not like us. Or do you know something about them that us folks out here in the sticks don't?"

She paused for breath, and Skin tried to slip a word in edgewise, to no avail.

"And do you know how crazy it's making *me*, knowing you're right there, risking your life, and all we can do is watch it on our damn wallscreen?"

"But," Skin began. "I just . . ."

"Yes?" Lisa said.

"Just let me . . . I want to . . . Ah, *shit.*"

"Mm-hmm?"

Skin swallowed and gave a short nod, his face burning. He'd never been able to argue with her worth a damn.

"What time did you say you'd get here?" he said at last.

Ten minutes later, after Lisa switched views to let Skin watch Randy sleeping in his crib, Skin clicked off the wallscreen.

The breeze blowing in his open window from outside had turned colder at last, making the weather feel a bit more like winter again instead of premature spring. Skin took a long breath of the cool air. His headache, thankfully, was starting to go away. They'd be here by lunchtime today.

He had no choice but to grudgingly admire Lisa. She would not take no for an answer, and she had a point: a family needed to be together at a time like this.

"That's my girl," he whispered with a smile, rubbing his eyes and finishing off the last of his coffee. Maybe later today, he decided, he could get some rest, once his family was there with him. It was going to be an interesting day, he could tell.

As he waited for Lisa and Randy to arrive at his hotel, Skin stood outside and stared at his hands. They were empty for once, instead of operating one of the handheld Netstreams the colonel had given him. A slight breeze blew the salty scent of the aliens across the river toward him. He stared at the slowly turning spires of the ship lodged into the black ground next to the river, wishing all the snow hadn't melted already. Everything looked dead now. Dead and muddy.

Lisa had originally wanted to meet him at the union so she could see the ship up close, but that had felt too risky to Skin.

As a sort of compromise, he'd managed to convince her to meet him at the hotel where the military had been paying for him to stay the past month.

Skin nodded at a pair of soldiers walking past, pulse guns in hand but pointed at the ground. He hoped Lisa would be able to handle the constant presence of soldiers and guns.

Just as he was getting ready to walk inside and grab his handheld Netstream to make a few calls and check his message boards, he saw a blonde head moving through the crowd of people and vehicles in the parking lot. Many people had gotten into the habit of parking their cars and trucks here and then walking across the river to see the ship. He also heard the high-pitched screams of a baby.

"Lisa!" he shouted, almost starting to cough from a sudden tickle in his throat. He bit back the cough and pushed his way through the crowd until he came face-to-face with his wife. "You made it!"

She was holding their squirming son Randy, his face red and streaked with recent tears. The two-month-old was catching his breath between screams. Skin wrapped his thin arms around both his wife and child and breathed in their smells of soap and baby powder and shampoo.

"We missed you," Lisa said as she returned his embrace. "You've been gone way too long, Tim."

"I know," Skin said. "I'm sorry."

"It's okay." Lisa passed Randy to him.

"Look at my big boy. I missed you."

Randy started crying again, throwing his little body back away from his father. Skin, caught in the middle of an unexpected sneeze, almost dropped him.

I'm out of practice, he scolded himself.

"Georgie wanted to come, too," Lisa said, glancing at the ship. Her eyes widened as she continued talking, machine-gun fast. "But I wouldn't let him. He let me take Mandy's car, though. It just about killed him, me coming here alone. At least he didn't make Matt come with me. Nobody's seen Matt in a couple weeks, by the way. So that's the ship, huh? Holy cow."

"That's it. I'm just glad you both made it," he said.

"So," Lisa said. She gave him a radiant, almost triumphant smile. "When do you think you'll be able to come back home?"

"Well," he began, "I'm not sure. But let's not worry about that now. I have some friends I want you to meet. Feel up for a walk?"

"This way?" Lisa said, nodding at the ship. "I can get Randy's stroller."

"Nah. I've got him. And we're heading over to the student union. We're taking the scenic route. There's too much activity going on by the ship right here. Plus, I want to show you my secret bridge."

"Okay," Lisa said. "But I do want to see the ship close up, soon."

Without answering her, Skin led Lisa along the river, past the view of the trucks, Hummers, vans, and cars on the other side of the water, surrounding the fenced-off ship. Lisa tried to ask him about the black hut-like structures inside the chain-link fence next to the ship, but he changed the subject, pointing out the geese to Randy before realizing his boy was napping against his chest. He barely felt Randy's weight in his left arm, and he coughed to clear a nagging tickle in his throat.

With the tall black ship now partially behind them, Skin exhaled, dispersing the sense of nervous tension he'd been feeling ever since they'd started walking within sight of the ship. The grass on either side of the wide sidewalk was trying to grow back here, and the early afternoon sun was warm on his face.

He almost felt like they were back home, strolling through Bancroft on their way to a football game at the high school.

Brown and slow, the river flowed past them on the right, broken only by a series of bridges.

It would be even better if I wasn't getting this stupid cold, he thought.

He pointed at a narrow footbridge, the last in a series of bridges for half a mile or so.

"There's my secret bridge," he said. "It's my shortcut from the hotel to the union, where my office is. Shontera and Toshera are meeting us in the union for lunch."

With Randy resting against his chest, propped up by his left hand, and Lisa holding his right, he led his family across the river, over the concrete patio filled with chained-down metal tables and chairs, and into the side exit of the student union. Waiting at a table near the windows were Shontera and Toshera.

He made the introductions, and they sat down to lunch.

In the past few weeks, Skin had worked closely with Shontera, comparing their experiences and theories about the aliens. With Lisa here, he realized to his own surprise that he'd never felt any knee-jerk racism toward the nonwhite people he had recently met. It was a small-town mentality that his buddies Matt and even Georgie had shared with and ingrained in him all his life.

Ever since he met her, he barely even thought about the fact that Shontera and Toshera were black, just like it hadn't registered with him that Ally was of Chinese descent. He wondered what Lisa thought of the new company he'd been keeping.

Earlier that day he'd tried getting hold of Ally as well, but she was almost always off getting more footage somewhere. And he knew better than to try and track down Joshua or Shermie, with their hectic schedules with the colonel.

He felt the tickle in his throat growing into the start of what was probably going to be a sore throat. He knew he needed to get more rest, but he'd been amazed at how much work he was able to get done, living by himself without Lisa to drag him off to bed, not to mention no Georgie and Matt around to help him get drunk on homebrew and high on filtered joints. He didn't have to worry about being too drunk to function anymore. Matt would give him hell for such behavior, he knew.

Skin gave a start at the thought of his former friend, and a sneeze escaped his mouth almost before he could slap a hand up to block it. He hadn't thought of Matt in what felt like ages.

Next to him, Lisa gave Randy a bottle while Shontera explained how they had arrived there with Father Joshua a month ago, hair-tentacles and all.

"I'm surprised you brought your baby here," Toshera said when Shontera had finished telling about meeting the Elders.

Shontera sucked in her breath and grabbed her daughter's arm. "Toshera! Don't be rude."

"It's just . . ."

"Toshera," Shontera said, her voice icy. "That's enough."

"No," Skin said. "If you don't mind, Shontera. What were you going to say, Toshera?"

"Go ahead," Shontera said.

"Well . . . It's just that a lot of the aliens are sick, and I think the people—the humans—around here might be getting sick too. Like it's contagious."

Lisa's eyes had grown wide. "Why didn't you *tell* me?" she whispered to Skin as Toshera continued talking about her headaches and the sick kids in her classes at school.

"I *did* tell you," Skin hissed back. "You just didn't listen."

"I'm sorry," Shontera interrupted, watching Skin and Lisa's conversation. "We're not making the best first impression here, are we? Toshera's been having headaches again, and it helps her to think that she's not alone in her suffering."

"Mo-om," Toshera said. "That's not it. Tell them about Nonami, at least."

"Have I told you about her?" Shontera asked Tim. "She was the Wannoshay I met in the brewery, the one who saved my life. Toshera thinks she saw Nonami—I wish I could pronounce her real name for you, but I can't do it without embarrassing myself. Anyway, Toshera may have seen her near the Mother Ship recently. But it's so hard to tell. There are so many Wannoshay around the ship these days. And I can't imagine how Nonami could've gotten here, or why she'd make such a trip."

"Good point," Skin said. "Who would have thought that we'd all end up here like we did?" He took Randy from Lisa and did his best to burp him. "We all have a lot to learn about the aliens."

"But at least we've got good folks like Tim here, working himself to death trying to help them." Lisa's voice had started off with an edge, but then she softened. "You folks are all doing good work here, you know," she added.

"Thanks," Shontera said. "We've had some success, but not as much as we'd hoped. People are still scared. And the aliens are still sick."

"Hey," Toshera asked. "Who's *Tim?*"

Skin pointed at himself and winked at Toshera. "Skin's my nickname."

"Shontera," Lisa said, leaning forward. "Tell me about Nonami, if you could."

Skin looked at his wife, her eyes filled with a mixture of fear and fascination, surprised by how young she looked. The frown she'd been wearing so much in the past few months had aged her. Now she looked beautiful, listening to Shontera tell her of the first day she'd met Nonami and how the Wannoshay woman had grabbed the beer bottle with her foot, saving it from exploding, though Nonami couldn't prevent the brewery from the same fate.

As he listened, Skin realized how badly he'd missed Lisa in

the past month. He leaned closer, smelling her perfume and shampoo, mixed with the smell of baby powder coming from his baby boy. He rubbed his son's tiny back, feeling the little ridges of his spinal column rise and fall under his fingers. He inhaled deeply, feeling something rattling in his chest to accompany the tickling soreness in his throat.

Before he knew it, the sky had turned dark outside the windows and most of the afternoon had disappeared as they talked.

Skin sat up and stretched, his throat aching. He must have dozed off at some point, catching up on his lost sleep from the night before. The women had let him and Randy take their naps.

"They're closing up for the day," Shontera was saying to him. The small restaurant inside the union was lunch only, and all the other tables had their chairs stacked on top of them. The wait staff sat in the corner, smoking filtered joints and waiting for them to leave.

"It was so wonderful meeting you," Lisa said, shaking Shontera's hand, then Toshera's. "We've got to keep in touch."

Skin felt his old headache returning as he got to his feet, and Randy started to squirm in his arms. For the first time in months, he felt a strange heaviness in his limbs, as if the gravity of Earth had been notched up to twice its normal strength. For a few painful seconds, as he felt his head reel, he worried that he'd drop his son.

Then the feeling passed, though his headache remained. Skin thought of Toshera's dire prediction about the contagiousness of the disease—or diseases—plaguing the Wannoshay.

Surely, he thought, their body chemistry is too different to infect us with any disease, right? Then he thought of the *War of the Worlds* vid he'd downloaded late one night at Matt's, and he shuddered. Hadn't a simple virus like the common cold killed all the invading aliens? Okay, it was science fiction, but it could easily be true. Couldn't it?

He walked outside, holding Randy close to his chest as the young boy began squirming. In the cooling air, Skin heard nothing other than the flap of wings from two geese on the sidewalk in front of him. Everything else in the area was deadly quiet.

Lisa, Shontera, and Toshera followed him outside, where night had fallen. Their happy chatting died away as soon as they entered the still air. A pair of streetlights lit up the sidewalk leading back to Skin's favorite bridge, but the rest of the world was hidden in darkness. Far off in the distance, an engine roared into life.

"Tim?" Lisa said. "Everything okay?"

"I don't know, actually," he said, pacing around the cement patio outside the union. Something was missing. He stopped walking and stood still, holding his breath.

"Wait," Lisa said. "There was a different sound this morning. Like someone was singing, maybe? But not just one person—"

"Everyone," Skin finished for her. "The Wannoshay camped out around the Mother Ship are always singing. All of them, at once. At least, they *were* singing. Now, I can't hear them."

He looked at Shontera and felt his wide-eyed look of fear mirrored in her dark brown eyes.

"I think you should all get back inside," he said. He handed Randy back to Lisa, who stared at him without saying a word as he pulled out his government-issue glasses. He put them on, dialed up a higher magnification and night-vision, and aimed the glasses at the landing site.

The Wannoshay inside the fence—there were hundreds of them in there now, an impossible amount—stood outside their black tent-like structures, arms raised to the sky. They were all looking up at the Mother Ship. Some were perched on top of the black metal houses, and all the alien structures—huts, tents, and Mother Ship—were glowing with a strange heat that the night-vision glasses easily picked up. More Wannoshay were appearing with each passing moment. They stood still as statues, arms raised as if waiting for something to fall that they would need to try and catch.

Skin felt both his sore throat and his rattling chest constrict, as if the air he'd inhaled was turning against him. Somewhere someone was running, footsteps slapping against concrete. He blinked his glasses into higher resolution so he could scan the Mother Ship, but he could find nothing out of order. As he looked, he again heard the rumble of a big, idling engine—gas-powered, he guessed from the sound, instead of electric—mixed with the growing sound of the footsteps.

In the cool night air, Lisa stepped closer to Skin. The footsteps became a muffled scuffing sound that could have been a pair of hands along with a pair of feet hitting the ground. The footsteps and handsteps—if that was what they were—grew louder.

Skin stared at the ship for a few moments longer, running his gaze from right to left as if he were tracking a deer in the forest. He couldn't figure out what it all meant.

And then, running away from the shadows of Hubbard Field as if he'd just burst out of the tiny chapel next to the ship, Awoyana the Wannoshay rushed forward on all fours toward them.

Skin relaxed at the sight of his alien friend even as Lisa hissed next to him and stepped back, covering Randy's head with her hand. Awoyana had arrived at the Mother Ship a week ago, and Skin was about to call out to him when the young alien stumbled.

Skin caught him just as he fell to the sidewalk, but holding onto Awoyana was like trying to hold onto a smooth-faced, quivering boulder. They both slid to the ground. Skin blinked off his glasses and looked down at the Wannoshay panting in his arms.

"Late," Awoyana said, shaking like a Blur junkie, though Skin had been convinced Awoyana had gotten off the drug. "So many late. So-many-lost-their-minds. Blurred. Late-ones, want-to-kill-us-all. Late. Something . . . had-to-be-done."

Skin took Awoyana's short-fingered hands in his own. He could feel the raised scars on the back of the alien's hands, the swirls inside of an octagon design that was unique to Awoyana. He took a breath, inhaling the other man's loamy scent. Randy was crying again, and Lisa was calling out his name.

"Awoyana?" he said, looking at the black scar on the alien's forehead from where Georgie had shot him. Would that ever heal? Skin wondered before looked back into the alien's eyes. "Why did your people stop singing? What's happening over there?"

A look passed over Awoyana's face, confusion mixed with what looked like guilt. He squinted all three of his flat black eyes in Skin's direction, twitching again. He looked as if he had just woken up from a deep sleep.

"Singing? I . . . do-not-know why-it . . . stopped." Awoyana pushed his way awkwardly out of Skin's grip and began talking even faster. "I-never-listened-to-them, never-did. But *you* must-listen-to *me.* Gather-your-people. Ask-no-questions. Something-had-to-be-done, something-to-get-people-to-act. Something *big.* It-happens . . . soon."

"Okay," Skin said. Awoyana was trembling so much he could barely hold onto him. "Okay," he repeated.

"Thank-you," Awoyana said, relaxing in his arms at last. His voice began to lighten and slow down its frenetic pace. "I knew you would understand, knew-you-would. Gather your people to you and get-away-from-here, get away, away, away . . ."

And then Skin felt everything suddenly snap into focus—the

field, the silence of the aliens, the presence of his wife and child next to him and Toshera and Shontera behind them, and Awoyana's scent of mud and salt in his nose.

"What did you *do,* Awoyana?"

But Awoyana simply rolled away from him, onto all fours.

Skin stood up to take another look at the field through his glasses again. Some of the cars and trucks that formed part of the outer barrier around the Mother Ship were being moved away from the chain-link fence. A handful of Wannoshay appeared to be directing traffic, and amazingly, humans were cooperating with them.

To the south, Skin saw a lone truck sitting across the street from the Mother Ship, idling with a low rumbling sound.

"Shontera," he said. "Take everyone back across the river bridge and find someplace safe in the hotel. Once you're there, get the colonel on your Netstream. Lisa, you and Randy go with her. I have to go help. Something bad's happening down there."

"Tim," Lisa called, "this doesn't even concern us."

"But it *does,*" Skin said. Before he could say more, the two streetlights above them went black with a popping sound, and the union behind them was plunged into darkness as well. Across the river, lights still burned, but on this side, the power was gone.

Over on Hubbard Field next to the Mother Ship, the strange globe lights of the Wannoshay were still lit, casting a whitish-yellow glow into the night. Silent as a whisper, Awoyana had slipped away into the darkness.

"Get back to the other side of the river," Skin said to Lisa. "*Please*. I'm sorry, Lisa."

As soon as the words were out of his mouth, the gas-powered engine of the truck roared into life. For a long, painful moment, the engine's revving grew louder. The revving was interrupted by a belching backfire as the driver put the truck in gear, and it leaped forward.

The truck was aimed at the Mother Ship, and it was picking up speed.

"You fuckers," Skin whispered. "You stupid fuckers."

With his military glasses on, he saw it all, unable to look away and too far away to help. He watched ghost-soldiers step in front of the oncoming truck, their high-tech uniforms glowing light green in the black night, blasting the truck with their pulse guns. Through the thunder of the guns, the truck kept coming, its windshield gone and the driver turned to a fuzzy, unfocused shape behind the wheel.

Then the truck crashed into the soldiers, sending them flying before it burst through the chain-link fence and slammed head-on into the Mother Ship.

Chapter Twenty-Five

A single light shone in the smudged-over window of an office in the Iowa Memorial Student Union, where two men worked on their separate projects long past quitting time and the start of nightfall. Shermie Powell was busy looking at old Wantaviewer footage, while Father Joshua McDowell was staring at a book he'd completely forgotten about until his recent talk with his ailing friend Johndo.

With the soft burble of four different Netstreams the only sound in the office, Joshua turned to a new page of the metal book of the People he had stored in a lower drawer of his desk. Almost a year had passed since he'd last looked at the book, and the text and even the metal looked unfamiliar and somehow dangerous.

He closed his eyes for a moment and ran a hand over his forehead, feeling a slight spin of fatigue-induced vertigo as he tried to refocus his eyes. The inconstant letters and symbols of the People's language had a way of making his vision double.

It goes back to him tomorrow, he thought, eyes still closed.

All last night and all day today Joshua had been thinking about the Elder's confession to him yesterday. To leave so many behind, even if there simply hadn't been room—he could barely fathom the weight of the decision and the depth of responsibility and guilt Johndo and the other Elders must feel. Somehow it had been enough to make many of them sick, even those who were not involved in the actual decision.

After a bit of a struggle, his eyelids wanting to remain closed, Joshua opened his eyes and looked across the office at his fellow collaborator. Bouncing in a slender metal chair from the Mother Ship that he had affixed to the office floor, Shermie watched all four different 'Streams at the same time. He murmured orders into the remote that were too low for Joshua to hear, working his way through a cached version of all the movies of Wantaviewer. His thick gray hair had come loose from his ponytail, falling onto his lined face.

Joshua smiled as he looked at the shiny black suit with the too-wide lapels that Shermie wore tonight, the same one Shermie had been wearing under his heavy orange poncho on the day they'd first met. It was so worn it was shiny, but Joshua liked that suit. It gave Shermie a nice touch of class.

"Everything okay?" Joshua asked him.

Shermie was mumbling in frustration as year-old images of Winnipeg and Ally, a.k.a. Wantaviewer, and her friends spun past on the four split-windows of the wallscreen at different speeds, both fast-forward and reverse.

"The quality of these movies," Shermie said in a hoarse voice as he lit another cigarillo. He raised the office's only window, scummed over with smoke and fingerprints, and fanned smoke out it with his hand. "I hate that Ally deleted the originals. These versions are crap. Girl doesn't even seem to feel bad about destroying all that work."

Turning his attention back to his own desk, Father Joshua had a brief moment of disorientation. Feeling strangely disconnected from his own body, he touched the metal book on his desk next to his portable Netstream with an almost numb hand.

How did I end up here? he wondered. I was supposed to have a good church and a congregation, and be thinking about retirement, not working long days in an office next to an alien mother ship.

He turned off his Netstream and pushed a liquid symbol around on the metal page of the book in front of him. The strange gray-and-white material reformed itself with the touch of his finger. It shifted from a spiral to a pair of triangles, without any logic or reason.

"Prone to senseless outbursts," he muttered. He wondered if Juana still had her faith and her desire to do good works.

"Oh the hell with it," Shermie said on the other side of the room. "I can't watch that grainy shit any more," he said. "It's killing my eyes."

With a final sigh of exasperation, he keyed off the wallscreen and dropped the remote onto Joshua's desk.

"Hey, Father," Shermie said. "Everything okay with *you?*"

"I'm just tired," Joshua said. "Tired of looking at this book, tired of this office. Tired of waiting and preparing and hoping." He closed the book and pushed it forward on the desk so he could rest his elbows on the flat surface.

Bright yellow-white globes, perched on top of black metal cylinders, lit up the field, their glow spilling onto the streets surrounding it. The encampment had swelled to easily a thousand of the People, if not more.

Many of them, for some reason, now stood outside their metal huts, gazing up at the Mother Ship as if they were expecting something to happen. And, as usual, they were singing. Through the partially open window, Joshua had been unconsciously listening to the high-pitched tones and notes rising from the field full of tightly packed People. Now that he had stopped working, the Wannoshay song made his eyelids grow even heavier than before.

Time to get some sleep, he decided, pulling his gaze away from the window.

When he turned around, about to say something to Shermie,

the humming song of the People outside came to an abrupt stop.

"What the hell's going on down there?" Shermie left his wallscreen and stood next to Joshua.

They stared down at all the People gathered below them; lit up by their yellow lights, the tall beings were standing around, watching the Mother Ship. For the first time ever, none of the aliens were twitching or hitting one another in the almost absent-minded way they did. Joshua squinted, wishing he had his glasses with him. Something felt wrong about the area just outside the southern edge of the chain-link fence, but he couldn't see clearly enough with his old eyes to know for sure what it was.

"Shermie—" he began, but stopped short when all the electrical equipment in their office went dead.

"Damn," Shermie said. He reached inside his coat for his lighter, his face glowing orange from the fresh cigarillo he'd lit just before the power went out.

"This can't be good," Joshua said, his head beginning to ache in the sudden silence. "Let's go see what's going on."

Joshua found a hand light from his desk and popped it on. The light flickered red and then covered him in a pink glow. Jogging with Shermie down the darkened hallway in the suddenly silent student union, Joshua's chest felt tight with fear. He wished he would have taken one last look out the window before they left the darkened office, and in that moment he realized he'd been expecting something like this for weeks now.

Father, watch over us, he thought. All of us.

Outside, more and more lights from the People were popping on across the encampment, making up for the dead streetlights. The globes, attached to the metal huts or carried by the People, now encircled the Mother Ship, illuminating it from all sides except for a gap in the lights in the south-facing sides of the ship. Farther to the south, out of the darkness, came the barking cough of a big gasoline-fueled engine.

"Get everyone you can out of the ship," Joshua said into his military transmitter, his voice loud but calm. He switched channels and repeated the message.

Grabbing Joshua's light stick, Shermie pointed at the unlit gap of the ship.

"That's where we need to be," he said as they circled the chain-link fence protecting the Mother Ship.

As they half-walked, half-ran toward the unlit section of the fence, Joshua heard the mad revving of the truck engine, and then he saw it. The dirty white pickup truck was across the street from the field, and it came streaking through the darkness. It bounced down the curb and crossed the street with a squeal of tires. The truck's headlights were dark.

Joshua was close enough now to see that the unlit gap had been cleared of all military and civilian vehicles, and his chest gave a hollow thud at the sight of the ten-foot-wide strip of land leading right up to the Mother Ship.

"Oh Father," he whispered. "Oh no."

The truck was riding low to the ground, its lower bumper throwing up sparks as the truck jumped onto the curb on the near side of the street. The laden truck was almost at the darkened gap.

"Security!" Joshua shouted into his transmitter, hoping the colonel and his people had heard. "Incoming!"

Shimmering ghost-soldiers flickered past Joshua and Shermie, and the thunder of their pulse guns filled the air. The driver of the truck was hit, but the vehicle kept speeding up.

It crashed into the front line of soldiers. Some of the pulse guns hit home and blew out the front tires.

The truck began to swerve, but it still made it to the chain-link fence. It blasted through the fence and plowed through the black metal structures of the encampment of the People.

Joshua heard the unmistakable thuds of vehicle meeting flesh and bone, human and Wannoshay. He felt each impact deep inside his chest, as if someone wracked with Blur and wearing metal-tipped boots was kicking him.

In the instant before the impact, Joshua saw the big white bags piled in the back of the pickup, and he saw the dark jacket of the slumped, bloodied driver. The truck's engine, most likely rigged to keep accelerating with or without a driver, roared even higher, like a shuttle during takeoff.

Then the truck hit the Mother Ship, and the night exploded.

Less than a minute later, Joshua opened his eyes to discover he was lying on his back twenty feet away from where he'd been previously standing, and his chest was aching. The impact of the explosion had thrown him away from the Mother Ship and covered him in bits of hot black metal.

The ship itself was still intact, but its upper levels were leaning hard to the south, looking like a giant black question mark. Around him, the Wannoshay dove onto the flames of the burning truck and tore holes in the sides of the ship to get the People inside free.

Joshua brushed the cooling bits of metal off his black clothes and pulled himself to his feet. Next to him, Shermie was working his way up as well.

"Got to get to the Elders," he said. "You okay, Shermie?"

"Think so," the older man said as he stood up. "I may not be able to run, but I can walk okay, I think."

Joshua felt a twinge of pain even deeper inside his chest as he straightened up. His ears were ringing, and he could smell the dangerous odor of gas, fire, and burnt rubber. The truck had left a twenty-foot deep indentation in the lower level of the ship. Already the broken metal from the impact was starting to mold itself back into shape.

All that was left of the truck was a burning husk of metal and a single black truck tire, sitting on its side, flat.

Joshua couldn't seem to find his own breath. The truck's sudden appearance and the explosion it caused had happened so quickly that his mind hadn't had time to process it all.

Shermie pulled on Joshua's arm, his strength surprising the priest. As they hurried toward the ship, they both began talking to the People in their native language, the words almost second nature to Joshua now, trying to figure out what had happened and how the truck had gotten through so easily.

But the People weren't talking. If they weren't tending to the injured or trying to douse the flames of the suicide bomber's truck, they were simply standing and staring at their ruined Mother Ship.

When he was almost aboard the ship, he looked over at tiny Danforth Chapel, sitting only a few feet away from the ship. In the past month, he'd spent many afternoons in the small brick chapel that was nearly hidden by the shrubbery and leafless oaks surrounding it.

He felt a mad desire to run into the chapel and lock the door behind him so he could sleep off the ache inside his chest, but the feeling was fleeting; he knew that his days of turning his back on his people were over.

Inside the ship at last, he heard the big structure groan and creak around him, and he felt something press down on his eardrums with a subtle pressure. A double line of liquid lights popped on in front of them as they hurried down to the main hold where the Elders congregated every day.

As they half-ran, half-walked down to the lower level of the ship, he felt another tugging sensation deep inside his sore chest, but he couldn't stop now if he wanted to keep up with Shermie. Panting with each step, he felt his left arm start to go numb.

Not again, damn it, he thought. Give me more time, Father.

Shermie was pulling away from him. Joshua fought for breath even as he continued down into the heart of the ship. The slick, unshining black wall gave when he pressed his right hand against it for support, and the greasy feel of it made him pull his arm back in surprise. Above them, something heavy crashed against the metal ceiling.

Just a little farther, he thought.

His left arm hung at his side, useless now. He walked as fast as he could down the last hallway toward the room of the Elders. The ship, normally frigidly cold, felt thirty or forty degrees warmer than usual.

He could just make out Shermie standing stock-still in front of the entrance to the room of the Elders, where whitish-blue light flowed out like fast-moving smoke. The pressure of the ship pounded louder and harder than his own irregular heartbeat.

From outside, the sound reaching them through the hole blasted into the side of the ship, came the sounds of a second revving engine.

Not another one, Joshua thought again. We've got to get the Elders out of here.

He gritted his teeth and took another step. His eardrums ached, and sweat dripped into his eyes.

Inside the room, all eight Elders had gathered together, linking hands in song. Johndo stood at one end, uninjured but still obviously sick. He was singing even as his eyes opened and closed at random intervals and his shoulders twitched. Three of the Elders, a woman and two men, were bloodied from the explosion, while a fourth was propped up in a metal chair with bands wrapped around her, keeping her from falling over.

Joshua realized the fourth Elder was Iyalloshay, though he could barely recognize her through the burns covering her face and her staring eyes. The truck had hit the ship, he realized, just below where her lab had been located.

Help them, Joshua wanted to say, but he didn't know who he was addressing anymore. His body and mind felt like they were all going numb on him.

In the center of the circle of the leaders of the People, a black disc hovered and spun, and spilling out of the disc was a smoky energy. Next to him, Shermie stared in wide-eyed disbelief.

The energy swirled hypnotically, and Joshua forgot about his strange mix of pain and numbness in his upper body. He watched the smoky energy spread to the walls of the ship and head downward. Toward the hole in the ship made by the truck.

Just as the energy of the Elders had begun to move faster down toward the damaged section of the ship, the energy suddenly broke apart and disappeared. With more effort than it should have taken him to move his head, Joshua looked and saw that injured Iyalloshay had fallen forward. She was now lying completely still.

White beams of energy began flowing upward out of her in a manner that had become all too familiar to Joshua in the months since he'd first encountered Matthew and the nameless boy in the Minnesota camp. As her lifeless body lifted from the indentation she'd made in the metal floor, he braced for the upcoming impact even as his knees buckled on him. His entire upper body was numb.

Wild energy, he thought.

Outside, the roar of the second truck grew louder, closer.

"Get out," Joshua tried to yell. "All of you, out."

But his words were drowned out by the competing noises around him: the desperate song of the seven remaining Elders, the swirling energy loud as a tornado building inside of Iyalloshay, the roaring engine of the vehicle outside, the banging and popping sounds coming from the upper levels of the ship, the pounding sensation in his ears, and the moans and cries of the sick and dying People and humans all around them, inside and outside the Mother Ship. Joshua was in the middle of a vortex of energy and sound that sucked away his breath and thoughts and left him numb and reeling.

And then it all stopped.

The wild energy that he'd been expecting to rush at him from Iyalloshay never materialized. The beams of light had been absorbed greedily by the Elders around her. Two of the injured Elders were now standing straighter, as if already Iyalloshay's dying energy had fortified them.

Joshua was having trouble understanding what his eyes were telling him.

Shermie, still staring at the swirling energy of the Elders, took Joshua's left arm and, without looking away, draped it over his bony shoulder. Joshua couldn't hold on. Too tired to keep moving, he sank into the cushion-like black metal of the ship floor, just inside the room of the Elders.

Iyalloshay was gone. Her body had been completely absorbed by the other Elders, and the black disc in the middle of the seven remaining Elders was resting on the ship floor.

"Jerusalem, surrounded," he whispered to himself. "We're . . . too late . . ."

His breath was coming in gasps now. His heartbeat sped up, then slowed down.

Outside the ship, something exploded.

Shermie made a final attempt to get Joshua up off the floor, but Joshua shrugged out of his grip.

Father, if you can hear me, forgive me, he thought. His chest was now numb. I'm a weak man, and I'm tired. Let me rest here.

Joshua's heart beat one more time, a contraction of the

bloody muscle inside his chest that seemed to take forever to complete.

The pressure in his head tripled and quadrupled, and then suddenly disappeared. He could no longer inhale.

His vision went white, shifted to gray, and resolved itself in blackness. And then, for the second time in his life, Father Joshua McDowell's heart stopped.

Chapter Twenty-Six

When the lights went out, Ally was walking back to her editing room in the student union after another long day of getting footage inside the mall camp. She didn't even have time to swear before she heard the mad roar of a truck engine and the firing of the pulse guns, followed by the explosion. Wishing for the first time in weeks for a couple capsules of Blur, she broke into a run toward the Mother Ship.

As she ran, she tried to load a fresh mini-DVD into her portable recorder and ended up dropping half of the new discs on the ground.

"Fuck it," she said, not even bothering to pick up the empty discs sticking up like little blades from the muddy ground next to the sidewalk. "No time."

With her eyebrow camera on and the new disc in place and recording, she turned to her left down a side street and saw the smoke coming from the Mother Ship. The lights of the Wantas were still burning, illuminating the smoke and damage. Biting back a moan that she didn't want recorded, she walked as fast as she dared while recording the damaged ship, a part of her hating the way she was being so careful about getting good material.

The top of the ship looked like it was trying to bend itself away from the student union next to it. She magnified her eyebrow cam and saw the gaping hole in the lower section of the ship and the smoking remains of the truck. At this magnification, she could see plenty of purplish-red and plain old red blood covering the aliens and humans in front of the ship.

She almost started screaming when she saw a bloodied human head lift itself up off the ground and rush off toward the ship. But then she realized she was seeing the exposed skin and clothing of the ghost-soldiers. Part of his invisible camouflage had been torn free from his body, exposing his head.

She was half a football field away from the ship and the chaos around it when she heard the roar of another big engine off to her left. The engine revved itself to an almost unbearable level, to the point where she thought the muffler would blow off.

Instead, the truck downshifted and launched itself down the sidewalk next to the bridge, aiming right for the gap in the gap left by absent trucks that had been parked there earlier.

"No!" Ally screamed, and she wasn't alone. The masked protesters that she and everyone else called the ET freaks spun away from where they'd been tearing apart the smoking remains of the first truck and rushed straight at the new truck.

She'd been almost running toward the oncoming truck, not thinking of what she was going to do to stop it, when she saw the ET freaks line up in front of it, creating a human wall a dozen people deep. The truck showed no signs of stopping, and in that instant Ally was back in Winnipeg, watching the Blurred aliens get hit by cars or injure each other in their confusion.

In the next few seconds, time took on an expanded quality that she'd always thought of as super-slo-mo, just like in the old vids. Sometimes she got the super-slo-mo effect when she took too much Blur and her senses were overwhelmed by so many stimuli that her brain somehow was able to slow her perception of time so she could take it all in without her head exploding.

She heard and saw the round-faced man behind the wheel of the truck, screaming in a desperate, angry voice that he wasn't stopping, he was *not* stopping. He wore the dark blue colors of the suicide cultists, but he didn't have the mesh cap. Instead, his jaggedly cut blonde hair stood up at wild angles from his scalp.

Ally saw all of this, processed it, and tucked it away inside her brain all in less than half second.

In front of the truck, none of the ET freaks moved except for a man in gray ski boots, a brown bathrobe, and a dark green rubber mask. He looked like the Creature from the Black Lagoon right after stepping out of the tub, but Ally doubted the Creature had ever carried a rocket-propelled grenade launcher like the one this man held in his hands.

In another half a second, the grenade launcher was pointed at the pickup truck.

"Please be loaded and ready to fire," Ally whispered.

She stopped hurrying toward the destruction caused by the first truck and the oncoming destruction of the second truck. Instead she stopped, plucked her camera from her eyebrow, and held it in her right thumb and index finger, pointing it at the truck like the world's smallest gun. Pulse guns thundered as the few remaining soldiers who were able to open fire on the truck did so, blowing out the front tires.

The man in the mask and robe calmly adjusted his aim, and with a loud hiss and a pop, the grenade launcher burst into life. The night air filled with yellow-tinted smoke as the Creature from the Black Lagoon shot a grenade through the windshield of the onrushing truck.

For a frozen second, Ally could have sworn she saw the grenade bursting through the windshield and through the back window of the cab, landing in the midst of the man-sized plastic bags piled high in the bed of the truck.

Fertilizer, she thought, with a grim, numb certainty.

Then the night was shattered by another explosion as the

truck was turned into a fireball.

The shockwave knocked her off her feet and onto her rear end, but she was able to hang onto the camera and keep on taping even as she hit the ground, hard. She turned her head in time to see the truck veer off into the river, missing the Mother Ship and, miraculously, all of the ET freaks that had been standing in its path.

A dozen of the bigger masked men and women ran into the night in the direction of the second truck, making sure no more trucks were coming. The leader of the ET freaks gave one last look at the burnt wreckage of the second truck, now almost completely submerged in the river and unrecognizable.

He lifted his mask and spit on the ground, and then he tossed the grenade launcher away with contempt before joining the others as they cleared debris from the Mother Ship and helped the wounded get to safety.

Standing halfway between the ship and the student union, Ally kept recording, tears streaking her face, as the Iowa City Fire Department arrived and continued the evacuation of the Mother Ship started by the mix of Wannoshay and humans at the site. She felt tired, suddenly, as she sat in the cold mud and watched the different groups working together, helping each other.

"This is what it took," she murmured, not caring anymore if it was picked up on her footage. Her tears cooled her hot face, scalded by the fire of the truck explosion.

As she felt the adrenaline finally begin to leave her system, she got ready to stop taping and help with the recovery. She froze when she felt something tugging at her stomach, and when she inhaled it hurt.

Afraid to look down, she ran her right hand down her side, to where the pain in her belly was. Her hand wrapped itself around a thin piece of metal. A moan escaped her as she ran her hand around her side and stopped at her back, where the rest of the thin metal cylinder protruded almost half a foot out of her back. The metal was tacky with her own blood.

"Oh Jesus H," Ally whispered.

She looked down and gave a whimpering sob. Over a foot of what looked like the old-fashioned radio antenna to a big fucking truck was sticking out of her stomach just below her ribs.

"Help," she tried to shout, but all that came out was a whisper, and then shooting pain hit her.

Ally's camera slipped from her hand, and it seemed to take forever for the expensive piece of equipment to drop to the ground next to her. Her body followed the camera as she dropped onto her right side, and she landed on top of the camera. It snapped underneath her, followed by a red blast of pain that came from the antenna lodged in her belly.

"Piece of total fucking shit," she tried to say, but all that came out was long, drawn-out groan that lasted right up until blackness filled her vision.

Chapter Twenty-Seven

Skin knew the driver of the second truck.

In the moments following the first explosion, he had taken one look behind him in the direction where he hoped Lisa and Shontera had taken the children. The women had only moved twenty feet away. He was about to yell at them to move when he heard the second truck. He almost dropped his military glasses at the familiar sound of the truck's rotten muffler and roaring ten-cylinder engine.

"Can't be," he said as he slapped on the glasses and zoomed in on the onrushing truck. It was the color of dark blood in the night vision, and the driver's face was a round white ball behind the wheel. Jaggedly cut hair fell into the driver's eyes. His old buddy Matt's eyes.

Skin didn't want to believe it, but it made too much sense not to be true. He'd heard that truck roar up to his trailer too many times in the past ten years to not recognize it, and Matt had last been seen in the company of his new friends, the suicide cultists.

Too far away to be able to do anything to stop it, Skin could only watch. At this magnification, he'd been able to see Matt's mouth form a perfect circle as he screamed in his mad charge at the Mother Ship. The pulse guns blew out his tires and burst through the windshield while the grenade from the leader of the ET freaks ripped through his truck.

"No," he hissed, steeling himself for the second explosion.

He wouldn't realize until later that the second truck had missed the ship altogether.

His anger fueled him now, giving him the strength to run down into the chaos surrounding the ship without another look behind him at the three women and his son. With the help of the military glasses, he'd found the gap in the vehicles around the ship. He thought immediately of Awoyana.

Something had to be done, Awoyana had said. *Something big.*

Passing through the ruined chain-link fence and running through the ruined alien encampment, Skin pushed through the crowd in front of the damaged Mother Ship. The injured would need his help inside, and he had a feeling the Elders were still in there. The ship wasn't going to hold together much longer.

He ran up the hatch leading into the ship, no longer thinking but simply reacting. The inside of the ship felt too warm, and on either side of him he heard deep shiftings in the walls accompanied with the cries and moans of the injured. He ran down the side hallways, passing bleeding aliens and humans, all of them on their way out.

He was sweating even harder now, forcing himself to go forward into the growing wall of heat, until he arrived at the room of the Elders.

Sprawled just inside the room lay Shermie and Father Joshua. Both of them were unresponsive: Shermie stared blank-eyed into the room, his back against the wall, while Joshua lay on his side, eyes closed.

Skin stepped inside the room of the Elders, where the sounds were dampened. He looked down at the two older men sitting in silence in the otherwise empty room with the ship falling apart around them, feeling a sense of panic. Joshua looked ashy and didn't seem to be breathing.

Just as he'd done with Georgie a few months earlier, as easily as he'd caught the boulder thrown at him by the young Wannoshay outside Macy, Nebraska, Skin scooped up Joshua and hoisted him into his arms.

The priest was cold to the touch. Skin nudged Shermie hard with his boot.

"Come on, Shermie. Wake up! We've got to *go.*"

Shermie's eyelids fluttered, and with an effort, the old man pulled himself to his feet.

"What about the Elders?" Skin said, already heading up the corridor leading out of the groaning, shifting ship. Outside the room of the Elders, the barrage of sounds drowned out his voice. Almost impossibly, he could hear the song of the aliens starting up again outside.

Shermie waved Skin on, a few steps behind them.

"Go," the old man shouted when he caught up to Skin, his voice almost lost in the cacophony around them. "They're gone."

The crashing sounds from above them were now blending together into a roar. Skin hurried up the sloping hallways even as the walls of the Mother Ship began to turn to liquid on either side of him. He knew they'd never make it out before the ship disintegrated around them. He checked their position, took another dozen steps up the sloping hall, and then he set Joshua down. The priest's head lolled to one side, lifelessly.

"Stand back," he said to Shermie, then he added softly to himself, "Oh fuck, this is gonna *hurt.*"

Skin gathered in his thin body all of the strength that had been with him since Awoyana had touched him last November, and he slammed both fists into the wall of the Mother Ship.

The liquefying metal bulged outward from the force of his blow, stretching impossibly outward in the two places where his fists had struck it, and then the wall burst outward.

Skin screamed as white-hot agony shot through his fingers, hands, and arms. Cold air rushed in through the newly made hole in the ship, and four-fingered hands reached inside, widening it.

Skin nearly fell to the floor of the ship, but the roar filling the ship from all sides goaded him out through the hole. With the help of Shermie on the inside and the aliens rushing up to them from the outside, he was able to pull Joshua out, and then Shermie.

His hands were starting to scream with pain now, and he would have fallen to the ground next to the broken ship if Shermie hadn't been there to pull him away. He could tell from the way they were bent that most of his fingers and knuckles had been broken.

The aliens had already taken Joshua away, and Skin saw the stricken priest's body floating eight feet above the ground in the arms of the Wannoshay, heading toward the student union. The world began spinning once he saw that, and the pain in his hands made him want to vomit. Above him, the ship rumbled and groaned, and popping sounds came from the upper levels, as if shots were being fired.

"Just a little further, kid," Shermie said, leading him away from the dying ship. The strength of the old man's hands on his shoulders was surprising. "The ship's going to blow."

Skin was able to take another two dozen steps before sinking to his knees.

"That's *it,*" he said. His mangled hands and fingers had already swollen to twice their size. "I'm out of miracles, Shermie."

He sank to the ground and rolled onto his back, and the impact sent fresh agony through his hands and arms. He was too tired to scream. He could only look up, at the sky overhead.

The smoke suddenly cleared, and Skin could see stars spread out in the night sky above him. He needed to find the Little Dipper before he closed his eyes. He remembered that constellation, and he wanted to teach its shape to Randy the first chance he got.

Next to them, almost forgotten by him in his agony, the giant black shadow of the Mother Ship had already shrunk to half its original size, and the popping sounds were growing louder.

We're going to need some more miracles, Skin thought. He'd found the Little Dipper, but it was no consolation. He sat up, cradling his hands, and watched the alien ship shudder and pop in front of him. And we're going to need them soon.

Less than a minute later, the Mother Ship completely collapsed in upon itself.

Chapter Twenty-Eight

Nowhere near the bridge they were supposed to be crossing, Shontera stood holding onto her daughter in front of her, unable to let the Mother Ship out of her sight. Skin's wife Lisa gripped her tiny son to her in much the same way. The sight gave Shontera just a bit of comfort in this night of explosions.

"Tim," Lisa said in a small voice as her husband ran into the darkened fray around the damaged ship with his military glasses still on his face.

They stood frozen in the darkness as the echoes of the second explosion began to fade from their ears. Finally, Toshera wriggled from Shontera's grasp and replaced her own glasses with the military glasses the colonel had lent them.

"Mama!" Toshera shouted from behind the glasses. "It went into the river! The truck didn't hit the ship!"

"Please let that be the last of the cultists," Shontera whispered. "No more. Please."

"Is that who you think did this?" Lisa said.

Shontera borrowed the glasses from Toshera and saw the flames of the second truck go out in the river.

"They're going to need help with all the hurt people over there," she said to Lisa after she'd given the glasses back to Toshera. "Want to try to get back inside the union?"

Instead of the uncertainty and panic Shontera had been afraid of seeing, Lisa's face transformed itself with her confident smile.

"Yes," she said. "I want to do something to help, not just

stand here waiting for something else bad to happen. Let's go."

They hurried across the darkened lawn toward the union, accompanied by the comforting sounds of the alien songs starting up again. Toshera held tight to Shontera's hand, and she had the glasses on again, giving a play-by-play of what was happening.

"The ship's shaking, sort of, like it's melting or something. Up top all of the spikes have fallen down, and—did you hear *that?* Stuff must be falling over inside there. And down at the bottom, the Wannoshay are pulling everybody out of the ship. I think most of the people are going to be okay. And over there's—"

"Okay, honey," Shontera said. "Watch where you're going, now. Put those glasses away, and put on your regular glasses."

"Just one more look . . ."

Shontera led Lisa and Randy back toward to the outside wall of the union as a squadron of mostly-invisible soldiers thundered past on their way to the ship. Along with the soldiers were at least a dozen aliens, galloping on all fours.

"Come on, Toshera," she hissed.

"Wait!" The panicked fear in her daughter's voice turned Shontera's blood cold. "Mama, I see Ally! Over in front of the union. And she's hurt!"

"Where?" Shontera reached for the glasses, but she'd already caught sight of her new friend sitting in the mud, surrounding by running soldiers and aliens and the wounded. Nobody seemed to notice her. "Oh, Ally."

Threading their way through the crowded field, Shontera thought of Nonami finding her in the brewery that day, carrying her out to safety when Shontera hadn't been able to move. As they grew closer, she could see the blood covering Ally's coat, turning her black jeans shiny. She needed Nonami here to carry Ally away to safety.

Shontera couldn't figure out why Ally was holding what looked like an old radio antenna in her hands until she reached her, just as Ally toppled over onto her side.

"Ally," she cried out. "We're here, girl. Wake up!"

"Shontera," Lisa said, her voice calm and cool. "Take Randy, please. We've got to stop the bleeding and get her inside. I saw a bunch of EMTs just inside the entrance on our way over here. We need to get her into the union, so long as we don't hurt her."

Shontera took the baby as Lisa dropped to one knee in the mud and tied one of Randy's blankets around Ally's abdomen. Ally tried to scream, but her breath wouldn't come.

"Hold your hands here," Lisa ordered Ally, placing each of Ally's hand around where the antenna had entered her abdomen. The blanket was quickly soaked in blood, but the flow seemed to have slowed with the pressure.

Shontera stared, sickened by the blood and the injury, but amazed at the control Lisa was showing.

"It's okay," Lisa said to Ally. "I'm a nurse."

The three of them lifted Ally to her feet, and this time Ally was able to find her voice.

"Give me something!" she said in a hoarse voice that made Shontera's skin turn cold. "Blur, morphine, fucking coke, anything, god, it fucking hurts!"

"Let's get you over there," Lisa said, leading them toward the union. She took Randy smoothly from Shontera while propping Ally up. Still screaming and demanding drugs, Ally was able to walk, but Shontera didn't let dare let go of her. Toshera was three steps behind, alternating between watching Ally and watching the ship.

Shontera had forgotten about the Mother Ship, but now she heard the low groans coming from the top of the ship. They were almost at the union when Toshera called for her.

"It's falling! Mama, the *ship!*"

The three women turned and followed Toshera's pointing finger. Even Ally was shocked into silence as the black ship warped the night sky, turning the stars into red and green and blue smears where the topmost levels began to distort the blackness with waves of energy. A sudden series of cracks and popping sounds came from those shimmering levels of the ship.

The singing of the Wannoshay all around them reached a high-pitched crescendo and then it stopped for the second time that night.

For a long moment the Mother Ship stopped shimmering. The alien lights all over the encampment went bright white, illuminating the strange angles covering the eight-sided ship, showing the alien power and craftsmanship that had brought the Wannoshay ships to Earth.

Shontera thought for a brief instant that the ship would hold. But then a wave of smoky energy rose up from the ruined south-facing walls, and the popping turned into a deep, thunderous cracking.

"Tim?" Lisa whispered next to Shontera.

With a final doomed sound that shook the earth, the Mother Ship began to implode.

"Hurry," Shontera said, needing to get away from ship before they were caught in yet another explosion.

Once they were almost inside the doors of the union, Shontera and Lisa turned to watch. The top of the ship sank faster and faster, as if the ship were eating itself. With a final rush of air and heavy *thwump* of molten alien metal dropping to the ground all at once, the Wannoshay Mother Ship fell.

It crashed to the ground, and then it simply disappeared.

Chapter Twenty-Nine

That night lasted forever for Toshera. She'd only stayed up all night once before, and that had been because of her stupid headaches. But tonight, there was nothing that could have made her close her eyes and go to sleep. So much was happening; she didn't dare stop and rest for fear of missing something. Luckily the power came on an hour after it had been knocked out, so Toshera was able to see her mother become, without a doubt, her hero.

Too busy with the sick and injured, nobody was talking about the ship, but Toshera knew where it had gone. In the past few weeks, she'd been watching the Wannoshay while her mother had worked to try to get people to like the aliens again.

She'd done research on the tunnels from all types of 'Streams, and she'd actually seen some of the tunnels next to the Mother Ship, though the Wannoshay did a good job of hiding their work.

You just had to know what to look for—piles of dirt next to the hunks of black metal, lots of aliens appearing all of a sudden in one spot, like magic. It was like the car with the clowns at the circus her mom had taken her to see once when she was a kid. The clowns had to come from somewhere, because they sure couldn't all fit in that tiny little car. Just like the circus clowns, the Wannoshay were using secret tunnels.

And that was where the ship was now, Toshera knew. It was filling the tunnels underneath the field. Their metal was all bendy, and it probably got so hot it melted.

So what was going to happen, she wondered, when the metal cooled off?

She'd wanted to tell her mother about her theories about the ship all night, but her mother had been too busy working with Lisa to get the piece of metal out of Ally's stomach—Toshera couldn't watch *that*—and then she'd gone on to help more of the hurt people. Toshera did her best to keep up by delivering blankets and running for gauze and bandages for the medics, but all the blood and screaming made her want to run and hide.

During one trip back to the storage room, she'd seen the Netstream reporters outside, filming the empty place where the ship had been, so she knew the rest of the world had heard the bad news. Doctors and nurses and other emergency workers who lived close by were coming here to help as best they could.

Not five minutes after seeing the reporters with their cams attached to their eyebrows or held in their hands like marbles, Toshera saw something else that made her want to run away in fear.

Plowing through the crowded field, she saw a group of bloodied and burned Wannoshay carrying Father Joshua high above their heads. They were almost running with him, and when Toshera saw the pale color of his skin, she thought he was dead.

"Mom," she tried to say, but all that came out was a squeak.

She pulled open the outer door with a numb hand and let in the aliens. Hunching low on their way through the door, the big Wannoshay men carried Joshua at chest level. One of them had his round hand over Joshua's heart, his short fingers splayed out and wriggling.

She wanted to follow them, but she couldn't bear seeing Father Joshua in such bad shape. She wiped tears from her eyes, and when her vision cleared, she saw two more figures hurrying toward the union. One was old and hunched, but he moved more surely than the thin, bent-over man next to him, holding his hands away from his body at a weird angle.

"Skin and Shermie," she said to herself. "Skin and Shermie!" she shouted, bursting out of the door. "Come here! Everyone's inside!"

As she held the door open once again, Toshera stared at the black gloves on Skin's hands, trying to figure out why he was wearing them. Something looked wrong about them.

When Shermie walked past, patting her head, she saw what the problem was. Skin wasn't wearing gloves. Those black and swollen things at the end of each wrist were his *hands.*

Biting back a flood of questions, she reached up and put her hands on Skin's side opposite from Shermie, propping him up but making sure she didn't brush up against his ruined hands.

"This way," she said, turning right at the top of the steps inside the union. She aimed Skin at where she'd last seen her mother and Lisa. The room had quickly filled to overflowing with injured humans and Wannoshay.

"Tim!" Lisa's voice echoed through the high ceilings of the union's second floor atrium. Lisa passed Randy to Shontera and rushed around half a dozen aliens lying on the floor, covered in blood-stained blankets. She rushed up to where Skin and Shermie stood reeling on their feet. Toshera hoped she wouldn't have to catch one of them if they fell.

"Your *hands,*" Lisa whispered, carefully pulling Skin close to her. "Oh God. What happened?"

"Show him a cot," Shermie said, "And he'll tell you all about it once he's got some painkillers in him. He's hurting pretty bad right now. But he got us out of the ship. He saved me and Joshua. Except Joshua . . . he . . ."

The old man looked so tired and sad that Toshera grabbed

his cold hand. She smiled up at him and ignored his body odor. Tears had worn tracks in the dirt and grime covering his wrinkled face.

"Do you need a cot, Mister Powell?" she asked him.

"Mister Powell's my dad, and he's been dead for years. But yeah, I'll take a seat somewhere, sweetheart. Only if you'll call me Shermie and tell me what happened tonight. I saw it all with my own old eyes, but I need someone young and smart to give me the details before I'll actually believe it."

Toshera found a pair of chairs in an alcove off the main room, within sight of her mother and their other new friends. She began talking to Shermie as they watched the doctors and nurses help the wounded. She showed him who Lisa and Randy were, while Shermie tried to keep her from looking at the crowd of emergency aid workers surrounding Joshua three cots down from where they sat.

Toshera had watched enough reality downloads from the 'Streams to know that they were doing CPR on the priest. She squeezed Shermie's hand tighter as she told him about the explosions and the trucks and the song of the Wannoshay from just a few hours earlier.

"Can you smell them anymore?" Shermie interrupted.

"What do you mean?"

Shermie pointed at the aliens lying on the floor barely ten feet from them.

"The aliens," he whispered. "They used to have all kinds of smells, sometimes sweet, sometimes salty, sometimes really stinky."

You should talk, Toshera wanted to say, but bit her tongue.

"Now, there's nothing. Not even with all of them in here. I can't smell 'em anymore. Maybe my old nose has just stopped working."

Toshera inhaled deeply, glancing at the purplish-pink blood

covering the arms and chest of the alien on the floor closest to her.

She shook her head. “You’re right. I can’t smell them either. Why is that?”

“Their sicknesses, I guess. Did you hear that people—humans—have started getting sick too?”

“I knew it!” Toshera shouted, completely awake now. “I think they were causing my headaches. Where’d you hear about this? About the Wannoshay making people sick?”

“Shh, girl.” Shermie patted her hand and nodded at her to sit down next to him again. Toshera hadn’t realized she’d jumped out of her chair. “I’ve been working with the colonel, and he has all sorts of ideas about the Wantas.”

“Wannoshay.”

“Yes, sorry. He thinks the Wannoshay might be using this sickness to get humans to act. I’m not sure if I believe him—I’ve been talking to the Wannoshay for over half a year, and I haven’t gotten sick, that’s for sure, and it’s impossible to figure out the logic of aliens—but he’s right about one thing. We’re making a mistake if we don’t help the Wannoshay.”

“People *are* helping.” Toshera pointed at Lisa and her mother. “What do you call *that?*”

Shermie gave a yellowed smile as he fumbled in his pockets and pulled out a plastic bag of cigarillos.

“I call that a good start. A very good start. Your mother is a good woman. That’s how it all has to begin, if we’re all going to survive.”

“You’re not going to smoke that here, are you?”

Shermie looked at the glowing lighter in his right hand and his cigarillo in the other.

“This? Oh no. I was just, ah, checking to make sure my lighter still worked. And it does. Good.”

Toshera gave him the eye until he returned the lighter and

cigarillos to his coat pocket with a sigh.

"Okay, missy, I've got a question for you," Shermie said when he was settled back in his chair again. The frenetic pace of the emergency workers had begun to lessen around them, and the pain-filled screaming and shouting from earlier had shifted into quiet moaning and whispered conversations. "Why do you think they *sing?*"

"The Wannoshay?"

"No, your Uncle Moe and Aunt Jane. Of course I mean the aliens."

Toshera let a jaw-cracking yawn slip from her mouth as she looked up at the ceiling of the union atrium. She followed the curving lines of the supports and columns surrounding the darkened sky lights and thought about the question.

"That's one of the ways they talk, I think," she said, still staring upward.

"Could be," Shermie said. "But my alien friends out on the rez hardly ever sang. They were younger, though. But all they wanted to do was talk and plan how to get the other aliens out of the camps. Here, all the aliens seem to do is sing, and . . ."

Toshera looked over at Shermie, whose voice was slowing down. He had his glasses perched on top of his head, and one of the lenses was missing while the other was cracked. His eyes had black circles under them.

"Sing and do what, Shermie?" Toshera urged him. With a surge of pride, she watched her mother stand up and pat the hand of an old woman she'd been caring for.

"Sing and . . . *wait,* I guess. They were waiting for something to happen, I think. Maybe they sing to try and understand what's happening, like we're doing right now, talking. Or maybe their singing had something to do with the attacks tonight. I don't know, kiddo. I just miss my friends and my neighbors. I'm ready to go back to Macy, Nebraska."

"Don't be sad," Toshera said, watching her mother turn toward a shadowy alcove off the main atrium. She couldn't see her mama's face, but something had caught her eye. A strange feeling filled her as her mother's shoulders tightened.

"Shermie?" she said, but the old man had dozed off in his chair. His chin rested on his chest, and he was snoring softly.

Holding her breath, afraid to wake him, Toshera slipped his reading glasses from his head, folded them, and placed them in the breast pocket of his shiny jacket.

Her mother was no longer standing next to the old woman she'd been helping. Toshera felt a moment of panic, like she used to feel when she'd wander off as a little kid and get lost at the mall or at school, and then she saw her mother standing in front of the alcove again. Suddenly, her mother ran into the alcove and dropped to her hands and knees.

Toshera left her chair and rushed over to where her mother was, and when she'd made it past the maze of injured in cots and on the floor, she found her mother bent over a Wannoshay. She ran to her side just as her mother whispered something under her breath. It sounded like a name.

She wrapped both hands around her mother's upper arm, afraid to look at the wounds covering the Wannoshay woman below them.

"How'd she get here, Mama?" she whispered.

"Toshera?" Her mother put her right arm around her while still holding onto a gray, four-fingered hand with her left. "What are you doing here?"

Toshera felt a jolt of electricity at her mother's touch, as if her mother had channeled the injured woman's alien energy into her. She closed her eyes and imagined the black metal of the Mother Ship filling the tunnels, forcing any of the Wannoshay down there out into the open air above them. She tried to take a deep breath; the vision was making her feel claustrophobic.

"Is it her?" She wanted to pull away and get some air, but instead she buried her face in her mother's shoulder.

" 'oshhh . . . 'oshera?" The injured Wannoshay that her mother had been helping answered in place of her mother.

Finally, forcing herself to turn her head, Toshera looked down at the alien's oval face, relieved to see there wasn't any blood there. She put a tentative hand on the Wannoshay woman's forehead, next to her half-open, sideways eye.

"It's you, isn't it?" she asked, and then she burst into tears. "Are you okay, Nonami?"

Chapter Thirty

Ally tried to count back through the recent weeks to the last time she'd felt this high, but when she ran out of fingers she quickly lost count. Too much time had passed, she decided. She let her hands fall back onto the cold floor of the union and made a conscious choice to watch the high white ceiling swim in her tripled vision instead. At least the pain in her gut was gone.

Screw Blur, she thought. Give me some opium-based painkillers any day. That way I can relax and not have to flash when it wears off or get shin splints from all my speed-walking and running around while I'm using it.

Somehow, the woman who'd introduced herself as Skin's wife, Lisa (Skin was *married?* Ally had wanted to say, but her mouth pretty much hadn't been working at that point), had found the drugs for her. Lisa had also found a doctor to remove the piece of metal from Ally's stomach.

Now, she was gloriously high again, with a thick piece of duraplast bandage covering her entire midsection from her beltline to just below her ribs.

She let the drug wash over her, enjoying the way she was floating ten feet above her own body. While she was up in the air, she was able to forget about Wantaviewer and camps and Brando and pickup truck bombers.

After ten minutes of mindless floating, she felt something shift in the big room of the union. She tried to turn and spin in midair to locate the disturbance, but she realized she wasn't floating after all, but lying on the floor with a moaning Wannoshay girl on her right and an elderly human man on her left.

Moving her eyes from side to side took a Herculean effort, and Ally swore she could hear the creak of her eyeballs in their sockets. Her breath was a series of tiny tornadoes entering and exiting her mouth. All around her were the injured and those rushing back and forth or leaning down over the hurt.

Her sore eyes were drawn toward two women, familiar to her even though they were facing away from her. These women were set apart from the rest of the room, bent over a hurt Wannoshay in one of the room's alcoves.

The weird tingling sensation—like hot air blown from a faroff fan—blowing onto her skin came from that alcove.

Her brain searched for the names of the two brown-skinned women with their backs to her, one about her age, the other young enough to be the first woman's daughter. She felt like she was scrolling and scrolling through an endless Netstream database until the names hit her: Shontera and Toshera.

The slight effort of raising her head from the floor for a better look was agitating the damaged nerves of her stomach. But when she saw the halo of light surrounding a second, shadowy Wannoshay figure inching toward Shontera and Toshera in the alcove, she couldn't look away.

Ally recognized that figure. She blinked and was back in the mall-camp, filming the last seconds of the Blur-addicted Wannoshay man's life. She'd been unable to determine the identity of the power-hungry creature wrapped in shadow—was it another Wannoshay?—before the creature had stolen the man's last bit of what Joshua would have called "wild energy."

And now, right in front of her drugged eyes, the wicked process was happening all over again.

Ally squinted and saw the short tentacle-hairs—like one of

the Elders—inside the moving shadows the creature was using to cloak itself. Now that she knew what to look for, she could see more of the shadowy Wanta. The creature was bundled up in one of the soldiers' invisibility jackets, and it was less than twenty feet from Shontera and Toshera.

"Late," Ally whispered. "You're late."

The electric sensation, as if a new power source had been started up in the air around her, suddenly shifted into high gear. With a moan that she could feel deep inside her stomach, she could suddenly smell every single Wannoshay around her. Wet dirt, burnt coffee, ammonia, cinnamon, cloves, salt—the barrage of earthy odors made her want to gag. But the smells focused her vision, and she could now see the hunched shoulders of the shadowy Wannoshay as well as the female's head.

She was as convinced as a drug-addled young woman could be that this alien was one of the Elders. On the floor of the union, the alien had left a widening trail of purplish-red blood. Ten feet from Shontera and Toshera, the late Wannoshay Elder was injured as well.

Late, she thought. Brando would have said you were late, Elder. Because I think that's what you are. An Elder and a thief. And you're too fucking late.

So why can't anyone else see you?

As Ally watched, helpless, the injured Wannoshay woman being tended to by Shontera began to shake. She threw her toe-fingered hands from side to side, and Ally felt her mouth drop open as the woman began to float into the air. She knew what that meant, and if she could have gone over to help somehow, she would have, but like the dying alien, her body was no longer cooperating.

Pulling Toshera close, Shontera tried to touch the female alien's hand. Ally could tell Shontera had known this woman, and she flipped through her mind again, searching for a name.

Nonami.

The dying alien woman swung her hands wildly, eluding Shontera's touch. Nonami kicked out at the air as she fought off her own death, and she shattered the walls of the alcove with each contact she made with her hands and feet.

Just five feet from Shontera now, the intruder made a whistling sound that cut through the babble of voices in the makeshift hospital ward to reach Ally's ears.

A trickle of white energy slipped out of the eyes of the floating, convulsing Wannoshay woman.

The energy was immediately pulled toward the shadow in a single line of light. Nonami only gave off a tiny rivulet of energy, not the flood that had come from the dying, Blurred alien in the mall camp.

Nonami was not yet dead.

Ally ignored the pain in her stomach and lurched up onto one elbow. Her vision went gray for a few seconds from the pain, and then the world turned completely black when she inhaled.

With all of her strength, Ally screamed her new friend's name.

"Shontera!" she shouted, feeling something tear inside her wounded stomach. "Next to you! Something's killing her!"

Moving in what looked to Ally like super-slo-mo, Shontera pulled herself away from Nonami in front of her to see the shadowy alien almost on top of her.

The two aliens were still connected by the glowing white ribbon of wild energy.

Shontera didn't hesitate. She reached inside her bloodstained coat and pulled a black metal spike from her inner pocket. Ally remembered a story Shontera had told her late one night about a pile of hair-tentacles lodged into a sign outside an abandoned landing site. This spike, Ally knew, had held the tentacles to the sign.

"Stop her," she whispered.

As the ribbon of white energy coming from the dying alien began to thicken and widen, Shontera lunged at the Elder and buried the piece of black metal inside the thieving Elder's mid-section.

The Elder's head snapped back, shaking loose more of the ill-fitting military jacket to expose the injuries on her upper body that she'd already sustained, before Shontera's attack. This Wannoshay was indeed one of the Elders they'd first spoken to last month, a day that now felt like years ago.

Shontera pushed against the gravely wounded Elder one final time. Like Nonami, the gravely wounded Elder lifted into the air with that push as life drained from her.

Please let this all be a hallucination, Ally thought, tears spilling from her eyes and doubling her vision as she watched the two dying Wannoshay women levitate six feet above the floor of the student union.

For a long, agonizing minute, Nonami kicked and fought against her combined wounds and sicknesses before her struggles finally ended. She went limp. The white light of her dying energy that she'd been holding back and protecting now spilled freely from her body and spread out into the alcove.

The dying Elder reached out two bloodied arms for Nonami's wild energy before it could spread. She pulled the energy into her hungrily, greedily, with the black spike Shontera had embedded deep into her stomach releasing its own purplish-red river of blood onto the floor.

Ally felt pain shoot up from her own wound just looking at the Elder's stomach, and she blacked out for a second.

In that second before her head hit with the floor and smacked her back into reality, Ally was zooming over black rocks in a frozen blue-white field, skimming over hundreds of vine-covered caves, and passing over a line of caves, unprotected and vulnerable.

Brando's home, she thought.

Too late to go back, she thought in a voice that sounded like her old Wannoshay friend. We must all look ahead now. We're all too late.

When she opened her eyes again, Nonami's body as well as her wild energy were both gone, and the Elder was still floating above the floor in the alcove. Shontera pulled Toshera away from the alcove, crying out a Wanta name that Ally couldn't recognize.

The Elder tried to contain Nonami's energy that was now coursing through her Blurred, soul-curdled body, but it was all too much for her. Her feet never returned to the ground to use the energy she'd stolen.

The dying Wannoshay whispered two words in her native tongue, and Ally was able to hear the words as clearly as if the Elder had whispered them in her ear. She held onto the alien words through her pain, repeating them until they were burned in her memory.

Outside, the night was starting to turn to day, but she barely noticed. She just kept repeating the words of the Elder until the light from the wounded alien grew bright as the sun.

She wouldn't know until later, when she found Shermie and had him translate, what the words meant: "Save . . . mother . . ."

The Elder had died, and the light of her wild energy was hundreds of times as bright as Nonami's had been. With a rush, the Elder's supply of stored energy, stolen from countless Wannoshay when they died, spilled out of her.

The blinding intensity of the light quickly broke apart into individual streaks of energy. Ally blinked and tried to deny with all of her agnostic energies what she was seeing, but there could be no other explanation.

In the flashing beams of light bursting from the thieving Elder, Ally could see eyes and stretched-out bodies with finger-toes at the end of them.

Wannoshay *souls.*

As she stared, Ally was able to understand what the Elders had been planning to do with all this stored energy. The souls moved toward the outer doors, aiming themselves with their last bits of wild energy.

Save . . . mother.

A final Wannoshay-shaped creature of light pulled itself free from the disintegrating husk of the Elder and paused. This last energy creature lifted its arms, and Ally could see a glowing face inside the light. Nonami.

Her lipless smile moved from mother and daughter to Ally, and then she began to break apart in front of Shontera and Toshera. Beams of light went out from her like tiny fingers, touching each person inside the temporary hospital ward.

Ally felt the pain in her belly disappear. She closed her eyes and almost allowed herself a smile through all of her tears.

Maybe, a voice whispered inside Ally's head, sounding just like her old friend Brando, it *wasn't* too late to go back, after all.

Chapter Thirty-One

While Ally was living through a reality that shimmered on the edge of a nightmare, Father Joshua was caught in a nightmare world that felt like no reality he had ever known.

He first saw fists and elbows, waving in his face or driving into his chest. Then there was darkness and peace, but that was shattered all too soon by a blue-tinged blast of electricity shooting from his chest into the rest of his body.

The pain returned along with a flood of sounds and smells. At first Joshua wanted that peaceful blackness back, but he knew it wasn't yet time for that. He fought his way back to those sounds and smells and let the people working on him pull him back to life.

After that, he slept, inhaling mud and salt and taking comfort from the dull pain in his chest and ribs.

He woke after too short a sleep with numbness in his chest and arms and what felt like fifty balls of cotton stuffed in his mouth. He was in the student union, but the room had gone completely silent. Outside, the sun was rising with an unnatural white light.

I'm still asleep, Joshua thought. Or I'm gone. Dead. In purgatory.

He sat up and looked at the sunlight. Something was wrong with that light. Next to him, he saw a pair of young People, covered to their chins in too-short blankets that left their finger-toes exposed. He could smell the musky scents of the People, but he couldn't hear them. A woman holding a small baby walked past, and Joshua could see that the child was crying, but he heard none of it. Nobody seemed to notice him.

In the blink of an eye he was standing. He touched his chest and felt no pain, just a sturdy pounding sensation under his fingertips. He let his arm fall to his side and walked in utter silence out of the emergency room of the student union.

He didn't remember walking down the steps or out the front doors, but suddenly Joshua was on Hubbard Field. The sun had dropped from the morning sky and taken up residence on the field, taking up the spot left by the Mother Ship.

It's gone, then, he told himself. Tell me the Elders and the other People made it out of the Mother Ship before it disappeared, Father.

Joshua stepped closer to the sun. After ten steps he realized his mistake: the sun was not yet risen, and this swirling ball of energy was something else, something alien. It was the wild energy of the People. More than he'd ever seen.

The streaks of energy crisscrossed and swirled through the air above the ground where the Mother Ship had once stood. Joshua caught a flash of something black and unshining underneath the busy streaks of white light.

Slabs of metal in their hands, the People on the field had been waiting patiently for this moment. Joshua's hearing had returned, and he could hear the People singing as they carried the metal from their lean-tos and huts toward the ball of shifting light.

The People stopped at the edge of the energy field and shoved their metal into it. With each new piece of salvaged Wannoshay ship, the shimmering ball of energy swirled a bit more frantically, exposing another fragment of the black structure taking shape underneath it.

A wind came up then, blowing dust into the air, shrieking in his ears and dissipating the song of the People.

The Mother Ship began to rise out of the tunnels, returning from its melted purgatory.

Joshua blinked and the ship was over forty feet high and still growing. Fewer and fewer streaks of white energy swirled around, and into, the remains of the ship.

Touched by a wave of fear for himself and for his dream, if that was what it was, he tried to move, to get away from the ship, but his feet were rooted to the muddy ground.

This had been their plan all along, he realized. Johndo claimed not to know where the wild energy of the dead had gone, but the Elders had been collecting it.

And once again, he thought, Johndo had not told me.

Even as the Mother Ship was still rising up from the ground, the People rushed into it, slipping into newly made openings that slid shut behind them, sealing them inside. The ship was now even bigger than its previous incarnation.

Other than being octagonal, the ship's new shape bore little resemblance to the original ship. This Mother Ship was taller than five of the original Mother Ships stacked together, and three times as wide. The spires were gone, replaced by curving armatures and graceful angles. It was wonderfully random yet otherworldly beautiful at the same time.

The growing sped up as the new Mother Ship began pulling nutrients from the dirt next to him. Clods of earth began flying past them, and the ship soon overtook the entire field, and its western edges splashed into the Iowa River. It kept growing, higher and wider.

The Mother Ship was back.

Joshua crossed himself, turned, and walked back to his makeshift bed inside the union, praying that this was no dream. If it was, he didn't want to wake up from it.

Chapter Thirty-Two

Skin stared at his wrapped hands in numb awe as he sat in front of the student union, in the shadow of the colossal new Mother Ship. The late-morning sun was bright in his face, warming him and his aching body. He'd just gotten back from spending the morning at the university hospital, and he'd left Lisa and Randy at his hotel so they could sleep.

After all that had happened, he was too wired to rest. He alternated between looking at his hands and the field in front of him, filled with wonder at all that had happened to him and the Wannoshay ship.

Hubbard Field had been transformed in the aftermath of the ship's rebirth. Anything metal—from the chain-link fence to the cars and trucks once parked around it, as well as iron from the rocks in the river—had been snatched up by the growing ship and absorbed. If Skin looked closely he could see an occasional muffler or metal fencepost sticking out of one of the eight sides of the ship. Rivulets of brown Iowa dirt stretched away from the base of the ship like tree roots.

Even now, hours after it had rebuilt itself with stolen alien energy and metal from other wrecked ships, the Mother Ship continued to inch higher into the sky.

Skin reached up a bandaged hand to shield his eyes as he looked at the distant spires of the ship's roof. The strange numbness in his hands distracted him from the ship.

He lowered his hand and looked at it. Surprisingly, there was no pain in either hand. He thought of Georgie and his state-of-the-art upright walker. Like his old buddy, Skin had also benefited from the latest technology; this morning's technique had used a new kind of glue that the surgeons injected directly into the bones. The glue adhered to the broken bits of his hand bones that he had shattered against the ship wall.

I really wish they would've knocked me out for that procedure, he thought, pacing around the crowded foyer of the hotel. He couldn't erase the memory of the five-inch-long, sixteen-gauge needle being slammed into each of his secured fingers. The popping of his bones as the needle broke through had been like tiny gunshots.

He wondered if there had been a limit to how long he could hold Awoyana's energy inside of him, giving him just enough strength to carry Joshua and punch their way out of the ship.

Skin looked out over the field and continued flexing his hands, surprising himself that he could actually do so. He saw Shontera and Toshera walking around and over the gashes in the torn-up field in front of the ship. He wanted to call out to them, but his throat was still killing him.

He watched them instead. Even though they both looked exhausted, they stopped and talked to people every few minutes, human and alien both. Sometimes Shontera would wipe her eyes, and Skin guessed she was still mourning the death of the alien woman from last night, the woman she called Nonami.

He thought he caught the glint of a lapel camera in Shontera's coat. He smiled, imagining Ally begging them to get footage for her while she recovered inside the union.

From the mother and daughter Netstream crew, Skin looked one last time at the Mother Ship. Most of the aliens were inside the ship now, including the surviving Elders. Skin wondered if Awoyana had survived the night.

Skin didn't even hear the small, short-tentacled Wannoshay

man walk up to him until the man spoke.

"You are one of them?" the alien said in a surprisingly clear voice. "You went inside the ship?"

Skin pulled himself to his feet from the step where he was sitting, surprised at how much effort it took him.

"Not late?" he said to the alien next to him. He hadn't ever spoken to a Wannoshay who stood eye-to-eye with him like this older man did, and Skin liked the sensation.

"You went inside with my friend, A-issha? I come to share my skills. To navigate."

"A-issha?" Skin squinted at the alien. "Navigate? Your friend?"

"I fear I am late, but not *late* like other Wannoshay. Late like humans are late."

Skin took a deep breath. "Okay, let's start over here. I'm Skin. What is your name? Your . . . *gahawa?* What do they call you?"

"Yes, Skin-from-*Nee-brash-yah*. We know of you. I am Wayandoshay, though my friend A-issha calls me by her own *gahawa*. She calls me Brando."

Skin wiped away a trickle of sweat that was sliding down the side of his face from the warm sun, and his fingers exploded with pain at the movement. But he barely felt it as he looked into the three black eyes of the gray-skinned being in front of him. A smile broke out over his haggard face.

Finally, he thought. Finally something good was happening after the insanity of last night.

"Brando," Skin said, still grinning like a fool. "Have I got someone who'd like to see you. Would you come inside with me?"

Ally Trang was dying to get out of the sick ward. She was glad to see that Father Joshua was awake and responsive and all, but she didn't feel sick or hurt anymore. All she felt was impatient to be out and about—too much was happening, with nobody to film it. She'd sent Shontera out that morning with her spare lapel camera, and she was praying that Shon had gotten footage of the ship rebuilding itself.

She had her bandage tightened and cleaned and was about to slip out when Skin came walking up, followed by someone she thought she'd never see again.

"Look who I found outside," Skin said, "looking for his old friend A-issha."

"Brando!" Ally shouted, regretting it immediately as a hint of pain flickered in her gut.

Brando took Ally's hands in his own and held them tight to his chest. For the first time ever, Ally felt the deep thudding of a Wannoshay heart. It beat clearly through his thin shirt and rough gray skin.

"I was almost *late*, coming to see you, A-issha." Brando's mouth barely moved with his words, and his touch filled Ally with a peace that no drug had ever done for her.

"But you made it," she said. "You made it here."

Brando rested a hand on Ally's forehead and kept Ally's hand tight in his other short-fingered hand, and he didn't say a word.

"Listen, folks," Skin said, "I've got to go get some sleep and see my wife and kid. Take care, okay?" He walked off, pausing by Father Joshua's cot before hurrying out of the union.

We made it, all of us, Ally thought. *Almost* all of us, she added, thinking of Nonami from late last night.

"A-issha?"

Ally looked up at Brando with a start. She must have drifted off for a moment there.

Good drugs, she thought again. Good drugs and good friends—what more do you need in this life?

The thought would have made her laugh if she wasn't afraid it would make her stomach hurt all over again.

Brando took his cool hand from her forehead and watched her with his third eye closed.

"What is it, Brando?"

"I came to find you, and to see the new Mother Ship. I am needed there."

"Really? What for?" Ally fought the urge to sit up straighter, and she hated not having her camera with her. Shontera better be getting some great footage, she thought.

"Talked to the others," Brando continued. "Only three of us survived. Some died in landings, some died in camps, some died in explosions. Only three . . ."

"Three? Three what?" Ally's joy at seeing Brando again, after thinking she'd never encounter him again, was replaced by a feeling that it was happening again. She was losing him again.

"I am a Navigator, A-issha. We must leave soon."

"What do you mean," Ally said, " 'we'? I'm not going nowhere, big guy."

"We shall see," Brando said, and placed his flat hand on her forehead again. Ally's eyelids closed, even though she was aching to stay awake and go outside.

Before she fell into a deep, healing sleep, untouched by a single bad dream, she heard the soft scuffle of Brando's bare feet as he left her side, on his way to the Mother Ship.

The next morning, at almost the exact moment when it had first started rebuilding itself the previous day, the Mother Ship stopped growing.

The width of two football fields, side-by-side, the Mother Ship now reached over twenty stories into the air. Its irregular sides were a mixture of Wannoshay and Earth metals. Once word got out that the ship was in need of metal, the donations came quickly, especially from local wrecking companies overstocked with old gas-powered, obsolete vehicles.

A flattened Ford Escort, along with dozen other wrecked cars, made up a large section of the wall of the ship. For another hundred yards on all sides of the ship, the soil had been drained of all minerals, leaving it bleached and lifeless.

The new and improved Mother Ship was a jagged black castle with a moat made of sand.

At sunrise, the Elders announced that the ship would be leaving soon for the Wannoshay home world. Now that they had a Navigator, they would need a small crew to keep the ship running. The rest of the space in the hollowed-out ship would be saved for the People of the Twilight and the long journey back to Earth.

The remaining Elders—only five had survived the explosions and their aftermath—offered Joshua, Shontera, Ally, Shermie, and Skin the option to travel with them on their mission home.

Shontera and Skin were too devoted to their families and too bound to restarting their interrupted lives here on Earth to accept the incredible offer. They turned down the aliens' offer.

Ally considered it seriously, especially with the knowledge that Brando was going as well, but she had work to do on Earth. With her Wantaviewer Netstream, she wanted to make up for the chunk of her life she'd lost thanks to Blur. She said no.

Shermie thought about it just for a moment, but everything changed the moment he saw his fellow Macy natives Rich and Rich's family pull up in their old pickup. After too much time away, the Indians were on their way back home. Shermie also said no.

The instant the question was out of Johndo's mouth, however, Father Joshua McDowell agreed—without a moment of hesitation or a trace of doubt—to travel to the stars with the Wannoshay.

Chapter Thirty-Three

On a cool, breezy day in April, less than a year and a half after the People first crash-landed onto his planet, Father Joshua McDowell left Earth aboard the new Mother Ship. The ship blasted away from its new home, starting on a round-trip journey that it would not complete for many Earth decades.

With his old friend Johndo there at his side to talk him through the bumpy rise into space, Joshua vowed not to forget any of what was happening to him. The tiny laser-pulse transmitter and the even-tinier lapel camera in his shirt pocket represented his attempts to keep the people of Earth from forgetting. He had only a short window of time to use them both, but he knew exactly what he would do and what he would say.

With his blood pounding inside his head in spite of Johndo's calming voice next to him, he saw, for the first time, his home planet from space.

At this distance, the ball that was Earth was filled with a delicate beauty that gave him a sense of peace, after so many years of turmoil. His heart beat strong and true, no pain left in his chest any longer.

Quite possibly my final look at Earth, he thought. Though I doubt it.

Johndo patted Joshua's hand and left him to prepare the rest of the skeleton crew for their newly made casks. According to Brando's calculations, they would soon need to enter the long sleep that would keep them safe between Earth and the Wannoshay home planet. To ease their sleep, the Mother Ship had created individual casks sized for each Wannoshay and human on the ship.

Joshua still had half a day left—I can't think in those terms any longer, he reminded himself—before he was scheduled to enter his long-term sleep. They would be leaving the solar system by that point, and just before they did, he needed to complete the task he'd agreed to carry out for an old friend.

Until that time, to keep him from panicking every time he glanced out of the octagonal-shaped window next to him, he picked up the sharp metal stylus that Johndo had given him.

He tapped the stylus tip on the metal wall next to him, activating a heat coil inside the metal barrel. When the tip was glowing red, he opened up Johndo's metal book for the first time in months. He hadn't gotten around to returning it to his old friend after all.

He marveled once again at the way the cold metal yielded to his touch but never bent. Inside the book, the empty pages filled him with hope and more than a hint of youthful exuberance. He turned to the first blank page, closed his eyes, and took a deep breath. He pictured in his mind the symbols of the People's language.

If I'm going to do this, he thought, I need to do it right.

Opening his eyes, he started by writing the current date, even if that information would soon become meaningless on his journey. He watched in amazement as the heated stylus in his hand began shaping the whirls and zigzags of the People. A pleasing scent of hot metal tickled his nose.

It is all right to doubt faith, Father Joshua wrote as the Wannoshay Mother Ship sped away from Earth. *Just as long as you are able to find your way back to that faith, at the end of the day. For it will still be there, waiting for you, an integral part of your true history. All you have to do is look around you to find your own true faith, for it is everywhere. It is you.*

It is you.

Even as night fell, North Myrtle Beach was almost unbearably hot by the end of May. Shontera and Toshera Johnson, however, had no complaints about the heat. They both sat on the back deck of their new beach house as the sun went down at their backs, and Shontera savored the sound of the ocean less than fifty feet away. When she was able to pull her gaze away from the darkening waves to check her handheld Netstream, Shontera saw that her weeklong project had finally completed—a search of the Netstreams for William, Toshera's father and her former boyfriend.

"Bingo," she said with a smile.

"You found him?" Toshera asked. "After all this time?"

"He's in Durham, the little shit. Living with his momma again, looks like." Shontera laughed along with Toshera. "Now that your mom knows some high-tech tricks for the Netstreams, we'll make sure he starts paying child support again."

And we'll also make sure you know it was me who did this. That's what you owe me for raising Toshera alone for the past few years, working all those long days at the damn brewery while you were out running around and being irresponsible. You owe me that much.

"When are you coming inside?" Toshera said, standing and stretching next to Shontera. "I'm tired."

"In another minute or two," Shontera said. She did a double-take at her daughter in her bright red bathing suit, without her glasses. Every now and then she forgot that Toshera no longer needed them anymore. Shontera had arranged for the lasix surgery before they moved to Myrtle, and Nonami's last wave of energy had ended the headaches that had been plaguing

Toshera for years.

Toshera's poor eyesight and headaches, along with the internment camps and the labor farms and the alien sicknesses, were now all part of the past.

"Well, I'm going to bed," Toshera said. She kissed her mother on the cheek and went inside. "Good night."

Shontera watched Toshera walk back inside with a surge of pride and happiness. We did the right thing, coming here, she decided. She'd always wanted to live next to the ocean; even with all the chaos of the past few years, that desire had never gone away.

Shontera clicked off the Netstream and leaned back in her reclining chair. The waves rolled toward her and receded, flashing stars and moonlight with a sound that made her eyelids heavy. The stars made her think of all her old friends had done for her, including one special person in particular.

"Thank you," she whispered, and carefully pronounced a tongue-twister of a Wannoshay name: "Oyallohawna.

"But you'll always be Nonami to me," she added, and the waves blurred with her sudden tears.

Shontera blinked and smiled, thinking about a raised foot with finger-toes, holding up a brown bottle of beer.

Still smiling, she looked up at the stars starting to pop out in the sky above her, and she sent another thank-you to the night sky, out toward where she guessed Father Joshua was heading. It was as accurate a guess as any could be, and even if her best estimate wasn't exactly right, it was at least made in good faith, and that was all that really mattered.

Ever since Joshua had blasted away from Earth with the Wannoshay, Ally Trang, a.k.a. Wantaviewer, had been unnaturally, inhumanly busy.

She'd gotten back all of her street and 'Stream cred when she ran the first images of the Mother Ship rebuilding itself, thanks to Shontera's camera work, and she hadn't stopped there. There had been too many stories for her to capture and record onto her Netstream. She'd also uploaded stories about the detainment camps being disassembled by crews of humans and Wannoshay, the use of Wanta tech by the military, and the construction of new homes being built for the aliens underground, close to the now-fenceless factory farms.

Wantaviewer was *back*.

What the Netstreams didn't show were the nights and weekends Ally spent in the Blur recovery houses in and around Iowa City. She worked with both human and Wannoshay addicts, but most of her time was spent with the aliens. The *People*. She had enlisted the help of Thumper for this, once her Wannoshay friend was clean of the drug. Ally still missed Brando, but her work kept her from feeling his absence too deeply. He'd always be there in her work.

In the middle of June, she'd received the message she'd been expecting for so many long weeks. It arrived at the astronomy lab on the University of Iowa campus, carried on pulses of narrowly focused laser light produced by a transmitter on the Mother Ship. The astronomers had been out of their minds with joy since its arrival.

Her first upload of the footage from her message came on the first day of summer, at noon central time. Ally's American friends had wanted her to wait and run it on Independence Day, but she refused; if everything worked out as planned, this would be a day that went beyond countries and borders.

This would be a day that went beyond *all* boundaries, a day that would allow people to once again lift their gazes to the stars, after so much time spent staring at the ground.

This would be a day, Ally hoped, that would let everyone look up again with hope.

At eleven-thirty a.m. on the first day of summer, Skin sat back in his easy chair and clicked on the wallscreen he had finally finished paying for. He was surrounded in his trailer by friends and neighbors, and the air was filled with the laughter of small children and the same anticipation that came with a Christmas morning.

He gazed at the children on the floor, playing with his son Randy, and grinned. Lisa sat with the other women gathered at the kitchen table, and the men lounged in chairs in the living room, talking loud and laughing while they drank the latest batch of Skin's homebrew.

The room went silent when Skin surfed over to the Wantaviewer 'Stream. Everyone knew about the upcoming footage, and the hum of anticipation intensified.

They were interrupted by a knock on the door. Mandy stood up from the table to get it, but Skin waved her away and handed the remote to Georgie in the chair next to him.

He walked over to his front door, and standing outside were three Wannoshay. A flash of panic filled Skin at first, wondering why they were here, but then he remembered hearing about the Wannoshay child who attended Randy's daycare.

"I invited them," Lisa said. Her hand was on Skin's back, rubbing him between his shoulder blades in a tentative manner.

Skin was already moving. He opened the screen door and smiled at the two adults and their child on his doorstep.

"Welcome!" he said, his fear melting into a sudden, bright sense of rightness. Not being scared for the first time in years felt unbelievably good. "Please come in."

These are the first aliens to ever set foot inside our trailer, he thought. But I'm sure they won't be the last. The Wannoshay weren't aliens anymore; they were *neighbors.*

Georgie rolled up to them in his upright walker. "Hey guys, sorry to interrupt, but the download's almost ready." He nodded at the three Wannoshay and gave them a smile. "I'm Georgie, by the way, and this is Lisa and Tim, but we usually just call him Skin. Can I get you a beer or something from the fridge?"

"Thank you for inviting us into your home, Skin and Lisa and Georgie," the female Wannoshay said, enunciating carefully. "We are Yialli and Hiyowana, and this is our child Oyalla."

"Come on in," Skin said. "The show's starting."

Once the two adult Wannoshay had found a space against the wall to brace their long backs as they squatted, everyone settled in to watch the footage from the Wantaviewer Netstream. Georgie rolled back in with a beer for Yialli and Hiyowana and settled back into his chair just in time for the start of the download.

The image flickered with static for a moment, and then Skin felt tears tickle his eyes as Father Joshua's red face filled his wallscreen. He reached for Lisa's hand and pulled her into the chair with him. The children quieted and the adults inched closer to the screen. The image was crystal clear.

"I have been blessed," Joshua began, "by all the wonders I've been able to see on this magnificent ship. Words can't describe it. But before I even try, I want you to take a look at this."

The perspective swung around to an octagonal window set in the black hull of Joshua's ship. Space was black and somehow blurry, Skin was somewhat disappointed to learn. But then the image corrected itself, as if compensating for the speed of the ship.

A robin's-egg blue planet hung in the black field of stars, with a wide ring and two reddish moons surrounding it. The ring was made up of rocks that looked tiny from the distance, but were probably close to the size of Mount Everest, Skin guessed. Bluish-white clouds covered most of the planet, but as the camera zoomed even closer, a spot in the northern half of the planet cleared, and dark reddish-brown land came into focus.

This was another world, Skin thought.

He laughed out loud in surprise, and then swallowed hard, wanting to cry. It all felt like too much information, especially smelling the salty-sweet smell of the three aliens squatting not even five feet from him.

Tialli, Oyalla's mother, winked her three of her eyes in succession at Skin and then gave him a smile. He inclined his head, trying his best to imitate Awoyana's bow from long ago, even though he was still sitting down in his chair.

The wallscreen faded to black after Joshua finished his description of the ship, ending with a final message honoring the memory of all those who had lost their lives in the past year and a half. Names began to scroll up the screen, human and Wannoshay.

Skin felt his eyes burn at the number of names moving up the wall at a slow crawl. He couldn't help but look for Awoyana's name, but it was nowhere to be found. He breathed out a sigh of relief tinged with disbelief at so many names.

As soon as the transmission ended, he grabbed the remote and repeated the entire transmission. Without a word, they watched it all over again.

At the end of the day, after three more viewings of the downloaded footage, with the sky growing dark and the stars beginning to pop out, Skin gathered up his family and friends and led them outside.

"Somewhere out there in all that blackness," he said to the kids around him, pointing at the scattered stars, his voice a bit hoarse, "there's a ship with our friends on it. And in who knows how many other places, there are more ships out there with people on them that we don't know."

Skin lifted Randy up higher and moved closer to Lisa, reveling in the closeness of friends old and new. Georgie and Mandy and their girls were on his left, gazing at the stars, while the Wannoshay on his right hummed softly together.

"At least," he added, "we don't know them *yet.*"

Epilogue

I feel an immense pleasure, tinged with a sense of sadness from all of our losses, to be able to take my book of ongoing words from the Father Joshua's sleeping hand and add another chapter to the true history of my People.

As my old friend and the rest of my sparse crew sleep for the duration of the trip—everyone but my Navigator and myself—I find I have too much to say about what is coming for the People of Wannoshay for me to sleep.

I write about what is in store for both Peoples, Dawn and Twilight, and I hope that we are not too late in returning. I want to write about our dying sun, how I wonder if it gives off any light at all anymore. I melt the names of all the People of the Twilight I know into the book, the People I hope to gather into our rebuilt Ship. I leave extra pages for all those I do not know.

I write about my hopes for the success of the cure for the wild blood and the guilt-sickness and the Blur. How I hope that the casks we have waiting for the People of the Twilight will cure them of their violent ways.

I write, and as I do, I feel the familiar heaviness of guilt—my own and that of my people—begin to lessen. Our true history is taking its final shape. No longer curdled, my soul feels unfettered, strong. Free.

I know that now, when I finish writing this portion of the true history of all of my People, I will be able to sleep on this journey, and with all of my being, my heart, and my healing soul, I look forward to that long-needed, much-deserved rest.

ABOUT THE AUTHOR

Michael Jasper grew up in Dyersville, Iowa (home of "The Field of Dreams"), but he now lives with his wife Elizabeth and son Drew in Raleigh, North Carolina. A graduate of the Clarion Writers Workshop and the North Carolina State Creative Writing Program, he works as a technical writer at a software company and squeezes in time for his writing in the early hours of the day.

Publishers Weekly called his 2005 short story collection *Gunning for the Buddha* from Prime Books "evocative and vivid." His fiction has appeared in *Asimov's, Strange Horizons, Writers of the Future, The Raleigh News & Observer,* and *O. Henry Festival Stories.* His website is at www.michaeljasper.net.

ABOUT THE AUTHOR